"HELP! MURDER . . ."

He reached the corner where the road rose. Fleming paused and turned. The man was closer. No more than thirty feet away. The man stopped and smiled disarmingly. He looked familiar.

Fleming unshouldered his bag and started toward him. "Who are—"

"Hello, friend!" Two bulky men stepped swiftly from the shadows of the narrow street and threw their arms around his shoulders.

Jay Fleming opened his mouth to yell, but he choked on his own scream as a massive hairy hand smothered his face. Heart beating wildly, Jay twisted from side to side.

"The briefcase," he heard the one on his right yell in English, "and the suitcase, too."

The men dragged him toward a narrow black alley, and the awareness electrified him: They were going to kill him . . .

LEWIS PERDUE

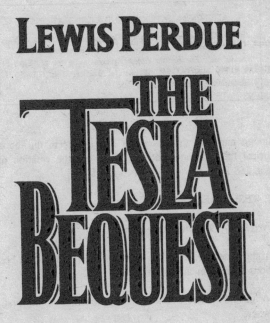

THE TESLA BEQUEST

PINNACLE BOOKS NEW YORK

Although many of the characters and events in this book are historical fact, the incidents described are the creation of the author and have no basis in historical fact.

THE TESLA BEQUEST

An original Pinnacle Books edition, published for the first time anywhere.

First printing/August 1984

ISBN: 0-523-42027-7

Can. ISBN: 0-523-43303-4

Cover art by Dan Wagner

Printed in the United States of America

PINNACLE BOOKS, INC.
1430 Broadway
New York, New York 10018

9   8   7   6   5   4   3   2   1

To Iris and Percy

Foreword

The Tesla Bequest, like my other books, is based on a great deal of factual research.

I first became interested in Nikola Tesla more than twenty years ago when I believed I was destined to become a scientist. It was at this time that I built a Tesla Coil. From plans in an electronic magazine, I built a device that emitted huge arcing bolts of electricity. It would light up flourescent lights in the next room without any wires attached. It was a miniature of the original that Tesla built for his experiments on the wireless transmission of electrical power through the earth.

I soon discovered that Nikola Tesla developed the foundation for our entire modern electrical culture.

Back around the turn of the century, another genius, Thomas Edison, had built all his devices around direct current electricity—the sort of stuff that runs flashlights, car batteries and other small appliances. Direct current's largest problem is that it doesn't travel well. Alternating current, which waits for you today in your wall sockets, was thought to be impossible to generate reliably. Tesla was laughed out of his college physics class for suggesting that he had developed a way to produce it. And after immigrating to America where he was hired for a brief time by Thomas Edison, Tesla continued to be the butt of his employer's ridicule concerning alternating current. They laughed when he sat down to invent.

But today we have alternating current because Nikola Tesla invented it. The 110-volt juice in your wall is 60-cycle current because that's what Tesla wanted it to be.

Aside from inventing the form of electricity on which our society is based, Tesla had an amazing repertoire of interests. He was experimenting with wireless communication a decade before Marconi. He laid the foundation for robotics back in the 1890s—principles that are valid today. His theories were used as a foundation by the great Nobel Prize winners in physics: Einstein, Compton, Millikan, Franck.

And for more than two decades before his death, he claimed he had invented a powerful "death ray" which would make modern weapons obsolete. The U.S. Government pretended not to take Tesla seriously, but when the inventor died in 1943, it seized all of the Tesla papers it could get its hands on and classified them top secret.

Those papers are still classified top secret today. As part of her research to write a recent biography of Tesla, author Margaret Cheney (*Tesla: Man Out of Time*, Prentice Hall, 1981, $16.95) made a number of Freedom of Information Act requests to many government agencies asking for access to Tesla's papers.

After repeated denials that the government had any of Tesla's papers, the Defense Department finally admitted that it had Tesla's research documents, but refused to release any of them, saying that they were still classified for national security reasons. This was in 1980.

What is in those papers that the government feels obliged to keep secret nearly forty years after Tesla's death?

The Tesla Bequest

Chapter One

New York,
January 7, 1943

The sounds of killing bled softly into the night. On the disheveled bed in the Hotel New Yorker, the old man lay clutching his chest as if he could strangle the crushing pain within it. He knew he was dying; he had no idea he was being murdered.

He was a tall, angular man with an elongated triangular face mantled with a full head of snowy white hair, normally swept back immaculately from his face. Tonight, it lay in disarray on his pillow as he rolled from side to side in pain.

His dark mysterious eyes peered out from under heavy eyebrows that formed a shallow "v" across his forehead. It was the face of a harlequin, and for most of his eighty-six years he enjoyed using his unusual countenance to unnerve people. He reveled in being the bizarre—some whispered, "mad"—scientist. Tonight, the face showed only pain and fear.

Nikola Tesla remembered the first time the pains had come. It had been January 4, just three days before, as he was preparing to visit his laboratory. He had agreed to meet his assistant, George Scherff, in the evening. The pain subsided, and since Scherff had been so keen on going ahead with the experiment, Tesla pressed on.

But in the middle of the experiment, the pain returned without warning, sharp and discomforting, but nothing like tonight. Nothing in his life had ever hurt as much as this.

He returned to the New Yorker, where he had lived for

several years. It was a nice hotel, though not as comfortable (or as expensive, he reminded himself daily) as the Waldorf, where he'd once resided for more than a decade.

His mind wandered now among the foggy banks of pain. He had held court at the Waldorf. Whenever he dined, the cream of New York society never failed to drop by and pay homage. Those had been halcyon days.

But no one had paid him homage when he returned from his experiments on January 4, his face gray and drenched with pain, his hands shaking as if he'd seen his own ghost.

He had his meals brought to his room, and on January 5, after the maid finished cleaning his room, he had her hang out the "Do Not Disturb" sign on the doorknob. She was the last person to see him alive.

Tesla's mind was too clouded with pain now to make connections. He made no connection between his pain and a conversation he had had a month before with an engineer associate. Tesla had told the associate then that the experiments with the wireless transmission of energy had been completed and perfected, along with his work on tapping the vast energy reservoirs of charged electrical particles trapped in the magnetic fields of the earth's upper atmosphere.

Tesla also failed to connect the paralyzing pain with the two young scientists who had shown up shortly afterward, asking to examine his papers. For the last two weeks, he had allowed them to borrow small batches of the papers for overnight study. Painfully, Tesla tried to focus his eyes on his bedside clock. It was 10 P.M. One of the youngsters was due soon to return the last batch. He didn't want the young man to see him like this; it would be too embarrassing.

Tesla struggled to the door of his room and opened it. The "Do Not Disturb" sign was still in place. "Good," he mumbled to himself as he closed and locked the door. It wouldn't do to be seen in such a state.

A final connection Tesla failed to make that fatal night was the taste his milk had developed in the past two weeks. He had given up hard liquor and meat years before and drank two quarts of milk a day instead. Lately, he had noticed, since about Christmastime, the milk had tasted a bit odd. He had asked the hotel to return the milk several times, but when the replacements arrived with the same almost imperceptible taste, he decided his palate was to blame, and continued to drink it.

The pain started a week or ten days later, but Tesla never connected it to the milk. He had no way of knowing that the bitter taste began when the hotel kitchen hired a new assistant. Nor did Nikola Tesla notice that the polite young engineers didn't return all the papers they borrowed.

The missing papers had not been taken far. No farther than the next room. As Tesla lay back on his bed, trying to find a position to diminish the pain, a room service clerk made his way slowly up the hallway and rapped lightly on the door of the next room. Wordlessly it opened and the clerk stepped in.

"You should have put more in," said Steven Strand, as he closed the door behind the clerk. He was a short, stocky man with fair hair and a complexion to match. His suit coat was thrown across an armchair. He looked comfortable in his suit pants, suspenders and white long-sleeved shirt. A loosely knotted tie hung from his open collar.

"I couldn't put any more in," the clerk responded defensively. "He would've tasted the stuff for sure." Strand just glowered.

A voice drifted in from the bathroom. "Is that Tony?"

"Yeah," the clerk answered. A second man walked into the room. He was dressed just like Strand, but was taller.

"He's suffering something terrible in there," Erick Hoffman said. "I don't like it."

"Look," Tony said as he walked agitatedly about the room, "I'm giving him what the lab tells me to give him. I can't help that—"

"Calm down," Hoffman said. "We're not blaming you."

"We only did what we had to do," Strand muttered. "Only what we had to do."

"It is really worth it?" Tony asked.

"Yeah," replied Strand. He walked over to a desk in the middle of the room.

"Just take a look at these." He pointed to a stack of papers. Tony looked at them but the clouded look of confusion remained on his face. He couldn't understand the papers.

"So?" Tony asked.

"If what this old man has written is true, we're going to have one of the most awesome weapons in the world. These are just the tip of the iceberg. When he dies, we get the rest. They must be in his room."

"So why do we have to kill him?" Tony asked. "Why make the old man suffer?"

"Because he's refused to give us the plans," replied Hoffman. "Insists that if the country wants the weapon, he'll build it himself, but he wants to work alone, without interference. He even threatened to destroy the papers if we tried to do otherwise. He just doesn't realize that the government—"

"And the government's war contractors," Strand interrupted.

"And the government's war contractors don't have any place for eighty-six-year-old men who limp around dark labs in the middle of the night. We have to control production."

"And the price charged from the production," Tony said bitterly. "You're afraid that the old man will do it for free or somethin'. That your fucking company won't make any profit from it, right?"

"It's a tough world, Tony," Strand said. "You either live with it or . . ." He held up his hands and shrugged, a malevolent smile on his face.

Minutes later, at 10:45 P.M., Nikola Tesla died.

New York,
January 12, 1943

More than two thousand people spilled from the pews and jammed the aisles of the Cathedral of St. John the Divine. Nikola Tesla might have been strange, but he was loved.

Two days before, New York Mayor Fiorello LaGuardia took to the airwaves of WNYC radio to deliver Tesla's eulogy. Eleanor Roosevelt wrote to Tesla's family expressing her sorrow. A trio of Nobel Prize winners in Physics—Millikan, Compton and Franck—who had all based some of their prize-winning research on Tesla's accomplishments, joined the mourning, calling Tesla, "One of the outstanding intellects of the world who paved the way for many of the important technological developments of modern times."

In the front row of St. John the Divine sat the Yugoslavian ambassador to the United States, the Governor of Croatia, a former Prime Minister, and Tesla's nephew, Sava Kosanovic, a Yugoslavian diplomat and soon to be ambassador.

In a small room above the altar, three men who cared little for Nikola Tesla crouched by two small peepholes, peering at the mob below.

"Christ," Tony the clerk said, "it's going to take weeks to identify all these people and track down the leads." He pressed the lens of his camera to the peephole and took another shot. Down below, Bishop William T. Manning began the service in English. "It's a dead end, I tell you," said Erick Hoffman, his squat body dressed in the same clothes he'd worn since the death vigil in the room next to Tesla's. The air was getting ripe in the confined space.

"You've got a better idea, I suppose." Steven Strand frowned. He had managed to change his clothes since that night. Aside from hastily snatched bits of sleep, the three men had not left each other's company for the better part of a week.

"Mr. K is the answer," Hoffman said, referring to Sava Kosanovic. "A diplomat or not, I say we talk to him about what got removed from the safe. Charge the fucker with burglary or something."

When Tesla's room had grown silent on the night of January 7, the three men had prepared themselves to break into Tesla's room and crack a safe he had installed there. But before they could enter, one of the hotel's maids disregarded the "Do Not Disturb" sign and found Tesla's emaciated lifeless body. She called the police from the room telephone and stayed there until they arrived, leaving the three men no opportunity to get in unseen.

Assistant medical examiner H. W. Wembly examined the body and fixed the cause of death as a coronary thrombosis. "No suspicious circumstances," Wembly wrote on his report. It wouldn't be the only time in his career that he was fooled. As time passed, the three men sweated in the next room, desperate for the endless stream of visitors to cease. The body was taken to the Frank D. Campbell Funeral Home at Madison Avenue and 81st St. But even with the body gone, the people didn't leave. Somebody called Kosanovic arrived with a locksmith who opened Tesla's safe. The FBI arrived shortly after Kosanovic left with the safe's contents.

"I still don't know who the hell called the Bureau," Strand groused. Down below, Bishop Manning's voice droned on.

"What a fucking mess," Strand continued. "First the Bureau and then they turn things over to the Office of Alien Property. Hell, Tesla's an American citizen. What's the OAP got to do with anything?"

"Maybe somebody found out," Hoffman mumbled. "Maybe they were on to our effort."

"Nah," Strand countered. "Maybe the government's just being its usual screwed up self." Hoffman grunted noncommittally. Tony the clerk said nothing, just kept on taking picture after picture.

"At least we got to the warehouse first," Hoffman said after a while. Strand grunted. "Could you believe how much stuff was there?"

"Look at my eyes and ask me that," Strand said wearily. They had spent the greater part of the past three days in the dusty, stale loft of the Manhattan Warehouse and Storage Company going through Tesla's effects which were stored there. There had been more than eighty trunks and boxes to go through.

"We missed something," Hoffman said in a worried voice. "I'm sure we missed something."

"Sure we missed something," Strand said. "We always miss something. Nobody bats a thousand. But I'm sure that what we were looking for wasn't there. We didn't miss that. Somebody down there has it. I'm sure of it. It has to be that goddamned Kosanovic. It has to be."

Tony the clerk continued his steady clicking.

Soon the tenor of the funeral services changed. The Very Reverend Dusan Sukletovic was concluding things in Serbian.

"Now that is a nice eulogy," Strand said quietly.

"I didn't know you spoke Serbian," Hoffman said.

"There are a lot of things you don't know about me. A lot of things."

The way Strand said it made Hoffman shiver.

When the service was over, the cathedral was filled with the great hushed human noises that church crowds make when they are finally set free.

"Time for us to get out of here," Tony said. "My knees are killing me."

Hoffman murmured his consent.

"Great idea," Strand agreed. "But first, I want to show you guys something." He fumbled in the deep pocket of his suit pants and pulled out a small vial. Tony and Hoffman had bent over curiously to see what Strand had produced. In the dim light it was hard to discern the object, but when Hoffman did, he jerked away from the huddled group, his fingernails and shoes scratching against the rough wooden floor as he scrambled for the entrance hatch. "No, goddamn it!" Hoffman shrieked. "Not me, not me!"

Tony looked at Hoffman curiously, and then he heard the vial hiss. An almond scent quickly filled the confined crawlspace. Tony collapsed on the floor a split second before Hoffman did. Hoffman's hand clutched at the latch of the crawlspace hatch for several clumsy seconds and then fell across his chest, motionless.

Methodically, Strand strip searched the two men, removed all their identification, grabbed Tony's camera and the exposed films and crawled over their nude bodies to the access hatch. The almond mist was Prussic acid. It stops the heart almost immediately unless one takes an antidote before exposure, as Strand had.

"You see, Hoffman," Strand said without emotion. "There were a lot of things you didn't know about me."

Chapter Two

The plain log cabin rested comfortably in a stand of hemlock trees. A graceful curl of white smoke wafted from the stone chimney and swirled among the light snow that drifted downward in the darkening evening. Around the cabin, tire marks in the faint coating of snow led to eight vehicles. They ranged from a Rolls Royce Silver Shadow to an olive-drab Chevrolet with U.S. Army insignia and serial numbers stenciled on the side.

Inside, sitting around a rough-hewn oak table were eight men, eight powerful men who had been summoned to the cabin by one of the others. Each had been assigned a code name by that man.

At the head of the table sat Diamond. Diamond was the chairman of a defense company which made billions supplying weapons to defeat the Axis. Around him sat Corundum, Jade, Onyx, Malachite, Obsidian, Beryl and Topaz. Corundum was a young member of the Roosevelt "brain trust," albeit a hawkish one. Jade was a banker, a power in international finance. Onyx had spent World War II using the weapons that Diamond's company produced. The war had made him the youngest general in the armed forces. Obsidian came from academia, a physicist, a major cog in the Manhattan Project that developed the atomic bomb. Beryl was the director of research and development for the second largest defense contractor of World War II; Malachite, the chairman and

8

founder of Beryl's company; and Topaz, a rising star in the largest oil company in America.

"I think, gentlemen, that the answer we develop here today may well have a decisive hand in maintaining the current status of the United States as the foundation for freedom in the Western world," Diamond said, fixing each man with his eyes as he spoke. "It's plain that the present administration has neither the guts nor the foresight to keep Chairman Stalin and his allies from cutting us up piecemeal.

"I have selected each of you to be present here today because each of you has publicly stated your support for the continuation of a strong national defense. The rest of the country is weary with war. We are not, by nature, a militaristic nation, and because of that, it is difficult for the public to support the notion of a strong peacetime military establishment. .

"But we are entering a unique period in which wars are going to be fought in bits and pieces and won or lost in bits and pieces." Diamond paused to look at Onyx, who nodded grimly. "I believe that it will be increasingly difficult, as the weeks and months of this new era wear on, to convince the public, and through them the Congress, to fund the weapons the United States will need. Simply put, we are entering an era when Congress and the people will not have all the foresight and knowledge to make these decisions intelligently. The democratic process, as valuable and cherished as it is, simply is not in a position to keep us as strong as we need to be." Through the room swam murmurs of agreement and concern shared by each of the men.

Diamond paused and looked past the table of powerful men, through the small panes of glass in the cabin's front door, through the snow at the distant lights of Front Royal, Virginia some fifteen miles to the north. As a boy, he had helped his father build this cabin, cutting the logs, trimming them—by hand, fitting each one of them together and chinking the cracks in between to keep out the wind which now whipped impotently outside. He and his father had built everything his eyes could take in now, the stone fireplace, all the furniture, including the massive slablike table around which they sat.

America was like this cabin, he liked to think. For many years, he had helped cut the logs and fit the timbers of the country, had bent his back to produce the weapons and material needed to beat all enemies. He was proud of his country and the role he played in helping it through the war. He would be damned if he was going to let a bunch of weak-willed shits give it all up to the Communists. His son had died at Iwo Jima, and now the peace-minded politicians wanted to forget his blood and the blood of millions of others and forfeit all of the progress they had made for peace and freedom in the world.

"Because of this lack of national resolve and foresight," Diamond continued, "I believe it necessary that we, as concerned citizens—citizens of some power and influence— take the initiative against the day when the political process will have failed us in this most important of areas." He turned to the man called Onyx, who, for the occasion, had dressed not in his usual military uniform with its many battle ribbons, but in a dark blue banker's suit. "General . . . Onyx, please excuse me." He flashed an embarrassed smile. "It's difficult growing accustomed to these names. But believe me, gentlemen, the coming years will prove the wisdom of their use. Now, Onyx. Will you take up here with your proposal?"

Onyx, a tanned, lean man with close-cropped hair nodded respectfully and stood to address the group. Three chairs away, Malachite shifted uneasily in his chair. He believed in a strong defense, had spoken out publicly about the need to maintain military strength following World War II. But as he sat, he felt like he was sitting in on the preliminary planning sessions of a military coup in some banana republic.

"I believe that Mr. . . . Diamond has summarized the problem succinctly," the military man called Onyx began. "The problem lies in the fundamental nature of our society. Instead of a monolithic structure—like the Kremlin—to make decisions, our national defense complex is a sprawling, frequently chaotic network, ranging from defense contractors, to Congress, to the military. And superimposed on that network are the public and the media who, depending on the effectiveness of whatever demagogue comes along, might be persuaded to elect a Congress full of pacifists, ready to turn the country over to the Russians lock, stock and barrel in exchange for some vague promises of peace.

"Our national defense complex has no coordination," Onyx continued, "nor is there any constitutional mandate providing for any defense system. Technically, the President should fill this purpose, but things have grown too complex for one man to handle. Besides, the President, like Congress, is subject to the whims of the electorate.

"We are all men who have given of themselves to protect this great country. We have helped guide this country through the greatest threat to its security since it won its independence. *We* can be the coordination for the national defense complex. Through our own knowledge and the knowledge of people we influence, we can make sure the nation will always have the resources to defend itself."

The room fell silent. Only the soft whispers of the wind outside and the occasional popping of a log in the fireplace interrupted the silky weave of quiet. All eyes focused on Onyx.

"A number of developments growing out of the last war have suggested ways for us to make sure that weapons research and development will continue to be conducted and that the industrial plant of the United States will always be in a state of readiness to respond to a war *regardless of whether or not the Congress and the President support us*. In addition, I believe that we must act to make sure that Congress does not deprive the nation of the most effective weapons. I believe we can make the system work for a better defense.

"Our biggest allies are recent changes in the way the government structures the contracts awarded to companies, and the burgeoning secrecy system which has accompanied the recent development of scientific research for military purposes. For that we have the Manhattan Project to thank. Let's take the contract system. Increasingly the government is granting weapons research projects on a cost-plus basis. The government bears all the costs and then tacks on a certain margin for profit. In addition, with the increased specialization of weapons, the military has strayed from competitive bids, toward negotiated, single-source contracts. When you combine these two factors, you have a gold mine for defense contractors. Costs can be hidden in a thousand different legitimate places. Extra, unseen profits are built into the system. We can use this! Gentlemen, this is where we will receive the funding for continued research and development and for weapons production—even if Congress fails to act responsibly. They do not have any authority over the weapons we develop in this manner.

"Finally," Onyx concluded, "the growing classification system offers us many opportunities to keep our activities confidential. As you know, one of the significant advances made in security classification during the Manhattan Project was the 'need to know' concept. A person cleared for, say, 'top secret' doesn't have access to all top secret documents, just the ones he needs for his own work. That was how we were able to employ tens of thousands of people all over the country to work on the Manhattan Project, with only a couple of dozen aware that they were working on the atomic bomb. The rest knew they were conducting secret research, but they had no idea to what end. I predict the 'need to know' concept will gradually grow more restrictive and segmented as the years pass. Splitting up a project into a dozen or two dozen different locations makes it physically demanding and difficult for an auditor to oversee every phase of a project. The small segments are easier to hide, easier to maintain secrecy. When there's nobody in the whole damn plant who knows the ultimate use, it's hard for something to slip out. Ultimately, we can make even the largest of projects invisible for all practical purposes, and *this*, gentlemen, will enable us to do what we desire without fear of outside scrutiny. We can direct the vast resources of the military and defense establishment for our own goals, and secrecy and segmentation will keep them from knowing they are working for us."

Onyx looked slowly about the room as he took his seat. He saw general agreement and some confusion. Only on the face of the industrialist called Malachite did he read hostility.

"That presented things rather well," Diamond complimented the general, and then turned his attention to the remainder of the group. "I think we can continue here with—"

"I would like to discuss the constitutionality of this matter," Malachite broke in angrily. "It sounds like we're plotting to take away Congress's rightful powers . . . and the President's as well. Have you forgotten, General, that the President also serves as Commander in Chief of our armed forces? I scarcely believe what is being discussed here." Malachite scraped his chair backward and rose to his full six-foot, three-inch height. He was a distingushed, gray-haired gentleman with chiseled features.

"If I heard you correctly, General," Malachite continued, "you propose that the military and the defense industry put their heads together to secretly siphon off money to build weapons that have not been approved by either the President or the Congress." He looked angrily about him. "General, I think that what you're proposing could be called treason. You could be shot for it. I think—"

"Oh come now!" A blustery man with a florid face rose to defend the proposal. His code name was Topaz. "I don't think you have to slander the general. He makes a great deal of sense. A President is elected every four years, Representatives every two, Senators every six. All those boys have to be running all the time, and they're going to parrot whatever will get them elected. If turning all our battleships into scrap metal will get them elected, then this is what the politicians will do. We cannot rely on them to keep our country strong. Why, look at what happened after the First World War. They just about scrapped the entire military."

"But I believe what we're doing is not only unconstitutional, it's also illegal," Malachite persisted. "We would be better off redoubling our traditional lobbying efforts."

"Come off it!" Topaz insisted. "Do you think the way you have been buying Congressmen and Senators is any better? No! Because you've spent millions on politicians who have a short memory once they get elected. Your system might be accepted, but it's inefficient and a waste of money. You're better to—"

"I still don't like it," Malachite's voice thundered, "and I'm having no part of any of this." He strode to the door, plucked his coat from the antler of a stuffed deer's head, and without saying goodbye, walked into the night.

An electric silence hummed through the room as the seven remaining men stared at the door in wonder. Diamond cleared his throat. The sound was startling.

"Please excuse me for a moment," he said as he moved toward the only other room in the cabin. There, after closing the door, he made a telephone call, and then returned to the assemblage. Six pairs of eyes searched his. He smiled reassuringly, then took his seat and resumed.

Peter Fleming, founder of Fleming Industries, the largest manufacturer of radio and radar equipment for the military, drove slowly and erratically toward his home in the exclusive Washington suburb of Chevy Chase, Maryland. He would have preferred to have his chauffeur drive him, but Liam Fitz-Gerald—that old fool!—insisted no one be present at the meeting but the principals.

Fleming's entrails seethed as he drove along. Code names! Secret weapons! FitzGerald had lost his bloody mind, Fleming thought. It *was* treason. Pure and simple. Fleming would have no part of it. Malachite! Fleming snorted in derision. What had FitzGerald started?

Anxiety nagged at the old man as he negotiated his car along the winding two-lane highway east toward Washington. The snow was falling heavier now, the car's headlights turning the soft snow into dizzying psychedelic streaks. He switched on his low beams, but that failed to help significantly. He muttered under his breath. He hated to drive.

Fleming wished he could dismiss FitzGerald and his concept as just a rich old man trying to indulge his fantasies of power. But FitzGerald was indisputably one of the most powerful men in America. And the people he had gathered together matched him either in power, influence, wealth or all three. And it was a seductive idea. Governing the nation was growing too complicated, too technological, too dependent on split-second decision making to trust it to the hands of an electorate which was—often as not—ill-informed and tended to vote their guts rather than their brains.

The thought bothered Fleming. He believed in the system. But . . . times were changing, the world was changing. Perhaps it was time for some sort of modification to the democratic process. It concerned him that FitzGerald might be right, that it might be necessary to sneak about in order to give the American people what was best for them.

Fleming began to debate with himself when a pair of headlights appeared in his rearview mirror, grew large suddenly and then sped past, just as the two cars reached a blind curve.

"Damn fool!" Fleming cursed aloud as he slowed for the curve. No reason to drive that recklessly. The old man had no doubt that he'd have to stop a few miles down the road to help the man out of a ditch or worse.

Getting back to his debate, Fleming decided he still believed in the system, believed that Americans could make the right decisions at least as often as dictators could, perhaps even more often. He wasn't ready to jeopardize that system. Not yet, not without a hell of a lot more evidence.

He let his mind freewheel, concentrating on his driving. He had almost succeeded in calming his anger and anxiety when he came around a curve and spotted two tail lights on the shoulder. A man stood beside a car, waving a flashlight. It was the same car that had passed Fleming at such a high speed. I told you so, you damned fool, Fleming thought as he slowed. The man probably ran out of gas, burned it up speeding down the road.

Fleming pulled off the road and brought his car to a halt. The driver, a man in his late thirties, smiled gratefully and strode quickly to Fleming's Packard. Fleming rolled down his window.

"Thanks for stopping, mister," the man said. Fleming looked at him closely and started to admonish him for driving so fast when he saw the man's smile vanish. The man swiftly drew an object from the side pocket of his heavy parka. Too late, Fleming recognized the revolver.

The founder and chairman of Fleming Industries saw the flash of the first shot and blinked to protect his eyes from the heat. The slug obliterated his right eye and most of the right side of his brain. He didn't hear the second shot.

Chapter Three

The aircraft carrier *John F. Kennedy* smashed through the cold green waves of the North Sea as it made a broad circle fifty miles east of the Dutch polder city of Leeuwarden. In the distance, gray storm clouds, like floating granite mountains, lumbered toward the mainland. The North Sea was never a congenial host, particularly in December.

"Why did we have to come out here?" asked a tall, black-haired man. His voice was unsteady from his shivers. He had come on short notice and had not brought a warm coat.

"I'll get you a parka from the ship," said the other man, equally tall, about six feet one. His voice was steady and confident. "U.S.S. John F. Kennedy" was stenciled on the back of it.

"I don't want a parka," said the first man. "I want to know why we're here." He had a hard time sounding stern and demanding, since the cold made his voice quaver.

"You'll see," said the man with the parka. "Just have a little patience."

The first man stamped his feet on the metal deck of the bridge overlooking the flight deck. Down below in the icy wind that knifed in off the sea, a crew was readying two F-16's. A small wisp of steam curled from the flight catapult and was quickly snatched away by the wind. The flight officer said it was blowing steady at thirty knots. It would get worse when the storm arrived.

16

The first man, Bogdan Subasic, cursed the superior who wouldn't allow them to go back inside and cursed himself for not bringing warmer clothes.

"You're not very pleasant when you get like this, Bogie," Don Reese yelled over the wind. "Why don't you let me get you a coat? We'll be out here for a little while yet."

When Bogdan made no reply, Reese picked up the intercom and asked for another parka. They had worked together for a long time, and Reese knew his partner's moods.

"I still don't understand why you don't just tell me what's up," Bogdan asked. Down below, one of the stiletto-nosed F-16s was making its way into position on the catapult in preparation for takeoff.

"It's because I don't know the answer." Bogdan stared at him, amazed.

"You're shitting me, Don," Bogdan said. "That's not like you. We've always—"

"Hold on," Reese said, holding the palms of his hands in front of him. "All they told me was to bring you out here, get you a good look at Jay Fleming and what he does, let you know what you'll be working with."

"But as control officer, you—"

"That's another thing," Reese said, his voice showing his doubts. "I'm not your control officer in this one. I—"

"But who—"

"You don't have a control officer this time. You report directly to Graham Kingsley."

Bogdan stopped stamping his feet. "The advisor to the President?"

"The same."

The F-16, this one with the round red, white and blue marking of the Royal Netherlands Air Force, was roaring and shaking now and Reese couldn't hear Bogdan's comment. Suddenly the catapult roared forward in a fog of steam. The F-16 dipped slightly as it left the flight deck and slanted upward.

They stood silently as the next F-16, this one with the star and stripes of the United States, was maneuvered to the catapult and launched. So Jay Fleming was the one, Bogdan thought.

Graham Kingsley had summoned Bogdan more than five

years ago, summoned him to meet with a select group of leaders from the government, the military and private industry, and for five years he had helped them assemble the project.

He had been working on a long series of not-quite-bogus assignments dreamed up by Kingsley and forwarded to Subasic's section of the Defense Intelligence Agency by the President. It was necessary for Bogdan and the Committee to have the support mechanism of the agency behind him, but it was just as vital that no one in the agency know exactly what he was doing. He filed two reports, one to Reese, the other to Kingsley.

For the past two years he had gone through thousands of names. They needed a person whose reputation was unassailable, who had no former connection with intelligence activities, who had a deep knowledge of physics, and who had supreme confidence in his physical and mental abilities.

Fleming's name had, as it were, been spit out of a computer, along with twelve other names. Bogdan had been amazed at the computer, operated by the National Security Agency. They called it Big Brother. Bogdan knew that if the American public knew the detail with which the agency watched their lives, there would be an outcry that would shake the nation right down to the last brick in its foundation. Bogdan had mixed emotions about Big Brother. On the one hand, it helped him with his job. On the other, he hadn't been able to get a printout of what Big Brother knew about him. He didn't like that.

Of the twelve names furnished to him by Big Brother, Bogdan had added his own intensive observation and had weeded out eight of them as being unsuitable. It somehow made Bogdan feel superior to know he had information that Big Brother didn't.

After investigating and observing the top four candidates, Bogdan gave three names to the Committee. Fleming's name was at the top of the list.

The warm feeling he got now from knowing the committee had agreed with his choice helped insulate him from the grasping, clutching wind that tore at his coat and hair and trousers.

He didn't need to watch Fleming today. It was all for Reese's benefit. Reese had been told that Fleming's life was in danger because the Soviets lusted after his brain and the ECM devices it created. Maybe, Bogdan thought, but that's not why he was there. It was true, Fleming's life would soon be in danger, but not from the Russians. An overrated threat if there ever was one.

Yes, Bogdan thought as he resumed his foot stamping, he knew all he needed to about Jay Fleming.

Fleming was the grandson of Peter Fleming, the founder of Fleming Industries. He was handsome, a bit short at 5'8" but well-muscled with the shoulders of a college wrestler. He had majored in physics at Cornell, been a fighter pilot in the Navy, and then went to work with Fleming Industry's aviation division in Santa Monica, California. There he had major disagreements with the chairman of the company, and despite holding more than seventeen percent of the company's stock, lost a management battle to have the chairman ousted. Fleming left the company and started a smaller company, ECM, Inc., which specialized in electronic countermeasure devices used to jam enemy radar, misguide attacking planes and missiles and generally confuse the enemy. He had been enormously successful. Every airplane in the U.S. Armed Forces carried one or more of Fleming's devices. Today, Bogdan knew as he looked at the two F-16s in the sky, Fleming was here to show the Dutch Air Force why it needed his newest state-of-the-art devices. To prove his point, Fleming—his F-16 equipped with new ECM pods—would allow the Dutch fighter to fire its full complement of live, armed Phoenix, Sparrow and Sidewinder air-to-air missiles at Fleming's unarmed plane. Bogdan knew that Fleming's agreement with the Dutch Air Force brass required him to take no evasive action. The Dutch general agreed that if Fleming's plane survived they would equip the entire Dutch Air Force with the new ECM pods. It was a billion-dollar contract.

Bogdan had no doubts that Fleming would succeed.

A steward brought Bogdan a parka identical to the one Reese wore, and he slipped gratefully into the warmth still lingering from the heat belowdecks. He'd have agreed to the coat much sooner, but he knew how keenly Reese was tuned in to his moods. He had to act annoyed, as if he didn't know what was happening.

Turning around, Bogdan looked up at the assembled brass in the glass enclosed section of the flight control bridge. Looking back down, Bogdan could see the flight crews, catapult operators, ordinance crew and other personnel standing still, legs wide for balance as they looked skyward at the two F-16s. They looked like the kind of crowd that comes to a bullfight to see the bull win.

Overhead the rolling thunder of the jets' exhaust passed back and forth as Fleming and the Dutch pilot awaited word from flight control to conduct the test.

Huge, clinch-fisted bolts of lightning reached from the approaching storm clouds and smashed at the sea, lighting up the inky blackness on the horizon. Finally the two jets leveled off at the same altitude, Fleming in front.

A loud murmur of excitement rose from the crew on the flight deck as the Dutch plane released six air-to-air missiles and pulled away to make sure that a malfunctioning missile didn't backtrack. Bogdan watched as the streaks from the missiles closed on Fleming's jet. Then just as quickly as they had been fired, two of the missiles exploded. Seconds later, Bogdan watched in amazed respect as two more of the missiles plunged suddenly toward the sea.

Fleming's F-16 maintained its speed and altitude as the two remaining missiles closed in on it. Several plane lengths behind Fleming, they lost their propulsion—Bogdan saw the flames of their exhausts disappear—and dropped harmlessly into the North Sea.

A great cheer went up from the flight deck. Fleming had pulled it off once again.

"Why in hell would a guy gamble with his life like that?" Reese said finally. "Even for a billion-dollar contract?"

Bogdan Subasic looked at him. "Just crazy, Don. Just crazy . . . like you and me."

But Bogdan knew that Fleming wasn't crazy . . . and he wasn't a gambler. That's what made him perfect for the job.

Air Force Colonel Martin Wayne Copeland sat uneasily, gripping the arms of a leather upholstered wingback chair in the General's waiting room. He was alone.

Copeland looked at the Seiko quartz watch he wore on his left wrist. It was 6:31 P.M. He had a 6:30 appointment, and had been sitting in the room for nearly half an hour. He had left his cramped office at the San Diego Intergovernmental Weather

Research Center at 5:30. The trip to the General's office, located near Lindbergh Field, usually took half an hour, but Copeland had left himself plenty of time to get stuck in rush hour traffic that hadn't emerged. He wished he had brought something to read. Well, he would just have to count on General Jerry Patterson's well-publicized penchant for being on time. Copeland hoped he would be. He didn't know how much longer he could keep this thing inside of him. He felt like he was going to explode.

Colonel Copeland looked around him at the floor-to-ceiling bookshelves, the leather upholstered couch, the oriental rugs on the floor, the dark wood furniture, dark wood paneling, dark wood floor. He had been in this room many times, and it never made him comfortable, despite attempts to make it look like a snug corner at a London men's club. All that wood, the smell of leather, the aroma of good Cuban cigars smuggled in through an Air Force officer's international connections, served only to remind him that he had fallen off the ladder.

He was forty-eight years old and had been passed over for promotion to general six times. Others in his position had opted for civilian life. Most of the officers he graduated from the Air Force Academy with were either generals by now, or pulling down a healthy income in private business.

"Why don't you take the hint, Martin?" They asked him over drinks. "The money is a lot better out here." Copeland never knew how to answer them when they brought it up. He was a good officer. His record proved that. He had earned the Distinguished Flying Cross during his two combat tours in Vietnam. Had enough citations to paper the walls of a fair-sized house. For everything from bravery to efficiency to service beyond the call of duty. Most of them weren't bullshit.

Copeland shifted uneasily and looked at his watch again. 6:32. He wasn't an ass-kisser. He said what he thought. He acted on what he believed was right, not what he felt was most profitable. That's why he was the oldest colonel he had ever met.

After he was passed over the last time, and after he refused to take the hint and draw early retirement, they stuck him here. Not that he disliked San Diego. He actually liked it a lot. But he had a hard time convincing himself that he was doing something worthwhile nursemaiding a bunch of snot-nosed bureaucrats and corporate princes. The Intergovernmental Weather Research outfit was a jury-rigged batch of people from private corporations and government agencies all working together on a project he was supposed to keep secure.

He hadn't known the first thing about security when they offered him the position. Copeland's specialty had been in Tactical Air Command strategy. But the position was an ultimatum, take it or leave it. So he took it. He only needed two more years to be eligible for full retirement but he had thrown himself into the task with the energy he had once reserved for knocking Russian Migs out of the Southeast Asian skies. That, he knew now as he fidgeted in his seat, was why he might just be throwing away his entire career on this fine December afternoon in southern California, less than two weeks before Christmas.

At 6:33, General Jerry Patterson opened the hand-oiled walnut double doors and exploded into the waiting room.

"Martin!" The general smiled broadly as he stretched out his hand, "How the hell are you?" Copeland winced inwardly at the bogus greeting. Patterson and he had never gotten along. But the general, consummate politician that he was, always smiled when he stabbed you in the back.

"I'm fine, General," Copeland responded as he debated whether to salute or to shake the offered hand. Finally, he decided to shake the hand. It was an ebullient, well-practiced handshake, not too firm, not too soft.

"Well, come in," the general said, stepping aside with a flourish. "Come on in. We've been talking about you."

Copeland's bowels turned to lead. "We?" he managed. "But I . . . that is, when I spoke to your secretary I asked that—"

"Yes, yes, of course you did," the general plowed on through Copeland's stammer. "And I read your rather cryptic memo. Must say it was rather mysterious . . . have to agree with you though about the need to tighten up what gets passed around to whom. Surely does seem like a problem. Surely does. But I don't see any crying need for a private meeting. In fact, the more minds we have on a problem such as this, the greater our chances to come up with the best solution. That's what you want, isn't it?" The general stared at him, the challenge to argue plainly in his eyes. Patterson always liked a good fight. Well, Copeland thought, I'm not going to give him one tonight.

"Of course, sir," Copeland responded. "That's what we're all after. May I ask who you invited?"

"Surely, surely," the general responded, smiling the little victory smile Copeland knew so well. "As a matter of fact, even before you sent your memo, I had an appointment on a similar topic already scheduled with Steven Strand. He's in there now waiting for us. Let's not keep him waiting, shall we?"

Copeland felt his anger building. Strand was Director of the Intergovernmental Weather Research Project and what Copeland had come to tell the general dealt substantially with Strand's abuses of his position. As a civilian, Strand had no authority over Copeland. But Strand and General Patterson worked hand in glove. What Copeland had to say would have been difficult enough alone with the general. Copeland felt like smashing the general in his ruggedly photogenic face and walking out. But he controlled himself. There was more at stake here than the pride and career of one has-been Air Force colonel. He summoned his resolve and walked into the office. He felt like a condemned man and wanted to ask for a last cigarette. Only he didn't smoke.

Chapter Four

The President stood rigidly, his head bowed as if in prayer. His rich shock of silver-gray hair fell over his forehead as he concentrated on the task before him. He took a deep breath, held it for a long moment, let it slowly out and missed a two-foot putt.

"I don't suppose you'd give that one to me?" the President asked his closest adviser, Marshall Dodd. The Constitution had no definition for Dodd's duties, but like aides to the Presidents who had come before him, he had the President's trust, his ear, his respect. In many cases, Dodd made the President's decisions for him.

They had been teammates on the crew team at Yale, rooming together in the shabby little apartment in New Haven. Marshall managed his friend's campaign for student body president—and all the campaigns afterward. Through the House and Senate and now the Presidency, Marshall Dodd had never been far from the side of his friend. He was a tough man, "doctrinaire," some said. He was not known for his sense of humor.

Dodd watched the President's ball roll past the cup and come to a stop six inches away. He pondered the President's request as he would one asking for a first strike on Moscow.

"With all the respect due the office, I—"

"Spare me the horseshit, Marshall," the President interrupted. "Are you going to give me the stroke or not? Just say

24

so. Don't give me a campaign speech." The President stood erect, his chin pointed like the defiant prow of a warship, mock anger on his face. It had been like this for nearly four decades. In the first years of their friendship, Dodd's unyielding manner had made him angry. Now . . . now he simply accepted it, as he had come to accept so many unacceptable things in the world. Inwardly the President sighed. People had called him "expedient." Others, "the great compromiser." Regardless of the epithet, he knew they thought he was wishy-washy, Dodd included. Shit, it didn't bother him anymore. He was President, wasn't he? And they weren't.

"All right." Dodd's lips curled into the tight, close-mouthed grimace that he called a smile. "No point."

"You're a hard man, Marshall, a hard man." Dodd smiled a broad campaign smile. The President sank his last shot and the two men shouldered their bags and headed for the sixteenth tee at the Chevy Chase Country Club. They were followed at a respectful distance by the entourage of Secret Service agents. The two men always came here when there was something to discuss that required absolute secrecy. The President actually cared little for golf, thought it a waste of time. No matter, he did it to indulge Dodd.

They walked from the green, past the sand trap in silence. Overhead, a 767 whispered softly out of the scattered cloud cover, gently losing altitude for its approach into National Airport. On this December day, the sun was warm, breaking a string of gray rainy skies.

"Mr. President." Dodd always spoke formally when he had bad news. "I believe I can now confirm our earlier conversation, the one concerning the Tesla weapons research. I'm not happy to say this, but we have definitely lost the project." The President jerked to a halt and turned to face his adviser.

"Lost?" the President's face turned from quizzical to disturbed. "I don't understand 'lost.' How in hell could we have lost an entire goddamned secret weapons research project? You lose your keys and you lose a golf game, and some people lose their minds like I think I am when I hear you talk like that, but you don't just lose a secret weapons research program."

"I understand your confusion, but—"

"Confusion, hell!" the President exploded. "I'm not confused. You're confused. Don't tell me we lost a project. Find it."

"That's what we've been trying to do since I originally voiced my concerns to you. I think I may have some good news. I think I may know how to find the project."

"You had better," the President said, uncharacteristically angry at his old friend. "It's going to be my ass, not yours or anybody else's, if the Hill finds out that we've lost something of this magnitude. How could anyone lose a top secret project, Marshall? How? I still don't understand."

"The danger is inherent in the classification system," Dodd began patiently. "It's really no problem at the lower levels of secrecy, because so many people know about it. Auditors and others can keep tabs on what is going on."

"Yes, I know, and so can the Russians and the Chinese and the Israelis and anybody else. Yes, yes, I know all that. Just tell me—"

"That's what I'm trying to do now," Dodd said, exasperated. "As we increase the levels of secrecy, fewer and fewer people are brought into confidence. At the highest level—and this is where the Tesla weapons project was—only three or four people knew of the overall plan. One of those was President Roosevelt, and he's dead. And we don't know the names of the other three."

The President dropped his golf bag noisily. "There have to be records. In the Pentagon archives. In a sealed dossier. Somewhere. Nothing happens in government that doesn't leave a trail of paper a mile wide."

"You're absolutely correct," Dodd replied. "We know there's a trail of paper, but we don't know what it looks like."

"I don't follow," the President responded.

"As far as any government record goes, there never has been a Tesla weapons project. There are no records, no documents, no trace whatsoever of this project. Not as anything organized."

"Then it doesn't exist, and our problem is solved," the President said. "It was just a rumor, like we thought it was?" A smile was beginning to return to the President's face.

"Not exactly," Dodd continued. "The project exists. A little piece of it gets done as part of one legitimate project, another piece in some other research lab. The work performed is so similar to the bona fide research that we don't know which part is for the Tesla weapons project and which is for the legitimate purpose.

"All we've been able to do is uncover the odd project here and there, scattered throughout the entire military and private industry research and development establishment. All of the work is paid for with funds allocated for other projects. But the research actually performed is usually so closely related to a validly funded project that it has been impossible to prove anything."

"Give me an example," the President said, perplexed.

"Well, one of the bits we uncovered had to do with an Air Force–funded research project on the upper atmosphere," Dodd said. "The purpose was to gather information about the Van Allen belts."

"The what?"

"Radiation belts. A scientist named Van Allen discovered years ago that the earth's magnetic field captures some of the charged particles given off by the sun and actually stores them in regions high above the earth. They are high energy areas and can interfere with radio communications. That's why the Air Force wanted the research done. But, apparently, the same team of scientists also collected a lot of data about the radiation belts that were unnecessary for the Air Force's purpose."

"Information needed for the Tesla weapons project?"

"Precisely."

"So it seems like a fairly easy case to trace the people who gave them the instructions to do the additional research, then we nab them, use them to trace the location of this phantom project and shut it down before those vultures over on the Hill find out about it."

"I thought the same thing," Dodd said. "But no one seems to know how the instructions for the research get into the guidelines. I talked personally with the young Air Force auditor who discovered the work on the Van Allen research project, and with the scientists in charge."

"And?"

"And they weren't much help. It turns out that the instructions for the additional research were made orally."

"How could—"

"I asked. It seems that an Air Force officer with the proper clearance and credentials visited the scientist. Suggested that since he was already doing the project, maybe he wouldn't mind collecting a bit more information at the same time."

The President was incredulous. "And he agreed?"

"Think of it, Mr. President."

"Don't call me Mr. President. We've known each other too long."

"Think of it," Dodd continued. "You are a scientist whose bread and butter depends on the Air Force. In comes this Air Force officer who has all the clearances he needs. He's been validated by the classification system. And he asks you, sort of as a favor, to include a few more items in the research you're doing. The items he wants aren't very hard to do, won't take up much time, won't cost very much—in fact the additional costs can easily be absorbed into the budget. He's a high-ranking officer and you figure he can help you to get the next contract if you do him a favor here. Now wouldn't you go along? The officer knows every detail of your research, how much you've got to spend, what you're planning to do and how you're planning to do it. If he knows that much about this secret project, then you figure he's okay. Plus, he's got all the badges and clearances. What would *you* do in a case like that?"

The President looked away from his friend, tilted his head back and pinched the bridge of his nose between thumb and forefinger.

"Do what the man asked," the President said, returning his gaze to his advisor's face.

"Of course you would," Dodd said.

"But I'd remember the man's name," the President responded. "An IOU is no good unless you know where to redeem it. I'd get the man's name, his phone number and address."

"The scientist did just that."

"So who was the officer?"

"Colonel Edward Barney."

"So let's talk to Colonel Edward Barney."

"We have a problem."

"Which is?"

"Barney died in a training accident off the California coast in 1984."

The President closed his eyes as if in pain. "Before or after he supposedly made this request of the scientist?"

"After."

"How soon?"

"About twenty minutes."

"Any way it could really have been Colonel Barney?"

"None."

"What you're telling me, then, is that someone pretending to be Colonel Barney, using his clearances, his name . . ."

"And his uniform and badges," Dodd added.

"And his uniform, gained entrance to the lab, asked the scientist for a favor and then disappeared?"

"It was timed precisely," Dodd said, "with the real Colonel Barney's flight proficiency exercise."

"An exercise that resulted in his death."

"A dead end."

The President leaned over to pick up his bag, and rehoisted it to his shoulder. He resumed the walk toward the green of the sixteenth hole. When they arrived, the President dropped his ball into the washer.

"So, that leaves us trying to find whoever is to receive the information, am I correct?"

"The information, as per their agreement, was sent by the scientist to Colonel Barney's home, by courier. Neither the courier nor the information has been seen since."

The President cursed under his breath.

"It has happened in a number of cases," Dodd said. "We are running computer checks, but we can't possibly investigate every death of every officer in every training accident since 1943. Besides, much of the scientific research that might be useful to our phantom project is conducted in universities or in labs owned by corporations. It's entirely possible that some of the research has simply been contracted for, paid for and delivered without any sort of contact with the classification system. There are millions of places for the pieces to be hidden. Too many for us to find without getting hold of one of the primary people, one of the people who actually knows the location of the lab where all the little pieces of the project are brought together."

The President straightened up and dried his soapy golf ball

with a towel. "You said a few minutes ago that you have a solution."

Dodd hesitated. "I hope it will work."

"Tell me, man," the President said. "If we don't clear this thing up, if someone in the press or on the Hill finds out about it, then we can kiss a second term goodbye. Do you understand?" Dodd nodded gravely as the President searched for his favorite wood with the battered brass faceplate. He found it, stood over the ball and took a tentative practice swing.

"Take a real swing," Dodd said. "Open up, get warmed up. Take a couple of genuine swings and keep your left arm straight. You're bending it a little."

The President glared at him, but followed the advice nevertheless.

"Well," the President said as he approached the ball for his drive, "get your plan together and make it work."

"I've got meetings scheduled for tomorrow with our top people."

"You'd better make sure this thing gets sewed up tight and soon, and that it won't get out to anyone."

"It won't," Dodd said. "It won't. I'm taking it up with Graham Kingsley."

"Good man," the President muttered. "Next to you, the best."

"I thought you'd see it that way. I'm going to put him in charge of the entire thing," Dodd said. "With him at the helm, nothing can go wrong."

"It better not," the President said. "It sure as hell better not." He took a swing at the ball and sliced it toward the edge of the fairway. Two Secret Service agents hit the dirt.

"Shit," the President muttered.

Chapter Five

Amsterdam,
December 15

Broad, dense curtains of rain stormed across the open spaces of Schiphol Airport, filling the gutters with torrents that swirled like molten brass under the glow of sodium vapor street lights. Traffic limped past the stand where recent arrivals, frazzled, jet-lagged and still groggy from one too many scotches at thirty-four thousand feet, sparred for the few taxis.

Jay Fleming strode through the clean modern airport, miserable as could be. Water squished in his thoroughly soaked penny loafers and trickled from his hair and down the back of his neck. Fatigue started to creep up on him, just as it always did when the pressure was off.

He had been so high after concluding the sale to the Dutch Air Force that he gave his pilot and co-pilot the evening off and flew the company's Gulfstream jet to Amsterdam himself. There were concluding formalities tomorrow at the palace, but the real work was over. The trip from Leeuwarden had been hairy. The storm Fleming had carefully watched that afternoon from the aircraft carrier had turned out to be particularly mean, even by North Sea standards. He'd not had a single moment's rest.

He taxied the Gulfstream up to the general aviation terminal at Schiphol and got drenched by the storm as he sprinted the forty yards across the apron to the terminal. He was a fast runner, even with his briefcase and the canvas bag he carried slung over his shoulder. But in the fifteen seconds it took him to reach shelter, he had all but drowned.

The wet wool of his navy blazer and gray slacks smelled like a herd of drenched sheep. His yellow button-down shirt was open at the collar, and a tie hung limply over his belt buckle. He had a lean muscular face, tanned from sailing, his favorite sport. His bright, piercing, aquamarine eyes were streaked with the angry red of fatigue.

Fleming made his way down the escalator. At the bottom, he shifted the bag to his other shoulder. As he did, he looked up at the escalator and caught the eye of a tall man, well-dressed and dark-haired. The man seemed embarrassed and looked away quickly. Fleming thought he recognized him from somewhere, perhaps the aircraft carrier. But the man showed no sign of knowing him. It happened frequently these days as he traveled from one country to another. There were always people around he thought he recognized. If he had tended toward paranoia, Fleming might have thought people were following him. He slung the bag over his shoulder, picked up his briefcase and walked on, following the signs marked "Ground Transportation." The man walked on ahead of him and disappeared into a side corridor. So much for spies.

Fleming joined the frantic clamoring for a cab, and after about ten minutes of jostling and jockeying reached an empty one, opened the door and plunged in. He gave the driver directions to his hotel in Dutch, and then sagged into the upholstery of the taxi as it threaded through the rain-snarled traffic.

Fleming felt his body begging for mercy, for a good night's rest, yet his mind raced on, not yet ready to put aside the events of the day. The Dutch Air Force brass had been delighted with the ECM demonstration, and agreed to their bargain to purchase. But where the Air Force left off, the finance and banking and purchasing agents began. The toughest negotiators in the world, but reliable. Once they made a commitment, their word was sure as death and taxes.

Fleming closed his eyes now, trying to give his harried thoughts some rest. He loved doing business with the Dutch, but they always left him exhausted.

The cab picked up speed. Fleming cracked open his eyes and saw they were free of the airport traffic and making their way onto the broad concrete ribbons of the A4, heading northeast into Amsterdam. The tires hissed along on the rain-sodden pavement, giving off a steady, soothing noise that almost lulled him to sleep.

The driver said, in Dutch, "I don't mean to pry into your business, sir, but do you have a companion who might be following you closely tonight?" Fleming bolted upright in the seat, wide awake now.

"What makes you think that?" Fleming peered out the rain-streaked back window. It was impossible to see anything but a mass of headlights smeared into fluid abstract patterns.

"A car behind us has consistently been making the same lane changes I have."

"Another taxi?"

"No," the driver responded. "I think it is a Mercedes. A sedan, but not a taxi."

Fleming squinted as he gazed at the lights behind, but the rain made it impossible to see.

"No," Fleming said finally as he turned around in his seat, not entirely comfortable with his answer. "There is no reason for anyone to follow me. I am just a businessman." Of course, he conceded, he could be a target for kidnappers, either political or financial. That he made only defensive devices cut little mustard with fanatics. He was a warmonger in their eyes. There was an upsurge in anti-American sentiments these days. Perhaps a Dutch branch had it in for him. And there was always kidnapping. Businessmen all over the world were being ransomed for millions.

He had been arguing with his company's security chief for several years about precautions. Fleming had always resisted. He didn't want to be tied down. Being surrounded by bodyguards, unable to take a solitary walk, or having to travel with an entourage was just another form of being held captive. He'd take his chances, thank you.

"You speak very good Dutch for an American," the driver said. "Most Americans never bother to learn the language."

"I like Holland a lot. I come here frequently," Fleming explained.

"Do you always stay at the same hotel?"

"Yes, why?"

"There are many evil people about these days. It is not like it used to be. Businessmen are sometimes the targets of these people. I would take precautions, if I were you."

Anxiety twisted in Fleming's chest. "Why are you telling me this?"

"I am a professional driver," the man said proudly, "and I am taking a chauffeur's course so I can go to work with one of the large corporations. They are teaching us many things there, how to drive defensively, methods for escape, how to recognize a potential assailant, how to recognize a tail . . . that sort of thing."

Fleming let out a long quiet sigh as he leaned back on the seat. He wanted to laugh, but stifled it to avoid hurting the man's feelings. His class had probably studied the chapter on recognizing tails that very day, and now every car on the highway was a potential kidnapper. Fleming leaned his head back, trying to squeeze away the tension. He stared idly out the window at the approaching lights of Amsterdam. They passed cars; cars passed them. None of them contained kidnappers.

As the driver skillfully maneuvered off the A4 at Amstelveense Weg, Fleming had the feeling of coming home. It was odd, he thought, every time he had visited here, even the first visit, he had the warm secure feeling of coming home. Of all the cities in the world, this was as close to home as he ever got. And, yes, he always stayed at the same hotel, the Ambassador, a small, unpretentious, but very comfortable hotel in the old section of town overlooking the canal named the Prinsengracht.

Traffic thickened as they approached the old quarter, with its tall, narrow houses and twisting cobbled streets that ran along the canals. The rain had nearly stopped now, but its aftermath still snarled traffic, even as midnight approached. They turned onto the Prinsengracht, creeping along. When the traffic had slowed almost to a halt, Fleming tapped the driver on the shoulder.

"I'll get out here. No reason for you to get stuck in this mess."

"Are you quite sure?" He gave Jay a concerned look in the rearview mirror. "It's really no problem. I'd hate for you—"

"Not to worry," Jay interrupted. "I'm still soaked from the downpour. Besides, a little bit of exercise will do me good. If I walk, I'll get to the hotel faster and be able to change into some dry clothes."

"But—"

"No buts," Jay said, proffering a handful of guilders that included an ample tip. "Take this. I'll be going." He was faintly irritated at the driver. He was a nice enough sort, but his James Bond driving course was getting on Jay's nerves.

He stepped to the pavement, hoisted the bag over his right shoulder and with renewed energy picked up his briefcase and walked toward the Ambassador. Somewhere behind him, he thought he heard another car door close. But when he stopped to turn around, he saw nothing and resumed his march.

The rain had tapered off to a fine mist which gave all the streetlights a halo to wear. They resembled giant Christmas candles. Christmas. Hell, he hadn't thought about it for weeks, and it struck him now that the holiday was less than two weeks away. That depressed him. Where would he spend it this year, he wondered, as he walked steadily along the uneven brick sidewalk. There wasn't much reason to go back to the states for Christmas. The family gatherings depressed him now that his folks were dead. Killed on Christmas Eve by a drunk who ran them down with his car just three blocks from their home in Syracuse. They had been on their way to some friends' house to exchange gifts. The photographs taken by the police department showed brightly wrapped packages scattered in the snow near their twisted bodies. It had been hard to tell which were the gifts, and which were clumps of snow dyed red with their blood.

He had been in the Navy then, stationed on the *Forrestal* on sea duty, and had gone ashore on liberty that night. He never got over the fact that while he and the other members of his wing were partying at a sleazy bar in Singapore, his parents had been crushed to death by a drunk driver out on parole from his last conviction. Fleming hadn't learned about their deaths for two days. The man who killed them had died shortly afterward of a heart attack. Merry Christmas.

Forcing thoughts of Christmas from his mind, Jay stopped to fill his lungs with the sharp cold air. It cleared his head, summoning some untapped energy source. After ten minutes of walking, he had gained several blocks on his taxi. Just past the next bridge glowed the lights of the Ambassador. He heard footsteps behind him. He stopped. The footsteps continued for another pace and also stopped. Fleming turned and looked directly at the tall, dark-haired man he had spotted on the airport escalator. At least it appeared to be the same man. It was dark, the man was twenty or thirty yards away and silhouetted by the headlights of approaching cars.

Jay felt his heart pounding as he continued walking toward the Ambassador. It couldn't possibly be the same man. He was tired and his mind was open to suggestion. Damn the taxi driver for getting him started on this. Behind him the footsteps resumed. Jay walked faster; the footsteps accelerated.

Suppressing the urge to run, Fleming walked on, listening to the steps grow closer. What should he do? Should he do anything. He'd feel foolish if he ran, and the man behind him turned out to be nothing more than a neighborhood resident hurrying home. He thought of facing him and quickly discarded that notion for the same reason. If the man really was following him, he might be armed, and the confrontation could turn ugly. Besides, Jay told himself, what could the man do? There were people all around, witnesses. But it was dark; the man would be hard to identify. Fleming quickened his pace.

He reached the corner where the road rose. To his left, a narrow bridge clogged with traffic crossed the canal. To the right, a pedestrian street too narrow for cars ran between four-story buildings for a short block before crossing another bridge, this one across the Keizergracht. Fleming paused and turned. The man was closer, no more than thirty feet away. Fleming was sure it was the man at the airport. The man stopped and smiled disarmingly. He looked even more familiar.

Jay yelled as he unshouldered his bag and started toward the man. "Who are—"

"Hello, friend!"

Two bulky men stepped swiftly from the shadows of the narrow street and threw their arms around his shoulders. To the drivers stuck in traffic, it must have looked like two friends greeting a drinking buddy.

Jay Fleming opened his mouth to yell for help but choked on his own scream as a massive hairy hand smothered his face. Heart beating wildly, Jay twisted from side to side, but his assailants were huge men who picked him off the ground and carried him away from the traffic, into the shadows.

"The briefcase," he heard the one on his right yell in English, "and the suitcase too." From the blackness of a narrow alley less than four feet wide, a third man darted out and grabbed his suitcase and briefcase.

The men dragged Fleming toward the narrow black alley and the awareness electrified him: they were going to kill him. But who were they? Why would they want to kill him? He strained violently against his captors, but one held his right arm and the other gripped his neck and face while pinning Jay's left arm behind him. Fleming jerked and struggled, tangling his legs with those of the captor who covered his mouth. They stumbled against the rough brick wall next to the alley. Quickly, Jay sank his teeth into the palm held over his mouth, tasting the rusty salty taste of blood.

The man pulled his hand away from Fleming's mouth. "You little motherfucker!" the man cursed, loosening his grip. Jay freed his left arm and flailed desperately with it. He jabbed at the man with the bleeding hand and landed a blow to his head, sending him crashing into the wall. Jay followed that with a powerful kick to the abdomen, knocking him to his knees.

"Help! Murder!" Jay screamed as he punched and kicked at his assailants. He felt one punch and then the next slam home. The man on his right held on to Jay's arm, but the grip was weakening. Jay pounded him with his free fist, but the man was huge, easily six foot five and built like a fireplug. Jay's powerful blows seemed only minor irritations. Jay threw a knee at his groin, but the blow slid harmlessly off his thigh. Somewhere in the distance came the sounds of running footsteps. The third man returned. Jay screamed louder for help when suddenly a crushing blow smashed into the side of his head, above his left ear. He watched the ground push up towards him and felt the cold wet pavement slap him on the side of his face.

"You're a real asshole, Fleming," Jay heard a voice above him and struggled to move but his arms and legs disobeyed him. He lay there in a dark nightmare, listening to the men but unable to respond. "A real shit, that's what you are. And a traitor on top of it all."

A traitor? Jay struggled to make sense of the words. He had never betrayed anyone. Who were these people? Surely connected with the tall dark man who had followed him. But who was *he*? Where had he seen the man before? He felt his body rock as a shoe slammed into his side.

He heard the urgent rise and fall of a police siren, very faintly. Someone must have heard him, Jay thought gratefully, someone heard his cries and called the police.

"Quickly," one of the men ordered. Then Jay felt someone grabbing his legs, then hands under his armpits. Then seconds later, he felt his body drop again to the pavement; this time, there was pain. Jay tried to move his fingers and was rewarded by a tiny jerk.

"You had to let him scream, didn't you, Johnson," an authoritative voice complained.

"Shit, you'd've done the same thing, sir," the man addressed as Johnson replied. "Look at this." Jay knew he would be holding up his bleeding hand.

"Pussy. You're a real pussy, Johnson, you know that?"

There was no reply.

"Get to work, you fuck-ups," the authoritative voice said. "Let's get it done with before the police arrive." Jay heard shoes gritting on pavement. "The police . . . shit. How did I ever get stuck with you two anyhow?"

A dim light shone faintly through Jay's closed eyelids. A flashlight. Why wouldn't his eyes open? Jay wondered. He could see the red of the lids, he was conscious, yet he couldn't move. He listened to the men force open his briefcase, listened as they rustled through his papers. Then he heard his bag being zipped open. He tried again to open his eyes. The sirens grew louder.

"I don't see anything here," said one of the goons.

"Neither do I," said the other.

"Just take the briefcase," said the authoritative voice. "Leave the rest. Don't forget his wallet. And hurry up." It seemed like forever since the two goons had dragged him in here, but Fleming knew it had been only a few minutes. The police would arrive to carry away the body. It was a fact all over the world. Rarely did they interrupt a crime in the act. Practiced hands went through his coat pockets. They were unsnapping his wristwatch when footsteps reached his ears. Fleming's wrist, the watch still on it, plopped against the pavement.

"Somebody's coming," one of the men whispered. Jay heard them scrambling to their feet, heard the low metallic snaps of holster straps being opened, the swish of metal against leather as firearms were withdrawn. Fleming tried his right arm. It responded, a little slowly, but the strength was surely returning. He wondered if his voice worked, and if he should cry out for help, or to warn the person approaching.

But he had little time to think before the air was filled with a steady stream of little coughs. Fleming heard a syncopated musical scale of slugs as they slammed into bodies, brick walls and against the windows at the end of the alley.

Particles of brick rained on Jay's head and peppered the alley. He heard a grunt of pain nearby, and suddenly had the breath knocked out of him as a body fell on top of him. Something clattered to the pavement. As he lay there, pinned by the bulk of the body, Fleming heard more grunts, heard more soft thuds and finally, the rustling and heavy dropping sounds of human bodies striking stone.

"Fleming!" a voice called from out of the darkness. "Fleming, are you all right?" He opened his eyes but saw nothing. Slowly, Jay moved his hands under him and tried to push himself up, but the strength hadn't fully returned.

"Here," Fleming said weakly. "Under here."

Quick steps soon stopped next to Jay's head, and he breathed with relief as the inert body of the man on top of him was pulled away. Groggily, Fleming sat up and turned around to face his rescuer. Fleming thought he was hallucinating, thought the blow to his head made him see things that couldn't be there.

"You!" Fleming said, astonished.

"Yes." The man smiled. "Me."

It was the man from the airport. And in his right hand, he held a boxy weapon with a huge silencer.

"I'm sorry I didn't get here faster," the man said sincerely as he held out his hand to Fleming. "But I didn't want to follow you any closer for fear of alarming you."

Conflicting emotions flooded Jay's head: gratitude, anger, suspicion, fear, curiosity. Jay looked at the man with open-mouthed amazement, looked at the proffered hand of assistance and wondered whether or not to take it.

The man had a winning smile, a smile Jay was sure he had seen before. Though it was dark in the alley, Jay could see the man was over six feet. His long face looked Slavic or Greek.

"Come on, take my hand," the man urged. "We haven't much time before the police arrive."

Fleming looked at him. "Before the police arrive?" he said slowly. "But I want the police. These men tried to kill me."

"Yes, I know," said the man flatly. "But you don't want to be here when the police arrive. Think of the publicity. Will that help you conclude the sale you made today?"

"The sale I made today?" Fleming said absently as he looked up at the man, suspiciously. "How did you know about—"

"Later. Discuss it later." Anxiety grew in his voice as the sirens grew louder. "I know and that's all that should concern you. Come *on* now, move. You can't afford to be tied up with all this."

"Just what is all this?" Fleming asked, finally taking the man's hand. The grip was warm and firm, the arm which helped Jay up was strong and steady.

"I don't know," the man said. "But whatever it is, you have better things to do than spend the evening at the police station. It could get very complicated."

"That's fine, I just want to know—"

"They're dead," the man said angrily. "What do you want with the police? All they can do is fill out a report, waste your time."

"I—" Fleming stopped when the man pointed the boxy silenced weapon at him.

"Move," he said viciously. "Get your bag and briefcase and get the hell out of here. *Now!*"

Warily, Fleming nodded, and bent over to gather the papers which had spilled from his briefcase. A shattering pain stabbed at his head and he sat down heavily on the pavement, holding his head in his hands.

"Come on, I'll help you," the man said as he stashed his weapon in a shoulder harness and hurriedly began to gather Jay's belongings. Fleming watched in amazement. Who was this man who had followed him, saved his life and had now threatened it if he didn't obey his orders? He didn't like that. Never had liked taking orders. But the man held all the cards. He was big and had a powerful gun. There was no choice. When the hand was offered again, Fleming took it wordlessly and stood up shakily.

"Who are you?"

"No time," the man said as he handed Fleming his luggage. "Head that way"—he pointed toward the Keizergracht—"and walk around the block to the Ambassador. That way nobody should connect you with all this."

Fleming looked at the man as he would a lunatic. How in hell could somebody fail to notice him? He was staggering, his clothes must look like hell. He shook his head slowly, and then started for the mouth of the alley.

But when he reached the narrow, dark street, he saw no one nearby, no one to notice him, just the creeping traffic some twenty yards away. He looked down toward the Keizergracht where an identical stream of traffic crawled along. The motorists, their windows rolled up tight, had heard nothing. Most of the neighborhood's residents, in their shuttered homes, probably slept through it all, too. And the police? They sounded no closer than they had five minutes before, probably jammed in traffic with the rest of Amsterdam.

"Go on. Go on!" the man urged from the alley, and as if for motivation, pulled out his weapon and pointed at him. Jay ignored the pounding in his head and ran toward the lights of the Keizergracht. The man was crazy, Jay thought as he sprinted shakily toward the lights, the cars, toward sane people who had been calmly sitting in their cars, trying to get home, probably listening to Christmas music on their car radios.

Fleming reached the corner and leaned against the side of the building to catch his breath and watched for a moment as the cars passed slowly. One stopped in front of him, the occupants staring at him for a moment before roaring off. Jay caught his reflection in a pub window. His gray slacks were splattered with blood, his blazer torn at the shoulder and his face was caked. He picked up his luggage and hurried on to the hotel.

Bogdan Subasic secured the silenced Ingram MAC-11 under his left arm and swiftly set about relieving the three men he had killed of all their identification and valuables. Where had they come from? Was it possible that the Tesla weapons people had found out about things already? If so that changed the entire picture. It meant that there was a leak in the committee. One of the members was a spy.

How could that be? He wondered as he bent over and turned one of the dead men face up. The members of the group had been carefully selected, thoroughly checked out by every intelligence service in the government. There was no group more completely investigated. Perhaps one of these three gentlemen would yield a clue. He pulled out a long wallet and opened it. He couldn't read anything in the darkness so he retrieved the flashlight that had rolled across the alley, and shone it on the wallet's contents. There was a plastic identification card with the man's picture on it. Bodgan pulled it from its pocket with thin supple fingers and shined the flashlight on it. What he read knotted his intestines into a bowline. Wayne Maxwell Anderson—U.S. Central Intelligence Agency. Division chief. Subasic whistled softly to himself. What in hell did the CIA want with Fleming?

The sirens were growing closer now, and Subasic could hear the voices of anxious people, probably the police, as they shouted for room. Quickly, he finished ransacking the man's pockets, and turned his attention to the other two. He strained, turning them over. They must weigh two hundred and fifty pounds apiece.

What he found in the first hulk's wallet shocked him even more than discovering he had killed a CIA section chief. The hulk's name was Ramone Vitelli. He had a State Department identification card, but Subasic had seen State Department cards like this before. There was no doubt the goon worked for their covert actions group.

The other big man's wallet yielded the same thing. It was obvious the operation was run by the guy from the CIA. The two defensive tackles had been loaned to him, probably as a favor and on short notice, otherwise it would have been an all-CIA affair.

Hastily, Subasic emptied the wallets of cash and credit cards. He wanted it to look as much like a mugging as possible. They didn't need Dutch Intelligence poking through things. With a few telephone calls, it wouldn't go past the Amsterdam police.

Bodgan Subasic straightened his tie, walked calmly from the alley and turned toward the Keizergracht, his pockets filled with dead men's money. What did the CIA have on Fleming, and what did it mean? Had they chosen the wrong man?

Chapter Six

The coffee was thick, hot and fresh. Jay Fleming took a sip, and swallowed slowly as he savored the flavor, the aroma. The coffee and the way the sun shone warm and yellow in the early morning nearly made him forget the night before. But for the scrape under his eye, and a tender swelling on the side of his head, he could have dismissed the entire altercation as the twisted nightmare of a very tired man.

Jan Dijks, the waiter who looked after the Ambassador's small solarium-like breakfast room with its broad glass wall overlooking the Prinsengracht Canal, watched as a small frown passed over the face of their regular customer, Mr. Fleming of Santa Monica, California.

"May I get you something, sir?" Dijks asked in perfect English. "Some more coffee, another roll?"

"Thank you." Fleming surveyed the wreckage of his breakfast: Crumbs of bread, cheese, a smear of marmalade. Nothing else remained. "Some more coffee would be nice."

"Was everything else . . . all right?" The waiter persisted. He liked this courteous visitor. Mr. Fleming never treated waiters like lower-class beings. Dijks remembered the time a couple of years ago when Mr. Fleming invited one of the bellmen to accompany him on his evening exercise jog around the canals. The bellman remarked that he could not get the same running shoes in Holland. A week later, a new pair

44

arrived at the hotel, air expressed from California, a gift for the bellman. Fleming was like that.

"The breakfast? Yes, fine as usual," Fleming replied, somewhat preoccupied. Dijks turned to fetch the fresh coffee. It must have been the mugging last night, he thought. That would be enough to upset anyone. The story had gotten about the hotel quickly. Everyone was talking about how Mr. Fleming had entered the lobby, blood on his face, his hair in disarray, clothing sticking out of the corners of his suitcase. He had to hold his briefcase under one arm to keep the papers from spilling out. Attempted robbery, he said. He refused medical treatment, said he would call the police in the morning. The waiter resolved to do whatever he could to make Mr. Fleming more comfortable.

Jay accepted the fresh coffee graciously, and leaned back to enjoy the view. According to his Rolex, it was 9:53. The head of Fleming's Amsterdam officer, Pieter VanderJagt, was due at 10:30 to discuss the final papers for the Dutch Air Force ECM sale. Then they would both walk over to the royal palace to get the last of the formalities over with. Normally, they would have gone to the Defense Ministry at The Hague to sign the papers, but the head of the Ministry happened to be in Amsterdam that day.

Fleming thought about the night. Who was the mysterious man who had saved his life? Jay thought about what the man had said concerning the police. It *would* complicate matters. No matter how much he disliked it, he knew that appearances counted, and there was no way that he could prevent people from reading more into the incident than really existed. They could deduce that Fleming was involved in some very unsavory business, and that could only hurt him. He knew that in this business, it didn't matter whether or not you were guilty or innocent of something, just as long as people thought you were. If it appeared you were guilty, you were guilty. He had seen people more important than himself stumble because of rumors. Maybe the tall dark man in the alley had been right, Fleming thought as he stared off through the window. A glassed-in excursion boat pushed slowly along the canal. He had just about decided to order another croissant when he heard his name.

A bellman approached, carrying a long white envelope. "I'm glad I found you, sir. This just arrived by messenger."

"Thank you." Fleming accepted the envelope and tipped the bellman. Warily, he examined it. The envelope bore the return address of the Department of Physics, University of Leiden. Written in a crabbed, shaky handwriting was the name "F. Anderson." Jay turned the envelope vertically, and carefully tore off one end of the envelope. Franklin Anderson. Professor Franklin Anderson. Fleming had met him on a number of occasions, usually at NATO meetings. British, an expert on electromagnetic phenomena. Lately, Fleming had seen his name on articles discussing electromagnetic pulses from nuclear explosions. The note inside the envelope read:

"Exciting matters to discuss. Possible breakthrough. Can you visit after concluding ECM sale? Am most anxious to meet with you. Please reply soonest."

It was signed with an illegible scrawl that looked like a mass of tangled fishing line.

How did Anderson know he was in Amsterdam? And about the ECM sale? He thought about the professor. A harmless type, actually, who had produced nothing really worthwhile since the test-ban treaty of the early 1960s. Scientists—foremost among them, Anderson—had only begun to study the phenomenon of the electromagnetic pulses when the treaty was signed. Since that time, Anderson had been pumping a nearly dry well. Fleming wondered what this "possible breakthrough" might be.

Tomorrow *was* a free day. He had planned a walk around Amsterdam, a bit of sightseeing. He closed his eyes, remembering Leiden. He had stayed there with some students on his first visit to Holland. A summer abroad. Fleming had been taking courses at the London School of Economics. On a weekend whim, he took a backpack and sleeping bag and crossed the channel on a ferry from Harwich to Hoek van Holland. Two nights later he found a place to crash on the floor of a cold, crowded apartment overflowing with students.

Leiden. A bucolic little town with canals and old buildings and the oldest university in Europe. Or was it the second oldest? He couldn't remember. No matter, he thought, squinting into the bright sunlight. He would enjoy the train ride to

Leiden, if not the conversation with Anderson. A walk around the town would be delightful. After his meeting with Vanderjagt, he would telephone the professor. A breakthrough. He could certainly use one. He leaned back in his chair and tried to feel comfortable about things. But something still gnawed at his thoughts.

San Diego,
December 15

Was it something she had said? Alexandra Downing wondered. She sipped at her snifter of cognac and searched her memory. She couldn't understand what had made Martin so gloomy. He was like that. Just when she thought she had some insight into what made him tick, he changed signals.

They were nearly alone in the restaurant now. At 1:30 in the morning. Two other couples dawdled over drinks. The remains of dessert lay on the table. Martin's cheesecake had been dutifully played with, but not eaten, just as his lobster had remained half eaten and his wine half drunk. It wasn't like him.

She had never seen him like this, not in the six months she had known him. She took his hand and squeezed it playfully, but it lay inert, lifeless, as if the man inside the body had gone for a walk and left her here with the corpse.

Alexandra looked into his eyes. They focused on some spot beyond her, beyond the restaurant. She loved him and it hurt her to see him so vacant. Perhaps, she thought, it was the pain. He said it came back to him sometimes. She'd met Colonel Martin Wayne Copeland two weeks after his wife of twenty-three years decided one morning to leave. She was tired of his dead-end outlook, tired of being an officer's wife, sick of what she called his pig-headed adherence to outmoded standards. So she left him a note, a pile of bills for new luggage and wardrobe, $7 in their joint savings account and no forwarding address.

Not long after that, he took to long, thought-filled walks, depressed wanderings. On one such outing, he was strolling along the docks at the small craft marina in Mission Bay, dreaming of buying a boat and sailing off to Tahiti, or any other faraway place.

It was barely eight o'clock in the morning when Alexandra climbed the stairs through the companionway of her Morgan 41 sloop, trying to chase the sleep from her eyes and get a look at the day ahead. She stood there, half in, half out of her boat, when she found him gazing fondly at her boat. When their eyes met, he flushed and started to walk self-consciously away.

"Good morning," she called. He stopped and turned. She saw a tall, lean man with salt-and-pepper hair trimmed in the military fashion. He was dressed in khakis, a navy-blue polo shirt and black lace-up shoes. He had a flat stomach. His arms and shoulders were well muscled. He was forty or so. She particularly liked his eyes. They were brown, with golden flecks.

"You have a lovely boat there," he said awkwardly. He stuck his hands in his pockets and rocked back and forth on his heels, like a little boy caught with his hand in the cookie jar, vulnerable, lonely. Instantly, she wanted to help him.

"Thanks," Alex replied. "The perfect thing to say to any skipper. We all like to think ours is the most beautiful." A broad smile filled with white even teeth spread across his face. They stood there for perhaps half a minute before Alex broke the silence. "Coffee?" she asked. "I've just put on a fresh pot."

Hesitantly, he walked down the finger that ran alongside her boat and stared up at her, intrigued. She was young, he knew, younger than himself by almost thirty years. It turned out she was twenty-nine. She had hair the color of dark teak and cobalt-blue eyes. She was tall, about five-seven, with a lithe, muscular body.

Later, he found she had an overall tan, firm breasts, and some stimulating ideas about making love. But not on that Saturday afternoon.

She liked Martin from that first morning. He was considerate, with a strong sense of moral obligation. After they'd been seeing each other for a while, she found he had the strength and physique of a man half his age. He kept himself in shape.

But mostly, she liked him so much because he needed her. She needed that.

The restaurant was emptying. The other two couples had settled their check, and now the last remaining waiter looked at them hopefully, so he could go home. The sounds of San Diego Harbor washed in through a partially opened window.

Alex set her snifter down to one side of the table and grasped his hand in both hers. "What's the matter?" she asked firmly. "I have to know. I love you, you know."

Slowly his eyes came back from their journey, their focus finally finding her face. "I love you too," he said.

"I think someone may try to kill me," he said finally.

She sat upright. "Have you done something?"

"Nothing wrong," Copeland said flatly. His eyes returned to their private scene. "But I've caught others . . . no." He stopped himself. "It's better if you don't know."

"That's nonsense, Martin," Alex said strongly. "How can I help if I don't know?"

"You can't help me with this one," he said. "I don't know that anyone really can."

"That remains to be seen," Alex said. "Who did you catch and what did you catch them in?" They stared at each other, neither wanting to yield. Alex sighed. She let go of his hand and leaned back in her chair.

"I've caught them in the biggest threat to the Constitution this country has ever seen," he said. "There's no way they can let me get away with it."

"Let you get away with *what?*"

Copeland looked at her for a long time without answering. Alex was alarmed. He actually looked ill.

"I think I ended my military career this afternoon," he said softly. "They finally pushed me too far, and pension or no pension, I have to do what's right. And that means going to Washington to see if I can blow this whole thing wide open."

"What whole thing?" Alex asked.

"I can't tell you, now," he said. "If there's a possibility that I can get help in Washington, it's better that you don't know. They might even come after you if they thought you knew."

"They?" She said. "Who's 'they'?"

"Strand, Patterson. The whole bloody lot of them."

She started to speak and he held up his hand.

"Hold on a minute," he said as he leaned over to retrieve a large manila envelope he had brought with him. She had forgotten about it. He handed it to her. It was heavy and fat and sealed with tape.

"Put this in the safest place you can think of," he said. "Do you have a safe deposit box?" She nodded. "Good. First thing tomorrow—today," he corrected himself, checking his watch. "Put it there. If anything happens to me, open the envelope. It'll explain everything."

She felt tears filling her eyes. "They're going to kill you." She stood up and went to him, oblivious to the waiter, who was shooting them a stare that could blister paint. Martin stood and hugged her. She buried her face in his hard muscular chest. "Please don't let them do that." Her tears came now. "I don't know what I'd do without you."

"It's something I have to do," he said sadly. "It's important."

"More important than you and me?" Alex looked up at him, tears streaming down her cheeks.

"I didn't think that anything could ever be more important than you and me," he said. She saw the moisture building in his eyes too. "But this could affect millions . . . tens of millions of people. If I'm right, there is no way they can let me live.

"The only saving grace in all of this, is that they don't know about you," he said. "You're safe and I want you to stay safe. If anything does happen to me, follow the directions in the envelope *to the letter*. I've set things up so you can get things moving without revealing yourself or exposing yourself to any danger." He sniffed and withdrew his right arm from around her so he could wipe away a tear.

He held her differently tonight, fragilely, as one would hold a cherished piece of porcelain. He had always treated her gently, but never like this. In his eyes she saw the reason. He never expected to see her again. She caught a sob, and hugged him with all her strength, praying he was wrong.

Chapter Seven

Night comes early to Amsterdam on winter evenings. By four, the sun is well on its way toward America, leaving behind, on most days, a flat sky the color of wet cobblestones. But on this evening, as Jay Fleming walked slowly north along the Damrak toward St. Nicholas Church, the sunset spread warm reds, oranges and yellows across the sky. Amsterdammers, scurrying home, paused to enjoy the unusual sky, remarking that such beautiful scenes always seemed to follow terrible storms like the one they had experienced the night before, as if God was rewarding the survivors.

Fleming, on foot, had stopped for a light at a huge intersection, trolley lines, canals and sidewalks tangling in front of the central train station.

"A wonder, yes?" A stooped woman swaddled in scarf, gloves and ankle-length coat addressed Jay as they waited for the light.

"Yes," Jay agreed, "a wonder." She smiled, then hurried across as the light changed, disappearing into the crowd anxious to get the next train home. Fleming walked slowly, envying them their sense of purpose.

The afternoon, he supposed, should have been a triumph. The Dutch government had signed the contract to equip all their military jets with his ECM equipment. Jay had aced out the giants in the defense industry to do it: Raytheon, Hughes, Fleming Industries, Allied Defense . . . none of them had really come close. But, then, none of them had come close for years now.

No, his triumph had been hollow. And hanging over it all was the tender place on his head reminding him that he had been a target, was probably a target still, of people with no faces, no names. He wanted to chuck his work and find out who was after him. The thought exhilarated him, pleased him far more than the success of the afternoon. A mystery. There were no longer any mysteries to solve in his business.

Fleming looked up at the ornate facade of the train station. Even when he wandered, his unconscious led him to points of embarkation. He glanced about for a moment, then started back the way he had come. The walk was the important thing, not the destination. As long as he could remember, his desire had been to move, to go, where had never been important. Being in movement was what mattered. And blasting along at mach 2.3 was the ultimate movement.

He cursed himself for ever leaving the Navy. All he'd ever really wanted to do was fly. There had never been a time of his life when he had felt more alive than in the Navy: the challenge of flight, dogfights, landing on the pitching, rolling deck of an aircraft carrier in rough conditions. They had tried to get him to stay, had offered every inducement allowed by law and more than a couple that weren't. But he had been flattered and he believed the flattery when a group of stockholders from Fleming Industries convinced him to leave the service and "take his rightful position at the helm of the great worldwide corporation your grandfather founded." And he had been caught up in it all. The company, they said, needed him to get rid of Steven Strand, a man who was ruining the company and along with it the great name of Fleming.

At first, the corporate game was a challenge, full of the same sorts of dogfighting that characterized aerial combat. But when he realized his corporate wingmates would just as soon shoot at him as at the enemy, he knew he had made a mistake. But by that time, it was too late. He had been led into what the *Wall Street Journal* later termed "the bloodiest corporate management slaughter in American history."

The stockholders who initially couldn't live without him struck a deal with Strand that left Fleming out in the cold, an orphan sitting on the curb in front of his own home. He left with his huge block of stock intact, and his pride down in flames.

After being forced out of Fleming Industries, Jay had searched for some way to avenge his embarrassment. As a pilot, he had seen all the things that were wrong with the military's electronic countermeasures. ECM devices were supposed to confuse enemy radar, confounding their anti-aircraft missiles, but the ones he had used, including the Fleming system, were simply not reliable.

Some of the stockholders in the corporate bloodbath had not deserted him, had, in fact, been as embarrassed as he had. With their venture capital, he started ECM, Inc. and two years later, Fleming Industries had folded its ECM division, buckling under the competition. Jay had rubbed Strand's nose in a prominent pile of manure. The stink was spread across the covers of every business and defense publication in the country.

But that was the last time Jay really enjoyed the company. He had founded it to embarrass Strand, and he'd accomplished his purpose. That was three years ago, and the company, despite its continued success, no longer gave him a sense of satisfaction. Now it was just another company.

At the Dam—the huge open square next to the Royal Palace—Jay headed east along the narrow twisting alleys that led toward the Zeedijk: the nightclub and red-light quarter. Along the tree-lined canals, near churches and homes, stood establishments of every sort, catering to every taste: shops offering pornographic films and magazines; clubs featuring sex, on film or live on stage; shop windows with naked women lounging, displaying their wares for all to see. Throughout were some of the best restaurants, bars and musical entertainment in the city. It was the perfect place to distract Jay from the thoughts of the day, the aimlessness of his life, and a more pressing question: Why had someone tried to kill him the night before?

Along the Achterburgwal, street and sidewalk were jammed. Jay sidled through well-dressed businessmen, middle-aged tourists, college students, scruffy long-haired types selling hashish and the occasional sailor from the nearby wharfs. It was a shoulder-to-shoulder carnival crowd, moving nowhere fast, no one in a hurry. At the Casa Rosso, a pitchman exhorted him to come in for some sexy entertainment. Fleming smiled and walked on. Not tonight.

Next door, a group of college students, three men and two women, paused in front of a window, studying a prostitute like a laboratory specimen. Her heavy breasts were bare; thick pubic hair curled through a slit in her panties.

"I think it's gross," one of the girls remarked. Jay stopped for a look. Turning his head, he caught a sudden furtive movement. A man turned and walked away quickly. Jay caught his breath. "You!" he shouted, shoving through the crowd. "Stop! Stop, please!" The tall, dark-haired man rounded a corner, and turned up a narrow side street. Heart pounding, Jay struggled against the dense crowd. It was like trying to swim against the current.

"Excuse me, please," he said, first in Dutch, then in English. "Please let me by. I must get past. Please . . . pardon me."

Angry looks and curses in a half dozen languages followed his slow progress toward the corner. He *had* to reach the man, *had* to find out what had happened the night before.

"Watch it, asshole!" A man muttered as Jay jammed past him. He reached the corner and lunged around it. He stopped, adjusting his eyes. The street was more dimly lit than the Achterburgwal and less crowded. People walked dimly as shadows.

Fleming ran, his boots pounding against the pavement. He examined every face as he passed. Strollers gave him looks usually reserved for the insane. He spotted a man at the end of the block, moving quickly, purposefully, not pausing at the shop windows. Jay closed in quickly.

"I've got you now!" Jay cried, grabbing the man by the shoulder and spinning him around. The man staggered and slammed against a brick wall. *"Was ist?"* the man exclaimed in German. He was obviously a German tourist, terrified that Jay was about to mug him.

"I'm sorry," Jay said in English, and then in Dutch. His knowledge of German was rudimentary. *"Entshuldegung,"* he said. The man looked at Jay as if he were crazy, and then slowly his expression of fear and confusion turned to one of relief and then anger.

"A mistake," Jay turned and said to the crowd in Dutch and

then in English. "Mistaken identity." He turned suddenly from the German, forced his way through the circle of onlookers and broke into a jog. He continued along the alley for another fifty yards until he came to another intersection. Fleming looked up and down the cross street and saw no one resembling the tall dark killer.

Which way would the man have turned? Most people went to the right. But this man, Jay knew, was a professional. He would take the less obvious direction.

Fleming followed a narrow street to his left. It was hardly wide enough for a single small car to pass. As it curved slowly clockwise, numerous passages branched off it. Jay stopped to peer into the depths of each passageway; the light from the street scarcely penetrated the gloom. He could be anywhere. There was no hope of finding the man.

Walking unhurriedly now, Jay made his way to the end of the street. It ended in a "T." He saw no one in either direction. Fleming stood for a moment, empty defeat sweeping through him. His shoulders sagged as he sat down on a doorstep. For a moment he considered that he had imagined the entire episode, that his mind had been playing tricks on him, that the tall dark killer had not been near the Achterburgwal just a few minutes before.

Wearily, Jay closed his eyes and rubbed them with the palms of his hands. It was the work, he told himself. The prudence, the security, the safety was starting to dull his keen senses. In a few more years, all he'd be fit for was running a corporation.

Happy night voices filtered down the street from the right. Jay stood up quickly, straightening his sweater and vest and looking toward the voices. Emerging from the darkness into the cone of light shed by the streetlamp were four young girls, college age, he judged, all chatting animatedly in a language he didn't recognize.

Fleming turned to the left and walked ahead of them, heading for a bar he remembered, a small English style pub just up the way. He needed a drink.

The Mercedes stretch limo whispered to a stop at the curb in front of the regal, gray stone building in downtown Washington, D.C. The building, with its hand-carved parapets and Corinthian columns, seemed out of place amid the massive expanses of steel, concrete and glass that typified the structures around it. It was a relic of an earlier, more graceful era.

A starched doorman scurried from a sheltered entryway and opened the door. He snapped smartly to attention as a tall gentleman with glacial blue eyes and a thick white mane, carefully combed, climbed out easily.

"Good afternoon, Mr. FitzGerald," the doorman said with genuine affection. "It's good to see you again." FitzGerald smiled regally, said a few words of greeting, then hurried up the marble steps and into the foyer of the Shepherd's Club. Veterans of national politics said the Shepherd's Club sheltered more power under its roof than Congress and the White House combined. The club's members tended to agree.

Liam FitzGerald, chairman of ADI Inc., the eleventh largest industrial corporation in America, crossed the foyer with the wide confident steps of a giant. The hand-polished, black walnut door swung back slowly as FitzGerald approached. The cast brass numbers were all the club had for identification. No name plaque, no sign. Those who needed to know where the Shepherd's Club was, knew.

Inside, FitzGerald yielded his cashmere coat to one of the club's butlers and crossed quickly past the entrance to the formal dining room and into the main room with its oak parquet floors, dark wood paneling, comfortable arm chairs upholstered in oxblood red leather, expensively bound books in floor-to-ceiling shelves and racks of newspapers from all over the world. The flat winter sunlight filtered in feebly through a set of French doors, its rays shattered into rainbows by a cut crystal vase filled with fresh red roses. On the far wall, a club assistant had climbed the bookcase ladder to obtain a book requested by a member. The club maintained a full-time librarian and several assistants for its extensive collection.

FitzGerald surveyed the room quickly, returned the greetings of several members he didn't have time to speak to, and headed for the small elevator just off the foyer. Once inside, he pressed an unmarked button located just below the one for the subbasement. When the elevator stopped, doors failed to open until FitzGerald inserted a small brass key into the lock provided on the elevator's control panel. The door opened, FitzGerald stepped out, inserted the same key in a wall plate which would ordinarily have held a call button, and the doors closed and returned to their standby position on the first floor.

In contrast to the luxury of the main floor, the room in which FitzGerald now stood was stark. The walls were plain, unadorned by art. There were no windows, for this room was more than six stories underground, its walls built to better standards than most bank vaults. And it had its own vault.

Liam FitzGerald was known in the room as Diamond. And, as there had been for decades, there were Corundum, Jade, Onyx, Obsidian, Beryl and Topaz. Although some of the men behind the names had changed since 1947, their positions of power had remained. Liam had planned it that way. In here, the man became the position, became part of *this* structure and none other. It had worked for decades.

To the personnel who worked in the club, and to the other members, the Seven were the founders, the membership committee. None knew their true purpose. Not yet.

Diamond surveyed his realm. Beneath the plain oak furniture, the floor was covered with thin carpeting with no pad underneath. There was no place to hide a covert listening device. Even if one of the Committee of Seven were to turn traitor and try to smuggle one in it would be impossible since the elevator contained sensors to detect such listening or recording devices. The sensors were activated whenever the key for the meeting room was actuated.

The sensors, the vault, the impregnable room, the entire concept of the Shepherd's Club had been Liam FitzGerald's concept. He was the founding chairman of the club, the only chairman, in fact, the club had ever had since its birth in 1947. Presidents had come and gone, but FitzGerald had always remained.

FitzGerald pulled one of the chairs away from the table and eased himself into it to wait for the other six members. There was Jade, a vice-chairman of the Trilateral Commission, member of the Federal Reserve System, international banker, adviser to the World Bank and the International Monetary Fund. Jade influenced the Trilateral Commission and the Trilateral Commission influenced—some said governed—the world.

There was Onyx, a member of the Joint Chiefs of Staff, former head of the Strategic Air Command; Obsidian, physicist, now director of advanced weapons systems research for the Department of Defense; Beryl, founder and chairman of the Vanguard Institute, the country's foremost national defense think tank; Topaz, Chairman of the Board of Global Energy, a consortium of oil and other corporations secretly linked together by Topaz to avoid anti-trust regulations. Taken as a whole, Global Energy was twice the size of Exxon. Finally, there was Corundum, former university president, world renowned historian and political scientist, adviser to four presidents, a man whose quiet words had shaped the course of world events for three decades.

An impressive group, Diamond mused proudly, for he had selected them all. Four of them—Corundum, Jade, Beryl and Onyx—had been with the Committee of Seven since its conception in 1947. The original Topaz and Obsidian had died and replacements had been selected.

The Committee of Seven formed the nucleus of the Shepherd's Club, acted as an all powerful membership committee that recruited influential members from American government, industry, academia, banking. The primary attributes for membership were power, influence, and a commitment to a strong America as the foundation for a free world. Every member was a leader, a shepherd, dedicated to leading the United States to its proper destiny. The club provided these most powerful men with a private place to meet, to talk, to plan and to conduct their most confidential business away from prying eyes and eavesdropping ears. But even among this bastion of discretion, the Committee of Seven was the most secret among the secretive.

But that secrecy, he knew from his brief telephone conversation with Corundum, had been breached. FitzGerald stared thoughtfully past the vault and scowled. He drummed his fingertips against the tabletop. He stood up and paced around the austere room, and finally sat down again.

There was something about Corundum which was wrong, seriously wrong. Diamond had heard it in his voice. He took a deep breath and sighed. He didn't want to have him killed. Not yet.

Within fifteen minutes, the elevator had arrived and departed five times, leaving only Corundum unaccounted for. Diamond looked at the slim Piaget on his wrist and noted with a frown that the presidential adviser was twenty minutes late. The six members present spoke in cultivated, well-rounded voices of mergers, policies and decisions that could affect billions of dollars and millions of lives. Finally, shortly before 2 P.M., the elevator arrived for the seventh time.

"Please accept my apology, gentlemen," said Corundum as he stepped quickly through the doors and inserted his key in the slot. "I received an important last-minute call." The assembly murmured its acceptance.

The subtle rustling and scraping of men seating themselves filled the room for a moment. Corundum seated himself between Topaz and Obsidian.

FitzGerald noted the seating arrangement with disguised anger.

Corundum cleared his throat. "Thank you all for coming at such short notice, but you all requested to be notified immediately if anything unusual occurred." The presidential adviser studied each face carefully. "Something has happened. As we discussed at our last meeting, we have taken steps to use Jay Fleming as a Judas goat to see if he can lead us to the final set of Tesla documents and, not incidentally, prevent them from falling into the wrong hands."

"Any hands but our own are the wrong hands," Onyx muttered. Heads nodded in agreement.

"Quite right," Corundum continued. "That's what makes recent events so disconcerting. Fleming was attacked last night by three gentlemen working for the CIA." Diamond searched the faces of each member as Corundum dropped his bomb-shell, looking for the inappropriate reaction, an indication of guilt. There had to be a leak from within the Committee of Seven. Or just as bad, the involvement of Fleming in something which they didn't know about. FitzGerald prayed that his greatest fear over the years, the presence of a Soviet mole within his carefully selected group, wasn't coming true. But those were the only possible explanations for the CIA's rapid reaction. The committee had only reached the decision to use Fleming a week ago, and had only started twenty-four hours before. Not long enough to leave a trail that could be spotted. No, there had to be a leak. None of the men assembled about the table displayed anything other than shock.

Onyx spoke up. "You think there is a leak within the committee?" His voice was incredulous. He cast a skeptical glance around the table.

"That was my original conclusion," Corundum continued. "But there may be other explanations. We have no proof that the attack on Fleming has any connection to us. At this time, I'm more inclined to put faith in the theory that the attack was motivated by a corporate enemy of Fleming's, someone who lost one too many contracts to his company. That, of course, includes a dozen or so large American firms, and at least half that many in Western Europe. We should also consider the possibility that the Soviet Union has finally given up on trying to beat his systems, and has finally resorted to the sort of tactics they have long been known for. Which would mean the three agency men were traitors."

Jade interrupted. "In other words, your guess is that Fleming has been so successful he had to be eliminated. But, if there is more support for that conjecture than for the possibility of a leak, I'd like to hear it."

"I took the liberty," Corundum continued, "of checking with the Director of the CIA. The agency men were all on leave. Any action they took was not sanctioned by the CIA. I double-checked this with the covert operations chief. The three were on business for someone else."

"Why don't we direct Subasic to interrogate them?" Topaz asked.

"Because Subasic killed them when he saved Fleming's life."

"A damn shame," Topaz said. "We could have learned a lot from them."

"I'd believe that if I knew who was behind them," Jade said. "I've used the agency before. So have most large companies whose aims run parallel to the nation's. But usually somebody knows where the contract came from."

"Things are a lot more tight-lipped, even within the agency," Topaz said. "Ever since the press got hold of ITT's involvement with the Allende thing in Chile, the agency hasn't let things go beyond the people directly involved."

"Besides," Corundum said, "if someone had really known about our entire operation, the obvious target would be Bogdan Subasic. We can always get another Judas goat. But Subasic is really irreplaceable. He's been with us long, and he's completely loyal. He's also the weakest link. Any of us can be replaced and the operation would continue. But lose Subasic now, and we'd never prevent the transfer of those documents."

The conversation degenerated into a multitude of two- and three-person discussions. Finally, the chaos resolved with a consensus. Corundum had to be correct. Only removing Subasic would fatally destroy the plan, and no one besides Subasic and the Committee of Seven knew about the plan. The relief was palpable, as if a cloud of poisonous gas had lifted.

"Incidentally, what *did* happen to Fleming?"

"He was roughed up a bit, but nothing serious," Corundum said. "I received Bogdan's telephone call about 8:30 last night. He'd observed Fleming's flight demonstration, and then picked him up again at the airport in Amsterdam. As we had discussed with him last week, it was felt that we needn't follow him too closely until after we'd truly exposed him as the bait. Fortunately, Subasic did see fit to follow him last night, saw the agency men attempt to make off with him. Bogdan is trying to arrange some additional help from the Defense Intelligence people in Amsterdam, just as a favor for a few days until they get to Luxembourg where the rest of his men will meet him."

"What are the DIA people in Amsterdam being told?" Onyx asked.

"The same thing as the people we had already arranged for in Luxembourg, that the Russians are after Fleming because of his ECM developments. They have been told that the Russians would like to snatch him, and, at worst, kill him to deprive us of his skills. They have been told to kill Fleming rather than let the Russians snatch him."

"It would be ironic if that were as close to the truth as we now think," Beryl offered.

The room was silent for nearly a minute as the members of the Committee of Seven assimilated the information they had been given.

"I'd certainly like the opportunity to speak with Subasic face to face on this," Jade said. "Somehow speaking with him seems to generate ideas and solutions." Several others murmured their agreement.

"As you know," Corundum responded, "Subasic must stick with Fleming until the end of the operation, barely a week from now. If we don't locate and obtain the documents before next Friday, I'm afraid we're going to have a very, very tough road ahead."

"Yes, yes. I know," Jade said, irritated. "I don't expect to see him here. I was just saying that he seems such an outstanding catalyst for solving problems."

"We *could* arrange to meet with him in, say, Luxembourg," said Onyx. "No problem for me to arrange the flight. To avoid raising eyebrows, and safeguard the future of the Committee, I could arrange three or four flights with a variety of destinations. Brussels, say, Amsterdam, Paris, and one to Luxembourg."

"Why don't we think about that," Obsidian suggested.

"Of course," Onyx agreed, "just give me a couple of hours notice." He smiled. Being a member of the Joint Chiefs of Staff had its perquisites.

Obsidian took the floor. "Before we leave, I'd like to give some consideration to ethics. I am not entirely comfortable using an American citizen in a matter such as this without his knowledge. I agree that our mission is of the utmost importance," said the physicist. "We have the weapon substantially completed, yet the method of aiming it has still eluded us . . . and the Soviets. But does that justify using Jay Fleming as we are?"

"This is a war," Onyx argued. "We've got to do everything possible to make sure we win."

"Yes," Obsidian agreed, "but even in wartime we ask for volunteers. Don't you think we owe Fleming the right to volunteer for this?"

"Obsidian, my old friend," Diamond's powerful voice filled the room. "I agree that we are in dangerous waters now. I think we all would have liked to do things differently. But if you'll remember, Fleming turned us down, not once, but half a dozen times, when we invited him to become a member of the Shepherd's Club. If he had not done that, I don't think any of us here would have hesitated to talk with him confidentially about his task. But the fact is, he did refuse us, and he *is* the best man for the job."

"Still . . ." Obsidian's voice trailed off. "After this is all over, I'd like us to come to some sort of understanding before we undertake anything else like this again."

"Agreed," Diamond said.

The meeting adjourned, and one by one the members left as the elevator rose and fell seven times. As Diamond rode upward to resume his life as Liam FitzGerald, he worried about both Obsidian and Corundum.

He hoped they wouldn't require anything drastic.

Chapter Eight

Martin Copeland sat impatiently as General Robert Guereri spoke on the telephone first with one person and then another. All together twelve calls so far. The Secretary of Defense was in Kuwait brown-nosing Arabs. The Assistant Secretary that Guereri usually dealt with was at a NATO meeting in Brussels. Guereri's most powerful contact at the White House, Marshall Dodd, had been taken only hours ago to the George Washington University Medical Center with what might be a fatal stroke.

"Damn!" Guereri cursed softly. "Dodd was a helluva man. A decent one. The last of a breed." He slammed the receiver on its hook and tried yet another number. He spoke to a secretary. The National Security Adviser was out of town until Monday. Furious, Guereri slammed the receiver down again. It slithered off the cradle, squirted off the edge of his desk and yo-yoed up on the coiled wire.

Monday was too long.

"Christ, Marty," Guereri exclaimed when Copeland had explained the situation. "If half of what you say checks out, we've got to move and move now." And Guereri, reliable Bob Guereri, who had graduated from Officers Candidate School with Copeland, who never turned away a friend, got on the telephone himself and started making calls. It was nearly four o'clock on a Friday, and the Washington bureaucracy had slipped away early like cockroaches into the cracks of a wall.

Copeland knew they had to do something drastic, like reaching the President. He figured that if anyone could reach the President, Guereri could. Now, Copeland worried as his friend wordlessly picked up the receiver and began dialing yet another number.

Guereri looked over at his friend of a quarter century and felt nothing but pity. A good officer, an honest man, and General Guereri knew that whether Copeland's information proved out or not, the man's career was finished. You just couldn't tell your commanding officer to go fuck himself and then get on the next commercial flight to Washington loaded with top-secret documents. Officers couldn't afford those sorts of run-ins with superiors. Copeland had confronted more than his share during his career. Which was why he was still Colonel Copeland. But this, Guereri reflected, this Tesla Project took the cake. Copeland was sitting on something that could destroy the nation.

Copeland folded and unfolded his hands. He crossed his legs; then uncrossed them; then crossed them again. His palms were perspiring; droplets tickled his ribs, staining his shirt. He was pale, his face drawn and tight from fatigue and anxiety. After saying goodbye to Alexandra, he had driven straight to Los Angeles International Airport to catch the last nonstop red-eye flight to Washington.

Copeland tried to concentrate on his friend, tried to take his mind off the awful process he had set in motion. "Yes, yes, this is General Guereri at the Pentagon." None of the general's anger or frustration surfaced in his controlled, deep voice. "Certainly I'll hold." Guereri covered the mouthpiece and whispered to Copeland. "Bastards always have to put you on hold to let you know how important they are."

"Yes, I'm still here," Guereri said, and then almost immediately "good afternoon, sir. Good of you to give me some of your time. We have a crisis which the White House should be aware of, and I can't seem to raise the right people through normal channels." He paused and listened. "Yes, I called him. Yes, him too. That's why I took the extraordinary step of calling Mr. Dodd. Yes, tragic. I agree. What's that?" Copeland watched as his friend concentrated on the telephone. Guereri's face sagged. "Just a few minutes ago?" Guereri shook his head slowly as he listened further. "What?" he said almost vacantly. "Five o'clock. Certainly. We'll be right over. Thank you very much, Mr. Kingsley." Guereri hung the telephone up gently.

"Dodd's dead," he said faintly, then looked up slowly, pain in his eyes. "He was my grandfather's closest companion. Treated me like a nephew. Arranged for my appointment to the academy." Copeland got up from his chair and put a fraternal arm across his old friend's shoulder. They remained like that until it was almost too late to make the White House appointment on time.

"I'm a desk soldier now, Marty," Guereri lamented. "I can't take death anymore. Death is for young soldiers."

To save time, they took Copeland's rented car.

The afternoon commuter traffic was mostly heading out of the city, so they made good time, crossing the Memorial Bridge by the Lincoln Memorial, heading east along the Mall, then north on 17th Street toward the White House.

"I really think we've hit the jackpot this time," Guereri said as Copeland drove. "Graham Kingsley is the guy we would have had to go through eventually to get to the President. If anybody can get the President to act, he's our man."

The prospect buoyed Copeland's morale, helped to dull the sharp edges of the fatigue. He concentrated on the traffic, not noticing that a black government-issue sedan had picked them up as they left the Pentagon's massive lot.

Copeland pulled up to the gate near the west wing of the White House and handed his identification and Guereri's to the uniformed guard. The man made a telephone call, and then the gate swung open.

Minutes later, they were sitting on a Hepplewhite sofa, drinking bad coffee from bone china cups.

Copeland glanced nervously at his watch. The second hand seemed to make it round the face once an hour. He clutched at the briefcase lying on his lap. Inside, he knew, lay his destruction. The intercom on the dour-faced secretary's desk buzzed once.

A wood fire crackled and popped in the fireplace across from Kingsley's desk. Copeland couldn't help feeling awe as he greeted the man who, some said, exercised more power than the President. It was a magnificent office, fit for a ruler, with its walnut paneled walls, huge window viewing Pennsylvania

Avenue and Lafayette Park, its Matisse and Pissarro. And a
door leading directly to the Oval Office. That, Copeland
thought, said more about the man's relationship to the
President than all the campaign lore.

"Please make yourselves comfortable. By the fire," Kingsley said in a voice that immediately set Copeland at ease. He
and Guereri selected seats at opposite ends of the sofa next to
the fire. Kingsley chose an armchair next to Copeland and
soundlessly crossed his long legs. No one spoke. Kingsley
inspected first Guereri's face and then Copeland's with the
intensity of an artist who would later try to paint them from
memory.

"Brandy?" Kingsley said as he straightened up. Guereri
accepted; Copeland demurred. There was no telling what
alcohol would do combined with his weariness.

"Very well," Kingsley said as he rose from his seat and took
two cut crystal snifters and a matching decanter from a niche
among a collection of leather-bound books in a case by the
window. Copeland and Guereri exchanged looks.

After he had handed a snifter to Guereri and seated himself,
Kingsley finally got to business.

"General Guereri," he began, "tell me about this crisis so
urgent it can't be handled through normal channels." Copeland
detected impatience. Guereri deferred to Copeland, who
opened his briefcase and ran through the explanation he had
given Guereri three hours earlier.

"What I have here," Copeland said as he pulled out paper
after paper, "are invoices, coded cable traffic and other
documents, which, taken along with this"—he handed a sheaf
of papers to Kingsley—"prove that a group of American
military officers, civilian officials in the Defense Department
and a group of our largest military contractors have secretly
developed a powerful new weapon which they intend to use
toward their own ends. I received a copy of the memo by
mistake. A routing error. The memo and the supporting
documents also prove that these people have been carrying on a
foreign policy of their own without approval or knowledge of
the State Department and have been improperly using resources of the United States Government to do so." Copeland
paused. The man is made of steel, he thought, as Kingsley
calmly took a sip of brandy, set down the snifter and

thoughtfully examined the sheaf of papers, thumbed through the pages, and set it quietly down on the table.

"Why don't you start at the beginning, Colonel Copeland," Kingsley said. "I'd like to hear you, in your own words, describe this conspiracy. With your permission, I'll tape record the conversation so we may have a permanent record." Copeland nodded his assent, and Kingsley pressed the intercom button to summon his secretary. After she had provided him with the recorder, he sent her home. The look of relief on her face was almost heartbreaking.

Kingsley had difficulty with the recorder's controls and asked Copeland for assistance. "Thank you, Colonel," Kingsley said after the tape began to roll. "Now please begin."

The sun had long set by the time Copeland had finished. Kingsley had been attentive for the three hours it had taken to run through the entire story—how Copeland had received the document, how he had brought the matter to the attention of his commanding officer and been rebuffed, how, using the memo as a map, he had riffled through files in the appropriate offices to gather the supporting documents. He left out nothing save the envelope left with Alexandra Downing.

Finally, Copeland ran out of words. He felt drained, as if someone had just emptied his soul. For better or worse, Copeland had begun what his conscience had told him was right. In the ensuing silence, Kingsley just sat, looking at the two through eyes which hid from Copeland any clue of the thoughts behind. The sounds of traffic filtered softly into the room, the only other sound the erratic popping of a fire which had long since collapsed into a glowing pile of coals.

"Thank you," Kingsley said finally, pushing himself up from his chair. Both Copeland and Guereri rose. Copeland wanted to rush over and shake the man by the shoulders, demand an answer from him, inquire what course would be taken. He was owed that much, Copeland felt. He had run the most enormous risks, the least of which was to ruin a lifetime career. But he restrained himself.

"I believe that you have in your possession a potential crisis of the largest proportions," Kingsley said gravely, fixing the colonel's eyes with his own. "Although I have it all on a recording, I believe you should tell the President in person. I'd like for you to remain in Washington, as the guest of the White

House, until I can arrange a meeting with him, probably tomorrow or the day after."

Copeland's heart soared. This wasn't just another futile joust with the bureaucracy. Something would happen. Action would be taken.

"Thank you very much, Mr. Kingsley," Copeland said almost exuberantly. "You have no idea what it means to me for a man such as yourself to help see justice done."

"Colonel, I'm not doing this to help you," Kingsley admonished. "I'm doing this for the good of the country. But I will say that I greatly admire the courage and initiative it took for you and"—he looked at Guereri—"and for you, General, to bring this to my attention. I suppose we can all consider ourselves fortunate that the usual channels were unsuccessful, and that I happened to be in my office. Otherwise, the matter might have been batted about in channels until it was too late. Thank you." He shook both men's hands, and then accompanied them as far as the elevator.

Copeland felt as if he were skating on clouds as he and Guereri walked back toward the car. They walked in silence, each man trying to make his own separate peace with the evening's events. Copeland glanced at his watch and saw it was just after eight. He had been awake for almost forty hours now, but he felt refreshed, as alert as he did upon rising the morning before. For the first time since reporting the misrouted memo and its contents to his commanding officer, Copeland felt he not only had a chance to live, but might even salvage his career, and, beyond that, he might see Alexandra again.

Both men were silent as Copeland guided the car away from the White House and around the Ellipse toward the Pentagon. Guereri had spoken only to suggest that he take a cab back to pick up his car, but Copeland wouldn't hear of it.

That decision made life easier for the three men in the black sedan. The men had been talking amiably with a couple of Secret Service agents at the gate when Copeland's car passed through. They quickly said their parting words and piled into the car in discreet pursuit.

The Fourteenth Street Bridge over the Potomac is a maintenance engineer's nightmare. The sheer volume of traffic chews up the road surface and spits it out in massive potholes. Heavy equipment is almost always blocking one or more lanes of the span. On this night, as Copeland approached the bridge, he noticed the bright klieg lights and the heavy equipment. A crane was lowering entire sections of roadway into place. Traffic backed up as a flagman waved heavy equipment across the lanes.

Copeland's mind was deeply embedded in thoughts of Alexandra, and of what Kingsley had promised: the President. Tomorrow he would meet with the President.

"I've got a lot to thank you for, Bob," Copeland said gratefully. "You've really gone out on a limb for me."

"No sweat," Guereri said, knowing that when all the shit had finally hit all of the fans there would be plenty of sweat. "What are friends for?"

The flagman waved again, and Copeland thought he'd make it through, but no such luck. Copeland put the gear selector in park. A crane operator gently urged a Cadillac-sized plate of concrete into the air and swung it over the roadway. It passed out of view overhead. In front of them, workmen with ropes walked across the closed traffic lanes. Copeland thought the flagman was ready to wave them on when he heard a shout and a long ripping metallic screech like gears being stripped. He looked up and stared wide eyed as the roof of the sedan bulged for a split millisecond and then broke. A great sadness swept through his body. He would never see Alexandra again.

When the police arrived, they found a rental car about eight inches thick, resting underneath a slab of concrete. The wreckage oozed blood. Police also found a crane with a stripped gearbox, and the remains of Colonel Martin Wayne Copeland and General Robert Guereri. After a thorough investigation, officials found that at some point the crane had failed to handle the enormous weight of the concrete slab. Although one industrial expert suspected the gearbox had been tampered with, no conclusion was possible, given the condition of the gears. Police investigators were unable to locate the crane operator. He had been hired that day to replace the regular operator, who had taken ill following lunch.

And no one took notice of the three men in the black government-issue sedan with the black sidewall tires, as one of them made a dozen radio calls to people scattered around the Pentagon. Several different men from various locations near the accident site left their positions and headed home. They had been prepared to act, but none of them had seen the airport rental car containing Colonel Copeland and General Guereri. They were all just as happy to be backups. The pay was the same and it was easier this way.

"Accidents will happen," the crane operator said to himself as he turned the ignition of his car. He didn't wonder who the two dead men were. He was paid to make accidents happen.

Chapter Nine

Leiden, Holland,
December 17

Rain fell relentlessly from a slate-gray sky as Jay Fleming slogged away from the train station in Leiden. The university town was drowning under another storm. Jay cursed and ducked under the overhang of a department store, battening his overcoat against the plucking fingers of the wind. Gone was his hope of spending a relaxing, touristy day, reliving some distant memories. He regretted now his decision to take the train rather than drive out by rental car.

Rain pounded at his umbrella as he plunged once again into the downpour, heading south along the Steen Straat, his trouser cuffs now dark and damp. Professor Anderson lived just ten minutes from the station, in a canal house on the Apothekers Dijk.

The streets were sparsely populated. At least the heavy rain made it easier for him to spot anyone who might be following him. But he had begun to doubt the probability of that happening. During the hour-long train ride the thought that he might be imagining things continued to gnaw at him. Fatigue had probably caught up with him; he was actually just the victim of a mugging. His weary mind had invented the tall dark killer and the three dead men in the alley. He decided to visit the Amsterdam police before he left.

Fleming knew that whatever emerged from his visit with the Amsterdam police would not satisfy him. Either they had found three bullet-riddled bodies in an alley, or they had not.

Neither situation was pleasant, whichever it turned out to be. The first meant someone was trying to kill him and the tall dark killer was real. The second meant he was losing his mind. He preferred the first by far. Nothing concerned him more than the thought that his mind might be going.

He passed a triangular park. In better weather, tour boats hugged the piers, and lunchers ate here. Fleming was dismayed to see the shining reflection of a McDonald's across the canal. He marched on, across the bridge to the Rapenburg Prinsessekade, and then another short half-block to the Apothekers Dijk. The Rijn flowed obediently through the canal to Fleming's right. He walked along the glistening brick sidewalk, searching each door for Anderson's number. Just past the Kenne Wegst, he found it, a shabby four-story house, distinguished from its neighbors by its unkempt facade. Anderson, it looked, had fallen on hard times.

Up and down the Apothekers Dijk, front doors were well varnished, with polished brass knockers and nameplates. Anderson's tarnished knocker was mounted on a door weathered from neglect, the rich mahogany grain showing in only a few patches. Fleming struck the knocker three times. He heard the sounds of someone stirring within. Moments later, a chain clacked against the interior, and a solid lock thudded open. Fleming was startled by what he beheld.

Huge purple bags hung from Anderson's eyes, and around them the skin was a ghastly gray. His gray hair stuck out like handfuls of hay. The professor stared at him with rheumy yellow eyes magnified by very thick glasses. He wore a ratty brown cardigan sweater over a plaid shirt and brown tweed trousers. His hands shook, and he smelled dank, like a dark, wet cellar. Fleming wanted to turn around and leave.

"Good morning, Mr. Fleming," Anderson said in a shaky old man's voice. Anderson was fifty-three, but on this day, he looked seventy.

"Morning," Fleming replied as cheerfully as he could.

"I'm glad you could come," Anderson stammered. The two men stared at each other in a silence punctuated only by the thud of rain drops on Jay's umbrella. Anderson did not appear happy to see him.

Imagination, Fleming told himself. You're imagining it. Why would the man have invited you here if he didn't want to

see you? And why would he be afraid of you? Control yourself.

"Well!" Anderson said finally, breaking the spell, "please
come in. Come in out of the rain." He looked down at
Fleming's feet. "You're soaked. You must be miserable. Come
in, come on in." Fleming stepped onto the slate floor, folded
his umbrella and shook it outside as best he could before
placing it in a rack by the door. Anderson disappeared into a
dimly lit room to the left.

Fleming placed his overcoat next to another on a tree, and
followed his host. Anderson had sagged into a threadbare
armchair next to a window facing the canal. But the curtains
were closed tightly, giving the room a funereal air. A small
table with a brass lamp stood to Anderson's left, and on the
other side of that, another armchair, even shabbier than the old
professor's. Across the room, a sofa missing a cushion faced
Anderson. There was no other furniture. Impressions on the
carpet and faint rectangles on the walls indicated that paintings
and furniture had been sold. The entire room smelled like
Anderson.

What had happened to the man?

"My back," Anderson responded to Jay's curious look. "It
has troubled me for some time, and it grows worse with the
rain. I must find a more hospitable climate." Fleming noticed a
curious slurring of words, a fuzziness in his enunciation which
had been absent the last time he had met with the professor.
Anderson looked like a junkie on his last legs.

Jay crossed the room, heading for the sofa.

"No, *here!*" Anderson blurted abruptly, pointing urgently at
the chair next to him. Fleming looked at him oddly, then
complied. What breakthrough could this wreck of a man
possibly have made?

"I have some difficulty seeing these days," Anderson
explained, clearly embarrassed by his own outburst.

"Perhaps if we opened the drapes a bit," Jay suggested. He
stepped toward the pulls.

"No, please. The light . . ." He searched for the thought.
"The light is painful to my eyes, even on a day such as this."
Jay looked at him curiously, then slowly settled into the chair.

"Have I come at a bad time, Professor Anderson?" Jay
asked, hopefully.

"Most times are bad ones for me these days," Anderson replied, his voice filled with self-pity. "As I'm sure you are aware, things have not gone so well for me in recent years. First with the research, and more recently . . ."—he looked across the room, scanning the empty spaces in what had once been a well-furnished room—"my health." He shook his head as if remembering some sorrowful memory.

"You don't know how very fortunate you are," Anderson said, returning his attention to his visitor. "You have your health . . . that's so important. Your health."

"I'm very sorry, Professor," Jay sympathized. "Is there anything I can do?"

"For me?" Anderson said vacantly. "I only wish you could, but I believe I've passed the point where . . ." His voice trailed off, the effort to finish the sentence too much for him.

"Professor?" Jay said gently, trying to bring Anderson back to the subject without embarrassing him. Anderson looked at him curiously, leaning forward painfully in his chair. He bent over and pulled a manila envelope from under the chair. With great effort, he straightened up and set the thick package on his lap. Anderson peered at Jay, then into the envelope, shuffling the papers inside as if to refresh his memory. He gathered himself to speak. Jay edged forward. Abruptly, Anderson slumped in his chair, shoulders sagging, his hands resting lifelessly on the envelope.

"Here," Anderson said wearily. He picked up the envelope in both palsied hands and proffered it. "I can't do it. I can't go through with it all. Here, come take these."

Jay half rose and leaned over toward Anderson. The manila envelope slipped to the floor, spilling its contents at Jay's feet. Fleming leaned over to collect them; they all appeared to be photocopies, many bearing the seal of the U.S. Department of Defense. Others were copies of memos from the Department of Energy. All were stamped "Top Secret."

"The breakthrough," Anderson mumbled.

Fleming scanned the pages eagerly, holding them close to the window to catch the feeble light which filtered through the heavy drapes.

"These are very interesting, Professor Anderson," Fleming began hesitantly when he'd finished his cursory examination. "Quite honestly, I'm astounded to have you hand them to me."

"They wanted me to pretend they were my own work," Anderson said feebly. "They wanted me to pass the information along to you as if I had discovered it myself."

"Who are 'they'?" Jay asked. The hairs at the back of his neck began to tingle. Something was very wrong and he was sure it wasn't just his imagination.

"They?" Anderson squinted dully through his glasses. "They? Why . . ." He looked at the ceiling, then down at his hands. Anderson studied his hands as they lay in his lap. "I didn't ask."

"You didn't—"

"When someone arrives on your doorstep and they know the most intimate details of your life, including the sad shape of your bank account and the sadder state of your health and they know you have been selling your furniture and pictures and your family heirlooms to pay the mortgage, and these people who know so much then offer you enough money to make your life comfortable, you don't ask who they are. They were the sort of people who don't answer questions. Do you understand what I'm talking about?" Gripping the arms of the chair, Anderson leaned forward with a great effort, his face full of appeal. Then he saw the confused expression on Jay's face and, sighing audibly, slumped back into the chair.

"Why did they give you these papers?" Fleming asked. "Do you know what's in them?"

"Do I know what's in them?" Anderson retorted indignantly. "Who do you think I am? I was conducting research on electromagnetic pulses when you were still struggling with your first course in calculus."

"I didn't mean to imply . . ." Jay held out his hands, unsure what he hadn't meant to imply. "It's just odd that . . . these anonymous people would hand you a packet of top secret American documents for you to pass on to me. I just don't see . . ."

"The exchange of information was to get you here," Anderson explained. "It was the device to legitimize our visit. After we had talked a bit about my 'breakthrough' "—he pronounced it bitterly—"after we had talked, I was supposed to let you in on a rumor I had heard from a reliable colleague of mine."

"This reliable colleague being the same people who brought you the papers and the money?" Jay asked.

Anderson nodded. "I was directed to tell you . . . to tell you . . ." His voice was faint. Jay leaned over to catch the words better, an act which just happened to save his life. For as he bent over, the window behind him exploded with a swarm of slugs that ripped great holes in the drapes and dusted the room with shards of glass.

"Get down!" Jay yelled as he plunged to the floor. Anderson sat upright in his chair, his face a childlike mask of amazement. Jay lunged for the professor's legs and pulled him to the floor.

"No," Anderson said. "No, this isn't supposed to happen. They said I wouldn't be hurt if I cooperated with them. They said I wouldn't be hurt." He leaned against the chair and tried to pull himself up. Jay grabbed him by the back of his collar and pulled him back to the floor as another fusillade pounded through the glass, pockmarking the plaster wall.

"Stay down!" Jay commanded. He crawled to the front door to make sure it was locked. Jay returned on his hands and knees. "Do you have a back door?"

Anderson shook his head. "They promised I wouldn't be hurt," the decrepit professor protested in a childlike voice. "I must talk to them about this."

"Where is your telephone?" Jay asked. Anderson looked up at him blankly. "Telephone," he asked again. "Where is it?"

"Kitchen."

Glass gritted under Jay's shoes as he scrambled down the hallway toward the rear of Anderson's house. Fleming searched the room. He heard pounding on the door. People were attacking the thick wooden door with a sledgehammer. The blows echoed down the hallway like cannon shots.

After what seemed like eons, Jay spotted the telephone and dived for it. He pulled the receiver from its base and held it to his ear. There was no dial tone. The telephone was dead. Someone must have cut the wires. The blows against the door were more frequent; they echoed with the splintering complaints of wood giving way. The gunfire had stopped. Fleming ransacked the drawers in the kitchen until he found a sharp knife. He slipped it slantwise into his back pocket.

Anderson was curled fetally on the living room floor. Two wet red stains the size of a tea saucer glistened below his

shoulder blades. Outside men were whispering orders. They
would be inside in seconds. He shouldered the professor's frail
frame and sprinted for the stairs.

The stairs in old Dutch canal houses are nearly as steep as
ladders and not much wider. Jay stumbled up the steps,
Anderson's limbs thudding against the walls. Jay cursed under
his breath.

On the third-floor landing, Jay caught his breath. Downstairs
there were triumphant shouts as the door finally yielded and
men spilled into the house. Fleming switched on the light on
the landing and hurried up to the fourth floor. There were four
doors. With Anderson still balanced over one shoulder,
Fleming opened one, threw Anderson in the room and pulled
the door to.

The landing light for the fourth floor was in a small fixture.
Jay removed it and unscrewed the bulb. He crouched down
next to the stairs in the darkest spot he could find, waiting for
his night vision to develop.

Two sets of footsteps sounded on the landing below.
Centuries-old floors creaked and complained. Doors opened
and closed. One of the men issued an order in English for his
companion to continue. Everything depended on Jay's seeing
the man without being seen first. The stairs creaked slowly as
the man cautiously climbed. Fleming slipped the knife from his
pocket and cradled it in his right hand.

The light from the landing below cast a shadow of a man and
a long gun barrel against the door leading to Anderson's room.
Jay smiled faintly when the man snapped the light switch on
and off rapidly, cursing when the light failed to come on. A
red-haired head poked upward, searching warily from side to
side, followed by a thick bull neck that seemed to run straight
from the man's ear's to his massive shoulders.

Breathing evenly and deeply as he once had during the
foreplay of an aerial dogfight, Jay coiled in the protection of
his shadow. The man tried the switch again, then moved
upward. Hurry! Fleming silently urged. Hurry before your
eyes adjust. The giant stopped for a moment, looked around
slowly one last time and then quickly mounted the remaining
half dozen steps. His head almost touched the ceiling. He held
an Uzi machine gun with a fat cylindrical silencer attached to

the muzzle. Fleming noted with satisfaction the cavalier manner in which the giant held the Uzi.

The giant moved quickly to the first door on his right, which led to Anderson's room. Fleming tensed. The giant threw open the door and jumped back, covering the inside with the muzzle of the Uzi. Only the sucking sounds of Anderson's attempts to fill his punctured lungs greeted him. Emboldened, the giant held his Uzi with one hand and flicked on the light switch with the other. A flood of yellow light poured from the room and flooded the landing. Between the giant's spread legs, Jay saw Anderson lying in a widening pool of his own blood.

"Found one of them," the giant shouted in what Jay could swear was a Long Island accent. "Up here on the fourth floor." Jay heard quick footsteps below.

Fleming flung himself across the landing toward the back of the giant, who had started across the room toward Anderson's body. The giant was several long strides away. On Jay's second step, the old wooden floor groaned beneath his feet. The giant turned. Jay plunged the knife between his shoulder blades, near his spine. Jay let out a gasp as he collided with the giant's massive bulk. They both crashed to the floor.

The giant bellowed like a wounded elephant. He struggled to his feet, throwing Jay as a wild horse sheds a rider. Jay held on to the knife and it slid smoothly from its wound. The giant was on his hands and knees, still clutching the Uzi.

"What's going on?" asked voices from below. Jay heard their tread on the stairs leading to the fourth floor. Jay leaped on the giant's back and brought the blade across the side of his neck, severing the man's carotid artery.

The giant shrieked and rose to his feet, throwing Jay head first against the wall. The knife clattered against the floor. Dizzily, he struggled to his feet. The giant, bleeding profusely, grinned and raised the Uzi's muzzle. Jay heard faint footsteps on the stairs.

The giant's finger tightened on the trigger. Jay lunged. As he did, the giant's knees trembled, and by the time Jay had covered the six feet between them, the giant had crumpled to the floor.

Jay stood unsteadily for a moment, gazing down at the huge body. Suddenly the air was filled with the sounds of coughing. For an instant, Jay thought it was Anderson. Pieces of plaster

showered on him. A pattern of craters had grown on the
ceiling. At the stairway, a man hid in shadows, aiming a
silenced Uzi like the one the giant now lay on.

Jay rolled the giant's bulk off the weapon. More shots spat
softly from the stairwell, low and well aimed. Fleming rolled
out of the line of fire. He switched the fire selector from full
automatic to single shot. The clip must last. He spent one shot
on the overhead light, plunging the room into darkness. The
hall filled with noise as the surprised men on the stairs blasted
at shadows. All their shots were landing high. Jay crawled to
the door on his belly. A cluster of bright blasts illuminated the
hall for an instant. Jay fired two rounds. There was a scream,
then a body falling down the steep stairs.

All was silent. Jay retreated into the room, feeling his way
around in the dark. The floor was slippery with blood. Jay
fumbled with the Uzi, twisting the silencer. He wanted his
shots heard. Perhaps someone would summon help.

Minutes later, there was still no sound from the stairs. Far
below, on the landing on the third floor, the man Jay had hit
scraped and twitched. Fleming made his way to Professor
Anderson's body.

"Professor," Jay whispered in his ear. "Professor Anderson,
can you hear me?" The head responded with a tremor. Another
burst of silenced machine-gun fire whispered from the stairway. Fleming loosed two shots toward the stairs. Their loud
reports sounded like a bombardment in the small room. Jay
heard sounds on the stairs, not the uncontrolled movements of
a wounded body, but of a prudent man taking cover. Following
suit, Jay pulled Anderson toward the side of the room, out of
the line of fire. The professor groaned.

"Luxembourg," Anderson muttered. "Luxembourg . . .
Tesla papers . . . sold there . . . the missing ones . . .
must get them . . . vitally important to the Western world
. . . not let Soviets . . . Soviets—"

Another flurry of slugs poured into the room.

"Shh!" Jay cautioned. "They can locate us by sound."
From downstairs came a metallic clunk. Jay hoped it was the
sound of a spent magazine being ejected. Gambling, he sprang
into the center of the room and squeezed the trigger of the Uzi
three times at the stairs. The gun fired twice.

The man on the stairs cursed. Jay's hopes quickly soared and were just as quickly shattered by the unmistakable sound of a fresh clip being inserted, followed by more silenced bullets. As Jay retreated to the side of the room, he heard footsteps moving slowly downstairs. Perhaps he had wounded the man.

Out of ammunition, Jay set down the Uzi and crawled over to the giant's body. There were no full clips in his pockets. The man must have emptied them all firing into the house in the initial attack. Hoping his shots had been heard, Jay silently closed the door and locked it. He recognized the outline of a heavy chest of drawers against the wall. He slid it in front of the door.

Anderson filled the room with fatal, panicked notes. Jay returned to his side and tried to make him comfortable.

"Must . . . listen. Most important." Anderson took ragged breaths as he fought for strength. "Must go . . . Luxembourg . . . keep Tesla papers from Russians . . ."

"Did the men who paid you tell you to say this to me?" Fleming whispered.

"Yes . . ." Anderson answered with difficulty. "Said you . . . you were only person to stop exchange . . ."

"What exchange?"

"Russians . . . close to . . . completing their . . . must keep them from Tesla papers . . . the key."

"You say this is supposed to take place in Luxembourg. Where? What am I supposed to do? How am I supposed to prevent this exchange?"

"Make a bid . . . sellers can be bought . . . bank there . . . bank . . ."

"There are hundreds of banks in Luxembourg."

"Friday . . ." Anderson babbled a dying man's final delirium. "Must prevent . . ." he gasped . . . "before then or . . . too late." Then Anderson died.

Just outside the door the floor creaked. Then the doorknob rattled. Jay left Anderson's body and fumbled around on the floor looking for the knife. The door splintered and slammed into the back of the dresser. Sliding across the bloody floor, Jay lunged for the chest, slamming it back against the door. Slugs thudded dully against the back of the chest.

A body thumped into the door again and again. Jay's feet slid in the blood and the dresser made progress with every blow. The knife, he knew, lay somewhere in the darkness, but he dare not leave the dresser long enough to search for it.

Faintly, from the bowels of Anderson's house, Jay felt the vibrations of running feet. Wild talons of panic clawed at his chest. Reinforcements. The killers, whoever they were, had called for reinforcements.

He felt like crying. The vibrations grew louder; the pounding on the door ceased. Fleming shoved the chest flush against the door again and headed for the tiny draped window at the end of the room. He ripped down the drapes and crawled up on the sill. Four stories below, driving rain pounded garbage into pulp. No rooftops, no ledges, no escape.

He had heard of people surviving falls greater than this one—forty or fifty feet. Voices filled the hall beyond the door. Jay opened the window and sat, legs dangling into the alley. He looked down and started to feel the panic grow in his bowels. The ground spun dizzily as he steeled himself to jump.

He had started to ease himself off the window sill when behind him he heard gunshots. Then, "Police. Put your hands up!" and more gunshots. Behind him, he heard the chest scrape along the floor as people wrestled the door open. Fleming turned his head. Behind him, almost hidden in the dark, was a uniformed police officer.

"Don't shoot!" Jay called in Dutch as he eagerly climbed away from the window. "Don't shoot. I haven't got a weapon."

Jay reclined as best he could in the front seat of the unmarked police car. It traveled from Leiden to Amsterdam along the twin ribbons of the A4.

"A neighbor heard the shots," explained the ranking officer, a plainclothes detective with the equivalent rank of lieutenant. His name was Wilem VanDeventer and he was a tall lanky man with a long sad face and watery blue eyes. A little more than an hour ago, VanDeventer had followed the uniformed officer through the door. Fleming had been shaking then, and the tall lieutenant had put a reassuring arm around his shoulder and led him to the first floor while his assistants attended to the bodies, four of them: Anderson's, the giant's, the man Jay had shot, and the last man, killed in the shoot-out with the lieutenant's men.

Jay tried to explain that the men sounded like Americans, but the lieutenant insisted on giving him a drink of *oude genever,* the Dutch gin, and sent him back to his hotel with one of his men.

"There is plenty of time to fill out all the proper forms, isn't there now, Mr. Fleming?" VanDeventer had a disarming smile that inspired trust and confidence. "After all, none of these gentlemen are going anywhere, are they?" The lieutenant also had the habit of ending his statements with a question. It made it difficult to disagree with him.

Not that Jay had wanted to disagree. He had no objection to being driven back to Amsterdam in Sergeant Dukkers's unmarked police sedan. Dukkers would be back to pick him up the next morning to take him back to Leiden so that statements could be taken, forms filled out.

As the sedan passed Schipol Airport, the rain had tapered off to a miserable drizzle, and Jay was reminded of that other rainy night he'd spent in Amsterdam. So much had happened that it seemed impossible that he had flown the company Gulfstream in only the night before last. Someone *was* trying to kill him. That much was plain. The relief that he was not imagining things was replaced by a confused stew of emotions: the fear of being killed, the thrill and challenge of facing death once again, and the sadness of dragging in poor, sick Professor Anderson.

All this was new to Jay, this matter of people hunting people on land. He was familiar with the rules and skills of hunting and killing in the air, but here he knew he'd have to learn new tactics, new skills, new ways of thinking.

And until he learned them, he intended to take full advantage of the tactics and expertise of his chief of security, Douglas Denoff. Just as soon as he returned to the hotel, he planned to give Denoff a call.

Sergeant Dukkers merged from the A4 to the A10 heading directly north, then onto the S105 and straight into the old quarter. Soon the S105 turned into the Rozengracht. A few moments later they crossed the Prinsengracht Canal and turned left. Fleming's hotel was a few houses down.

Traffic on the one-lane street was, as usual, congested. But this time, Jay thought, he wouldn't get out for a little air. As they pulled abreast of the hotel and slowed to a stop, a small cloud of anxiety gnawed at Jay's mind. He tried to run the morning's events through his mind. In none of them did he remember telling Dukkers where he was staying. But things had been intense, chaotic. He must have told at some point.

Washington, D.C.,
December 17

"They've struck again."

"Goddamn it, Bogdan." Graham Kingsley strode agitatedly back and forth across the Persian carpet in his study.

"Three of them hit Anderson's house in Leiden."

"How is Fleming?"

"Fine," Bogdan Subasic replied as he paced the floor in the Amsterdam Hilton. He wished the telephone cord were longer. He wanted to take long angry strides. "Fleming acquitted himself nicely. He killed two of the three. Slit the throat of the biggest one there, a veritable ox. Took the dead man's gun, killed one of the others and wounded the third."

Kingsley nodded his head slowly to himself. Yes, they had indeed chosen the right man. Fleming was everything the dossiers, newspapers clippings and the bar stories said he was. Formidable. Once things were over, they'd have to watch him very carefully.

"And Anderson?" Kingsley asked after a long silence.

"Dead."

"Before or after he fulfilled his mission?" Kingsley asked.

"Judging by the length of time they spent together before the attack, I'm pretty sure that Anderson briefed him, although I understand that Fleming has the documents we gave to Anderson."

"The old fool!" Kingsley said.

"No harm done," Subasic said. "As long as Fleming's appetite is whetted, that's all that's necessary. All we need him to do is go to Luxembourg and start asking questions."

"Are you sure Anderson gave him the information about Luxembourg?"

"We can't be sure of that until he goes," Subasic said. "But we'll monitor his telephone calls. He does business with a small private merchant bank there by the name of Hartkemeier et Fils. If Anderson gave him the information, he'll broach the subject with his banker. You need a good banker as a representative in matters like this and we know that Fleming trusts Hartkemeier implicitly."

"Very well," Kingsley said. "But isn't there anything we can do about these attacks on Fleming? We're so close right now. It worries me."

"And me," Subasic agreed. "But *because* we're so close makes it difficult for me to act. I suppose—"

"It must be a leak within the Committee of Seven," Kingsley insisted. "That's the only way things could happen so quickly."

"I suppose we could arrange to have them put under surveillance," Subasic offered. "But that would be next to impossible given the way they all travel, and the fact that all of them employ intensive counterintelligence efforts. Gold, for example, has his telephone swept for taps each day. And so do the General, Hill and Rhodes. I can't see how it could be done effectively without being detected."

"Perhaps," Kingsley thought for a moment. There was silence on the telephone for nearly a minute.

"Yes, sir?" Subasic tried to prompt his employer into finishing the thought he had begun.

"Perhaps there is another solution to all this," Kingsley said. "During our meeting yesterday, the general offered to fly the whole committee to Luxembourg for the event. Perhaps I should insist on it. Get them all together there. Luxembourg's a small place. They'd all be on foreign territory. No way their counterintelligence efforts could be as effective as they are here in Washington."

"An excellent idea if it can be done," Subasic agreed.

"Then we'll do it," Kingsley said. "Can you handle the surveillance in Luxembourg if I get them all there?"

"It won't be easy—"

"I didn't ask if it would be easy," Kingsley retorted testily. "I asked if you could do it."

"It'll require calling in just about every IOU I have."

"Then do it. There'll never be a more important reason."

"Yes, sir."

"Call me if anything else develops."

"Yes, sir."

They said goodbye. Neither was happy. Kingsley wandered over to the French doors. Snow carpeted the forest floor, a winter expanse with gray-brown tree trunks. It was a comfortable neighborhood, Kingsley thought, comfortable and secure. But on this morning as he stood pensively searching for the key to this conundrum, he felt anything but secure.

Chapter Ten

Holland,
December 18

The silver Mercedes glided along the A4 from Amsterdam. Jay Fleming leaned forward to get a better look through the windshield. Ahead, he recognized the approach of the city limits.

"Another ten minutes or so, Mr. Fleming," the chauffeur commented when he caught sight of Fleming in his rearview mirror. "And no one following us." The driver hired by Doug Denoff had taken a circuitous route from the hotel, making unexpected stops and U-turns in the light Sunday morning traffic. The tactics had revealed nothing. The missing tail upset Fleming. He would rather know where his enemies were.

Jay sat back and peeked out the rear window for the hundredth time. The driver was a former Israeli commando. He currently worked for an international firm that protected executives, wealthy people, politicians and other targets for terrorists. The man was well-trained in looking for tails, eluding potential attackers, killing them if escape were out of the question. His name was Aaron Fiszmann. He had been born in Munich of parents who had survived Hitler's death camps. He was a beefy man with prominent muscles that strained at his dress suit. Fiszmann reminded Jay of the giant he had slain the day before. But in contrast to the dead giant, Fiszmann conducted himself with panther-like grace and awareness.

Doug Denoff had hired the former commando and the

specially equipped limo following Jay's telephone call. Denoff had initially insisted on hiring a small army. They had argued for more than an hour about security.

"Damn it, Jay, you've got the money," Denoff had argued, "spend it and stay alive."

"I'm not going to be a prisoner," Fleming responded. "I don't want to be a specimen in my own private zoo."

"Do you have any idea how many people's lives are depending on your staying alive?" Denoff countered. "What would happen to ECM if you died? The company, the people, their jobs? You can't just think about yourself. You have to think of others. We need you alive."

Jay had been adamant. One guard. That was all. And the armored limo. Nothing more. The limo had been driven in overnight from Brussels. It was one of scores which had flooded into that international city after a rash of attacks on NATO personnel and associates. It was equipped with armored doors, special tires which could be driven at high speeds even after puncture by machine gun fire, armor plate in the floor to guard against land mines like the one terrorists used to kill Lord Montbatten, gun ports in the doors, emergency radio transmitters, the works.

The whole setup seemed to close in on Jay as he sat in the rear listening to a cassette of Bach's *Brandenburg Concerto Number Two.* Denoff had a good point. There were hundreds of people whose quality of life depended on his staying alive. But where did that leave him? His success made him a target, and that put walls and perimeters around his life.

Denoff had been astounded to learn that all his attackers appeared to be Americans. He was even more astonished at the presence of the tall dark assassin who had saved Jay's life in the alley. Who were they all? Denoff promised he would make some calls to his contacts with the American intelligence agencies to see if they had any information that could shed light on the mystery. Perhaps, Jay thought, his meeting with the police in Leiden would help. Then, the following day, Jay was going to stop by the Amsterdam police to discuss the alley killings.

The Mercedes slowed for the first traffic light in Leiden. Fiszmann stopped the limo a full car length behind the next car. An escapeway, always an escapeway. The light changed and

Fiszmann skillfully guided the limo into the thick of Leiden's narrow small-town streets.

The traffic was light. Most people were either still asleep, in church or eating breakfast.

Jay looked out the side windows and looked at old brick buildings with white stone trim. Part of his solution, he felt, had to be in Luxembourg. Obviously someone—who, he couldn't imagine—had primed Professor Anderson to set him up. Someone was trying to manipulate him. But why? Why not approach him directly, ask him to go to Luxembourg? Why the elaborate charade? He was already going to Luxembourg, had to conduct business with his banker there. What did they want him to do and why him? Anderson, it was plain, was killed because of him. How would he tell the police that? Could they possibly believe him?

Fiszmann found the police station easily, and guided the Mercedes to a graceful halt at a visitor's space in front. Jay checked his watch. VanDeventer and Dukkers weren't expecting him for another three hours. When Dukkers had dropped him off the night before, the policeman had promised to return at 2 P.M. to drive him to the station.

Jay had not called. He wanted to surprise the two men. On the seat beside him was a plain white bag with two small boxes wrapped in gold foil and festively tied with Christmas ribbons. Inside each box was a three-carat, flawless diamond. It would put a child through a university or care for the widow of a slain officer. Jay felt it was inadequate thanks for saving his life.

He had purchased the loose stones at a famous Amsterdam diamond firm. The manager had been delighted to make such a sale so early on a Sunday morning.

The diamonds, Fleming decided, would be the perfect gift. They were good investments, couldn't be spent as readily as cash, but were liquid enough to be converted if an emergency arose.

After the car stopped, Fleming told Fiszmann he didn't want any doors opened for him—the Mercedes was ostentatious enough. Jay opened his own door and stepped onto the brick sidewalk. Fiszmann got out anyway and looked up and down the street with a mean, wary look. Jay stuffed the two diamond boxes into his windbreaker pocket and strode across the sidewalk, up the steps of the police station and in through the swinging doors. He thought Dukkers and VanDeventer would be surprised, but had no idea how surprised *he* would soon be.

The drapes were drawn; the "Do Not Disturb" sign in five languages hung on the doorknob outside; two men confidently shuffled through the haphazard pile of papers on the bureau.

"Here is it," one of them said softly.

"Wonderful," said the other. "Is everything in it?"

The first man spilled the manila envelope's contents on the bed and rustled through the pages which spilled from it. He compared the title pages with a rumpled list. After a moment he replied, "All here."

"Good. Now all we need is the letter."

The first man continued to shuffle through the papers. "Bingo!" he said triumphantly.

The second man smiled. "Check the waste basket for the envelope."

"It's been emptied."

"Wonderful. Let's go."

The first man slipped the letter into the manila envelope, tucked the entire package under his arm, and followed his companion from the room, carefully placing the "Do Not Disturb" sign on the doorknob inside. Outside, they headed north along the Prinsengracht toward the train station.

"Now wait just a minute!" Jay Fleming protested. "You *have* to have a Lieutenant VanDeventer and a Sergeant Dukkers. Perhaps you've made a mistake."

"We don't have an extremely large police force," the officer behind the desk explained politely. He was a young man, about twenty-five years old, with close-cropped blond hair and pale blue eyes. "And I assure you that I know the names of all the sergeants and lieutenants. There are only five lieutenants and none of them is named VanDeventer."

Jay Fleming looked at the policeman, trying to stay calm, fighting the anger and frustration that rose bitterly in his throat.

"Look," Jay said slowly, patiently. "There was a bloody shoot-out over on Apothekers Dijk yesterday."

"A shoot-out?" the police officer's eyes widened. "Here? In Leiden?" The policeman jumped from his chair and hurried into an adjoining room. He returned with a large burgundy-stained leather-bound book. "No," he said, scanning the pages, flipping one back and then forward again, examining both sides of the ledger. "There is nothing about a shoot-out here," he said turning the book over to Jay. "Look for yourself. This is the official log of all reported crimes and responses by our personnel. There is nothing more serious here than a motor vehicle accident."

Jay took the book and frowned at the page. Wildly, he flipped the pages forward and backward, his eyes growing wilder as he did. Finally he turned to the policeman and opened his mouth but could think of nothing appropriate to say.

"We are a fairly small town, Mr. . . ?"

"Fleming," Jay responded, distractedly. "Jay Fleming."

"Mr. Fleming. I can't remember the last time we had an incident involving a firearm, much less a shoot-out, as you call it. Where did you say this was supposed to occur?"

"On the Apothekers Dijk," Jay responded, slamming the book back on the desk. "And it *did* happen. I was there. I saw it! I killed two of the attackers. Your men—Dukkers and VanDeventer—saved my life. They know the entire story. They can confirm what I've said!" At a nearby desk, a plainclothes officer glared at Jay.

"But we have no Dukkers and VanDeventer." The policeman took the ledger and toyed with it on his desk. "And we have no report of any altercation on the Apothekers Dijk."

"But there were gunshots," Jay persisted. "Neighbors heard them. They called the police."

"Mr. Fleming," the policeman continued patiently, "you saw for yourself. We had no reports of gunshots, or of anyone being killed by a gun."

Jay stared helplessly at the policeman, speechless. He looked first at the young man and then at the older plainclothesman at the nearby desk, and back again. This was madness. The police had come. People had been murdered. Anderson. The three attackers. He had copies of top secret American documents to prove it all happened. There had to be an answer, some proof the attack had happened.

"Wait!" Fleming blurted suddenly. "The house. The blood. There's my proof. Come with me to the house at the Apothekers Dijk. I'll show you—"

"Mr. Fleming," the young officer began. "I don't see what that will prove. I've already told you that we have no rec—"

"You must!" Fleming thundered, grabbing the officer by the lapels of his uniform coat. "You *have* to come with me. I'll show you the blood, the bullet holes, the smashed doors." He shook the officer urgently. "Come with me. I'll *show* you!"

"Mr. Fleming." Firm strong hands gripped Jay's shoulders. The voice was strong and soothing. "Please get ahold of yourself."

"I'm sorry," Jay apologized as he slowly released his grip. "I'm very sorry. I don't know what . . ."

"It's all right," the soothing voice said. Jay turned around and faced the plainclothesman. "Sometimes these mistakes happen to all of us. Why don't we go over to the Apothekers Dijk and take a look." He looked over at the young policeman who was rubbing his palms against the new wrinkles in his coat, trying to press them out. "It's not so far from here," he said to the young officer. "We'll go over and take a look. Sometimes we do make mistakes."

Jay looked at the two officers. He knew they were humoring him. It didn't matter, just as long as one of them went with him to the house. The proof would be there. He'd be vindicated.

"Mr. Fleming," the plainclothes officer asked. "You're Dutch?"

Jay shook his head. "American."

"American!" The plainclothes officer was genuinely shocked. "But you speak Dutch so well." He looked at Jay more closely and mumbled, "American." Then, in a normal tone, "And Mr. Fleming, where are you staying here in Holland?"

"The Ambassador. Amsterdam. But I don't see what relevance this has," Jay complained. He headed for the door. "I'm going over to the Apothekers Dijk right now. If you want to come, please do. Otherwise I'll buy a camera, take pictures and bring the evidence back to you."

"That won't be necessary," the plainclothes officer said. "I'll go with you." He passed a knowing glance at the younger officer and then followed Fleming out the door.

They rode in Jay's Mercedes, passing the ride without talking. When the limo turned from the Rapenburg Prinssekade, Jay's insides suddenly froze. Down the street, in front of Anderson's canal house, were a collection of construction vehicles. A long wooden chute led from the upper stories to the bed of a dump truck parked halfway on the sidewalk in front. Great clouds of dust rose from the back as debris crashed downward. The plainclothes policeman shot Jay a sideways glance. His eyes were heavy with disbelief.

Fiszmann pulled the Mercedes past the dump truck and parked on the sidewalk in front of it. Jay leaped from the Mercedes and ran to the entrance of the building. He braced himself unsteadily against the gaping hole where the doorjamb had once been.

"Pardon me, sir," a workman said as he pushed by with a shoulder stacked with lumber. Jay looked around as if he were seeing ghosts. Then, unaware of the plainclothes policeman behind him, he stumbled into the living room. The flooring had been stripped, along with the wall and ceiling plaster.

They were destroying evidence. He pushed his way past the plainclothes officer and rushed back into the hall. There was no work going on in the kitchen or in the other rooms on the first floor. Someone was methodically destroying the evidence. Jay ran to the stairs. The carpeting had been removed, the walls stripped. He paused at the landings on the first and second floors. There was no work being done in any of the rooms. Finally, knowing what he would find, but not wanting to see it, Jay slowly climbed the bare steps to the fourth floor. The landing and the room in which he had killed the giant was a shell.

Jay dropped to the floor and studied it carefully. There had been so much blood. Something must have seeped through to the subflooring. Workers held their tools and watched in amusement as Jay scrambled about the floor on his hands and knees, sweeping with his hands.

"You've got to stop them!" Jay demanded of the plainclothesman. "Stop them! They're destroying evidence."

"They're renovating a house," the policeman responded, exasperated. "There is nothing illegal about renovating an old canal house."

"But they've destroyed the—"

"They've destroyed *nothing!*" the man replied. "They are renovating a house. That's all. And I think perhaps it is time you realized that whatever you imagined might have happened here did not. Have you taken any drugs?"

Jay stared at him, slack-jawed.

"It's nothing to be ashamed of, Mr. Fleming. Many Americans, when they find drugs so readily available—"

"By God!" Jay bellowed. "I do not take drugs and if you're suggesting that I—"

"Please calm down," the policeman implored gently.

Suddenly Jay's shoulders sagged, his mind scattered in a thousand places. "I don't know what to say. This has . . . has never . . ." He looked over at Aaron Fiszmann, but the man's face was impossible to read. Too stunned to protest, Jay let the policeman lead him back down the stairs.

Chapter Eleven

Luxembourg,
December 18

Alexandra Downing slumped in the rear of the Opel taxi and closed her eyes tightly against the brilliant sunlight which flooded through the windows as they sped from the airport along the Rue de Neudorf. Her nerves felt like the ragged edge of a broken tooth. Jet lag twisted her thoughts, fatigue battered her body.

The past two days had been a blur. When she had returned from the strange dinner with Martin, things on the boat were subtly out of order. Nothing she could put her finger on, just an envelope that didn't seem to be where she'd left it, a stack of sweaters too close to the rear of a locker. Someone had searched her boat.

She worried about Martin all the next day, not for his physical well-being, but because she thought he was suffering a nervous breakdown. What he had told her at dinner seemed preposterous, melodramatic, paranoid. She suspected the strain of watching his career stall had done it. She had heard of things like that. A man's life is suddenly going nowhere, then a few bad breaks drop out of nowhere, and suddenly even the sharpest minds see shadows moving in the graveyard.

She sat around all day, staring at the envelope he had left for her. Should she open it? She had promised not to unless something happened to him. She had promised, and despite her raging curiosity, she resisted. More than anything else in the world, she wanted to turn an unviolated envelope back to him when he returned, safe.

Only he didn't return safely. She was stunned when the telephone call came that night. Martin carried her telephone number in his wallet because he was terrible at remembering numbers. He even carried his own number there because he regularly forgot it.

In the back of the taxi, Alexandra felt the tears welling up again in her eyes. She blinked them back as she fumbled through her shoulder bag in search of another tissue. Her search turned up nothing. Damn! She had run out on the plane. She wiped the tears away with her hand and thought of the boxes and boxes of tissues she had cried into tight little paper balls.

Her husband Mike had died suddenly in his sleep. An aneurysm. In his sleep a weak spot in an artery behind his forehead ballooned beyond its capacity and spilled death across his thoughts and his handsome face and his loving manner. She had been a widow at twenty-seven.

Mike's death left her rudderless. She had been teaching journalism at UCLA when he died and suddenly the life drained out of her. For two years she had been fighting the administration; they would rather spend money on new athletics and landscaping projects designed to make the campus look like a country club than on resources for teaching. She had taken the fight to the media, to the legislature, and had all but won when one morning she woke up and Mike was dead beside her.

Life seemed to hurtle downhill after that, gaining speed like a luge. She quit—to the administration's delight—sold all the furniture, moved out of the apartment, and moved aboard the Morgan 41 sailboat on which she and Mike had experienced some of their most wonderful times. Her savings, Mike's life insurance, and the sale of everything that didn't fit on the boat made her financially secure. For the past two years she tried one thing and another. She taught part-time at a community college, worked on boats, studied for and received her Coast Guard captain's license, took people out on charters, taught aerobics at an exercise club, even started to write a novel.

At first, she dated many men, most of whom she met at the health club. Then she tired of men she didn't really like and gradually withdrew. And one morning she climbed on deck and found Martin looking fondly at her boat.

As soon as she had gathered her wits following the telephone call, Alexandra retrieved Martin's envelope from its hiding place in the bilge. She carefully unsealed the plastic and with quaking hands, tore open its seals. Inside was $25,000 in assorted bills and a note from Martin.

"If you are reading this note," it began, "then I am dead. But I want you to remember that I will love you always. Your love, even for as short a time as I have known it, has been the most cherished experience in my life.

"The money you find has been borrowed against my military pension. I want you to have it. I want you to call Lee Goldberg in Brussels, 87-91-44. He is a long-time friend who works in the intelligence section of NATO. He is a trusted and knowledgeable man. Call him and say, 'Tesla lives.' I have sent him a separate package of information and documents via international courier. He should receive them by Monday. He has instructions to deal with the package in the event that you call.

"He doesn't know who you are. Nor should you reveal your identity. This is a dangerous thing I have stumbled on, and it would certainly mean death if you were known to be associated with it. Please follow these instructions to the letter. Ask for Lieutenant Colonel Goldberg—I've given you his home telephone number—speak only the two words, then hang up. If everything goes according to plan, you will hear nothing, for the matter will have been cleared up discreetly. A very embarrassed United States government will see to that. If things do not happen accordingly, it could mean the death of millions and the destruction of our country as we know it.

"But, my love, don't try to do anything else. Set the process I have built into motion and then take cover. And always, always remember that I love you more than life itself. Goodbye. Martin."

"Tesla lives," Alexandra said softly as she opened her eyes and stared blankly out the window at Luxembourg. The modern steel-and-glass skyscraper of the parliament of the

European Community hovered over the landscape, an intrusion upon the quaint and medieval architecture that seemed to characterize the city of Luxembourg.

She thought back to the Saturday afternoon she had received the phone call. She had thought about calling the police, the FBI, someone. But the police said Martin had been killed in a freak accident. Who was going to believe he was murdered? The only evidence she had was the note and the money. So she called Lieutenant Colonel Lee Goldberg.

But she said a lot more than "Tesla lives." They talked. He was a worried, polite man who had once served under Martin in Vietnam. Goldberg's respect for his former commanding officer was undisguised, as was his shock at learning of the death.

"The stuff he sent was powerful," Goldberg said. "Sizzling. But I never thought they—"

"Who's 'they'?" Alexandra demanded. Goldberg hesitated. Martin had enclosed a note about her in his package. The note warned Goldberg that Alexandra would probably disregard his plea to stay out of the matter and that he would have to tackle the difficult job of dissuading her.

In the end, he'd failed, and agreed to meet her in Luxembourg. Alexandra knew he would try to put her on the next plane back to the States. She knew he'd fail again. She loved Martin for wanting to protect her, but she had never needed protecting before.

Alexandra Downing sniffed, wished again that she had a Kleenex, then leaned back in her seat and watched the medieval city of Luxembourg draw closer.

Belgium,
December 18

The white Cessna *Citation* with the red-and-gold insignia of the Global Energy Corporation whizzed south-southwest over the flat landscape of Belgium. Bogdan Subasic stared out of the window at the earth, looking at the towns and rivers and woods that read like a roll call of bloody battles: Bastogne, Liege, The

Ardennes, Dunkirk. Subasic sadly shook his head as he envisioned the bodies.

The buzzer from the cockpit intercom dragged his thoughts back to the present. He picked up the receiver of a red-and-gold telephone on the table next to him.

"Yes?"

"Your call is ready," came the voice of the co-pilot. "You'll need to insert the receiver into the descrambling modem to make any sense out of the message."

"Of course," Subasic said flatly. He slipped the receiver into a receptacle which linked the scrambled message from Washington, D.C. to a microcomputer which would reassemble the scattered bits of electrical energy into the voice of the person on the other end. Subasic picked up another receiver hanging on the side of the microcomputer. The clicks and squeals and squawks coming from it hurt his ear. He held the receiver away from his head until all the transmitters and scramblers and computers and satellite relay links cleared their electronic throats.

"Bogdan?" asked the voice from the earpiece.

"Good afternoon, sir," he responded. "Or should I say, good morning? It must be—"

"Eight in the morning," replied Corundum. "But let's eliminate the pleasantries. How is he? Where is he?"

The anxiety in Corundum's voice disturbed Subasic. The presidential adviser was usually unemotional.

"He's fine, now," Subasic said, "and he's about ten minutes ahead of us, at the controls of his company jet. As you can well imagine, he was shattered after he left Anderson's home."

"That was a remarkable job." Corundum offered a rare compliment. "Having the crew out there that fast on Sunday."

"Thank you," Subasic said graciously. "But money does speak a multitude of tongues. They actually began Saturday, shortly after we cleared out the bodies. I imagine there will be hell for someone to pay in a few weeks, though."

"Why?" Corundum snapped anxiously.

"Permits," Subasic said. "There are no building permits for the construction. Sooner or later—and probably sooner because the Dutch are pretty efficient—some bureaucrat is going to discover it. But that won't be for a while. Besides, there is no way it can be traced to us."

"Good."

"At any rate," Subasic continued, "Fleming's chauffeur drove him back to Amsterdam. Fleming seemed like a new man when he got out of the limo. He stepped quickly, vigorously, as if he'd come to some decision during the drive. It didn't take him an hour to get packed and out to the airport. He's flying the wings off the Gulfstream right now, hell-bent for Luxembourg."

"How do you know?"

"Compass heading," Subasic said, "plus he filed a flight plan at Schipol before he took off. Also the tapes of his phone conversations. I just finished going over them a few minutes ago. He's taken the bait."

"Wonderful!" Corundum sounded happy, then commented, "You said he looked as if he'd made a decision. What's your guess?"

"On what the decision was? I'd say he's mad. The tapes of his phone calls with his offices in Luxembourg and Santa Monica yesterday were tentative, unsure. I think he doubted his sanity for a while. Now I think he's decided that someone has it in for him and he's going to go to the mat with him."

"That's important. Very important, because someone does indeed have it in for him. Have you made any progress on that score?"

"None," Subasic said, embarrassed. He squirmed in his seat as if Corundum were just feet away. "I still can't figure out why the CIA is after him."

"But I—"

"I know you checked with the Company, but you must realize that the CIA has never been under control. It *could* be a Company operation without the director or the dirty tricks division knowing about it. It might be something classified beyond your reach." Subasic waited for the outburst. Corundum was a proud man who liked to believe nothing was beyond his reach. But the man kept his anger in tow.

Breathing a sigh of relief, Subasic continued. "We ran an Interpol background check on the men we found in Anderson's house. They were contract killers. One of them was Wolfgang Kleiderman, a high-priced killer who normally works for the Hamburg underworld. The second man was a character from the Amsterdam docks known as 'The Hammer.' He's the one

Fleming stabbed to death. We haven't got a make on the third one yet. So far, there's nothing to connect them firmly with the Company boys who assaulted Fleming in Amsterdam. Whoever is orchestrating this thing is being very crafty."

"Too crafty for my liking," Corundum snapped. "And I don't think we're going to make any progress on getting the committee to Luxembourg. Diamond was incensed when I suggested it; Topaz insisted that such a gathering would not only serve no purpose, but would also attract attention. And on second thought, I tend to agree. It would be hard for such a large group to escape the attention of the KGB. And you know they're going to be edgy with the transfer scheduled for this Friday."

"A very good point," agreed Subasic, who hadn't liked the concept from the beginning.

"As a security precaution," Corundum went on, "the remainder of this operation will be conducted by you and me. None of the other members shall know anything until after the transfer has been thwarted. We simply don't have the time to smoke out the traitor, but neither can we allow him—whoever he is—to sour this most important operation."

"I must remind you that is a violation of the charter of the committee," Subasic cautioned.

"You've done your duty by warning me," Corundum said testily. "I'm aware of the extraordinary situation. I will be prepared to accept the responsibility at the next committee meeting."

"May I also remind you that, according to the working arrangements laid down by the committee, I am supposed to notify the chairman, Diamond, if any such deviations from policy are requested?"

There was angry silence on the line. Corundum's furious breathing conveyed more than his words possibly could have.

The arrangement was one of the checks and balances written into the committee's charter to assure that a power-hungry, or insane member couldn't subvert the power of the committee and its projects to his own ends.

Subasic struggled with conflicting emotions. On the one hand, it was a violation of a very important check on the abuse of power. On the other hand, the committee was faced with the indisputable presence of a traitor, quite possibly a Russian mole, who had attempted twice to kill one of the key players with less than a week left in the operation. Unprecedented situations required unprecedented actions. Violating the charter of the committee might be the only way to salvage the operation. And, Subasic told himself, it would be for less than a week. Full disclosure could be made after that without jeopardizing the action.

"I will respect your decision," Subasic said finally. "But only for as long as it takes to complete this operation. Following that, I'll expect complete disclosure to the full committee. We'll be fine if the traitor is receiving all his information through the committee. This may be only a minor hindrance if he has his own intelligence contacts."

High-tech static filled their long silence.

"We can pray that is not the case," Corundum responded gravely. "Although I agree it's likely. Each of us on the committee has his own constituency in the intelligence community, and none of us would—given the necessity—lack the means to build such a separate intelligence system." He made this last statement with what sounded like a weary sigh. "And one last thing," Corundum concluded, "I am concerned about the acceleration of violence in all this."

"As I am also," Subasic responded. "But it has been unavoidable. I—"

"I'm not convinced that it has been unavoidable," Corundum interrupted. "Perhaps our planning needs to be tightened, security arrangements revised. I don't know. But I *do* know that you and Fleming are leaving quite a trail of bodies behind you. A trail that can't help but be noticed sooner or later. We *must* make sure this doesn't backlash on us one day."

"Yes, sir," Subasic said, chastened. "I'll do my best."

"I know you will," Corundum said.

They said goodbye and Subasic held the receiver to his ear for a long time, listening to the stew of electronic parts talking to each other, before he finally hung up the receiver and slumped against the window, worriedly running his long fingers through his hair.

He gazed contemplatively down at the landscape. Shadows had already engulfed all of the low-lying areas. Only the tallest buildings, hills and treetops were still bathed in daylight.

Subasic wanted to be down there, strolling along some rustic country road.

He wanted to free his mind of the terrible discipline that staying alive in his business required. He wanted to stop killing, he wanted out of this jungle. But he knew that the only path out of it lead inexorably to his death.

Luxembourg,
December 18

The dimly lit interior of the Brasserie Goethe swarmed with the massed bodies of afternoon drinkers. The air, redolent of pungent French cigarettes, hung in foggy layers so dense they barely budged when the front door swung open, admitting a blast of the crisp December wind.

Along the marble-topped bar, solitary drinkers nursed their beers. Most of the patrons were men, most spoke the curious Letzeburgesch, a dialect that sounds like a mixture of German and French. Some of the patrons spoke French—the official language of Luxembourg—some spoke German and still others conversed in English.

But at only one table in the room was Serbo-Croatian being spoken—the small round corner table by the half-curtained front window.

"Koliko dugo ste ovde?" asked a stringy middle-aged man with a pointed face like a ferret and very bad teeth.

"I've been here for about four hours," replied a tall, gray-haired gentleman who spoke imperfect Serbo-Croatian, rusty from decades of disuse. "I flew in from the United States via a commercial flight." The gray-haired man remembered the flight with evident distaste. He disliked having to mingle with ordinary people. He hated to be cooped up with them, breathing their stale breaths, feeling the moist fetid presence of their perspiration on his skin. As in this place. But he had to meet with this smelly little Serbian with his foul-smelling breath and rotting teeth, his oily hair, crudely cut, and the pickpocket's gleam in his yellow eyes.

The American was sixty-four years old, but his taut facial

muscles and the fluid movements of his conditioned body made
him seem decades younger. He knew this and liked it. More
than once, his physical presence had been his decisive edge in
negotiations with lesser men. He was a panther in the
boardroom, cunning, strong and fast. People who knew him
feared him; just beneath his urbane veneer was an almost
palpable violence.

He was dressed in navy-blue pinstripes and highly polished
Italian loafers. He looked like a successful corporate executive, which is what he was. But he was not talking business
mergers with the ferret-faced little Serbian here in Luxembourg. The American was here on a mission of larceny and
violence. He regretted having to ally himself with the man in
front of him. But he summoned his best friendly face and
addressed him with flattering respect. The Serbian smiled. The
American hoped he would still be smiling when he died.

"Have you determined yet where the exchange will take
place?" the American asked.

"Not yet," the Serbian replied. "They have the strictest of
secrecy. As you are aware, my position as an assistant military
attaché at the embassy makes me privy to certain information,
but only in a support role. As such, I cannot very well ask
questions. I must wait for the information to pass over my
desk."

"I understand," the American said, trying to disguise his
annoyance and impatience. He knew all about the little man.
His name was Milutin Szgety and he had worked at the
embassy in Luxembourg for three years. Months ago, before
the Committee of Seven decided to use Jay Fleming, the
American had used a banking contact in Luxembourg to locate
a suitable informant inside the Yugoslavian embassy. It was not
that the American thought that Subasic and the committee
would fail, it was just that he felt the need of a backup—and
backup that was loyal to him.

Szgety had come cheap. The balance in the special account
the American had set up for him at the Banque Generale du
Luxembourg would hardly buy a top-of-the-line Mercedes. But
to the military attaché it was a fortune.

"When will you know?" the American queried testily.
"When do you expect to learn of the location?"

"I am afraid that I may not have that information until a few hours before the actual transfer."

"And you still don't have the time either?"

A worried shadow covered Szgety's face as he nodded. He was anxious not to offend this wealthy, powerful man. The little Serbian was worried by the frown on the American's face. There was anger in the eyes, and beneath that, something that made Szgety shiver. The Serbian attaché was grateful when the meeting ended.

As Szgety walked through the door and into the gathering darkness, Steven Strand stared after him and wondered if the man had been a mistake. Strand sighed, dropped a couple of bills on the table and walked confidently into the night.

Chapter Twelve

The Colt .45 hanging comfortably in the side pocket of his wool overcoat, Jay Fleming followed Aaron Fiszmann into the still darkness of early morning. They could see their frosty breath in the dim illumination of the street lights. Both men scanned the street suspiciously, but saw no one.

Jay turned and with one leather-gloved hand tried the doorknob of the apartment building. It was locked. Fleming looked upward at the old graystone building with its parapets and stone carvings. The four-hundred-year-old building stood in the center of the old medieval portion of Luxembourg city. It was one of the few buildings on top of the old city that had a view of both the European Center to the northeast and the breathtaking Petrusse River valley to the west and south.

The old city fortress of Luxembourg—once called the Gibraltar of the North—sits atop a massive wedge of stone pie with precipitous vertical sides one hundred and fifty feet high which come to a point at the confluence of the Petrusse and Alzette rivers. Though the city itself contains a mere two hundred and fifty acres, the impregnability of the fortifications, and their strategic location to trade routes, inflated Luxembourg's influence in medieval times far beyond its size. This crucial role in European wars and political affairs for more than five centuries led to its development as a modern center of banking, commerce and politics. The site of the European Parliament, Luxembourg draws prominent politicians from all

106

over Western Europe, also making it an ideal place for foreign companies.

The building in front of which Jay now stood contained offices for ECM, Inc. and apartments for Jay and for other ECM executives. The upper two floors were used for meetings, receptions and whatever other official entertaining was necessary.

Without further thought, Jay turned toward his huge bodyguard and followed him down the narrow cobbled street toward their rented car. It looked just like any other rented car, a tan BMW with nothing unusual about it. But it didn't come from Hertz or Avis, but from another of Denoff's contacts. And like the Mercedes limo they had left in Amsterdam, the BMW was armored all around, and equipped with special tires and a powerful engine.

The BMW had been waiting at the Luxembourg airport when they had arrived the night before from Amsterdam. Also waiting were the Colt Jay now carried and a few items which Fiszmann had requested. Jay was beginning to appreciate the complete professionalism of his security chief, Doug Denoff. It was as if Denoff had been preparing all along for the attacks which were now being made on Fleming's life. Jay had always thought of Denoff as just a worrier. Now, as he stopped beside the BMW and waited for Fiszmann to open it, he realized that worrying was part of Denoff's job. It was now part of his own, too, Fleming thought as he pulled open the door and slid into the passenger's seat. He watched through the windshield as Fiszmann checked under the hood for signs of tampering, and then got down on his hands and knees to inspect the undercarriage with a flashlight. Warily, Jay slid his hand into his coat pocket and felt the cool metal of the Colt. He looked around at the street, wondering if another trio of killers was about to burst out of one of the dark, narrow alleys.

Jay almost wished they'd come at him now. He was ready, exhilarated by the thought of impending combat. He felt more alive right now than he had since leaving the Navy. He was the hunter again. And he was the hunted. The thought raised the small hairs on the back of his neck. This time, the battlefield wasn't the air above Vietnam, but the ancient streets of peaceful Luxembourg.

He was ready now, on guard. The attacks in Holland had

taken him by surprise, and the antics at Anderson's house the previous day had momentarily dazed him. Someone wanted to kill him, and failing that, to discredit and disorient him. If it hadn't been for the faint stains of blood he had found on the sub-flooring in the upstairs room of Anderson's house, Fleming knew he might still believe he had cracked up. But they had been there, and those few drops, seeping through the flooring, had formed the axis around which he spun a new equilibrium. By the time they'd arrived back in Amsterdam, the fighter pilot had taken over from the executive. He was angry and determined and deadly.

Jay was smiling when Fiszmann finally finished his inspection and approached the driver's side of the BMW. Jay had decided that he would share duties with Fiszmann. He wasn't going to sit idly by while someone risked his life for him.

Fiszmann's lips parted into a grim little smile; it was the most expressive he ever got. Jay watched Fiszmann intently. He was a young man, perhaps twenty-six or twenty-seven, yet his dark, almost black eyes belonged to an old man. They were filled with pain. Jay wondered what could happen in a man's life to fill his eyes with that much sadness so early.

Fiszmann climbed in, locked the doors and turned the ignition key. The engine came quickly to life, the carefully muffled motor disguising the growl of the powerful engine. Silently, Fiszmann guided the car away from the curb and down the twisting lane.

When they reached the Rue du Chimay and turned left, Jay checked his watch. It was just after six.

"Don't worry," Fiszmann said. "We've got plenty of time."

Jay nodded and returned his gaze to the yellow penumbras the headlights cast through the darkness. Fiszmann guided the BMW north along the Cote d'Eich and then left on the Rue de Beggen. They drove north out of the city into the Luxembourg countryside, toward the tiny village of Echternach, some thirty kilometers away.

They made very good time on excellent roads, and it was 6:25 when they reached the iron gate guarding the turnoff to Max Emerson's estate. A massive stone wall, fifteen feet high, stretched along the road in both directions, disappearing into the darkness.

A sentry carrying a Heckler and Koch machine pistol

stepped from a glassed-in enclosure and walked up to the
BMW. The man wore an all-black uniform with the stylized
head of a fox over his right breast. The medallion on the man's
billed cap duplicated the emblem. Inside the guardhouse, a
companion looked at them warily.

"Good morning, sir," the sentry said in a polite, yet
threatening manner. "Would you please state your business?"

"Jay Fleming to see Mr. Emerson," Fiszmann responded,
matching the sentry's tone inflection for inflection. The sentry
walked back to his post, picked up a telephone and spoke on it
for a few moments before he returned. This time he wore a stiff
smile on his face, as if the expression were actually painful.
The gate began to part.

"Please drive in," the sentry said. "Stay on this main road
and do not get out of your car until you reach the inner
compound. If you have some sort of mechanical malfunction
with your auto, please stay until help arrives. There are several
dozen mastiffs which are allowed to roam the area behind this
wall," he droned in a voice that sounded like a stewardess
asking people to fasten their seat belts and to bring their seats
to a full upright and locked position for landing. "The mastiffs
are trained to kill. If you have not arrived at the inner
compound in five minutes, a car will automatically be
dispatched to assist you. So, gentlemen, please do not under
any circumstances get out of your car or open your windows
until you are *inside* the inner enclosure."

Fiszmann nodded, and drove through the gates.

The well-maintained tarmacadam road wound its way
through tall timber. Jay strained his eyes to catch sight of one of
the killer attack dogs they had been warned against, but when
they arrived at the gate to the inner compound, he was
disappointed. He wondered if there really were mastiffs out
there in the darkness, swarming through the shadows with their
black coats and deadly jaws. Fleming decided that, for his
money, he'd believe in the dogs. Max Emerson was frequently
full of idle boasting, but even more frequently, he delivered on
his promises . . . and his threats.

Emerson was an arms merchant, one of those private
entrepreneurs who buy and sell instruments of death. Now in
his late sixties, he had made his first fortune buying surplus
M-1s, old jeeps, bayonets and helmets and anything else he

could get his hands on after World War II. There were even rumors that he had bribed Allied soldiers into turning over huge caches of new weapons and ammunition, which he then sold to both Mao and to Chiang Kai-shek. He reportedly had men following both armies, prying rifles out of the hands of dead soldiers whose bodies were still warm and selling them to the highest bidder. Commmunist, capitalist, fascist, revolutionary . . . it made no difference to Emerson just as long as they had the money.

Today Emerson was a multimillionaire, and with the illusion of respectability that large amounts of money can create, lived in the style of a feudal lord. He no longer pried the rifles out of the hands of dead soldiers. He sold advanced jet fighters, and had lucrative contracts with arms manufacturers in two dozen countries.

Representatives of the world's largest banks, eager to mortgage developing nations to pay for the jets and napalm, were regular visitors to Emerson's estate, as were the chief executives of many countries and large corporations. Emerson dealt with them all on an equal basis, with a slightly condescending attitude.

For more than two years now, he had sent emissary after emissary to ECM, Inc., pleading for a contract to peddle Jay Fleming's devices. No, Jay had told him, for two reasons: one, because his devices sold themselves; two, the main reason, because Jay didn't want his ECM devices falling into the hands of the enemies of the United States. Emerson had chided Jay for his "naive" attitude.

Jay remembered their conversation now as he stepped from the BMW and looked up at the massive stone walls of the old eleventh century castle that Emerson had bought and turned into a modern day fortress. The battlements and towers were harshly illuminated by powerful carbon arc searchlights. If even half the stories Jay had heard about the place were true, it was more secure than Fort Knox, the Pentagon and all the Swiss banks put together. Now Emerson did all his business here following an attempt on his life the year before.

He lived in luxurious exile behind the ancient walls like some latter day Howard Hughes, guarded by a small army of former mercenaries and others he had met through the arms business. He claimed he had not ventured beyond the walls since the attack and would never do so again. Let his executives take the risks and do the work now, he was going to live to enjoy the exotic fruits of his tainted labor.

Jay's stomach rolled as he approached the door. He detested the man, and he detested the way he had willingly given up his freedom to conserve a few years of his life.

The massive dark doors opened as Jay approached the top of the stairs. Jay and Aaron stepped across the threshold into an entrance hall with an arched ceiling like a cloister. The hall stretched beyond them into the darkness. The gloominess seemed to sit palpably on their shoulders. It might have been unbearable had it not been for a display of jewels about fifteen yards from the door. They glowed and sparkled like a living thing under the scrutiny of strategically placed lights. A soft mechanical murmuring hummed behind them. The heavy doors automatically closed.

When they got to the jewels, Jay stopped, stunned more by the tasteless conglomeration of precious stones than by their fabulous worth. In front of him, rubies, emeralds, aquamarines and sapphires were set into a garish setting the size of a large dinner plate. The setting depicted the head of a fox.

Emerson liked to think of himself as crafty. After all, he enjoyed telling people, if he really was guilty of the many things the authorities said about him, why had he never been brought to task? He liked to think it was the result of a quick mind that thought like a fox and had chosen the fox emblem as the logo of Emerson Armaments. This ostentatious display of jewels seemed to sum up everything about the roughneck from Houston: crude, rough, unsubtle.

The jewels were not protected by a case of any sort. An obvious reminder that the room was being watched closely by Emerson's security people. Jay craned his head and looked about for television cameras, but saw nothing. He had to give Emerson credit; things had been expertly hidden.

"Gentlemen," a voice echoed from the gloom at the far end of the hall. Jay strained his eyes, trying to penetrate the darkness from the cell of glaring light that surrounded the jewels. Soft footsteps sounded evenly against the stone floor, followed moments later by the outline of a formally dressed butler. The man's face looked like he studied old English murder mysteries and intended one of these days to be the one who did it. "Please follow me." He commanded imperiously and turned on his heel.

Jay and Aaron followed him into the reaches of the entry hall, past rough pieces of furniture and walls hung with tapestries. There were no old suits of armor standing in the corner. Jay was disappointed.

They reached another heavy door at the end of the hall, this one slightly smaller, but no less sturdy than the one through which they'd entered. A numerical keyboard glowed softly on the adjacent wall. The butler turned his back to them as he punched in a code. An electrical catch buzzed, and the door swung open. Jay squinted as he followed the butler from the hall. ·

"Through there, Mr. Fiszmann." The butler nodded toward a door to the left. He turned to Fleming. "You'll please give me your coat, Mr. Fleming." Jay complied. "Through that door, please, Mr. Fiszmann," the butler repeated when Aaron hesitated. "You'll find your morning meal prepared. This meeting will be between Mr. Emerson and Mr. Fleming only."

Aaron looked at Jay like a mother turning her pre-schooler loose in the lion's cage at the zoo.

Jay nodded. "It's okay. We probably won't be long." They stood there for a long moment.

"Please, gentlemen," the butler repeated. "Mr. Emerson's time is extremely limited."

Jay shed his coat into the butler's hands. Fiszmann quickly reached out to take it. The Israeli and the butler dueled with their eyes a split second before Emerson's man relinquished Jay's coat. Fiszmann shot Jay one last look of misgiving, as Fleming turned to follow the butler through an ornate door to the right.

It was like trekking through a maze, up one long hall, down another. Left here, right there, through this door, past dozens of others. Everywhere there were little numeric keyboards. Nowhere were armed men or cameras or other surveillance devices obvious. The less the enemy knew about your defenses, the safer you were. Emerson obviously took the advice of the world's best experts.

Finally, the butler led Jay through an airlock chamber into a vast greenhouse-like room the size of a college basketball gymnasium. As soon as the inner doors closed, a great cresting tide of heat and humidity smothered them. It was a sweltering jungle, and Jay could almost feel the condensation on his cheeks, still cold from the winter outside.

He looked around him. The gray tendrils of Spanish moss hung from the branches of oak trees. Lush green vegetation choked a view of more than fifteen or twenty feet. It looked like a jungle. Somewhere, beyond a thicket of cane, came the sounds of water. Above them, the branches of trees reached toward the glass panels of the roof. Through the panels, Jay could see the first pink hints that the sun might rise that day. In wonder, Jay turned in a slow, stunned circle. It was grander than the botanical gardens in Vienna, though not as beautiful. There was a quiet menace here, something threatening, as if danger lurked somewhere in the bushes.

The butler cleared his throat, smiled indulgently at Jay and resumed the walk. Jay followed him along a closely clipped grass path that meandered through the greenery. Here and there a side path wandered off to some distant location. Perspiration quickly formed on Jay's face and under his armpits and dripped down his neck, along his ribs. It felt nearly a hundred degrees, with ninety percent humidity.

They came around a sharp bend, and Jay caught sight of a white wooden lattice gazebo woven thickly with wisteria vines. The lavender flowers were blooming under powerful lights high on the ceiling. It looked like the courtyard of an old Creole home in New Orleans's French Quarter. As they drew closer, Jay saw the corpulent figure of a profoundly obese man with thinning gray hair sitting at a glass table supported by wrought iron stands. He was dressed in blue seersucker and Jay could see that his hands shook perceptibly. It was Emerson. Spotted skin, pale as a toad's belly, covered Emerson's face. Jay stepped under the wisteria arbor and felt for the first time a hint of a breeze that must have come from silent hidden fans. The air was redolent of wisteria blossoms.

"Good morning, Jay Fleming," Emerson spoke in French with a hideous deep southern accent. The arms merchant pulled himself up and extended his right hand as Jay approached. "Glad you could join me for breakfast." Emerson smiled faintly. Jay felt Emerson's eyes take him in as though he were an undertaker measuring a prospective client for a coffin.

"Good of you to see me on such short notice," Jay said

graciously and added, "quite a . . . room you have here."
Emerson smiled victoriously.

"I got homesick for Houston several years ago," Emerson
explained, changing to English as he sat back down and
gestured for Jay to do the same. Jay chose a chair directly
facing Emerson. "So I found a company in England that makes
these things for, you know, dukes and that sort of shit. And had
the old boys build me one. They had a helluva time finding the
right kind of trees and stuff. Had to go back to Houston and dig
up a bayou. Damn it if they didn't bring the mosquitoes too.
Had a fucking time getting rid of them."

Jay nodded seriously, not sure where to begin, or whether to
begin at all until Emerson had finished with his monologue.
Jay took his napkin from the table, unfolded it and spread it
across his lap. A white uniformed black man materialized with
two silver coffee pots. He poured from them simultaneously.
Hot milk streamed from one, a chicory blend coffee from the
other. They melded into a uniform brew just slightly lighter
than the waiter's skin. Jay picked up the bone china cup and
sipped at the café au lait. It was every bit as good as the coffee
he remembered from the old French Market in New Orleans.

"Like it?" Emerson inquired, leaning toward Jay, elbows
cantilevered on the table. "I get the coffee special from New
Orleans. The same place I got the boy."

Jay smiled thinly. Fleming had come to obtain information,
not to fight the Civil War again. Emerson found in Jay's smile
whatever meaning he wished, and continued to prattle on about
the room, the castle, how much it had all cost, and why hadn't
Jay taken him up on previous invitations. He finished up by
asking what was so urgent about this morning's meeting.

The dreaded moment had arrived. He was going to have to
do business with this man. Jay had rehearsed the scene in his
mind a dozen times on the plane to Luxembourg and again that
morning on the drive out. But somehow, he found himself
unprepared.

Jay stammered, the appropriate words on a tall shelf just out
of reach. "When I called you yesterday I had just come from
Leiden. An odd thing happened there." Jay took a sip of the
coffee and gingerly replaced the cup on its saucer. He cursed
himself. He was never at a loss for words.

Emerson looked past Jay at something, then held up a hand.

"Just hold on a minute with your tale. I see breakfast coming. I'm sure things'll be better after we get a little food in your stomach."

Jay smiled genuinely and agreed as he watched the waiter set down before them large platters of scrambled eggs, browned sausage patties, biscuits, something that looked like a deep-fried plastic hose and finally an antique Limoges tureen filled with grits.

The waiter, a different black man than the one who had poured the coffee, served them both.

Emerson dominated the conversation while they ate, talking volubly. He talked about the many millions his security system cost, how much meat the mastiffs consumed, about his computers and how, through a sophisticated system, he had managed to steal into the computers of many of the world's corporations and governments.

"I'll tell you right now, buddy," Emerson pronounced it "rat now," "if I had to do it all over again, I'd go for computers. You can steal somebody blind and they'll never know it. And if you get caught, well, shit. They don't send you to jail, they hire you as a consultant to tell them how you did it."

Emerson had paid millions for the world's most advanced security system—much of which was predicated on keeping its components secret—and he had spilled most of its details to Jay in a wild torrent of vanity. Emerson ate hungrily, inhaling his food between words. Jay ate silently as he listened.

"Here." Emerson interrupted his soliloquy and proffered the platter with the fried plastic hose. "Have some of this. It's good stuff."

Politely, Jay took a small portion, cut off a bite and speared it with his fork. "What is it?" Jay said as he stuck the piece in his mouth and began to chew it.

"Chitlins," Emerson said. "Good, ain't it?"

"Chitlins?" Jay said as he swallowed. "What's that?"

"Hog intestines," Emerson responded. A flash of malevolent laughter glinted behind the arms merchant's eyes as Jay tried unsuccessfully not to grimace.

Emerson grinned.

The first waiter refilled their coffee cups and cleared away the wreckage of the southern breakfast. Finally, Jay recommenced the explanation for his visit.

"Someone has been trying to kill me," Jay said bluntly as Emerson gulped his coffee.

"The first attack took place in Amsterdam, the second in Leiden." Jay described the events of the past four days. Emerson leaned back in his chair and took it all in, his face a mask of alert indifference. When Jay had finished, Emerson sat up in his chair, fished around in an inner coat pocket and withdrew a cigarette from a pack of Camels, tamped each end thoughtfully on the table, then stuck it between his lips. His gold lighter was set with a jeweled fox head.

Emerson cocked back his head and blew out a cloud of tobacco. "So?"

Jay looked at him, momentarily taken aback. He opened his mouth and was about to speak again when Emerson said, "So what do you want to do about it? Rent a room in my maximum security Hilton?"

"I'd like some information," Jay said neutrally, fighting the provocation.

"Information?" Emerson responded and looked at the ceiling, at the rapidly lightening sky, as if Jay had presented a novel request. "From me?" Emerson said returning his gaze to Fleming. Jay nodded.

"Why me?" Emerson said.

Jay swallowed against the humiliating paces Emerson was putting him through. "Everybody knows you've got the best intelligence network within the arms community," Jay began. It was true. Emerson owed his great financial success to his thousands of informants, shills, dupes, compromised politicians, military officers, executives, and outright spies.

"All I'm asking of you," Jay pleaded, "is for you to tap your system and see who it is that's after me." Briefly Jay considered asking the man about any information he might have concerning the transfer of the Tesla papers that Anderson had told him about. Fleming decided against it. Emerson was the type to run off with the prize himself.

"You think it's someone in the arms business?" Emerson asked. Jay nodded. "Who do you suspect?"

Jay said he had no idea.

"What are you offering for this information?" Emerson said, leaning forward. "What have you got that could be worth this information?"

"A contract to handle my second generation ECM devices," Jay offered hopefully. Emerson smiled broadly and then shattered the quiet of the greenhouse with convulsive laughter.

"Your *second* generation devices?" A new fit of laughter seized Emerson. Tears ran down his cheeks. Then just as suddenly as it had begun, the laughter was gone, the smile replaced by a derisive glare. "Your second generation devices are worthless. Maybe I can sell a few to a banana republic here and there." The hospitable voice grew frost on the edges of the soft Texas vowels. "There is only one thing you have that I want. I want the rights to sell the same devices you just made available to the Royal Dutch Air Force."

Somehow Jay managed to keep his face impassive.

"I'll consider it," Jay responded. "But only if the information you have identifies the people who are trying to kill me."

Emerson's face betrayed nothing. Jay prayed his was equally blank.

"You're really scared, aren't you?" Emerson stated.

"Concerned," Jay responded.

"Why don't you go to the CIA?" Emerson queried. "Certainly you have contacts there. What about your own security system? Denoff is one of the best in the world. I offered him a job, you know. The little Jew prick wouldn't work for me."

Emerson shook his head sadly, as he got up. The breakfast, the interview, was over. Jay rose.

"Where you staying?" Emerson asked.

"The company apartment."

"When're you going to get yourself a *real* place to live?" Emerson asked derisively as he walked around the table and motioned Jay to follow him.

"Like this?" Jay asked as neutrally as possible. Emerson looked back to see if Jay was making fun of him.

"Yeah," Emerson said. And walked on quickly along the immaculately clipped grass path. The butler materialized at the door to the main castle.

"I'll be in touch," Emerson said. "But I'll tell you right now, I've already heard about things, and although I'm not in the habit of giving things away, I will tell you to watch out for the Russkies."

"The Russians?"

"They don't like you much."

"Why?" Jay stammered. "Why would they want to kill me?"

"Hold on a minute." Emerson stopped and held up his hand like a traffic cop. "Just hold on. I didn't say they were trying to kill you. Did I? All I said is that you should look out. They don't like you."

"But it might be them?"

Emerson nodded and then added, "And it might *not* be them." Jay had never liked the man less.

"I'll be in touch," Emerson repeated himself. "And don't you hesitate if you make up your mind."

"It all depends on what you come up with," Jay replied uncomfortably.

Emerson proffered his hand at the airlock. Jay looked at him and turned away without taking it. As the door of the airlock closed, Jay heard the Texan laugh victoriously.

Chapter Thirteen

Raoul LeClerc was rarely thankful. But on mornings like this, he said a silent word of appreciation to the medieval fortifiers of the old city of Luxembourg for the foresight that allowed him to secretly stash a virtual supermarket of weapons beneath the city streets, and right underneath the noses of the police.

Beneath the cobbled streets of the old town were hundreds upon hundreds of tunnels and passages that once connected the forts and cannon stations. Except for a couple of sections which were kept open for tourists, the passages and underground chambers had been sealed off, bricked up or built over for hundreds of years.

The passages remain, but most of the tunnels are out of sight, nearly forgotten and almost inaccessible. There are no accurate maps of the huge rock honeycomb, luckily for LeClerc, who rented a ramshackle stone house in the old city, an ancient stone house whose lower cellar dated from about 1300. The cellar of the house communicated with the elaborate system of passages beneath the city.

LeClerc bent over a low bench which rested in the center of what had once been a powder magazine, some seventy feet below the Place Guillaume. The vaulted ceiling was about thirty feet at its greatest height. Feeble light from a battery lantern scraped against the ragged edges of the stone. The odor of gasoline permeated the chamber and gave LeClerc a persistent headache.

He was a short, wiry Parisian with oily black hair and tiny eyes that glared at the world. His attempt at a beard clung to his jaws like a moth-ravaged fox pelt, his mustache just a ragged shadow on his upper lip. The skin over half a dozen angry pimples shone tight and full on his cheeks.

A steady stream of curses in French and Russian floated through the air as he used a wooden spoon to stir a mixture of laundry detergent flakes and gasoline in a large gallon jar that had once contained pickled eggs. He added detergent, and then more gasoline, and then more detergent.

Anxiously, he glanced at the cheap plastic digital watch on his wrist. He had to hurry. The others would be meeting him in front of the Excelsior in a little more than an hour.

As he stirred and mixed, LeClerc cursed the lateness of the assignment. He would have preferred to spend more time in preparation, to use more professional devices. But no, the man—an American, judging by the accent of his French—said it must be done this morning. Barely six hours had passed since the call, and less than four since LeClerc picked up the money, taped under a rubbish can in the park next to the Citadel St. Esprit. He hated Americans, but they paid well.

He brought the lantern closer and inspected his handiwork. He stirred the substance in the jar once again, and lifted the bowl of the spoon upward and let the jelly-like mixture drip slowly back. A thin slash of a smile opened across his face, revealing crooked teeth.

He set a quart mayonnaise jar on the workbench and filled it with the mixture, then screwed on the lid tightly and wiped away the excess with a rag. He closed the large gallon jar. Taking the electric lantern and the filled quart jar, he walked to the entrance to the room. Bending over, he set the trip for the boobytraps that would kill anyone who entered without his permission. LeClerc was whistling an off-key rendition of the Star Spangled Banner as he mounted the steps.

"You military men are all so frighteningly similar somtimes," Alexandra Downing said as she sat sipping a mild Ceylon Breakfast Tea in the Excelsior Hotel's dining room. Across the table sat Lieutenant Colonel Lee Goldberg from NATO intelligence.

Alexandra had called him immediately after checking into

the Excelsior the day before. He had insisted on taking a day of leave from his job in Brussels to come talk with her.

He was a tall, thin man whose dark brown hair and eyes seemed to shine in the bright sunlight that cascaded through the windows.

"How are we so much alike?" Goldberg asked a little insecurely. He was more than mildly unnerved by Alexandra. It was more than just her connection with Martin Copeland, or the fact that he had been killed. *She* would have made him nervous under any circumstances, with her assertive, straight-forward manner. She was direct without being abrupt, aggressive but not a bully. He had known women like that before, but none so attractive and delightfully feminine.

"The way you insist on playing the gentleman. Not," she said, leaning over and putting her hand lightly on his elbow, "that it's bad. I rather enjoy it. But it seems so inbred in military officers that I wonder whether it's real or just another regulation."

Goldberg looked at her, uncertain how to respond. She caught his confusion.

"It's all right, Colonel," she said lightly, her smile infectious in the early morning light. He crossed his legs, uncrossed them, shifted in his seat, took a sip of coffee and tried to smile. His smile came out like the grimace of a prisoner being interrogated.

"I'm sorry if I've made you feel uncomfortable," Alexandra continued. "It's just that there's something about you that reminds me . . ." A light mist swept across her eyes for an instant. She smiled bravely. "Let's just drop it," she said. "I shouldn't have brought it up."

They looked at each other for several moments. Goldberg poured more tea for her and more coffee for himself from the silver pots left on the table. He looked out the window at people strolling past on the sidewalk, their images softened by the sheer curtains that hung from a brass rod.

"Thanks for inviting me to breakfast here," Goldberg offered, trying to break the awkward silence. He looked around at the elegant surroundings. "A real American breakfast," he said, glancing at the menu. "The place I'm staying is not as fancy as all this," he said, his eyes taking in the cut glass chandeliers, the brocade wall paper, the plush carpets. "An officer's salary doesn't go too far." He laughed as if to say it didn't really matter.

Alexandra remembered the money Martin had left her in the envelope. So much work, so little to show for it. She wanted to cry, but she resisted. There would be plenty of time for that as soon as she discovered who had killed him and why. She would not let his sacrifice be useless.

"My pleasure," she replied. Goldberg looked at her oddly for an instant as if he'd momentarily forgotten his last statement during the long pause. "But it's a bit close to the kitchen for my liking," she added as a waiter rushed passed them and was swallowed by the swinging doors beside their table.

"But," Alexandra continued, her voice all business now, "We're not here to have a nice little vacation in Luxembourg." She fixed his face with eyes that held him with their intensity and determination. "I appreciate your concern for me in trying to keep me out of whatever—whoever—killed Martin. But I will not sit around and play the mourning woman." She felt her voice start to crack. She looked down and took another sip of tea while she composed her thoughts.

"You said over the phone the other night that you were going to respect Martin's last wishes. That you were going to handle the matter yourself and keep me out of it." Her voice was growing stronger. "Is that still your decision?"

Goldberg nodded and started to speak, but Alexandra cut him off.

"Hear me out," she said, raising her hand. "I know that something is supposed to happen here in Luxembourg soon. 'Tesla lives,' that's what he told me to tell you. It has something to do with Tesla. I know that he invented some weapons and a lot of his papers are still classified secret by the U.S. Government. Furthermore, I know that Martin sent you some information, information that got him killed." She paused and took a breath. "I also suspect that the materials he sent to you were classified documents. So now, I'd like to tell you what I'm going to do if I don't get access to those documents: First, I'm going to go to the nearest NATO security office and tell them you are illegally in possession of classified documents." She saw the flash of surprise in his eyes and knew she had scored a point. "Secondly, I am going to go to every police agency, every university, every military consulate in Luxembourg and tell them that something awful is about to happen with regard to some Tesla invention. I don't know if that's the story or not, but it'll be close enough so that if the people involved in it hear about me, I'll get a visitor.

"Now, Colonel Goldberg," she measured her words carefully, "if you want to adhere to the spirit of Martin's letter—rather than to the letter itself—and help me stay alive, please give me access to the documents. Otherwise, I will have no choice but to go my own way and I have no illusions that any 'visitors' that turn up will be friendlier to me than they were to Martin."

Goldberg looked at her a long time. He massaged his chin as if he were trying to remold a lump of clay. He ran his fingers through his hair. He hoped he would never have to cross wits with someone like her again.

"You know that it's illegal for you to possess those classified documents?" he asked feebly. "I could still turn those documents in and not be legally liable," he said.

"Would you?" Alexandra asked, suddenly concerned.

"Of course not," he replied indignantly. "I owe my life to Colonel Copeland. When you owe your continued existence to someone, you don't go by the book if they ask a favor of you."

"Exactly my point," Alexandra pressed. "Don't go by the book. I don't give a damn about violating national security laws if it means finding out who killed Martin, and preventing them from doing whatever it is that he died trying to stop." Their eyes locked like they were connected by invisible controls. Alexandra saw a decision brewing behind his. "Did you bring the documents with you?" she persisted.

He nodded. "Back in my room at the Hotel Central, near the train station."

Good, she thought. If he had really been determined not to let her see the documents, he'd have left them in Brussels.

"If I *did* let you look at the documents," he began slowly, picking his words carefully, "what would you intend to do?"

"That depends on what was in them," she replied. "I imagine—"

The noise of angry chants filtered in from the street. Alexandra turned and through the window saw a mangy group of protesters carrying signs in French and English. They wanted Luxembourg out of NATO and American nuclear weapons out of Western Europe.

"Goes on all the time," Goldberg remarked with disgust. "There must be some official they don't like staying here at the hotel. This is where most dignitaries stay when they visit." He watched them silently for a moment and then continued, "I guess what they want is Russian nuclear weapons in Western Europe."

"They mean well," Alexandra said as she turned back to face Goldberg. He continued his scrutiny of the small gathering. There were probably no more than a dozen in all, and the police hadn't arrived yet.

"Good intentions don't keep you safe," Goldberg rebutted. "I suppose that most of them mean well, but the ones who don't—" He looked up suddenly as something beyond the window caught his attention.

Alexandra watched as the muscles in Goldberg's face tightened, and his eyes grew larger.

"Get down!" Goldberg shouted, leaping from his chair just as the window exploded, showering the dining room with glass.

Excellent, Raoul LeClerc thought as he marched up and down the sidewalk among the dozen or so anti-nuclear protesters. The anonymous American's information was uncannily correct. The man and woman were just where he said they would be. There would be no need for him to kill them separately in their rooms. It was better this way, he told himself as he edged his way to the periphery of the group.

It wasn't a very large group, he thought ruefully, but they were vocal, very vocal. All in all, not a bad group for such short notice. He had called Emil Boncoeur minutes after talking to the American. Boncoeur was a student at the university and had received a lot of publicity recently as a leader of student protests against the United States and its nuclear weapons. He'd told Boncoeur that the American Assistant Secretary of Defense was staying at the Excelsior before speaking to the European Parliament. Boncoeur had even apologized a few minutes ago for the lack of a larger crowd.

"The holidays," he lamented. "All of the students have

already headed home for Christmas. Any other time . . ." He'd shrugged his shoulders. *C'est la guerre*.

What a wonderful naive fool, LeClerc thought as he reached the other side of the street and propped his protest sign against a parked Citröen. In the distance he heard sirens. The hotel's management must have called the police. No matter, he knew as he unshouldered a small battered canvas backpack and set it on the hood of the Citröen. He unbuckled it and withdrew the jar he had prepared that morning. Also from within the sack, he pulled out a fireworks device the Americans called an M-80. With a piece of silver duct tape, he fastened the M-80 to the side of the jar.

As he finished his preparations, he watched with satisfaction as one of the demonstrators, whipped by the talented Boncoeur to a high pitch of indignation, bent down and pried loose from the street a round gray paving stone. He heaved it at the hotel's dining room window.

It was a beautiful sight, LeClerc remarked to himself. The broad expanse of plate glass seemed to dissolve at once, cascading down like an avalanche of ice. That's when LeClerc pulled a disposable butane lighter from the pocket of his jeans and lit the fuse of the M-80.

The dining room reverberated with the screams of panicked diners, the thunder of the shattered window and the clashing and clanging of silver flatware, crystal glasses and fine china. It sounded like someone had thrown a bomb into a symphony orchestra during the *1812 Overture*.

Alexandra looked just in time to see the window bulge under the impact of the paving stone. Suddenly strong hands hurled her toward the safety of the kitchen. She cartwheeled into one of the swinging doors and fell, half in, half out of the kitchen. A waiter, anxious to avoid the violence, stepped on her as he retreated to the kitchen.

Alexandra struggled up into a crouch. Ahead of her, Lee Goldberg stood like a statue, looking out the window. He screamed an obscenity that she didn't understand. Its intonation was clear. Bright red blood trickled down his khaki shirt where glass apparently had dropped on him. Madness crested through the dining room like thundering surf.

"Lee," Alexandra screamed as she struggled to her feet,

leaning on the doorjamb for support. Behind her, helping hands grasped her elbows. "Lee, be careful. You're injured."

Raoul LeClerc heaved the jar with all his strength and watched with pride as it arced neatly across the street and through the hole left by the paving stone. He started to run, but was transfixed by the figure of a man in military dress who had suddenly stood up. The man in the uniform looked like an American football player, and the gray, tumbling jar hurtling toward him was the football. It was a perfect scene, Raoul thought when the man raised his arm in anger. It looked as if he were trying to catch the ball.

And then the window was filled with flame.

Alexandra heard a sharp explosion and instantly the dining room was transformed into a raging hell. Flames flowed liquidly across the floor, clinging to the walls and ceiling. She threw an arm up to cover her face as the heat of the fire grew instantly unbearable. And in the middle of it, a sight no human being should ever have to see, Lee Goldberg, a human wick in the heart of the flames. A low inhuman moan of pain and anguish howled from his throat and quickly grew to a high pitched shriek of terror. Her legs quivered with indecision, wanting badly to run to his aid, knowing that she must save herself if she was to be any good to him.

Wicked, hungry flames drove Alexandra back to the safety of the kitchen as she watched Lee Goldberg leap into the street. She ran through the kitchen and made her way to the exit leading to the service elevator and from there to the lobby.

As she sprinted through the chaos in the lobby, heading for the front doors, all she could think was, I'm a lightning rod for death. She lunged between two elderly ladies and sidestepped a bellman carrying a multi-colored parrot with one leg manacled to a perch. *"Merde!"* the parrot squawked. *"Merde, merde!"*

The revolving doors were jammed, so she made for the swinging door used by the bellmen to transport luggage. She hit the door at a slow run, leaning into the polished brass crossbar when suddenly someone jerked it open from the outside, sending her face first onto the sidewalk. She broke the fall with her palms and quickly regained her feet. Frantically, she elbowed her way through a cordon of bystanders and gawkers.

When she finally gained the other side of the crowd she

beheld a sight that could not have appeared even in Hieronymus Bosch's worst nightmares. Lee Goldberg had fallen, somehow made his way to his feet again, and had stumbled into the street in pursuit of . . . only he would ever know. Fierce flames leaped off his body and drove back a pair of men who had tried to use their coats to beat out the flames. She walked nearer, and froze as he sank slowly to his knees and toppled forward, his body rapidly consumed by the flames.

The stench of burning flesh filled her nostrils and twisted her insides with nausea. Someone arrived with a small red fire extinguisher just about the time she doubled up and left the remains of a genuine American breakfast all over the paving stones.

Chapter Fourteen

Luxembourg,
December 19

Fiszmann advised returning to Luxembourg via a different route. It would discourage a potential ambush, he said. Jay had voiced no objection, although he was slightly annoyed at having to alter his route for unknown pursuers.

Sitting in the passenger seat next to Fiszmann, he fumed silently over his meeting with Emerson and wondered how anyone could be so perfectly despicable. The man had no morals, no ethics, no loyalties save to himself and his money. Jay twisted uncomfortably in his seat, smarting from the humiliating meeting with the arms merchant. "Sooner or later," Emerson had once said, "everybody has to deal with me." Jay had resisted, he had come to enjoy the feeling of superiority every time his colleagues in the defense industry complained about how difficult it was to deal with Emerson. Nobody liked the fat arms merchant, but they all did business with him.

Jay grew alternately ashamed of himself and then angry that events had forced him to do commerce with the Texan. Somehow, he resolved, he would get the information from Emerson and leave the man holding an empty bag. It would make him a serious enemy of the man, Jay knew, but who needed him as a friend?

Fleming turned his thoughts to Anderson's statements involving the Tesla papers. They obviously had something to do with the attempts on his life. Somebody wanted to manipulate him. Just as obviously, someone else was trying to kill him. Locate the first party, he thought, and you're a step closer to the killers. Who had he gotten himself caught between? What were the names of the players? Mentally, he tallied known enemies, people who disliked him or could profit from his death. The list read like a Who's Who of the defense industry.

Most of the major arms manufacturers resented him because ECM, Inc. refused to accept a cost-plus contract, and in the entire history of its existence had never charged the government for a cost overrun. Fleming won contracts on the basis of competition. He built the finest components and made a handsome profit on them.

ECM's record embarrassed the entire military-industrial complex. And his prices forced other companies to lower their bids. The amount of gravy the big companies had to trim from their profits was reason enough for some corporate executive to pull a few strings with the CIA and have him killed.

But that didn't explain the fake cops in Leiden or the tall, dark-haired man in Amsterdam. Someone wanted things kept out of police hands. And somebody else was trying to interfere. And somehow he was the key in a mysterious plan, important enough that both sides were willing to go to enormous lengths. For what?

And then there was Emerson's cryptic statement subtly pointing a finger at the Soviets. What did they want? His devices? It was possible, but not likely. Jay knew that any Russian attempt on his life would provoke an espionage war. Though Fleming was disliked by his arms industry colleagues, if he was snatched, they would all become targets. But that didn't rule out the possibility that he had gotten caught between the Russians and someone else.

The riddle ran in dizzying barrel rolls through his mind. He resolved to see his entire staff in Luxembourg to work on the problem as soon as they returned.

Jay looked at his watch. The alternate route was taking nearly twice as long. They were, according to the signs, about twenty-five kilometers from the city.

Seeing, but not really enjoying, Jay watched the forested countryside sweep by on the other side of the tinted, bullet-proof glass. The two-lane concrete road snaked through the forest, roughly following the course of a rushing stream which glinted white and foamy in the patches of sunlight that broke through the trees.

The road crossed and recrossed the stream, only occasionally climbing above it to cross the modest bluff here and there where the gentle streambed turned into a ravine. They had passed through at least one tunnel.

Traffic was surprisingly heavy, Fleming thought, with an abundance of trucks and transports. Twice they had been forced to stop while an oversized truck crossed a narrow bridge.

Jay looked over at Fiszmann. He seemed totally attuned to his task, eyes darting alertly from road to rearview mirror, examining each vehicle that approached, scanning the onrushing roadside for possible trouble. He drove fast, using the BMW's superior power and handling to pass slower traffic and sail around the road's many curves.

"What do you make of Emerson's estate?" Jay asked Fiszmann. The bodyguard glanced over briefly at Jay. His look had a way of stifling small talk.

"I'd say his security was pretty formidable," he responded crisply, all business. "I'd hate to have to break in by myself."

"Impregnable?"

"Nothing's impregnable," Fiszmann said professionally. "You could drug his dogs—lace their meat with tranquilizers, or shoot them with a tranquilizer dart gun. You'd have the inner compound to yourself then because they couldn't mount motion sensors or trip wires . . ." He paused and thought for a moment. "Although they might put tripwires or infrared sensors above the ground . . . perhaps at shoulder-level. Those wouldn't be tripped by the dogs.

"The outer and inner walls, of course," he said warming to the challenge, "would be no problem, as long as you didn't step on top of them or interrupt any sensor beams. You'd have to stay clear of an area two or three feet above the wall.

"But inside the compound . . ." His voice trailed off. "Inside would be a different story. Old castles are built to take almost anything. The doors and windows are the weak points, and they're well secured. The only way to get inside would be to blast your way in with explosives, or to be invited as we were this morning. And once inside . . . well, you saw the electronic combination locks on the doors all through the place.

"I'd say Emerson has a remarkably secure setup," Fiszmann concluded, nodding his head, lecture over. He turned to Jay and said, "I wouldn't get any ideas about waltzing in and lifting that fox head." He smiled the little narrow grimace. A few teeth showed this time.

Fleming silently toyed with schemes to keep anything really valuable out of Emerson's hands. Jay resented having to do business with him, but he was the quickest way of unraveling the problem of who was trying to kill him. There must be a means to compel the arms merchant's assistance without delivering the most recent generation of ECM devices to him—which was tantamount to sending them air mail to the Kremlin.

Fleming's reverie was interrupted when he felt a surge of speed from the BMW and heard the engine growl.

"What's up?" Jay asked.

"I think someone's following us." He looked in the rearview mirror.

"Which one?" Jay asked as he looked at the traffic behind them.

"Possibly the Jaguar sedan, the dark green one."

They took a curve, and when the road straightened, Jay saw the Jaguar surge around a delivery truck about a hundred and fifty yards behind them. Then behind that, another Jaguar, this one midnight-blue, cleared the truck. They gained on the BMW as Fiszmann pushed the car ever closer to its limits. Jay glanced over at the speedometer; the needle rested against the extreme right end. The last number was two hundred kilometers per hour.

Trees and road signs blurred past as Fiszmann drove like a maniac. Behind them, the Jaguars were slowly closing in, but were still too far away for Jay to recognize any faces behind the windshields.

Fiszmann maneuvered through the sharpest curves, blasting past slower moving traffic on blind turns. Somehow, the Jaguars kept up, gaining with every move and countermove.

"Get in the back," Fiszmann ordered. "In the black attaché case, you'll find a Uzi. Can you use it?" Jay replied that he could, and climbed hurriedly into the back as Fiszmann took another curve. Jay felt the rear of the BMW slide as the speed

surpassed the tires' ability to hold the road. The right rear
wheel left the concrete with a hard whump and scraped along
in the gravel of the narrow shoulder as Fiszmann fought for
control.

Jay pulled himself up to a sitting position and between
frantic thumps of his heart admired the remarkable, almost
meditative calm which molded Fiszmann's face. He seemed
unconcerned by a skid at one hundred and twenty miles per
hour. Jay wiped the perspiration from his upper lip.

They had to slow the BMW to get it back under control, and
by the time they did, the Jaguars had closed half the gap
between them. Methodically Jay unlatched the attaché case and
pulled the well-oiled submachine gun from the molded foam
inside. He inserted a 32-round clip in the grip and slammed it
home.

As Jay moved to the right side of the car and began to unroll
the window, a drumroll of slugs ripped into the trunk of the
BMW and turned the rear window into a crowd of webs.

"Wish we had the Mercedes," Fiszmann commented. Jay
agreed. Where the Mercedes had a small gunport in the middle
of the rear window, the BMW had none. He would have to lean
out the window to shoot.

Suddenly they careened around a sharp curve to the right,
throwing Jay across the car, and exposing the half open rear
window to the gunmen behind them. It was an opening not to
be missed. Slugs slammed viciously into the door, and climbed
upward toward the open window. Jay dropped the Uzi and
lunged for the window handle as the first rounds wove their
spider webs in the bulletproof glass. A round embedded itself
with a hollow thump in the upholstered door pillar inches
behind Fiszmann's head. He didn't flinch. Then, they were out
of danger as the road straightened, presenting the armored
rump of the BMW to their pursuers. Jay looked at the hole
behind Fiszmann's head, started to make a comment and
decided against it.

"Always roll down the window *behind* the driver," Fiszmann instructed. "The only thing that gets exposed is the
passenger side, and then only if we take an abrupt left-hand
turn." There was no rancor in his voice. Yet, Jay felt chastised.
He had a lot to learn.

Slugs continued to pelt the rear of the car. Jay unrolled the window behind Fiszmann. With his thumb on the fire selector button, Jay squeezed a long burst at full automatic. Pieces of the roadway leaped up like popped corn as Jay struggled to aim the gun. As the clip emptied itself, a covey of slugs burst through the green Jag's windshield. The tempered glass disintegrated. The Jag fell back immediately. Wind at a hundred and twenty miles per hour can make driving without a windshield difficult. The blue Jaguar immediately passed its wounded companion and resumed the pursuit.

Fiszmann looked in the sideview mirror. "Well, one thing in our favor. They've got stock cars. Aim for the driver or the tires." Jay fumbled to eject the empty clip. He succeeded and then rammed another one home.

"Try selective fire," Fiszmann suggested. "It'll conserve the ammunition. All we've got is in the case. I wasn't counting on a long firefight." Four more full clips rested in their molded compartments in the foam.

The icy morning air parted Jay's hair as he again leaned out the window and fired a three-burst round at the Jag which was now almost bumper to bumper with the BMW. The burst missed as the car swerved to the right out of Jay's line of fire. Fiszmann edged to the right shoulder so Jay could get a better shot but as he did, the Jaguar slammed into the rear, sending a shudder through the BMW's frame.

"Hold on!" Fiszmann shouted as he stabbed the brakes, flinging Jay forward. An intense dull pain radiated from Jay's ribs as he banged into the front seat. The maneuver failed; the Jag's driver, anticipating Fiszmann, had already braked. The rear of the BMW swerved as the car started to spin. Again, Fiszmann skillfully regained control and rapidly accelerated.

"No doubt about it," Fiszmann said with new respect in his voice. "We're dealing with professionals."

Jay struggled back to a firing position as Fiszmann swerved to foil the aim of the Jag's gunman. Jay fired another burst at the approaching vehicle. It was now practically on their bumper. The slugs sprayed impotently across the pavement.

Jay ducked as they rounded a left-hand curve that left Jay's side exposed. Slugs buzzed in through the open window, slashing the air above Jay's head and pounding into the back of the seat and the doors at the other side of the car. Despite the freezing wind whistling in through the open window, Jay felt sweat trickling down his forehead and soaking his eyebrows. As the road straightened again, he wiped his moist eyebrows.

"Jesus!" Jay shouted, "this is insane!" He leaned out the window and prepared to fire again. But before he had a chance to pull the trigger, Fiszmann shouted, "How good are you at praying?"

Fleming spun around. The road was running straight between the stream on the right side of the car and a sheer bluff some forty feet high to their left. Directly ahead, a narrow outcropping of the bluff reached down and crossed the road like the paw of some giant animal. The highway engineers had constructed a short tunnel through the outcropping. On the other side of the tunnel, Jay saw the speeding hulk of a gasoline tanker as it moved toward the center of the road in order to negotiate the tunnel. There was no question of stopping.

The dark mouth of the tunnel loomed ever larger as Fiszmann pressed the accelerator to the floor. The tunnel swallowed them. Sunlight still shone on the tanker as it approached from the other end. Jay felt his sphincter muscle tighten as he watched the lumbering mass of the tanker grow larger. The driver was blinking his lights now and Jay could hear his horn. Smoke billowed from the tanker's rear wheels as the driver tried desperately to stop.

Jay could make out the Elf Aquataine lettering on the tanker now. He worked his tongue against the roof of his very dry mouth, as the Fiat emblem on the truck's grill raced into focus. A tiny voice in the back of Jay's head told him to be thankful it would be over quickly. He wouldn't feel anything at this speed.

The truck hovered before them like an onrushing mountain as the BMW burst into the bright morning sunlight. Fiszmann jerked the wheel to the right. The edge of the tanker's fender raked ear-splitting grooves along the side of their car and then raced like a freight train into the tunnel.

The BMW's right wheels were lifted off the pavement, and for a long sweaty second, Fiszmann struggled to maintain equilibrium. The car seemed to slither along, the front and rear never quite lined up.

Then, Jay found himself trapped inside a giant kaleidoscope; left became right, and up, down. He dropped the Uzi and clutched at the buckle of a seatbelt that had hit him in the face.

He felt his legs slam first into the ceiling and then the floor. One instant he was standing upright on the rear door, and the next he was on his head. The Uzi slammed into his left kidney and Jay prayed it wouldn't fire. The screams of tortured metal filled his ears with a pitch that started as a screech and fell into a groan, and then finally stopped altogether as the BMW came to rest on its right side.

Jay didn't hear the collision in the tunnel, but instants after the BMW came to a rest, the earth rumbled and seemed to buckle under him. Fleming struggled painfully to his feet, and stuck his head out of the still open rear window in time to see angry tongues of yellow and black and red and orange leap from the mouth of the tunnel. He dropped to his feet as the shock wave and bone-numbing amplitude of the blast slammed into the wreckage of the BMW and punted it like a soccer ball off the road shoulder and down the short embankment into the stream where it came to rest, this time on the roof. The gasoline tanker had made one hell of a bomb.

Just before he ducked, Jay had seen the blue Jaguar on the other side of the road, its hood intimately embracing a power pole girder. The tanker must have collided with the green Jag, the one with the shot out windshield.

Icy water cascaded into the overturned BMW and shocked Jay like electric wires. He lay still for a moment, taking inventory. His ribs hurt from the impact with the seat. His head throbbed. He probed a sharp pain on the side of his head with one finger. It came back red. Slowly, he tried to move arms, legs. Everything seemed to work.

Cautiously he shook the grogginess from his head and crawled forward on his hands and knees toward Aaron's inert body which was cuddled up like a sleeping child in the curve of the windshield.

"Aaron." Jay shook him. There was no response. He was out cold. Trying to gain some leverage with his legs, Jay grabbed Fiszmann's belt and dragged him backward. Jay tried to open first one door, then the other. They were all jammed from the impact. Finally he pulled Fiszmann to the open rear window and shoved him through into the water. Jay followed him out, and took hold of him before the water carried him off. With his other hand, he clutched at a rod on the BMW's undercarriage.

The BMW had landed just upstream of a gravel bar, and the current had quickly carried the car against the sediment, hood pointing upstream. The window faced the deeper part of the stream where the current snatched at them and threatened to pry loose Jay's grip on the unconscious Fiszmann. The muscles in his forearms ached. He began to shiver uncontrollably, further loosening his grip.

Then the current lifted Fiszmann's legs, and his body floated gently across the surface. Jay relinquished his grip on the BMW and let the current carry him toward the gravel bar, kicking desperately with his legs to avoid being carried into the middle of the stream. Then he felt his feet scrape against the gravel. Fleming switched his grip on Fiszmann and turned over on his belly. He crawled painfully out of the water and onto the bank of the stream, where he collapsed, breathless, numb. His legs felt like two frozen beef shanks. Clumsily, Jay crawled backward, pulling Fiszmann with him. The air hung heavy with the acrid odor of gasoline and burning rubber and paint. The smells reached Jay's nose only faintly. The cold continued to seep through his entire body. When Fiszmann was clear of the stream, Jay struggled to a sitting position. He no longer felt any sensation in his limbs. He had to watch them move to know where they were.

Fire, he thought, hungrily gazing at the inferno that raged on the roadway some twenty feet above him. The mouth of the tunnel was nearly one hundred yards away, but the blast had scorched a black smear along the bluff above the road that extended almost to the spot where the BMW had left the road. A pall of black hovered above the scene, cutting off the sunlight like a shroud. To his left, near the tunnel's flaming mouth, Jay saw a burning stream flowing toward him. He coveted the fire, the warmth.

He shook his head and drunkenly climbed to his knees. Leaning over Fiszmann, he slapped the man's face.

"Aaron," he slurred and then cursed his tongue for being so lazy. But he was so tired. He wanted desperately to lie down, take a little nap, like Aaron. The man obviously had the right idea. Just a little refreshing nap and he'd be able to—

"Stop!" He said out loud. His voice came strangely to his ears. "Just stop, Fleming. If you go to sleep you're going to die, you fucking fool." There, he thought. That was better. His voice would keep him awake. "Okay, now, you're going to get old Fiszmann here, and drag him and yourself up there to the road where you can get some heat."

Somehow, he struggled to his feet and leaned over to slip his arms under Fiszmann's armpits. That was when he noticed that Fiszmann's head rolled in ways that God had never designed it to. His neck had been cleanly broken and he was very dead.

Jay set him down gently, and swayed like a lone tree in a thunderstorm as he fought to stay erect. He looked down on the perfect, unmarked body. There was not a visible wound, not a scratch, not a bruise.

"You shouldn't be dead," Fleming mumbled to no one. "I'll go get help."

The rocks and gravel didn't hurt Fleming's cold anesthetized legs as he stumbled, fell, regained his feet, and fell again making his way to the embankment. It sloped steeply from the road to the streambed. When he reached it, panic seized him. It looked like Everest.

Steadying himself with one arm against the rip-rap placed to protect the roadbed when the stream flooded, Jay looked dizzily upward and then started to climb. He told himself that the jagged pieces of rip-rap should hurt, but he felt nothing. Each foothold, each handgrip took a supreme effort. He wanted to sleep. Then the scraping of footsteps filtered over the edge of the embankment like tiny pebbles of sound. Jay's spirits soared. Someone would help him.

"Help!" he cried feebly. "Down here! Don't go away! Help." Moments later the outlines of two men were silhouetted dimly against the roiling smoke overhead. "Here!" Jay waved the frozen piece of meat attached to his left shoulder.

Then suddenly, his mind went as cold as his body. Jay watched stupefied as one of the men raised a handgun and aimed it at him. Jay decided it was time for his nap.

For a people who profess undying devotion to the functional and disdain for the decadence of Western culture, Russians have an irresistible attraction to the more ostentatious examples of capitalistic and monarchic architecture. In London, the Russian embassy occupies a massive stone mansion on a private street that borders the queen's own roses at Kensington gardens. In Washington, D.C. the Russian embassy conforms grandly with the opulence of Embassy Row. Luxembourg, however, outdoes them both. The Russian Embassy is housed in the Chateau de Beggen, as fine an example of feudal comfort as can be found in Europe. Situated a few miles north of Luxembourg between the villages of Beggen to the west and Dommeldange to the south, the chateau offers both comfort and isolation. Forest surrounds the chateau on two sides, a highway on the other two. No one can pass without being observed by the security staff.

Obsidian was comfortable in these surroundings, for they matched or even exceeded the luxuries provided by the Shepherd's Club in Washington. But he was decidedly ill at ease with Russians who now leaned forward to catch his words. Not that Russians in general made him nervous. On the contrary, as a physicist specializing in national security issues he had frequent contact with Russians. But he didn't feel comfortable sitting there in the luxurious paneled room, in front of a crackling fire, sipping fine cognac from a cut crystal snifter and talking treason with the KGB. Uncomfortable or not, he told himself, Jay Fleming had to be stopped.

"You've taken a considerable risk coming here like this," Pasha Belenko observed as he brought his snifter to his lips, his bright olive-green eyes fixing Obsidian's with a skeptical glance. Belenko was a young man, probably no more than thirty-five. He stood five-eleven with an athletic body, broad shoulders, sinewy neck. His carefully tailored Savile Row suit gave him a powerfully elegant look. A scar below his left ear disappeared inside the collar of a light blue broadcloth shirt. His thick, light brown hair was cropped short, just barely longer than a military cut. There's a White Russian inside there somewhere, Obsidian thought.

"Yes," Obsidian responded hesitantly. "I have taken a risk. But I believe it sufficiently balanced by the gravity of the matter."

"Yes," Belenko agreed, nodding his head slowly, never letting his eyes stray from Obsidian's. "You've been quite plain about that. I have found your explanation thorough and convincing. But still . . ." He sighed softly. "You have taken a great risk, and you're asking us to take an even bigger one."

"I realize that, but you *must* stop Fleming!" Obsidian

pleaded. "I have just about run out of resources. Can you imagine what is going to happen if he succeeds?"

Belenko nodded noncommittally, his face, his eyes betraying none of the thoughts in his head. "There is the possibility of postponing the transfer."

"That was a risk I considered before contacting you," Obsidian said. "It is something to consider."

"Not really," Belenko countered. "The Yugoslavians are ready. Postponement might ruin it altogether."

Obsidian leaned forward in his chair. "But to let it fall into the hands of the Committee of Seven . . ." He left the sentence unfinished.

"Disaster," Belenko stated flatly. "An unmitigated disaster. I agree."

The young KGB agent set his snifter on a table next to his chair and rose to his feet, crossing over to a bookshelf. He pulled a hefty volume bound in red leather. He flipped through several pages.

When he returned to his seat, he held out the book, not as an offering but to exhibit it.

"Comrade Lenin had many things to say about risks," Belenko began. "Most of them had something to do with the West, and most of those were warnings against trusting Americans. I have read Comrade Lenin's words. I believe them."

Odsidian's spirits fell.

Belenko continued, "But Comrade Lenin also said that sometimes we must take a chance on those we don't wholly trust. I don't trust you. I believe some of what you say. And most of what you have said has merit. If you have lied, you will die, just like Jay Fleming. Anonymously."

Belenko took the book and left a frightened man sitting in the elegant room.

The lobby of the Hotel Central swarmed with tourists on a budget and a host of men in the military uniforms of half a dozen nations. English was spoken in small huddles throughout the lobby.

Alexandra Downing made directly for the women's room where she repaired the damage to her makeup and straightened up her clothing. She took a wet paper towel and dabbed at the drying flecks of half-digested food that spotted her outfit. Her stomach still quivered and she wondered if she would get sick again. The image of Lee Goldberg's corpse appeared everywhere she looked. She closed her eyes and massaged the lids with weary fingers. The image was indelible.

What had Martin gotten caught up in? Who could possibly be so fiendish as to kill people like that, in a way designed to inflict the maximum amount of pain? She looked at her watch and again tried to sweep the image of a fiery Lee Goldberg into some dark corner of her mind. There were two deaths to unravel now.

Hurriedly she swiped at the drying specks that dotted her shoes and stood up and surveyed herself. Stay away from bright light, she told herself, and you'll look just as respectable as ever. She snapped her purse shut, and set about attending to the vital task at hand.

The delivery man was standing at the reception desk with the flowers when she stepped back into the lobby. She took a seat and waited for someone to come take the flowers to the room. Anxiously she glanced at her watch. A minute passed, then two, then five.

At last a uniformed bellman collected the flowers and carried them toward the elevator. She rose from her chair swiftly and followed him, loitering beside the elevator. The doors opened and disgorged three U.S. Army officers and a family of six. The bellman waited for her to board.

No, she thought. He'll also ask me what floor I want.

"One second," she said to him. "Could you hold the elevator for just one second? I see a friend I want to say something to."

"Certainly," the bellman said reluctantly.

Alexandra stepped to one side, out of the bellman's sight, said hello to a totally surprised stranger, and then hurried back to the elevator. To her relief, the bellman had already punched his floor. The button for the seventh floor was lighted.

"Your floor, please?" the bellman said with a polite French accent.

Alexandra smiled. "Seven."

They rode up in silence. Alexandra looked over at the arrangement of flowers: a dozen roses. She recognized her handwriting on the envelope attached, and knew the card inside was blank. Happy funeral, Lee, she thought, as tears came to her eyes.

The door opened and, as she expected, the bellman waited for her to debark. She did and turned right. Not for any good reason. She walked slowly and heard the bellman make his way toward the other end of the corridor.

Alexandra walked slowly until she heard the bellman's key slide into the keyhole. Then she abruptly turned and strode down to the open door. When she arrived, she knocked delicately.

"Pardon me," she said as politely as possible and stepped into the room. The bellman set the roses down on a dresser with a laminated top and turned toward her.

"Yes," he responded. "What can I do for you?"

"Would you be so kind as to purchase a bottle of liquor for me?" she asked as she fumbled with the latch on her purse. "I forgot it, and I'd like to have some when my friends arrive this afternoon." She withdrew a handful of banknotes.

"Of course," he said as he stopped beside her. "What kind would you like?"

"Frangelico," she responded and pulled off enough bills to buy two bottles and pressed them into his hand. "Here. This should be enough. If it isn't, I'll reimburse you when you return."

The bellman smiled broadly at his chance to make a nice profit on the "markup" of the liquor. He didn't count the money, but he could assure her that the bottle would cost more than whatever amount she had given him.

As coquettishly as she could, she took his arm and smiled at him and led him toward the door.

"I *knew* you would do it," she said, trying to remember old Marilyn Monroe movies and the breathless way she talked. They approached the door, and he looked up at her. Confusion and lust swirled in his brown eyes. As she led him out of the room, he didn't notice the piece of masking tape she placed over the door latch, and he didn't pay any attention when she, not he, closed the door.

Raoul LeClerc sped south along the autoroute d'Esch, past the village of Kuelebierg on a Honda motorcycle he had stolen just after the rally. That had been one fine fire, he thought. And the way that American officer danced in the street was one fine sight. Serves the bastard right, he thought, the way the Americans dropped napalm on Vietnam.

Just after he passed the soccer fields, he pulled the Honda toward the shoulder, and then off the road entirely. The road was surrounded here by the trees of the Bois De Cessange. He dismounted the bike and walked it down the brush-covered slope and into the woods. When the terrain flattened out, he mounted the Honda again and rode slowly among the trees until he came to a narrow dirt road where the second half of his payment would be waiting. He had arranged for the American to leave the second payment at the bottom of a rubbish barrel next to the jogging trail. LeClerc had used it before. The maintenance people only emptied it every couple of weeks.

LeClerc's anticipation mounted as he saw the yellow barrel in the distance. He gunned the Honda and sped down the road. Less than a minute later, he braked to a skidding halt, leaped off the bike and killed the engine. He waited a few moments, listening, looking. Satisfied that he was alone, he eagerly strode to the barrel and dug at the garbage, throwing it on the ground in great handfuls. Finally he spotted the brown wrapped box they had specified.

With trembling hands, he pulled the box out and brought it to the bike. For a moment, he thought about waiting until he got back to his house before opening it, but the suspense was too much. Excitedly, he peeled off the wrapping, and opened the top of the box, anxious to see the banknotes.

The tremendous roar could be heard as far away as Alzingen. Motorists on the autoroute slowed as first the light of the blast, and then the smoke, shot up from the trees. The police never did find enough pieces of LeClerc to make a positive identification.

Feverishly, Alexandra scoured Lee Goldberg's room. Others must know of the letter Martin sent and she was terrified that they would burst through the door at any minute. Or that the bellman would return to room 726 and find that no one there ordered a bottle of Frangelico. He was sure to take another look at the room where he had met the strange woman.

She had gone through Lee's suitcase, through the pockets of his bathrobe, had even torn the sheets and blanket off the bed and looked under the mattress. And still she had found nothing. She listened to the blood rush in her ears. Her heart all but stopped every time she heard the elevator stop on the seventh floor.

The packet of documents that Lee said he had brought with him to Luxembourg was nowhere to be found. She sagged on the bed and considered the possibility that the killers had been here before her. That they had broken into the room as she and Lee sipped coffee.

No, she upbraided herself. That's no way to think. She sprang from the bed and looked around the room. Where could something be hidden?

She got down on her hands and knees and tugged at the wall-to-wall carpeting. She unzipped the covers on the sofa and chair cushions and pulled them off. She unscrewed light fixtures, even pulled a nile file from her purse and unscrewed the plates covering the electrical outlets and light switches.

There was nothing taped to the backs of drawers or the bottoms of any of the furniture. She jerked the grill off the ventilating system, dismantled the table lamp, left the back of the television lying on the floor. She pulled all the pictures off the wall and took the frames apart.

Time was growing short. She looked at her watch. The bellman had been gone almost fifteen minutes. Plenty of time for him to return and start getting suspicious. If he saw the room . . .

Desperately now she attacked the bathroom, unfolding every towel, ransacking Lee's toilet kit. She took the top off the toilet tank and peered in.

She was sitting on the edge of the toilet, aimlessly letting her eyes wander about the bathroom, when a slightly green patch of grouting between two tiles in the shower caught her attention. She looked at the tube of Crest on the counter.

Anticipation rising in her breast, she rose and stepped into the shower. With the nail of her index finger, she scraped at the green patch. It filled the underside of her nails. She sniffed at it. It was toothpaste! She retrieved her metal nail file and scraped carefully at the patch.

Ten minutes later, she stood before a very crowded reception counter.

"I'd like to get the papers I left in the safe deposit box," she said, proferring the key to a harried clerk. "Room 715." He hastily took the key without noticing the tiny fleck of green toothpaste still clinging to the inside of the keyring hole.

Alexandra Downing didn't notice the trim middle-aged man with the bald head who stared at her as she stepped into the morning sunlight with a bulky brown envelope under her arm.

Chapter Fifteen

Luxembourg,
December 19

The blizzard hurled black snow from a black sky. He soared through the blizzard, safe, secure. The world couldn't hurt him here. There was no pain, no thought, no trouble. Jay Fleming tumbled through the blackness. But here and there, gray began to shine through, a ray of sunlight behind strange dark clouds.

"He's taken quite a beating," a voice reached his ears from beyond the gray. "Are you sure you won't allow me to admit him to the hospital?"

"It is really necessary?"

"Only if complications develop. He's in good shape, sturdy. The ordeal might have killed others. Just keep him warm and I think he'll be fine. His body's warming up now. You did well, not warming him up too fast. He'll have a pretty severe headache when he comes to. Also a bit of stiffness all over. He was pretty well battered, but not too severely in any one place."

Jay Fleming tried to fly away from the gray. It shone with pain, with tension.

The voices receded, a door clicked silently shut somewhere on the other side of the gray. Jay found a black spot and glided toward its velvet comfort.

"He went to visit Emerson," Subasic said wearily as he sat on the sofa in the sitting room of the Hotel Intercontinental. His socks were still wet from where he had slipped off the narrow path around the the tunnel area. His suit coat hung limply over the arm of a chair by the window. His heavy gray wool overcoat, stained where Jay Fleming had bled on him, lay in a heap by the bedroom door. Subasic spoke quietly on the telephone. He didn't want to disturb Fleming. Not yet, anyway.

"What the hell did he do that for?" demanded Corundum's anxious voice. Subasic held the receiver tighter to his ear, as if the voice coming through the earpiece might carry through into the next room. His employer sounded overwrought.

Corundum spoke again. "Do you have any information that Emerson is playing a role in all this?"

"No," Subasic answered. "I don't think Emerson is involved with this. But he does have an excellent system of informers. I think Fleming went to Emerson in an attempt to find out who's trying to kill him."

"Have you gotten anywhere with that?" Corundum pressed.

"No," Subasic said. "The man I killed this morning was a former member of the Special Air Services. So was his companion. Both are . . . were mercenaries. I assume the other two killed in the crash with the gasoline tanker were SAS also, but there's no way of telling. Everything in the tunnel was incinerated. There was nothing left but bits of twisted metal where the vehicles had melted from the intense heat."

"Mercenaries," Corundum repeated thoughtfully. "CIA in Holland. Mercenaries in Luxembourg. It sounds as if our mysterious assailant is running out of options."

"That is *one* possible explanation," Subasic responded as diplomatically as possible. He didn't want to jump to conclusions, even if he did tend to agree with Corundum.

"Well, in any case, I want us back on track," Corundum demanded. "We're running out of time."

"Mr. Fleming." The voice came out of the gray.

Go away.

"Mr. Fleming, can you hear me?"

Yes, damn you. Leave me alone. The black world trembled, then diffused to gray. *Leave me alone, whoever you are.*

In the fog of semi-consciousness, Jay Fleming remembered. Remembered a man pointing a gun at him, remembered Aaron Fiszmann's cold peaceful body, remembered being tired.

"Mr. Fleming?"

Jay remembered that voice from somewhere, somewhere beyond the fog.

The gray world soon turned red and Jay recognized the backs of his eyelids, glowing crimson with bright light beyond. Reluctantly, he swallowed, then cracked one tightly squinted eye. Sunlight poured through an open window. He raised his right hand to block it out. The hand felt heavy, like a piece of dense wood. Pain throbbed in his head and a score of locations from his feet to his neck. He wiggled his toes; his calf muscles hurt. He swiveled his neck; those muscles hurt, too. In the pit of his stomach he felt something that was either hunger or pain. Perhaps both.

Jay gradually took in his surroundings, one sliver at a time: a room, a door opening into a bathroom, a dresser with a mirror, cream-colored walls. Everything glowed with the unreality of his drugged state.

"Are you all right?"

The voice came from the side of the bed. A blur stared down at him. Jay tried to see the face, but could only make out pieces. He blinked several times, and finally the whole face came into focus.

"You!" Jay said feebly, as he tried to sit up. Powerful hands clamped his shoulder and gently pushed him back onto the bed. Ineffectually, Jay tried to resist, but the man's strong arms were too much.

"You. From Amsterdam." Jay tried to form a coherent sentence. "Today, the accident . . . you saved my life again?"

"Relax for just a moment, please." The man spoke soothingly. Jay relaxed against the soft, cool sheets beneath him. "Let me do the talking for a moment," the man said. Jay listened carefully to the man's speech. He spoke English almost too well, as educated foreigners do. Behind the words was something subtly Balkan.

"Please, let me do the talking for a little while. You've had a rather difficult time today."

"Aaron?"

"He's dead, I'm afraid," the man answered sympathetically.

Jay sank slowly back and laid his aching head on the pillow. It was all true. The gasoline tanker, the killers in the Jaguars, Aaron's death. The reality he was assembling was considerably less appealing than the pleasant dark floating he had experienced. He closed his eyes and listened.

"My name is Bogdan Subasic." Jay listened to the voice as images played across the backs of his eyelids: the fight in the alley; Aaron; the dead men in the alley; Anderson; the policemen in Leiden; Emerson; the giant he had killed in Anderson's house. "I work for the United States Government, for a small, specialized intelligence operation that's part of the Department of Defense."

"Task Force 457?" Jay asked. He had heard of the special team whose alumni went on to form paramilitary companies who were hired by people with more money than morals.

"Of course not," Subasic said indignantly. "Those people," he said angrily, "are nothing more than fortune hunters. My group is composed entirely of naturalized citizens. Each of us was born something else—I was born in Yugoslavia—and we all made the decision to become Americans.

"Those people," Subasic spat, "support fascists, tyrants, for a profit. They bring death to line their own nests. I have seen the fascist. Sometimes he has the face of a Nazi, at other times the face of a Communist. But they are all the same."

Jay listened silently as the emotions in Subasic's voice grew warmer, rose closer to the surface.

"I'm sorry," Subasic said, breaking the silence. "It's been a long, long time, but such wounds don't heal quickly. The only people who have caused my people to suffer more than the Nazis were the Russians.

"You may find my passion odd, extreme maybe," Subasic said, "but you don't know what it's like to have enemy troops invade your home, eat your food, kill your loved ones.

"I tell you all this," Subasic explained, "to let you know how seriously I take my work. I am sorry we got sidetracked. Task Force 457 is a sore subject with me. Some of us do what we do because we believe that our tasks—no matter how distasteful we may find them personally—are necessary to make sure that the tyrants of the world don't gain the upper hand again."

"Where are we?" Jay asked when Subasic paused again.

"The Intercontinental Hotel. It's comfortable. Adjacent to the European Community."

They were silent for a moment as Jay formulated another

question. The task of thinking grew less painful by the moment. "Why here?" Jay asked. "Didn't I hear the doctor suggest I ought to be in the hospital?"

"Doctors are usually overcautious," Subasic replied warily, surprised that Jay remembered the conversation. What else had he overheard? "You're here because your life would be in danger in the hospital."

"Mind telling me why?"

"It's too easy to trace someone who's been admitted to a hospital. Right now the best chance you have of surviving is to remain out of sight, at least until you have some idea of who is trying to kill you."

Jay lay there silently, absorbing the statement. He thought about what Emerson had told him. "What about the Russians?" Jay asked.

Subasic shook his head. "Today's attack on you, as well as the ones in Leiden and Amsterdam, have none of the marks of a KGB operation. Realize, please, Mr. Fleming—"

"Call me Jay."

"Fine," Subasic agreed. "But please realize that I was there, and you are here because of that fact."

Jay opened his eyes and looked up at Subasic's face, trying to figure out if the Yugoslavian was trying to extract a show of gratitude. Jay was uncomfortable with the notion that he had been so helpless that someone had had to save his life three times. Having his nosed rubbed in it so soon was a little more than he could bear. But Jay saw nothing in Subasic's brown eyes that indicated anything more than the statement of fact.

"I thought the Soviets were capable of most anything," Jay said thickly. His lips still felt like some sort of synthetic material. He struggled to a sitting position.

"It's too much of a risk," Subasic said. "If it could positively be proved that they were behind the attacks on you, it would have.the most severe consequences."

"Like what?" Jay gave a cynical laugh. "Our usual response to Russian aggression is to draw a six-gun and shoot ourselves in the foot."

Subasic stared back at him stonily. They frowned at each other for several awkward moments, neither sure how to continue the conversation. Jay felt clarity returning to his thoughts. The pain killer the doctor gave him must have been a mild one. But as his head cleared, the pain in his body grew more intense. Nothing hurt enough to make him worry, but everything hurt a little. He used the three middle fingers of his right hand to scout the perimeter of the bandage on his head.

"The doctor put in about six stitches," Subasic said evenly. "I regret that I took so long in aiming at the man who got the drop on you following the accident. He managed to get a shot off just after my bullet hit him."

"Thanks," Fleming said self-consciously. "I don't know what I'll ever be able to do to repay you. I owe my life to you, several times over." Jay watched Subasic's face and was amazed to see him flush. He had more trouble accepting the thanks than Jay had in offering it.

"It's not a matter of repaying me," Subasic countered in a brusque, businesslike demeanor. "I saved your life because you have an important role to play in this whole affair."

Jay felt the warning bells ringing. "What whole affair?" he asked warily, and then abruptly, "This has to do with Anderson, doesn't it?" Jay sat up straighter. "Anderson said someone wanted me to come here to Luxembourg to find some Tesla papers. Someone who fed him some classified American documents. That someone would have to be well-connected with the American intelligence or defense community, wouldn't he?" Jay asked rhetorically as he scrutinized Subasic's face.

"You set that up, didn't you?" Jay charged. The cut over his temple throbbed. "You gave him the classified documents because you wanted to lure me here."

Jay swung his legs over the side of the bed and sat up. "You killed that man!" Fleming stood on legs of Jello and took a swing at Subasic. The Yugoslavian grabbed Jay's arm and spun him back into the bed.

"Listen to me," Subasic said in a calm, threatening manner. "I didn't kill Anderson. Yes, I gave him the documents and, yes, I asked him to tell you about the Tesla papers. But I *didn't* kill him. The same people who are after you killed him."

Jay looked helplessly up at Subasic. "Why? Why would you do something like this? Why use an old man? Why try to lure me here with a cock-and-bull story? Why do the Russians want to kill me?"

Subasic's face ran through a repertoire of emotions. Finally, he seemed to reach a difficult and perilous decision. He picked up a straight-backed chair resting in front of the dresser, and brought it bedside, straddling it backward. He looked ready to make a speech.

"What I have to tell you is very difficult for me," Subasic began, choosing his words carefully. "There have been some unanticipated problems which have lead to your being here this afternoon. I'm terribly chagrined by—"

"I don't give a rat's ass about your embarrassment, mister," Jay snarled. "What I care about is getting some answers. You may have saved my life, but I'm getting the feeling that my life would never have been endangered if you hadn't gotten involved in it." Jay glared up at Subasic, who struggled to retain control of his emotions.

"There have been some mistakes made," Subasic continued in a serious voice, "but they have been made for the best of reasons. We never intended to put you in any danger. But what is at stake could put hundreds of millions of people in danger. Some time ago, my agency learned that a Yugoslavian archivist at the Tesla Museum in Belgrade discovered a set of the scientist's papers that previously had been miscatalogued. He brought them to the attention of the director of the Museum who, in turn, told his superiors. Physicists from the technical university in Belgrade recognized immediately that the papers had great significance to weapons production. As you may know, American scientists have long suspected the existence of a set of discoveries pertaining to Tesla's work with electromagnetic pulses—"

"That's what Anderson said," Jay interrupted. "You rehearsed him well."

Subasic continued. "I learned about the papers through one of my contacts there and tried to acquire copies. But," Subasic's voice grew angry, "the Russians moved faster. Yugoslavia has always been a thorn in the Russians' side because we—they—refuse to submit to the Kremlin's orders. They have rejected Soviet puppets. Since World War II, Yugoslavia has been a top priority for subversion and political assassination for the KGB. But they have never been able to succeed, partly because the Yugoslavian secret police is so successful at smoking out the Russian puppets, but also because the cooler heads in the Kremlin realized that with all the different ethnic groups in Yugoslavia, any government incapable of unifying them would face the same overwhelming, organized guerrilla chaos that defeated the Nazis. But that hasn't stopped the KGB from bribing their way into the bank accounts of weak, greedy people."

Fleming concentrated on Subasic's eyes. They glinted like sunlight off wild water. Jay felt himself drawn deep into Subasic's narrative.

"These traitors," Subasic went on, "are ranking members of the Yugoslav government and have convinced others to trade the papers for a Soviet non-aggression pact. And you know as well as I do how seriously the Russians take their treaties. They are worthless paper backed by scheming and lies.

"But," Subasic's voice dropped wearily, "the Yugoslavians feel they will lose nothing useful. Which, for them, is true. But they are giving a technological advantage to the Russians which it may be impossible for the United States to overcome."

Fleming was tired of the traitors-versus-true-believers argument. "What kinds of weapons are we talking about specifically? I hope you aren't referring to Tesla's particle beam work. I've seen the papers and the designs aren't workable. His work is brilliant and visionary, I'll grant you that, but there are holes in the theory bigger than the ones anyone could hope to make with a beam weapon."

"No," Subasic said. "It's not a particle-beam weapon we're talking about, but something very different. It has to do with using the charged particles trapped in the earth's upper atmosphere as some sort of weapon. I'm not a scientist, so I can't describe it very well."

Jay looked up at the ceiling and massaged his head in thought. The heat produced by the fusion of hydrogen into helium reactions of the sun spins off many billions of tons of particles into space every day. Because of their immense energy, they speed through space without the electrons which normal atoms have; this gives them a positive charge. Most are either single protons—the nucleus of a hydrogen atom—or alpha particles—the nucleus of a helium atom. Because of the vastness of space over which these billions of tons of particles are spread, their density is very low, and most particles hurtle onward, never encountering any barrier to their rush towards the infinite emptiness of the galaxies. But charged particles are attracted by magnets.

High school physics students are taught that charged particles from the sun are trapped by the complex magnetic fields of the earth's poles. These reservoirs of trapped particles cause the brilliant displays of the aurora borealis in the arctic, and the aurora australis in the antarctic regions. Space exploration proved that the belts of charged particles could also disrupt radio communications and could, under the right conditions, disrupt other electrical equipment.

As Jay stared vacantly at the ceiling running all of these facts through his head, the light of something exciting glowed just beyond the horizon of his consciousness, like the glow that precedes dawn. He had these premonitions every time he finally cracked some tough problem with one of his ECM devices.

"Go on," Jay urged.

"Both the United States and the Soviet Union are working to develop this type of weapon," Subasic explained. "The Lawrence Livermore Lab in California and a dozen other research labs are trying to perfect the weapon. The United States is ahead—for now. But these papers will put the Soviets in the lead. As I understand it, this weapon can alter the balance of power irrevocably. It is devastating only to electrical and electronic apparatus and leaves no residual radiation."

"What you're talking about is an electromagnetic pulse," Jay said. "You're talking about producing an EMP burst without having to detonate a nuclear device to get it." Jay sat up suddenly, swinging his legs over the side of the bed. Subasic leaped up. His chair crashed violently to the floor as he poised his body for combat.

"Calm down," Jay said excitedly. "Calm down." The man never let down his guard. Jay decided he was glad Subasic was on his side. "Don't you see what this means?" Subasic peered at him warily. "If one side can produce a weapon that shoots bursts of electromagnetic pulses, then it would have a device that would attack and destroy everything electrical." Subasic picked up his chair and returned to his straddling position.

"Everything from computers to telephones, even circuit breakers in people's homes and the ignition wiring on their cars would be knocked out of action. The only people who would be hurt would be those who were in direct contact with those devices when the EMP burst hit." Jay spoke excitedly, waving his hands as he did. "And people with pacemakers. It would fry them . . ." His voice trailed off. He stared past Subasic. "Have you any idea what this would mean?" Jay now focused his eyes on Subasic's. "With a weapon like this, we could return any of our enemies to the pre-electrical period. To 1870 or thereabouts. They'd then be sitting ducks for even the most primitive conventional weapons." He sucked on his lower lip. "I hope I'm jumping to conclusions," Jay said. "But if the Tesla papers can make such an EMP weapon possible, we've got to do everything possible to prevent the exchange." He stared at Subasic for a moment. "And get those papers for ourselves." He tapped his lips with his index finger. "No," he said slowly, "no. I'm not sure it's wise for anyone to have those papers. I think the world would be better off if they were destroyed."

Subasic tried not to smile. Jay Fleming had just accepted the mission which the Committee of Seven needed him to accomplish. As for destroying the papers—he'd deal with that once they were in their possession.

"So this is what you were trying to lure me into in the first place." It was a statement. Subasic nodded.

"Why me?" Jay leaned back on the pillows, suddenly conscious of the pain again. "And why didn't you just come out and ask me to do it? Why the elaborate rigamarole?" Subasic opened his mouth to respond when Jay sat up again. "The Russians. Suppose the Russians got wind of this? Maybe that's why they're trying to kill me?"

Subasic shook his head vigorously. "Let me take those questions one at a time, if you will."

"Let's get some food first," Jay said, looking at his watch. "I haven't had anything to eat since early this morning. And it's almost 2:30."

Subasic walked over to the phone. "You might want to get cleaned up a little. The bathroom's in there." He nodded toward a closed door.

Less shaky than before, but with more pain, Jay stood, using the back of Subasic's chair to steady himself. The room did a half spin, then stabilized. Concentrating on remaining vertical,

Jay walked cautiously to the door, twisted the knob and pulled it open.

There was no window. Jay flicked on the light and closed the door behind him. A strange battered face he did not immediately recognize as his own stared out at him from the mirror. The bright white bandage attracted his eyes immediately. He probed at it, watching his fingers in the mirror. The gauze stood out in the midst of an unruly shock of dark brown hair. His face was covered with bruises and scrapes. A fleck of dried blood matted his right eyebrow. He rubbed it with his index finger and closed his eyes against the small dusting of dried blood that fell from it. A small mouse had welled up under his left eye, but did not affect his vision. "You've been hurt worse than this in fun," he said to the mirror.

When he returned, Subasic was back in his seat. But instead of returning to the bed, Jay walked, sure of his balance now, to a trio of easy chairs that surrounded a writing table by the window. He stood observing the traffic pass by below.

"What floor are we on?" Jay asked.

"Eleven."

"Room number?"

"Eleven-eleven."

Jay turned toward Subasic. "What's through there?" He pointed to the door next to the bedroom.

"A sitting room," Subasic said uneasily. Fleming had recovered faster than he had expected.

"Come on over here," Jay suggested, seating himself by the window. "I'm tired of playing the invalid."

Subasic took a seat facing Jay across the table.

Jay formed a steeple with his hands. "I've got some idea of what we have to accomplish," he said. "But before I agree to anything, you have to answer my questions. Why me? Why the charade? What's expected of me? And I want to know who is trying to kill me."

Subasic dipped his head in agreement. "Why you? I suppose it's a little too general to say that you were the best man for the job?" Jay nodded. "I thought so. Well, first of all, we needed someone outside our organization, someone outside the American intelligence apparatus. We feared if a known agent were to make an approach regarding the Tesla papers, the exchange dates or place might be changed. We'd lose track of it and have no chance whatsoever to intercept it." Subasic watched Fleming's face closely, looking for hints of confusion or disbelief. He found none.

"Another reason we chose you is your background as a fighter pilot," Subasic continued. "Fighter jocks have certain qualifications that we needed: nerve, composure under pressure, an ability to flirt with deadly situations. Finally, you have access. Here in Luxembourg, your company is well known, you conduct substantial business with the local banks. You are known and you know people. Even if we had an agent who filled all the other prerequisites, there is no way he could have the access to people and information you do, at least not in the short time we have to work with."

"How short *is* that time?" Jay asked.

"Four days now. What we have to do, we must accomplish by Friday."

Jay pursed his lips.

"That answers your first question," Subasic said. "Now for the elaborateness of the 'charade,' as you call it."

"Why didn't you just ask me?"

"I suppose we were afraid you'd turn us down. Would you have agreed if we'd approached you directly?"

Jay shrugged. "Maybe. I've been bored out of my skull lately. I might have accepted just so to keep from going crazy."

"That," Subasic said, "figured into our thinking."

"You *knew* I was bored?"

"We have an excellent information system."

"I see." Jay preferred the private things in his life to stay that way. "This time I'll let it pass, but I may . . ."

"May what?"

"Never mind," Jay snapped. "Continue."

Subasic wondered if Fleming had deliberately tripped him up. "I . . . we . . . felt it better not to risk telling you. We needed you so badly."

"That's very flattering," Jay said drily.

"The deception in Leiden was supposed to entice you here to look for the papers."

"And what would that have accomplished?"

"You would have made certain inquiries," Subasic said. "We would have kept a close watch on you—just as we did in Holland—to see who contacted you, where they stayed, what they did. We know the transfer and treaty signing is set for this Friday, but we don't know where or where the papers are being kept until then."

Jay glared at him. "What gives you the right to go around tinkering with people's lives? To trick me, to follow me around, to pry into my private life to . . ." Jay leaned rigidly forward, his mouth working furiously, his emotions blocked by the very anger he tried to express. He slammed his fist on the table.

Subasic flinched.

"A man is dead in Leiden because of you!" Jay thundered. "There are dead people in Amsterdam and Leiden. Your brilliant plan has totally fucked up so far. What guarantees me that the rest won't be equally screwed up?"

The room was quiet. Only Jay's angry breathing and the distant sounds of street traffic staved off total silence.

"Nothing," Subasic said finally. "I have nothing to guarantee that the rest of the operation will work."

Fleming's breathing slowed. He reclined in the chair. Tension crackled in the room. But after a moment, the taut muscles that held Jay's jaw rigid relaxed. He smiled thinly. "Now we're getting somewhere," he said. "I think you're actually telling me the truth."

Subasic unclinched his nervous fingers.

"But if I agree to go through with this insanity," Jay said levelly, "you must give me two things." Subasic raised his eyebrows. "First, the complete file you have on me, along with how you got the information and the names of the people who gave it to you."

"But that's—"

"Second, a signed guarantee that I'll get the first item."

"But—"

"That, as the terrorists say, is a non-negotiable demand," Jay emphasized. "You want me? Then I suggest you make arrangements."

Subasic opened his mouth to speak when a knock sounded on the door leading to the sitting room. The door clicked open, and an attendant rolled in a cart with an assortment of stainless steal covers, a bottle of wine, several beers, a carafe of coffee and a single rose in a bud vase. Wordlessly the man pushed the cart up to the table where Fleming and Subasic sat. He gave

Fleming a neutral look that could mean anything, and then turned questioningly toward Subasic.

"*Hvala Vam mnogo*," Subasic said. The man smiled, turned on his heel and left, closing the door after him.

Fleming raised his eyebrows quizzically. "And that was?"

"Serbo-Croatian," Subasic said.

"No," Jay said, "the man."

"Ante," Subasic answered as he pushed himself up from his seat and bent over the cart. "Like me, he is from Yugoslavia. Unlike me, he is still a Yugoslavian citizen." He lifted the covers off two grilled sandwiches and a tureen of thick soup that filled the room with the aroma of beef stock.

"A Reuben and a grilled ham and Swiss on rye," Subasic announced. "Take your pick." Jay reached over and grabbed the Reuben. "Soup?" Jay nodded. As he dished out a broth heavy with potatoes and chunks of meat, Subasic said, "My agency is very small—for two reasons. We save money, for one. But mostly we want to preserve security. We hire professionals, or borrow them from other agencies as the task demands. They never learn more than a little about the operation and are never offered the chance to learn more. It's rare for someone to work for us more than a couple of times and never on related missions. We have the tightest security of any intelligence or security apparatus in America," he boasted.

"We have no permanent staff hanging around an office water cooler or a favorite after-hours bar exchanging stories. The men who helped keep you under surveillance in Amsterdam were told that you were a kidnap target. They know nothing about the overall mission. And what they don't know can't hurt us. The men I used to extricate you from Anderson's house in Leiden were members of the Dutch Secret Service. They owed my agency a favor. They repaid it. Coffee, beer?"

Jay took a cup of coffee, sipped it black and then began on the Reuben. "That must have been one hell of a favor."

"Yes," Subasic said, "it was." Jay knew he wouldn't elaborate. The Yugoslavian used a small metal opener to pop the lid off a bottle of Mousel beer and took a long pull from it. He settled back with the grilled ham and cheese.

"Ante is helping me here in Luxembourg. He's a first-rate driver. Once had ambitions of being a professional racer. But he got caught up with me." Unanswered questions littered the landscape of Subasic's conversation like feathers after a cockfight.

"There is one other gentleman here whom you will get to know well. His name is Donald Sweeny. He used to work for MI6. He works for himself now. Both of them are absolute professionals. Dependable. But they know nothing about the Tesla papers and unless you make a grave mistake, they never will."

Jay took another bite of his sandwich.

It continued like that for the next two hours. Jay asking questions, Subasic answering them, mostly to Jay's satisfaction. The more Subasic talked, the less Jay was inclined to set off on his own. It was true, Fleming reflected, that his company put enormous resources at his disposal. But there was no way he could hire the expertise and experience he needed in time to beat the Friday deadline. On the other hand, Subasic's was a small group, but what it lacked in manpower, it made up for in speed and the ability to move unnoticed. Jay decided by the end of the afternoon that with a little help from his company and what Doug Denoff could dig up, they might have a chance at locating the papers.

With a little luck, he'd be back in Santa Monica by Monday with the Tesla papers and a hell of a story that he couldn't tell to anybody. Without luck, ten or twenty million people might be killed. He hated trusting to luck.

Chapter Sixteen

Luxembourg,
December 19

The secure telephone link between Luxembourg and Washington, D.C., crackled with static stirred up by a severe bout of solar flares.

"You have the girl?"

"Not yet. But we know where she is."

"Why are you hesitating?"

"Because we don't want another episode like the one at the hotel."

"That was certainly clumsy."

"I have taken care of the man responsible for it. I had no idea that he would—"

"All right, all right. You've apologized already."

"We're planning to take care of the girl tonight."

"Has she called the police?"

"Not yet."

"That's odd, don't you think?"

"She's very resourceful, and she's got the package of documents Copeland sent to Goldberg."

"You're sure of that?"

"Positive. She found the key to the hotel's safety deposit box before we did."

"How could you let that happen? Why wasn't Goldberg intercepted before he got to Luxembourg?"

"You forget we didn't know it was him. We had to follow the girl. We're lucky the surveillance on the boat paid off."

"All of your connections, all of the favors owed to us and she got away."

"It won't happen again. She's in her room right now. We'll have her and the documents before the night's over."

"You had better. She's too much of a threat. She's learned too much of our operation. Copeland did the impossible. He managed to pull all the threads of the project together."

"Well, we stopped Dodd before he could do anything. Have there been any hints that the authorities suspect anything?"

"None. The *Post* ran front pages stories on Dodd's death— invisible hand at the helm of the government, that sort of thing. And another on Guereri and Copeland. Those accidents were nicely arranged."

"Thank you."

"You earned it. But let's make sure you stay ahead of things now. Don't let Fleming get in your way. Kill him too if necessary."

"I don't think that's wise. The town is already crawling with security agents and investigators. They haven't totally bought the peace rally story. More murders might make operating here impossible."

"Well, arrange more 'accidents.'"

"Easier said than done. I do not have the depth of resources here as in Washington."

"Well, handle it the best. But get the documents."

"Very well, sir."

"Then, until tomorrow, Zbogom."

"Zbogom."

Money works wonders, Alexandra thought as she bent over the cart laden with towels and wash clothes and spare pillows and blankets. The powder-blue institutional uniform cut into her armpits, and hung loosely on her hips. The shoes pinched her toes. Only the blue chambermaid's cap seemed to fit right. For that she was thankful. The woman who had worn the uniform into the room had black hair. Even from the length of the corridor, the man at the end would have noticed the difference if she hadn't been able to tuck her hair into the cap.

Hands on her hips, she faced the large full-length mirror on the back of the closet door and surveyed herself once again.

Behind her on the bed sat the real chambermaid. She was several years younger than Alexandra but three children, a starchy diet and lack of exercise had already begun to give her a middle-aged appearance. Alexandra was four or five inches taller, but she hoped that wouldn't be noticeable from the length of the hotel corridor. Alexandra's pumpernickle tan matched the chambermaid's.

The chambermaid caught Alexandra's eye in the mirror and they both smiled. Alexandra gave her a conspiratorial wink. The chambermaid's face filled with sisterly patience. She understood this beautiful American woman's desire to escape the persecuting eye of her former husband. He had hired detectives to follow her. Men could be such swine! The chambermaid shook her head ruefully.

The Turkish woman squirmed, trying to get comfortable in Alexandra's clothes. It was difficult. The seams of Alexandra's nutmeg-colored wool skirt puckered her heavy hips and thighs. But it would pass at a distance. Above the skirt, she wore a white silk blouse with ruffles at the bodice and over that a rust and brown tweed blazer. It was an outfit that Alexandra had not worn in weeks. She didn't want the man at the end of the hall to mistake the chambermaid for her. Neither he nor the bald man looked particularly kind. She didn't want anything to happen to this sweet woman.

She had first noticed the trim, middle-aged, bald man on the way back to the Excelsior from Goldberg's room. The thick manila envelope seemed to burn in her hands like a deadly acid of some sort. It made her jittery. She looked about her frequently, but at first saw nothing unusual. She had walked past the Excelsior and stopped across the street to watch the firemen extinguish the last of the flames in the restaurant. A scorched pain burned in her chest as her eyes scanned the blackened patch of pavement where Lee Goldberg's charred body had finally fallen. His body had been taken away, leaving only the flame-darkened circle frosted with white powder from a fire extinguisher. A small cry caught in her throat, and she whirled suddenly away from the grisly image. A bald-headed man who had been walking toward her stopped suddenly and locked eyes with her. Alexandra was transfixed. He pivoted suddenly and strode angrily away.

He frightened her, and instead of returning immediately to her room, she clutched the envelope and made her way to a cafe. She drank cup after cup of espresso, trying to compose her frantic thoughts.

She obtained her key from the front desk and took the elevator to her room. The bald man was nowhere in evidence. But there had been a much younger, taller man with eyebrows like huge black caterpillars loitering at the end of the corridor on her floor.

She rushed to her room and bolted the door.

It had taken half an hour to concoct the plan, another half hour to set it up. Now, turning away from the mirror, she would see if it worked. The chambermaid stood at the door leading to the adjoining room. She produced a large key ring.

While the maid selected the correct key, Alexandra buried her leather attaché case under a pile of towels and made sure it didn't look suspicious. Inside were the envelope she had obtained from Goldberg's safety deposit box, her passport, money, airline ticket and other papers. She would replace her clothes and other effects as soon as she felt safe. Carefully folded under the attaché case were a pair of shoes and a change of clothes.

The chambermaid opened the door. Alexandra gave her a little wave with one cold sweaty hand and then wheeled the linen cart toward the door. Behind her, she heard the doors click discreetly shut.

Alexandra checked her slim gold wristwatch. The chambermaid had been in the room for about ten minutes. The man with the bushy eyebrows was sure to have noticed. Alex stopped the cart by the door, and after a deep breath, turned the knob and pulled it open. Moments later, she heard the door of the adjoining room open and then shut loudly.

Without hesitation, Alexandra wheeled the cart into the corridor and turned it quickly away from the man at the other end, careful not to let him see her face. She closed the door as respectfully as a chambermaid might.

Then, as swiftly as she dared, she pushed the cart down the hall toward the service elevator. She felt the blood pounding at her temples, as the wheels glided softly along the carpet. Was he following her? She'd never hear his footsteps on the thick pile. Frozen notes of fear played a chilling tune along her spine. She exercised a supreme effort to will her legs not to run.

Ante Dvorak's head spun, then he heard the click of the door up the hallway. From his seat in the little straight-backed chair between the two elevators, he turned his head and watched alertly as first one door then the adjacent one opened. He got to his feet.

Coming toward him was a slatternly woman with black hair and olive skin, dressed expensively in poorly fitting clothes. He decided at a glance it couldn't be the Downing woman. *She* was tall, with auburn hair and high cheekbones. He fantasized for a moment what she would look like undressed.

A linen cart emerged from the Downing woman's room and headed toward the other end of the corridor. It had been in there for at least ten minutes. So long, in fact, that he'd almost forgotten about it. Anxiety began to nag at him as he watched the cart and the chambermaid behind it slowly grow smaller in the long corridor. There was something familiar about her walk.

The woman with the olive skin blocked his way. *"Excusez-moi, m'sieur."*

"Oui?" he answered impatiently as he watched the chambermaid reach the end of the corridor and push the cart around the corner to the right.

"Avez-vous le temps?"

Dvorak looked at her, glanced down and saw she was wearing a cheap plastic wristwatch. What did she need the time for? Perhaps her cheap timepiece didn't work.

"C'est . . ." He looked up. As the chambermaid turned the corner, he caught the briefest glimpse of her profile. That proud head held high, the soft contours of her well-formed nose. There was no mistaking it. He snarled at the woman and pushed past her, breaking into a sprint.

"Courez!" He heard the woman shouting behind him. *"Il vient! Il vient!"*

Of course, the chambermaid. They must have switched clothing. Adjoining rooms! How could he have been so stupid? Ahead of him, he heard elevator doors open. He ran faster.

* * *

"Run! He's coming! He's coming!" Alexandra heard the chambermaid's shouts as she rounded the corner. The anxiety that had twisted in her guts transformed itself into a grasping fist of terror that tore at her insides. Ahead of her was a short hallway, a window at the end, the service elevator at the left, a utility closet on the right. Behind her, she heard the heavy rapid footfalls of her pursuer.

Panic tingled in her as she waited helplessly for the elevator to arrive, listened as the footsteps grew louder, closer.

Alexandra moved to the far side of the cart, ready to ram the man with it as he rounded the corner. The elevator came to a halt. The doors parted. A wizened old man in blue bib overalls stepped out of the car and blinked teary eyes at Alexandra.

"Good afternoon," he greeted her in French. She replied as calmly as she could. She quickly spun the cart and shoved it in energetically. The man's footsteps echoed in the hallway. Up or down? Down was to freedom, seven floors below. Her hand wavered in front of the lobby button. His footsteps grew louder. It was easier for him to run down. He could take the stairs and intercept her by hitting the call button on the wall. She heard his heavy breathing as the automatic elevator doors began to close on their own. Frantically, she stabbed the button for the fourteenth floor.

In horror, she watched as a hand darted into the rapidly closing door. But he was too slow. The doors closed. The last thing she heard was a pounding on the elevator door.

Dvorak looked up at the elevator floor indicator. She was going up! He smiled. The woman had trapped herself good now. He turned, surveying the hallway in a flash. The red letters of the exit sign glowed welcomingly from the short hall on the other side of the main corridor.

He dashed to the door and exploded through it, his long powerful legs carrying him up the stairs by twos and threes. With his strong sinewy arms, he hauled himself up the pipe bannister and around the landings. His breathing was fast and heavy, but regular, the cadence of a man in good physical shape.

At each floor, he peered out into the hallway at the elevator lights. Each floor was a mirror of the one below it. Still the elevator continued up. Dvorak said a quiet prayer of thanks for slow European elevators. He was keeping up with this one, just one floor behind. He'd never be able to do that in an American hotel.

The stairs ended at the fourteenth floor. He paused to unhook the hammer strap on the heavy Colt Python .44 magnum he carried under his left shoulder. He probably wouldn't have to use it. His muscular hands could snap her neck like a porcelain figurine. He heaved on the door and burst into the corridor. The linen cart lay in the middle of the hall close to the window. The window was open. Was she outside?

Swiftly, he made his way past the main corridor, and after checking to make sure it was empty, moved slowly toward the cart. The elevator doors were still open. She had been here only seconds before. He tugged at the utility closet door. It was locked.

Cold blasts of air sliced through the open window and set the sheer curtains on either side to dancing. With his right hand, Dvorak slid the Colt from its holster. It made a satisfying metal-against-leather murmur as it came free and deadly in his hand. He looked around and then moved cautiously toward the window.

Traffic progressed along the street below. Beyond was the greenery of the forest and the fields of the countryside. The gusts of wind brought tiny tears of irritation to Dvorak's eyes. He brushed at them with his free hand, and leaned on the window sill. The window opened onto a stone ledge about a foot wide. A stone parapet cantilevered out above the window. Plenty of room here for someone with a little nerve. And from what he understood of the Downing woman, she had an abundance.

Dvorak leaned out the window and peered left. The ledge was clear. Looking down at the street made him dizzy. He quickly turned to the right. The ledge was clear in that direction also.

An uneasy feeling grew in his chest as he slowly stood up. A noise behind him demanded his attention. Over his shoulder, he saw the linen cart hurtling towards him. He spun to face the danger, then whipped out the Colt Python .44 magnum. But as he brought the muzzle to bear on the woman in the chamber-maid's uniform, the cart slammed into him with surprising force. He felt the gun leap out of his hand as he lurched backward, grabbing for his balance. His hand closed on empty space. The low windowsill caught the backs of his knees and suddenly he was looking up at the sky. He heard a scream. Just before he smashed into the pavement with a symphony of cracking sounds, he realized the scream was his own.

Chapter Seventeen

San Pedro, California,
December 19

Brilliant sunlight poured down on the utilitarian beauty of the docks. On the far side of Wilmington Channel, the massive Chevron petroleum tank farm glowed in the intense light. Down toward the left, toward Wilmington, under the graceful green arc of the Vincent Thomas suspension bridge, container ships surrendered their cargoes of brightly painted semi-trailers. Here and there a pleasure yacht passed by incongruously. This was a working harbor of freighters and tankers, of fishing boats and the powerful launches that delivered men, supplies and heavy equipment to the oil rigs exploring for energy on the continental shelf offshore.

The chain-link fence leading into the yard of Offshore Technology, Inc. was locked and a burly former roughneck with four fingers missing on his left hand stood guard. A portable crane hoisted the last of three carefully crafted wooden crates—each the size of a small van—carefully onto the deck of a workboat. Workers scurried around the crates, covering them with plastic to guard against the errant wave, and then lashed them down with painstaking care.

The workers thought the crates were for an on-board computer meant to enable the oil rig to drill directional holes more accurately, and to keep track of drilling mud and other functions. Offshore Technology serviced a great number of offshore rigs, some operated by the big companies—Texaco, Chevron—and others by smaller independents. But none of these rigs was as poorly run as the one they were about to take the computers to. For more than three years, they had delivered boatload after boatload of supplies to platform Delta Zeus. Three years and they hadn't come up with a thing. No sign of either oil or gas.

Oh, they were clever with their security—all oil companies are—no one likes others to know what they've found. But there were ways of telling what was going on—the type of mud ordered, the equipment needed to drill for oil. By the estimation of everyone on the docks at Offshore Technology, from the foreman down to the lowliest laborer, platform Delta Zeus was a big loser that Global Energy should have abandoned years ago.

All of them would be astounded to learn that platform Delta Zeus, located thirty-five miles southwest of Huntington Beach, was never intended to produce oil. In fact they had never searched for it, not from the first day the semi-submersible rig had arrived on its long trip from Rotterdam. They would be equally astounded to learn that the three crates of computers weren't computers at all, but the final pieces in a lethal puzzle that had taken more than four decades to assemble. What they didn't know could kill them.

Luxembourg,
December 19

Steven Strand paced the oriental carpet of his lavishly furnished quarters, carrying the receiver in his left hand, holding the earpiece to his head with his right. He breathed deeply and heavily. The call from Washington had interrupted his nightly exercise.

"Subasic's no closer to unraveling the attacks," came the voice from the telephone.

"Do you suppose they're aimed at us?" Strand said as he stalked first one corner and then the other. He paused to admire his reflection, framed in a mirror surrounded by an ornate gilded frame.

"Of course the attacks are directed at us!" the voice stressed indignantly. "How in the world did you think—"

"No, no." Strand interrupted, as he turned away from his reflection, "I mean are the attacks pointed at you and me, as opposed to the committee as a whole? Do you suppose that someone else on the committee might be on to us? Trying to sabotage things?" The man was such a fool, Strand thought. They were all such nearsighted clowns. He relished the thought that he would be able to climb above all of them. And soon. It had taken him close to his three score and ten to accomplish it, but he would soon see the day when they would all acknowledge his superiority. He would have the respect he had always deserved.

There was silence on the line as the man in Washington thought. "As we've discussed before," he began, "that's a possibility. But don't you think that they would be going after Subasic?"

"Subasic's harder to get to than Fleming. Besides, at this late date, the death of either would be disastrous," Strand responded as he sat down on the edge of the bed.

"But who?"

"I'm sure it's neither the Russians nor the Yugoslavians," Strand pronounced.

"Ah, then you've made progress?"

"Some." Strand thought of his meeting with the embassy official. "Not enough, but that could change in the next few days." He got up from the bed and walked to a set of French windows overlooking formally kept grounds. There were neatly trimmed hedges and pea gravel walks. "Back to your notion of it being another member of the committee. Who? Diamond?"

"Absolutely not!" said the man from Washington. "The man's blind. He's a fool and he always has been. He believes in this project, and, more than anyone else on the committee, he trusts."

"Then who?" Strand pressed. "Eliminating you and me, that leaves four."

"There's a sure way to find out," said the man from Washington. "Eliminate them until we eliminate the attacks."

"You're getting bloodthirsty in your old age," Strand said.

"It has to be done sooner or later. Why not start sooner?"

"Because we may need them," Strand answered. "Among them they command a lot of influence. We may need that."

"We'll not need anything once we get those papers."

"Don't get ahead of yourself," Strand cautioned. "We have a ways to go yet. There's also the possibility we won't get them."

The voice in Washington turned frantic. "We can't even consider that."

"You'd better consider it," Strand said harshly. "It's always a possibility."

There was a pause. Then, emphatically, "We *must* get those papers. The fate of the United States, of the Western world depends on it. Without those papers, without the ability to use the weapon and use it soon, four decades of work will be for nothing. A lifetime of effort wasted!" There was despair in his voice.

"I know," Strand said soothingly. "I understand. The pressure rests heavily on us all. Just try to retain control for four more days. Just four more days."

"Yes," came the voice from Washington, "just four more days. You will keep me posted?"

"Haven't I always?"

"Of course." There was a long pause. "Well then, I'll talk to you tomorrow?"

"Certainly. Goodbye." Strand hung up the telephone and returned it to the bedside table. He looked at the foxhead tapestry on the wall, done in blues and reds. The only thing he didn't like about staying here was the omnipresence of that damned fox head.

Three thousand miles to the east, Corundum slowly replaced his telephone on the cradle and stared blankly at the dull, gray sky that hung over the nation's capital. It matched his mood.

Chapter Eighteen

Luxembourg,
December 20

It was midnight in Los Angeles when Jay Fleming reached Doug Denoff. The security expert had just returned home from one of his many forays into the jungles of the Southern California nightlife.

"Sorry to get you so late," Jay apologized. He leaned back in the armchair and propped his feet up on his desk. It was piled to overflowing with papers of every sort, mostly relating to the Dutch ECM sale.

"No problem," Denoff responded in a strained voice. In the background, Jay heard a woman's voice. "What's up? Is Aaron working out all right?"

Jay told him about the attack the previous day. In the earpiece he could hear Denoff ordering the girl out of the room. "I called a local synagogue last night, and they've taken charge of all of the rites and the burial. Would you believe that Fizsmann carried a copy of his will with his luggage?"

Jay heard Denoff's voice stumble. "He was the most thorough soldier I ever served with," Denoff continued after clearing his throat. Jay wanted to say something, but hesitated to break the silence.

Denoff had never talked about Fiszmann at any length before except to say he was a hell of a soldier with a hell of a history. Now, like a long distance eulogy, Denoff rambled mournfully on. The two men had served together in the Israeli army through the entire 1973 war and had formed a bond that only

172

men who had placed their lives in another's hands can know. They both left the army in 1980 for jobs with a private executive protection company. Jay had hired Denoff from that agency when ECM, Inc. was formed. Fiszmann worked for that agency until yesterday.

Denoff's anguish was undiminished from six thousand miles away. "He was the last one I thought would ever . . . he was so meticulous, such a professional." Then as if he had reminded himself of his own professionalism, Denoff's voice assumed precise, guarded tones. "Have you informed the company?"

"Yes." Jay's heart ached for his friend. "I understand there was no next of kin. At least that was what his papers said."

"Right," Denoff said flatly. "What can I do? Do you need me over there?"

"Without a doubt," Jay said. He nervously pulled a fresh sack of Corn Nuts from the desk drawer and popped one in his mouth. He sucked the salt off it a while before biting down. It made an audible crunch. "But before you get on the plane, there are a few things you must know."

Denoff listened attentively as Jay described the day leading up to the attack, his awakening and the subsequent revelations by Subasic and Jay's agreement to work with them.

At the mention of the attempted manipulations by Subasic, Denoff's angry curses crashed from the telephone receiver, violating every law of every nation about using obscene language over common carrier communications devices. But he quickly calmed when Jay explained the potential strategic importance of the papers.

"Now," Denoff said, his voice dropping, "if you'll hang up and let me get packed, I'll hustle my ass on over there before you get yourself into any more trouble. I know he saved your life, but watch this Subasic. He sounds like a strange character. I don't entirely buy his story. Something smells about the whole thing. Cover your ass, and cover it good. I know it's useless for me to say it, but you ought to find a dark armor-plated closet and hide in there until I arrive."

"Thanks for the warning," Jay said appreciatively. "I'll take it seriously. I agree. But as for finding an armored closet, I'd rather hunt than be a sitting duck."

"Yeah, okay," Denoff said ruefully. "Well, good night."

"Good morning," Jay said and thoughtfully hung up the telephone.

Fleming was bothered by Subasic's story, too. Something didn't ring true about it all. Why would Subasic's unit be so concerned about secrecy? Concerned enough to expend enormous amounts of money covering up the murders in Leiden and Amsterdam? And why would agents of the CIA be trying to kill him? What happened to the bodies? The dead men in Amsterdam and Leiden? And Anderson's? Jay grabbed a felt-tipped pen from the desk and made a note to ask Subasic about the bodies when they next met. Too many unanswered questions hung in the air. Jay had the feeling that the Yugoslavian was not telling him the whole truth.

What, for instance, happened the previous afternoon? During his session with Subasic, the telephone rang, and Sweeny burst into the bedroom, his face white and covered with sweat. He had hustled Subasic into the sitting room and, behind a closed door, held a frantic conference. Subasic had returned to the room, his face tight, a white ring of flesh around his tensed mouth. With an abrupt explanation he grabbed his coat and disappeared, leaving Sweeny to stand guard. With the stimulus of Subasic absent, the exhaustion of the day and the battering he had taken soon pressed Fleming into the welcoming arms of sleep. As he fell asleep, he wondered if Sweeny was there to protect him or to keep him from getting away. That question led to others, which ran through his mind as he slept.

When he had awakened this morning, Jay realized there were dozens of questions he had lacked the presence of mind to ask the day before. The trauma had diminished his ability to dissect the situation quickly and thoroughly.

Jay tossed a couple of Corn Nuts into his mouth as he hunched over the legal pad. On one sheet he had listed questions he expected Subasic to answer. The page was nearly full. On another, he had listed everything he knew about the Tesla papers and the plan to exchange them for a secret Russian non-aggression pact. The page was almost empty.

He knew the papers were supposed to be transferred sometime Friday. He didn't know who was doing the transferring, where or when it was to be done.

He did have an idea of what the papers contained. He knew the exchange had bypassed the normal diplomatic channels, and was being handled by special personnel flown into the Yugoslavian and Russian embassies for the occasion. Subasic had also told him that the delicate negotiations for the transfer of the papers had been handled by a neutral party, a banker and international broker with offices in Luxembourg, Vienna, Moscow and Belgrade. The banker, Ernst Fischer, was an Austrian who spent most his his time in his Luxembourg office. He had an international reputation as a catalyst for business deals, licit and illicit, between East and West.

Fischer frequently served as the glue that bound together mutually suspicious parties. Each trusted him, neither trusted the other. His bank might serve as escrow for the seller and appraiser for the buyer, assuring that neither side took advantage of the other. He was the mechanism for simultaneous execution of obligations. It had made him a very rich man.

But, although the banker was the protection that each side desired against the other, Jay agreed with Subasic that little protected Fischer from outsiders, like themselves. He was the weak link they had to snap in the next ninety-six hours or so. Jay decided to pay Fisher a visit, spread a little panic in the banker's life. He also decided to call his own banker, Len Hartkemeier, and have him set up the appointment with Fischer. Hartkemeier would understand.

Fleming shifted in his chair and looked past the desk to the gray clouds that plagued the sky. Perhaps they would bring him better luck than the brilliant day had yesterday. The intercom buzzed.

"Yes?"

"A package has arrived for you, Mr. Fleming." His secretary had a slight accent. "It came from the Davis Company but the gentleman insists on giving it to you personally."

Jay smiled. "Please send it in." The Davis Company was one of the foremost suppliers of weaponry and other accessories to the police agencies of the world. Jay had long been friends with the company's owner. Now the friendship might just save his life.

Fleming's secretary entered. She was a woman of medium height who wore her brown hair in a severe bun which pulled back the skin of her face like plastic wrap stretched over a melon. She looked like a matron in a women's prison, but she was very efficient. A tall, well-dressed blond man with the standard-issue poker face of the American Secret service followed her in. He held a carton the size of a case of champagne. It was wrapped in brown paper and bound with formidable straps of nylon-reinforced tape.

"Thank you," Jay nodded at his secretary. She retreated reluctantly through the door and closed it discreetly.

"Good morning, Hamilton." Jay stood up and offered his hand to the Davis Company's Luxembourg manager. Hamilton Steed, former Secret Service agent, former head of the Secret Service's European bureau, set the box down on Jay's desk and shook hands with him vigorously.

"Mr. Davis wanted me to make sure I got this to you personally," Hamilton explained.

"How is Gil?" Jay asked as he sat down and indicated with his hand for Hamilton to follow suit.

"Mr. Davis is fine. Told me to give you his regards, and ask when you're going duck hunting with him again."

"Good," Jay responded. "Give him by best, and my thanks." Jay grasped the box and turned it toward him as he pulled a letter opener from a stand on the desk.

"Everything's used," Hamilton said apologetically. "All we had were demo samples. The Hamburg sale cleaned us out of sidearms and body armor."

Jay tore open the box and pulled out a Smith and Wesson .357 magnum, a Bianchi Leather shoulder holster, a well-tailored vest and four boxes of cartridges for the .357. The vest was reversible, gray wool on one side and brown tweed on the other. He put the vest on and buttoned it up, leaving the bottom button undone.

"Looks good," Hamilton said.

"Amazing what they can do with Kelvar," Jay said. Kelvar was a modern plastic with greater penetration resistance than steel.

"What do I owe the company?" Jay asked.

"Nothing," Hamilton said. "Gil just said to bring more Jack Daniels with you the next time you two go hunting."

Jay smiled, and the two men shook hands in parting. After Hamilton left, Jay tried on the shoulder holster and adjusted the straps to fit his broad shoulders. With his coat on, there was no telltale bulge. He had been unprepared to defend himself until this point. From now on, he was going to surprise a lot of people. The first one would be Ernst Fischer. Jay grabbed the telephone and dialed Len Hartkemeier's number.

The pounding rose to a crescendo. Gunshots, explosions. Alexandra shook uncontrollably, trying to make the noise stop. She kept seeing Lee Goldberg's fire-charred body, kept hearing the inhuman shriek that came from within the fire, and the explosion. The bedclothes were braided like rope and damp with the sweat of nightmares. Droplets of perspiration had broken out on her face and coursed the valley between her breasts. Someone was knocking on the door with a heavy, exasperated hand.

A thin reedy voice filtered through the door. "Déjeunèr."

Alexandra dimly remembered filling out the little card with her breakfast order and hanging it on the door before she went to bed.

Hurriedly, she jumped out of bed and looked frantically around her for her robe. Then she remembered it was still in the room at the Excelsior.

"One moment!" she called to the person outside. "Just a moment please." She surveyed the room, spotting only her attaché case and a pile of clothes thrown over the back of a chair near the closet. She rushed to them and frantically started pulling on one item after another. Then the memories of that horrible yesterday ambushed her: Lee, the man with the bushy eyebrows who had tried to kill her, the flight from the hotel. Her blood started to chill as she considered for the first time that the man in the hallway with her breakfast might be with the killers.

Silently, she flew to the door and found it deadbolted and chained.

"Leave the tray in the hallway," she said through the door. "I'll get it when I'm appropriately dressed."

"Yes, madame," the man said politely, relief plain in his voice.

Alexandra listened to the delicate tinkling and clanking of dishes as the tray was deposited on the carpeting. Then there was silence. Her heart did a spirited salsa behind her breastbone. She stood there, ear to the door. She heard an elevator open, then close.

With trembling hands, she unchained the door. Was he still out there? She turned the deadbolt. You're making more out of this than necessary, she silently scolded herself. But what if he was waiting out there, waiting for you to open the door? She turned the door slowly, hesitantly, and then with a great fluid movement, flung it open. Nothing. No gunshots. No chloroform. No gorillas with lead pipes. No napalm. Only two hard rolls, three pats of butter wrapped in foil, four small wedges of cheese also wrapped in foil, three circular tins of marmalade, a stainless steel urn of coffee and a small pitcher of milk. Hardly a threat to the superiority of American ham and eggs, but an even less convincing threat to her life.

Nervously she laughed aloud with relief as she leaned over, picked up the tray and brought it into the room, closing the door with one foot as she did. She deposited the tray on a small round table in one corner of the room next to the window, and then pulled the thin cord to draw back the drapes. An anemic gray morning light washed in the room.

Alexandra sat down and poured a cup of coffee from the stainless steel urn stamped "Intercontinental Hotel." She sipped the aromatic brown liquid thoughtfully as she dredged up the details of the preceding night. After a quick dash into the utility closet to exchange the chambermaid's clothes for her own, she had taken the stairs down two flights to get away from the open window she had shoved the man out of.

Carrying her attaché case, she had walked briskly through the lobby of the Excelsior to the cashier and checked out. They could have her clothes. She was not about to risk her life for them. She thanked the doorman who held the brass and glass door for her, and tipped him as he fetched her a taxi. As it drove off, she didn't look back at the street where workmen were already cleaning up the debris.

She instructed the driver to take her to the information bureau by the train station, but it was closed. Inside the station, she feigned interest in the train schedules while she thought. The first thing she had to find was another place to stay. Pensions and small hotels were out. Desk clerks at those establishments would easily remember an American woman traveling alone. She needed anonymity. But Luxembourg was a town of less than eighty thousand. There weren't many large hotels. The Excelsior had been the largest and most luxurious.

A quick check through a guidebook she purchased at the train station listed only one other large hotel: the Intercontinental.

She had checked into the Intercontinental and after a desultory supper in her room, had fallen into a deep but disturbing sleep full of nightmares and demons.

She looked out at the threatening sky and then down at warmly bundled people carrying rolled umbrellas. She turned abruptly from the window and clicked on the television. She saw an old re-run of "Gilligan's Island" dubbed in French. Gilligan speaking with a suave Parisian accent almost made her laugh. Fear and depression sank into the corners of her mind. She took a deep breath and, suddenly hungry, set about demolishing her puny "continental" breakfast. She ordered another pot of coffee from room service, then cleared the remains off the table and set the tray in the corridor. She covered the small round table with the contents of the package Martin had sent to Lee Goldberg.

She saw page after page of statistics, apparently experimental data. The figures had been copied on a reducing machine and were difficult to read. There was a thick technical report dealing with some sort of weather experiment involving low-frequency radio waves in the ionosphere. Two memos and a cable seemed ominous. One memo, dated three years previously, touted a new weapon and described targetting difficulties. The second memo, only two months old, outlined a final targetting process. The cable contained a cryptic message to a Luxembourg banker, Ernst Fischer, from a man named Steven Strand, requesting an opportunity to bid on a consignment. The solitary word "denied" was scribbled in angry handwriting at the foot of the page.

There were also copies of newspaper clippings from all over the world, mostly dealing with electrical power outages, failures of radio or telephone systems, unexplained interferences with radar systems, massive breakdowns of computers. There was even a clipping from the *New York Times* about the great Manhattan blackout. None of it made any sense to her.

Meticulously, she examined every page, looking for some explanation, some Rosetta stone to decipher the papers. Martin had seen something here. What was it? She stared at the ceiling and sipped at the coffee trying to conjure up anything that might glue the pieces together. Something Lee had said, something Martin might have let slip.

She had faced this problem dozens of times before as a reporter. Piles of seemingly unrelated documents and sources and interviews swam randomly like great schools of fish in her mind until something clicked, one last piece of information, one last interview, one last something.

She looked at the daunting papers before her. It had been so long since she had tackled anything more intellectually challenging than grading final exams. For an instant, the task seemed impossible. She felt the energy drain out of her. Her insides felt empty. Sleep seemed like the best option. Depression crawled out of the corners of the room.

"Damn it, Alexandra!" she said suddenly as she stood up and walked angrily to the window. "You can't walk away from all this," she said aloud. "They killed Martin, they tried to kill you. You *can't* walk away from it."

Knuckles rapped politely at the door.

"Yes," she said, turning from the window.

"*Votre café.*"

Alexandra strode to the door, looked through a peephole she had not noticed before and opened the door for the white-coated waiter. He smiled gratefully at her generous tip and pulled the door quietly shut.

She sat back down at the table, poured a fresh cup of coffee and went over the pages again.

What had Lee Goldberg said at breakfast yesterday? Martin had warned him about her stubbornness. A letter. Of course. Martin would have written a letter to cover the documents, to explain their significance, to recommend some action. She mentally reviewed her search of Goldberg's room. She was confident she hadn't missed it. He might have been carrying it on him when he burned to death. Yet, she thought, it was the only likely place for such a letter.

Slowly, she shook her head and began to make notes on a piece of hotel stationery. The name Nikola Tesla continued to crop up in the papers. She decided she'd do more research on him.

Shuffling through the pages, she pulled out the cable to Ernst Fischer.

"Visit Fischer," she wrote. She stared at the name for a

moment and then underlined it, added an asterisk. He seemed like the logical place to start.

Strand. Steven Strand, the other name on the cable. It sounded vaguely familiar.

"Look up Strand," she wrote on the hotel stationery.

By the time she had finished, her list of things to research in the library included: "Intergovernmental Weather Research Project," which was on many of the letterheads; "Platform Delta Zeus," although she had no idea where in the world she'd find information on that; "General Jerry Patterson"; and "electromagnetic pulse."

She stared at her list. Not much to go on, but it was something. She had started out with a lot less on some of her more successful stories. As Alexandra ran her eyes over the list again and again, she felt something stir inside. She realized then how much she missed the thrill of the hunt, the challenge of the puzzle, the dogged pursuit of a story that epitomizes reporting.

Now, she felt that excitement again.

"For you, Martin," she said reverentially as she folded the piece of paper with her notes. "But for me, too. I never knew I missed this so much." She placed the paper in her attaché case and began to dress. She had clothes to buy, research to do, a banker to visit and a life to reclaim: hers.

Chapter Nineteen

The sky had brightened from battleship-gray to light pearl when Jay stepped from the hired limo in front of the Intercontinental. Hartkemeier had set up the appointment with Fischer and Jay wanted to change from his relatively casual clothes to something more formal—a uniform that a banker would respect. No reason to go into the meeting without every chip he could carry.

Subasic's man Sweeny stepped out first and scanned the street in both directions, craning his head at the upper stories of surrounding buildings. He nodded to Fleming.

Annoyed at the constraints imposed by the security, Jay grumpily slid across the seat and walked quickly across the sidewalk and into the hotel lobby. A long line snaked to the counter, mostly refugees from the Excelsior who wanted to get as far away as they could from the threat of violence. The morning news had been full of the bomb explosion in the hotel's restaurant, and the apparent suicide jump from the fourteenth floor.

There was also the spectacular crash and explosion of a gasoline tanker just outside town. Everywhere, on street corners, in cafes, in offices, people were buzzing with excitement. Nothing this dramatic had happened in or near Luxembourg since Patton had driven out the Nazis. Jay saw the bold headlines in the hotel newsstand.

He and Sweeny were waiting for the elevator when Jay decided he wanted a newspaper.

Sweeny wore an expression of dismay. He didn't dare tell his charge that he had drunk too many cups of coffee while waiting for him outside the banker Hartkemeier's office and needed to use the bathroom.

"Look," Jay said, watching Sweeny's irritation, "you go on ahead and go up. I'll be okay. I'll just grab a paper and be right up."

Jay watched Sweeny's face as duty dueled with one of nature's most compelling urges. Nature won.

"All right," Sweeny replied, "but don't tell Subasic."

Jay toyed briefly with the idea of taking a walk but decided that was pushing things too far. Instead he walked dutifully to the newsstand. He wanted to read about the deaths at the Excelsior and the tanker explosion. Too much was happening for all the events to be simple coincidence. The police admitted as much. Jay hoped some facts in the papers might add a piece or two to his own puzzle.

Hartkemeier had been helpful in helping to set up the appointment with Fischer. He told Jay that Fischer was a respected member of the Luxembourg banking and business community with "a certain reputation" for helping mutual enemies—countries or corporations—consummate deals of mutual benefit. Beyond that, there was little to know about Fischer. He didn't fraternize beyond the usual business meetings. He was trustworthy, not terribly cordial, kept to himself, lived in a comfortable unostentatious home in the country overlooking the Alzette River, was a widower and held honorary posts in a variety of charities and international organizations. Politically, Fischer went to great lengths to stay scrupulously neutral. This went back to his service in the Austrian government just after World War II when Austria had been under Soviet domination. He had been instrumental in negotiating a neutrality stance which satisfied both the Americans and the Russians. Secretly, Hartkemeier confided, Fischer seemed to hate Americans.

He leaned down to pick up a paper from the top of the pile. His shoulder brushed a woman.

"Excuse me, please," Jay said. "I didn't notice—"

She wore an expensive, though wrinkled, herringbone blazer and a charcoal skirt. "Oh," she said in a relieved voice. "You're an American."

She fixed him with blue eyes deep enough to drown in. They peered at him over high cheekbones. Her hair was the color of teak and came down almost to her shoulders. She was striking Jay decided, but she looked as if she had been traveling for days with no change of clothes.

Now why should I be relieved that he's an American? Alexandra cursed herself. The people who are trying to kill me are Americans. She studied his face for a moment, taking in the broad shoulders and lean athletic face with the strong jaw. His hair was dark brown, almost black, and framed a sun-tanned face that made his turquoise eyes stand out. He was dressed in a coarse Harris tweed blazer with fine threads of maize and chickory. He wore a vest that didn't precisely match the brown in either the coat or his dark brown wool trousers. Still, she found him attractive.

"Yes," Fleming answered. "Santa Monica," he said. "And you?"

"San Diego." Alexandra laughed.

Behind them, the manager of the newsstand, a lumpy woman with warts on her hands, listened to the conversation. She'd heard it thousands of times. Americans! They thought they were Marco Polo among the savages every time they went to Europe. No other culture seemed to carry the same ready-made fraternity membership.

"Californians everywhere," Jay said lamely and tried to make up for it with a smile. "You're staying here?" he asked, and then immediately regretted it. She stiffened at the question. A look of fear flashed across her face.

"No," she said hoarsely and then cleared her throat. "Just . . . stopping for the day. I'm on my way to Belgium." Fool, she scolded herself. He could be with *them!* "Please, excuse me," she said abruptly, taking a paper from the stack and setting it on the counter. "I'm running out of time. I have a tour to go on before my train leaves." She handed the woman behind the counter a banknote and waited for her change. "Goodbye," she said, looking nervously at Jay. She glanced around like a frightened rabbit alert for hawks and made for the door.

Jay watched her hurry into a taxi. Funny woman, he thought. First she looks at me with those wonderful blue eyes as though she wants me to take her away; then suddenly the blue turns to ice. He shook his head.

He paid for the paper and headed toward the elevator, intrigued by the incident. She reminded him of Helen. Dear Helen. Wonderful, loving Helen. A good wife, a good housekeeper. The wrong woman for him. The wrong woman to marry a fighter pilot. He remembered the first time their eyes locked. Across an oak table in the Cornell Library, the light playing in her eyes. He kidded her about her sorceress's eyes. He'd never forget the way they stared when he came home and found her dead. She hadn't even finished the note. It said, "I love you," but she couldn't bear knowing he mightn't come home one day. And Jay signed up for his third tour in Nam.

The elevator doors rumbled softly open. Two dowdy women debarked, followed by two even dowdier men. Jay boarded alone. Back into the corner went Helen. He had killed her. Just as surely as if he had forced the pills down her throat. Back in the corner she went, back where she couldn't hurt him so much.

Bogdan Subasic was waiting in the room when Jay arrived. His face was red with anger. Sweeny sat in one of the easy chairs by the window, looking like a chastened puppy.

"What are you doing, running off without an escort like that?" Subasic thundered before the door was completely closed.

"I'm not your prisoner," Jay said evenly.

"You could have been killed," Subasic said. "I don't think you understand. There are people out there just waiting for you to make a mistake."

"I don't think you understand. I'm not your prisoner," Jay repeated in a low voice. "If I want to get myself killed, then I'll get myself killed. I will not live in a cage and be led out on a chain."

The two men faced off, knuckles clenched. Suddenly Jay went to the small refrigerator that stood in one corner of the room and pulled out a bottle of orange juice.

After a long sip, Jay spoke, his voice calmer now. "What's with you, Subasic? Are you always like this? After all, you're the one who was supposed to be with me this morning and canceled out." Without waiting for an answer, Jay walked into his bedroom and stripped off his coat. He began to change for his meeting with Fischer.

Subasic followed him in.

When he spotted the shoulder holster, he said, "Where did you get that?"

"You're not the only friend I have, Subasic," Jay said.

Subasic sat on the edge of the bed. "You wanted to see me?"

"I'm going to see Fischer at noon," Jay said. "He sounded panicky on the phone. I told him I wanted to discuss the Tesla papers." Jay threw the holster and vest on the bed next to Subasic.

The Yugoslavian looked at the firearm. "May I?" he asked. Jay nodded as he slipped out of his shirt and trousers and walked to the closet. Subasic slid the revolver from the leather holster. He reholstered it and laid it on the bed. "Good choice. Now what is it you wanted to see me about?"

"You wanted to see *me*," Jay said. "Or have you forgotten? Last night. Before the phone call that tossed you on your ear. You said you wanted to run through things once more before I met with Fischer." Jay pulled from the closet a three-piece navy-blue wool suit with brass buttons.

Subasic's voice was weary. "I've been under a great deal of pressure lately, since that call."

"What was it about?" Jay asked.

"It doesn't concern you."

Jay hung the suit over the back of the nearest chair. "Anything that affects your frame of mind and your ability is my business. And don't forget it." Subasic glared up at him sullenly. Jay returned his attention to dressing.

Jay broke the silence. "Okay. You wanted this briefing, so let's get on with it. First, as you suggested, I am going to make him a money offer for a photocopy of the papers." Jay selected a pair of black knee-length socks from the drawer. "Tell me again how high your agency is willing to go."

"You must keep it under ten million U.S. dollars," Subasic replied absently.

"Hartkemeier said Fischer is a noted tightwad," Jay

commented. "He'll probably ask for the ten million and expenses for Xeroxing the papers."

Subasic's face remained an immovable mask.

Jay slipped on his pants. "Second, if, as you predict, he refuses, then I threaten to go to the Yugoslavians and tell them the Russians have bribed Fischer for the documents and that Yugoslavia gets no treaty. I also threaten to call the Russians and tell them that the Yugoslavians have sold the documents to the United States."

Subasic nodded. "That would ruin Fischer's most lucrative business—East–West deals. Plus, he'd have the Yugoslavians on his doorstep demanding their documents back even before you hung up the telephone. Fischer knows the Yugoslavians would probably kill him for the double cross. The Russians know this too."

"Why call them?" Jay asked. He buttoned up the white broadcloth shirt and fumbled through his bag for cufflinks. "That seems to complicate things unnecessarily. Don't you think the Yugoslavians are going to call them even before they call Fischer?"

"Maybe," Subasic said. "But I'm hoping the Russians will be angry enough at what they perceive as a Yugoslavian double cross that they won't communicate terms with them. It should keep them from comparing notes, and from realizing the emergency is bogus, at least long enough for us to obtain the documents. At the least, it ought to prevent the Russians from obtaining the Tesla papers. That would give us time to obtain them."

"And if the Russians find out we're behind it?"

"People could die," Subasic said unemotionally. "Some kind of war is not out of the question."

Jay finished dressing while Subasic took up the narrative. Jay would take a cab to Fischer's office, Sweeny and Subasic trailing as protection. They would stay out of sight since they were well known in intelligence circles. "Besides," Subasic said, "Fischer hates Americans, particularly intelligence agents. If he saw me or Sweeny, the operation would be out the window."

"Funny," Jay said as he adjusted the knot in his tie,

"Hartkemeier said the same thing. But he didn't have any evidence to support it. Do you?"

"Some files from the old OSS," Subasic said. "Americans who dealt with him in the negotiations wrote uncomplimentary reports. He was like a referee who always sides with one team. He always had a justification that stood up to scrutiny, but he always threw the dicey calls against the West."

Jay turned away from the mirror and grabbed the suit vest. He regretted that the Kelvar vest wouldn't match. "So how come he'll see me?"

"Greed," Subasic replied. "You're the head of a company that makes things he might like to sell. I gather Hartkemeier hinted as much when he called."

Jay nodded as he buttoned up the vest.

"He's not about to meet with an American spy like me," Subasic continued. "There's no percentage in it. But you could mean big bucks. Let him think so, at least."

Jay left the bottom vest button undone, and slipped into the shoulder holster. The Smith and Wesson nested snugly under his left arm. It felt good, Jay reflected. He would not be a sitting duck any longer.

After putting on the suitcoat, Jay turned toward Subasic. "Old files from the OSS? Why did you ask me to use my connections to find out about Fischer? Why didn't you tell me about the files before? I spent all morning making calls around town, calling in some IOUs to get information about Fischer."

"The OSS file is out of date—"

"Don't you have recent stuff also? Up-to-date information? A guy who regularly makes deals happen between East and West? Maybe some high-tech items here that might not be sanctioned by Western governments? Silicon chips, laser mirrors? Certainly you have a file on him. Or else you're even more incompetent than the newspapers make out."

Subasic looked embarrassed. "To tell you the truth—"

"Do that," Jay interrupted sharply. "Tell me the truth, all of it."

"The file we have on Fischer is embarrassingly thin. He structures his deals with the minimum number of people. His files are sketchy, even his personal telephone book has no more than the expected numbers. He seems to keep everything in his head. At least he keeps nothing extraordinary in his office."

"You know all this because your people have been through his office?"

Subasic nodded. Jay took a deep breath and let it out slowly as he sat slowly down. "This is also how you know that he has no vault at his office and that the Tesla papers aren't there?" Subasic nodded again. "Otherwise, you would have stolen them already and let the Russians and the Yugoslavians and Fischer have it out with each other?" Again, Subasic nodded, wearily. Jay massaged his jaw, pulled at his lower lip as he looked at Bogdan Subasic. "It makes you mad as hell to have to depend on an amateur like me, doesn't it? It really gets under your skin."

Subasic wearily brought both hands to his face and rubbed at his eyes. "It bothers me very, very much," he said. "You have no idea." The intelligence man's shoulders and face had lost the bristling authority they had radiated the day before. "Ante," he said in a low sad voice. "Ante was my half-brother."

"Was?"

"He died yesterday."

"The telephone call?"

Subasic's head bobbed in acknowledgment. "Out of the window of the Excelsior. It wasn't a suicide. I know that." Subasic's voice cracked for an instant. Then, like a juggler gathering up Indian pins after a mishap, he stood up straight, gathered his courage and walked to the window, shoulders square, head once again held high. "I'm his only surviving relative. And I can't claim the body." Angrily, he turned to face Jay. "But I'm going to do the next best thing. I'll find out who killed him and I will make them suffer for a long time."

"Do you know who?" Jay asked sympathetically. Jay got a glimpse of a tiny ray of humanity shining in the murky hard facade the intelligence man had built around him. "Is it the same people who are after me?"

Subasic shook his head. He got up from the bed and left the room. "Tell me when you're ready to go to Fischer's," he called back over his shoulder.

Jay snatched his shoulder bag from the floor and fumbled around in it for a package of Corn Nuts. He found one, his last. I wouldn't want to be the person who had killed Subasic's half-brother, Jay thought. He popped a couple of the kernels into his mouth. Whoever it was would die horribly. The thought made him shiver.

Chapter Twenty

Pasha Belenko pushed away the plate of veal his assistant had brought him and stared past his desk at the muddy gray clouds that scudded past one another over the bare winter landscape.

He was beginning to feel naked himself. Who had sent the prominent American to see him? There had to be someone behind it all, some ulterior purpose. Prominent Americans, influential people who ran government research institutions which performed tens of millions of dollars worth of classified defense work each year didn't just show up at the Russian Embassy in Luxembourg for no reason at all.

But he didn't for a moment believe the man's preposterous story about an exchange of some musty old papers by an obscure Yugoslavian scientist for a secret treaty. Hmmph! This Tesla had been dead for decades. Science had progressed light years since then. How had the American thought the ruse would work for even a second?

No, there had to be someone behind it all. He looked down at the list. He had many enemies. One didn't rise in the KGB as rapidly as he had without making enemies. Belenko's list contained mostly foreign intelligence services. There were too few opportunities for anyone he knew to have contact with influential Americans. One by one, he narrowed the list. Two Russian names remained. He would have the surveillance on them increased. As for the foreign intelligence agencies . . . he sighed and shook his head. Perhaps the act against

191

him was the beginning of a new campaign against Russia. Perhaps he wasn't the only KGB official who had been visited by someone like this man.

Sleep had come only fitfully last night as he struggled with the reason behind the extraordinary visit. He'd had no more appetite at breakfast than he had now. He closed his eyes and sighed audibly. The mere fact that such an American, one so closely identified with the right-wing, anti-Soviet faction of American politics—the mere fact that he had visited Belenko, had asked for him by name—made him suspect in the eyes of his fellow KGB officials. He could hear them now: "Why would such an American with known anti-Soviet tendencies have visited Belenko if Belenko hadn't invited the meeting, either by offering to perform a traitorous act or considering such acts? If he was truly loyal, the American would never have visited him."

The investigation that must follow, the interrogations, the harassment that would inevitably occur made his intestines churn.

But he *had* to file a report. Failure to file the report would sooner or later get him in worse trouble. The thought of defecting flitted through his mind as it did a hundred times a day. And as always he rejected it. His wife could go to hell, but his little girl . . . he looked at the color photograph of little Anna, nine years old, her bright blond hair plaited into a long pony tail as she struck a dramatic pose on the balance beam. Anna's mother deserved a gulag, but Anna—his resolve melted every time he thought of her being taken out of the special school and forced to attend a regular school with ordinary offspring of factory workers and street sweepers. No, he couldn't do that to her.

But what to do about the American? Damn him! Belenko's hands were in his lap, clinched into tight fists, the knuckles white. He decided to wait until the Deputy Foreign Minister had concluded his visit. He was supposed to depart on Sunday. Belenko decided he would send his report to Moscow on Monday. Perhaps something would occur to him by then.

Ante Dvorak's face resembled an uncooked pot of haggis. Even though the newspaper photographer had tried to take the picture from a discreet distance, the distinguished American known to his colleagues as Obsidian noticed that the man's face was a mess. So, for that matter, was the rest of him.

But who had killed him? Obsidian wondered as he sat at one end of the comfortable sofa of indeterminate design in the lobby of the Intercontinental. It hadn't been *his* people. Had Belenko lied to him about not helping? Russians were like that. Would never admit to helping a capitalist, even when their interests coincided—mainly because Lenin's dogma said the interests of Communism and Capitalism *never* coincided.

Obsidian scanned the paper with interest, keeping one eye on the elevators. He wondered if the spectacular bombing of the Excelsior was perhaps related to the equally spectacular explosion in the tunnel. The paper said more than a dozen vehicles at both ends of the tunnel had been blown off the road by the blast. Windows were shattered in farmhouses up to ten kilometers away.

As for the Excelsior bombing, the prefect of police said that some sort of homemade napalm had been used. The leader of the protest, a local college student, was being held without bail.

He turned the page to read the continuation of the stories, and skipped over a smaller story about an unidentified body being located near a jogging trail south of town.

At ten minutes before noon, his heart took an extra beat as Jay Fleming stepped from the elevator, preceded by Bogdan Subasic and trailed by a balding middle-aged man he didn't recognize.

Obsidian's hand reflexively dropped to the thin, soft-sided leather briefcase by his thigh. His fingers palpated the heavy metal object inside. It had cost him plenty. Gun control restrictions were murder in any European country, especially for handguns, even more especially for foreigners.

He resented not having the power to order more men into action here, to make sure Fleming and Subasic were stopped, that the entire operation was halted. If this had been Chicago or New York, or anywhere in the United States, the manpower would be available. But here, he could only call in distant IOUs—the men in Amsterdam who had once worked for the Secret Service—or hire them from the readily available pool of mercenaries, former soldiers and former security agents. They were eager, but the quality, as he had found out, was inconsis-

tent and hard to determine. He had help arriving in another
thirty-six hours, but he couldn't depend on what Subasic and
Fleming might accomplish in the meantime. With any luck, the
team arriving at his rented house shortly after midnight tomorrow would have very little to do.

As the three men left the hotel lobby, Obsidian picked up the
leather briefcase with the Heckler and Koch VP70 and four
extra clips of ammunition inside and strolled toward the exit.
He watched as a Volvo sedan was brought by the valet. The
bald man slid in behind the wheel. Subasic took the passenger
seat. Through the semi-sheer curtains, Obsidian saw Jay
disappear inside a taxi that nosed its way into busy noontime
traffic, followed closely by the Volvo. Only then did he walk
briskly out and into the cab waiting at the head of the line.

"*Suivez ce taxi, là,*" he said, pointing at Fleming's cab. The
driver looked back at him and shrugged. The well-dressed
American didn't look like a detective to him.

"*Vous avez des amis ici en Luxembourg, m'sieur?*" the driver
asked Jay as he peered curiously in the rearview mirror. The
echoes of a taxi driver in Amsterdam bounced around in his
thoughts. He turned around and watched as the Volvo with
Subasic and Sweeny matched every move made by the taxi.

Jay didn't like Subasic. The man was a fanatic and fanatics
were capable of acts that got them and those around them
injured. Jay realized Subasic would do anything, including
endanger his own life, to make sure the mission was accomplished. Later, Subasic had to be watched.

Jay answered the taxi driver in French. "I have friends here
in Luxembourg. They're in the Volvo right behind us."

The cabbie's neck muscles relaxed. His shoulders sagged a
little. From relief or disappointment?

The taxi sped along broad modern boulevards to the
narrower streets of the pre-war period and finally into the
cramped alleys of the old medieval town. As he watched
the world grow steadily more ancient outside his window, Jay
rehearsed what he would say to Fischer. He tried to picture the
office, but constructed only half an image. The cobalt eyes of
the woman at the newsstand kept crowding in. Here you are in
a foreign country with a firearm strapped to your ribs, followed
by a carload of armed men, about to set off a potential war

between two superpowers, and all you can think of are two blue eyes.

He was still thinking of the eyes when the cab pulled to a halt on the Rue Beck in front of a stately old stone building with two bronze lions fearlessly guarding each side of the steps. They had weathered to a time-worn patina of cupric green and ebony. Jay paid the driver. Sweeny steered the Volvo past the cab some twenty yards and up on the sidewalk across the street. Subasic nodded "all safe."

"Your friend," the taxi driver spoke. "He will get a ticket if he remains there long."

Jay thanked him and stepped out of the cab and quickly up the steps. The driver shook his head, then drove off. Neither Jay nor the two men in the Volvo noticed the cab at the far corner at the Avenue Monterey. It disgorged a well-dressed gentleman with a soft leather briefcase.

Fischer's waiting room was the antithesis of ancient old Luxembourg. Jay walked into a bright room furnished in the minimalist style. Three walls were painted a rich cream. The fourth wall contained a phalanx of windows. The polished wood floor was mostly hidden by a large deep pile rug, also cream, leaving a walnut colored perimeter. The furniture was glass and chrome and leather, Bauhaus imitations. Desert plants with sharp drooping leaves grew out of grayish stalks sprouting from mirrored cylinders in the corners. On the far wall was another door.

There was one other person in the stark, forbidding room. It was the woman with the cobalt-blue eyes. She had changed clothes. In place of the rumpled outfit, she now wore a navy-blue skirt and matching coat over a white blouse with a simple businesslike bow at the collar. Navy-blue pumps showed off her slim ankles. Most women would have looked plain in the outfit.

Jay smiled as soon as he saw her.

Her startled eyes threw wide puddles of blue at him. Her right hand flew first to her mouth, then plunged into the attaché case on her knees.

She seemed to stiffen as he walked toward her. The reaction confused him further.

"I'm sorry," he said lightly. "I don't *usually* have this effect on strangers."

"Mr. Fleming?" A harsh authoritarian voice sounded from the open doorway like the report of a small caliber rifle. Jay had not noticed the door being opened.

Jay faced the door. "Yes." The woman looked like her voice. She was in her mid-forties and had gunmetal eyes. Her brown hair was cut in a short, indeterminate style that displayed the prominent angular features of her face. Her nervous body quivered inside a severe suit. He wondered if she had decorated the reception area.

"Please have a seat." The granite jaw clipped each word. "Herr Fischer will be with you in a moment. He has had to rearrange his appointments to accommodate you," the voice said resentfully.

"Thank you," Jay said courteously. A kind word turneth away wrath, he remembered. It didn't work for Fischer's own *reichsmarshall*. She started to close the door when the woman with the blue eyes jumped up. Her attaché case slipped from her lap and thudded on the thick carpeting. Jay glanced down and saw that a great pile of papers had spilled out.

"Excuse me," she said firmly, her blue eyes burning. "But I've been waiting some time. Can't you tell me if Mr. Fischer is going to see me or not? I've come a long way to see him."

"Many people come a long way to see Herr Fischer," the woman replied icily. "And they have appointments. If you truly have business with Herr Fischer, then you must have patience." She ended the conversation by closing the door a little harder than was necessary.

Jay watched the woman with the blue eyes. She looked like she was struggling for air. She stared at the door as if she could melt it with the heat of her gaze, then turned her head and stared at him with infuriated eyes that accused him of depriving her of an appointment.

"I'm sorry," Jay said in the most conciliatory tone he could muster. "I really am." He took a chair across the room from her. It was the least threatening thing he could think of.

She looked suspiciously at him, and without taking her eyes off him, reached for the papers that spilled from her case. She grabbed a thick manila envelope and a handful of stationery with the Intercontinental Hotel's logo at the top. Underneath was a pile of American dollars, traveler's checks, an American passport, and a large handgun. Jay stiffened, his eyes wide with fright as his hand sought the comfort of his own gun's handgrip. Was she here to kill him? Had Fischer called someone?

She looked up at Jay, tried to shield the gun from his vision with the case. She caught the look of fear and surprise on his face and then quickly finished stuffing the contents back in the case and snapped both latches firmly.

If she was there to kill him, why hadn't she killed him that morning? She could have buddied up to him at the newsstand and shot him on the elevator. A voice in the back of his head reminded him that he wasn't the only person in the world whose life was in danger. He remembered the large amount of money in the briefcase, and considered it likely that she had the gun to protect that. It was logical. Here was a woman with a great deal of money waiting to see a banker and she has a gun for protection. It all made sense. All except the fact that, like him, she had arrived without an appointment. His curiosity was overwhelming. He *had* to know. He also wanted to see those blue eyes closer.

"Is this a stop on your tour?" he asked lightly. She glared back at him. "I'm Jay Fleming," he tried again. He watched her face reflect the battle raging behind it. Fear, uncertainty, anger, sadness. But not murder, unless she was better at hiding that than her other emotions.

Then her gaze softened, as if some tentative decision had been reached. "I'm Alexandra Downing," she said as properly as one might to a stranger on a train.

Jay smiled. He wanted to ask her why she was here, why she had lied to him, why she was carrying a revolver around in her briefcase. He settled for, "Too bad the weather's not as pretty as yesterday's."

She nodded, searching his face.

Alexandra willed her breath to come normally. Had he seen the gun? She was sure he had. His reaction was one of surprise, a normal reaction. If he was with the killers, he would have known that she had made off with the other man's gun. But this Jay Fleming had been surprised. His turquoise eyes had gone wide with fear. It wasn't the look of a killer. Perhaps he was safe. She examined his face carefully, the way he held his body, the tone of his voice. He had obviously been expected by Fischer, though on some sort of emergency basis. The Tesla papers? No, it would be too much of a coincidence. But, she considered shrewdly, he knew Fischer or was well enough known by Fischer to have the banker rearrange his schedule to fit him in. She pondered the treachery that had just grown full-blown in her mind and it made her feel guilty. It's your life, she thought. You have to do everything to save it, and to avenge the deaths.

She looked at him in a different light. "I don't suppose anyone comes to Luxembourg for the weather," she said warmly. "Although it is a beautiful city, especially in the spring."

"You've been here before?" Jay asked, pleased that her mood had shifted so quickly into a friendly one.

"As a student," she answered quickly. "The cheap airline fare I got landed here."

"That's funny," Jay said. "So did I. Came over here with my backpack and sleeping bag." He thought dreamily of the past.

She looked at him sympathetically. The way his eyes had drawn that wistful look around them made him seem vulnerable. Guilt pricked at her conscience. Don't get involved, she told herself. He has a way to get the appointment with Fischer that she knew by now she could never get on her own, but she'd have to be careful not to draw him into a situation that could get him hurt if someone attacked her again. She didn't want to have that on her conscience.

"What did you study in college," Jay said. Political science or maybe economics, Jay had guessed. She looked like a business woman. Probably had an advanced degree, MBA or maybe law.

"I studied journalism," she replied. "Northwestern."

"Good school for that," Jay replied, nonplussed. "Are you a reporter?"

She shook her head. "Used to be. Then I taught college. Right now I'm unemployed." And playing at James Bond, she thought. "What about you?"

"I own a company that makes electronic devices for the military." He watched a small frown ripple across her face. Was she one of the nuclear freeze types?

"How interesting," she said, not entirely honestly. Why

couldn't she seem to get away from military men? "What sort of devices?"

"Electronics countermeasures," Jay said a little defensively. "They help confuse enemy missiles, jam their guidance systems. That sort of thing."

Alexandra nodded and gave him a vague smile and thought about what to say next. She did know that she had to have time to talk to him, to convince him to help her with Fischer.

"Have you always done that?" she asked by way of keeping her end of the awkward conversation moving.

"No, I used to be a pilot. For the Navy." He smiled. "I got tired of the ECM—that's what we call electronic countermeasures—I got tired of devices that didn't work on our planes. So I decided I could do it better." It was partly the truth, Jay thought. Anyway, he didn't want to have to go through explaining the entire ordeal at Fleming Industries and that flaming asshole Steven Strand.

"And did you?" she asked. "Make them better, I mean?"

"A lot of people think so," Jay said, a bit embarrassed.

"Like who?" she persisted, not quite knowing why.

He told her about the Dutch government. Then she wanted to know how ECM devices worked. By the questions she asked during his explanation, he could tell that she had a quick mind. He was impressed. He told her about his office. She asked if she could see it.

"Of course," Jay said, surprised at this sudden show of friendliness. "But it's just an office. People at desks. We actually make the stuff in Santa Monica." She looked disappointed. "But I'll be glad to show it to you anyway if you'd like."

"Tomorrow, perhaps?" she suggested brightly. Deep furrows plowed across his forehead as if he'd suddenly remembered some distasteful chore.

"I'd like to say yes," he began, "but my business here is kind of volatile right now. I really can't make any appointments."

She *had* to talk to him and soon. Oh hell, she thought, it's a new age, might as well brazen it out.

"What about a drink this evening?" The words sounded strange to her ears. She hoped they didn't sound like a cheap come-on.

"Sure," Jay responded quickly, flattered that she had asked. It had saved him the trouble of asking her. "I'm staying at the Intercontinental."

"So am I," she said, forgetting her lie of that morning. "How about in the bar at . . . what's convenient?"

Jay thought about Subasic and Sweeny. He would have to get rid of them. And what if they had to suddenly go elsewhere? His face darkened. "I'm here with two associates. I'll have to coordinate things with them. May I call you at your room later this afternoon so we can set things up?"

"Of course," she said.

The conversation fell like a poorly-baked cake. Only the opening of the door into the inner office saved them the agony of trying to get the momentum going again.

The granite-faced woman gave Alexandra a sour look and then focused her venom on Jay. "Herr Fischer will see you now."

Jay rose. "See you later," he said to Alexandra.

She ignored Fischer's secretary and smiled. "Later." As she watched him disappear, she realized she was genuinely looking forward to seeing him again. And immediately, she felt guilty. Martin had been dead for such a short while. It seemed wrong to be interested in other men. She would just have to watch herself, she cautioned. She was on the rebound and that could be dangerous.

Alexandra checked her watch. The city library, according to her little tourist map, was just a block away, on the Rue Aldringen. She could look up all of the names and references she had pulled from the documents. It was obvious that the Nazi who worked for Fischer wasn't going to let her see him today, or perhaps any other day for that matter unless someone interceded. Someone like Jay.

On the other hand, she thought, if he *did* see her she wouldn't have to manipulate Jay Fleming. She could go about her task and not have to worry about her emotions. She had handled loss before Martin. She could handle it again.

There were good reasons for leaving and equally good ones for staying. She hated it when she couldn't make up her mind.

* * *

The Rue Beck was not a crowded street, but neither was it deserted. It was lunchtime. Some people strolled singly, others in pairs, looking for a restaurant to lunch in.

The well-dressed American with the soft leather briefcase fit unobtrusively into the foot traffic on the street. After paying the taxi, he paused at the corner and watched as Subasic and the other man he didn't recognize got comfortable in the Volvo. Sitting ducks, he thought. But the trick was to get them without being caught.

He stood there on the corner, not worried that Subasic would recognize him. He had shaved off his heavy beard, and now wore heavy-framed glasses rather than contact lenses. In a long face-to-face meeting the disguise wouldn't hold up. But here in Luxembourg, where Subasic did not expect to see him, Obsidian figured he could probably walk past the car on the other side of the street without being recognized.

As the American surveyed the street, a plan took shape in his mind. Less than ten minutes after alighting from the cab, a pair of businessmen deep in conversation about exchange rates and the strength of the dollar passed him. He quickly stepped away from the corner and followed closely, close enough for an observer to think he was of their party, but not close enough to invite suspicion. A single person stood out more than two or three. And even though he didn't think Subasic would recognize him, he decided that added caution wouldn't hurt.

As he walked along behind the two businessmen, Obsidian's eyes dissected the street and buildings around him. The alley was perfect, but there was no concealment. He rejected the foyers of several office buildings for the same reason. The businessmen formed a single file and squeezed between the Volvo and the building on its right. Obsidian followed them. When he glanced to his left, he was relieved to see both Subasic and the other man intently scanning the building across the street.

Obsidian passed a window painted white. It was covered with decorative iron grillwork. Some ten yards ahead, the businessmen pushed through the leather-padded doors of a restaurant. Above the doors hung a carved nameplate with gold foil outlining each letter, "Lion d'Or." Obsidian walked on alone. He thought he had found what he was looking for, but was too cautious not to take a more thorough look.

Within another thirty yards, he found two more suitable locations, but neither was perfect. He returned to the Lion d'Or and requested a table. The maître d' sized him up with a studied glance, and led him past a group who, judging by their disgruntled comments, had been waiting for some time, and seated him alone by a window. It was even better than he had hoped. He would be able to watch the Volvo in comfort. He ordered the wine list.

"I dislike waiting most," Sweeny commented as he lit a cigarette from the glowing butt of the last. "Waiting," he repeated flatly. "I almost prefer a day like yesterday to waiting."

Fool, Subasic wanted to say. The memory of Ante's grisly death mask filled his mind. Mikhail Dvorak was a farmer near Nova Vas. Both he and his wife had resigned themselves to childlessness when the shellshocked Bogdan Subasic stumbled onto the porch of their modest farmhouse. They had taken him in gladly and had loved him as the child they thought they could never have. Three years later, Ante was born, a grand surprise for the Dvoraks, and a source of delight for Bogdan.

But the joy didn't last. In a fit of collectivist passion, the Dvorak farm was confiscated by the Communist government and integrated into a larger commune. When Dvorak and his wife fought the confiscation, they were imprisoned. No one saw them alive again.

And now Ante was gone, Subasic thought bitterly. His eyes began to tear. Anger surged through him, the heat of its fury drying his tears. He would find the person who killed Ante. Revenge would be his.

"You're positive the woman pushed him," Subasic asked as casually as he could.

"There's no doubt," Sweeny said. "Everything points to it. He had gone to eliminate her and to retrieve the packet. And there's the chambermaid. I think the prefect will let us have a copy of her statement."

Subasic ran the facts quickly through his mind. After the death, the chambermaid had gone to the police and told them about her role in exchanging clothes with a woman who said she was trying to escape from a private detective hired by her husband. It was clear that somehow the woman had managed to push Ante from the window.

"May I see the photo again?" Subasic asked. Sweeny reached into an inner coat pocket and produced a copy of the woman's passport photo. Subasic took the small photo and glared at it as if it were a voodoo object that he could use to kill her through black magic.

"She's clever," Sweeny said. The hint of admiration in his tone angered Subasic even more.

"But not clever enough," Subasic said bitterly. "Not when it comes to my brother." He stared at the photo for a moment longer, imprinting its image on his mind and then handed it back to Sweeny.

"She won't last long. Believe me," Subasic mumbled.

Alexandra Downing looked at her watch again. Half an hour had passed and there had been no word from the bitch who guarded the gates to Fischer's office. She was incensed. Enough was enough. She picked up her briefcase, felt the heavy revolver slide to the bottom and walked out.

Chapter Twenty-one

Luxembourg,
December 20

Ernst Fischer was not a cooperative man, thought Jay Fleming. He sat on the other side of the massive walnut desk. Although the reception area and the outer office were stark, Fischer's own office was a sort of Bavarian Gothic, crowded with huge pieces of wooden furniture, heavy drapes, pictures, lamps.

Fischer used his desk like an ancient embattlement to fend off Jay's questions. He seemed to believe they would wound him. He was an obese man, close to three hundred pounds. Although he had not gotten out of his chair to greet Jay when he had been conducted in by the secretary, Mrs. Stahl, Jay pegged him at under six feet tall.

He had deep, piggy, black eyes like two pieces of coal pressed into a lump of bread dough. A multitude of broken capillaries covered his nose and cheeks like a fractured roadmap. He had that look of dissipated youth that old fat men have, caused by lard which prevents wrinkles from forming. He had a nasal problem and breathed heavily through his open mouth.

"Let's say, just for argument's sake," Jay persisted, "that what you say is true. That you have never heard of Nikola Tesla, any of his papers or any attempt to exchange certain of those papers in exchange for a secret diplomatic agreement." Jay leaned forward, placing his elbows on the edge of the desk. Fischer suddenly sat back in his chair as if he believed Jay was about to grab him by his thick throat.

"Let's just accept that for argument's sake, all right?" Jay smiled. Fischer wasn't agreeing to anything. "*If* that is indeed the case, then you won't mind my calling the Soviet and Yugoslavian embassies now, will you? It won't make any difference if I tell the Yugoslavians that the Russians offered you a great deal of money and the deal with the treaty is off." Jay leaned back in the comfortable old chair whose genteel leather upholstery was beginning to deteriorate. The mask of abject fear which had peeked from underneath Fischer's poker player face had made the morning worthwhile.

"And I don't suppose that it would make any difference to you if I called the Russian embassy and told them that you had decided to sell the papers to the Americans for a great deal of money." Great globular streams of sweat made glycerine tracks down the sides of Fischer's face. He moved to speak, but only a hoarse croak sounded. He cleared his throat.

"You make some preposterous statements, Mr. Fleming," Fischer began. "There is, of course, no basis in fact for your little fantasy." The banker reached into his desk drawer and pulled out a white linen handkerchief with a navy blue "F" monogrammed in script. He ran the handkerchief across his forehead, down both cheeks, erased the beads on his upper lip and dabbed at the sides of his neck. "I must make a note to have Mrs. Stahl adjust the temperature in here."

Fleming smiled comfortably. It was no more than seventy degrees in the office.

"But what you say intrigues me," Fischer said. He dropped the soaked handkerchief in the still open drawer. "In a purely intellectual way, of course."

"Of course."

"Now if such a situation did exist, and I must stress how preposterous it is to think that the security of an entire nation could depend on a handful of moldy old papers from a scientist no one seems ever to have heard of." His voice rose. "*If* it were true, how would I—hypothetically, of course—go about such a maneuver to satisfy the security of the papers from the Russians and from pirates such as yourself?"

Fischer paused. The office was silent save for Fischer's labored breathing. The sweat glistened again on his face.

"Hypothetically, of course," Jay prompted.

Fischer looked fearfully at Jay. "Well, if I were to undertake such a task, I would require that the papers and a signed, ratified copy of the treaty be deposited with me for issuance to the proper parties at a mutually agreed upon time." Fischer's voice grew more confident as he dropped into his secure, familiar world. "I would take those valuable instruments, and deposit them in the most secure place possible."

"Like a bank vault?"

Fischer ignored the interjection. "In order to assure that nothing of the sort which you propose could occur, I would further arrange to have the instruments placed in the trust of an officer with the proviso that they could be released only if I and the other parties concerned were present, and further, that they could not be released before Friday noon."

"Let's not talk hypothetically, Mr. Fischer," Jay said threateningly. "You mentioned Friday noon. I didn't say anything about that."

Fischer drew a fresh handkerchief from the desk and mopped the flood streaming down his face. Dark stains were spreading on his shirt collar. "Of course you did," Fischer complained lamely.

"No, I didn't," Fleming countered, "and you know it." Jay stood up and leaned across the desk. "You set up the arrangements, and you can unset them. Can't you Herr Fischer?"

Fischer mopped furiously. He discarded the handkerchief and rummaged about in the drawer. "That's quite impossible," Fischer said nervously. "Those arrangements, because of the delicate nature of the—"

"Cut out the horseshit, Fischer," Jay interrupted viciously. "You made those arrangements and you can change them."

"But to do so could ruin me," Fischer whined, still searching in the drawer. "To do so would require me to break the very strict banking laws of this country and would require me to induce another to do the same. I do not have the right or authority to ask that."

"Nothing is impossible, Mr. Fischer." Jay turned toward the door. "But I assure you that when I walk out of here, I will make those telephone calls. I have a feeling that it would be healthier for you to induce that other person to violate the banking laws than it will be to face the Yugoslavians or the Russians."

"But you're not going to walk out of the door to make those calls, Mr. Fleming." Fischer's voice had grown cold. Jay looked into the dark blind eyes of an old 9mm Luger.

"Don't be a fool, Fischer," Jay said. "I've got reinforcements outside who will make the calls themselves."

Fischer looked at him doubtfully. "But if I do give you the papers, I'll have the Russians and the Yugoslavians after me anyway, don't you see?"

"I've already told you," Jay said. "The U.S. Government will pay you ten million dollars. That's more than enough to have all of the plastic surgery, to buy all of the documents you need to vanish."

"But my business, Herr Fleming," Fischer said. "You forget that I have spent a lifetime building it. I am a powerful man. Money doesn't mean everything to me. I enjoy more the power and the influence it brings. Why, you'd be surprised at what I can—"

"Your business is finished, regardless of what you do," Jay said harshly. "If you cooperate with us, you will enjoy the rest of your life, and be sure it doesn't end on Saturday."

"You forget that I hold the gun right now, Mr. Fleming."

"And you forget there are two more people outside waiting to take over if you shoot me."

"Perhaps," Fischer said as he punched a black plastic button on a small box on his desk. "Frau Stahl, *Kommen Sie hier*."

Jay stepped aside as the door opened. Mrs. Stahl stepped through and looked at the gun in her employer's hand. She smiled as she moved out of Jay's reach and said, *"Jawohl?"*

"Ich musse haben drei Herren für diese Schwein," he said.

She nodded and all but clicked her heels together as she marched from the room.

"The men are to carry you out of here," Fischer said as he trained the muzzle of the Luger on Jay's chest. "And to take care of your friends. *Auf Wiedersehen!*"

Alexandra Downing stabbed repeatedly at the elevator call button. The creaky conveyance rattled slowly upward. She searched the corridor in both directions and found no stairway. Impatience chewed at her. She was annoyed at having wasted the time sitting in Fischer's waiting room. She told herself she should be grateful at the good fortune of meeting Jay Fleming, but her impatience failed to listen to her logic.

"Come on, come on!" she muttered quietly in the still corridor. She had work to do, research to conduct. Finally a light climbed slowly past her eyes and halted as the elevator car clattered to. She opened the door, stepped in and punched the button for the lobby. Reluctantly, as if the climb had winded it, the car jerked, shuddered and noisily descended.

Bogdan Subasic caught a glimpse of the black uniform in the Volvo's rearview mirrow.

"Uh-oh."

Sweeny's hand slipped inside his suit coat.

"No," Subasic cautioned. "Be calm. Traffic cop."

"Good afternoon, gentlemen," the policeman said in French. Subasic pretended not to understand the language. "English?" the policeman inquired tentatively.

Subasic gave him a grateful tourist's smile.

"Good," the policeman said. "I speak a little of your language. I wish to inform you that your vehicle has been positioned in a prohibited zone."

Subasic looked up at him, the confused tourist. "I'm very sorry," he said with a flustered look on his face. "We were waiting for an associate who has an appointment across the street."

"Yes, I comprehend," the policeman continued politely. "But it is necessary for you to move your vehicle so that I may avoid issuing you a . . ."—he looked upward as if a dictionary were printed on the bottom of the gray clouds— "citation," he said with a relieved smile.

Subasic and Sweeny looked at each other unhappily.

"Very well, Officer," Subasic said, and then to Sweeny, "Why don't you wait for Fleming by the steps? I'll drive around the block for a parking space."

The policeman looked from one man to the other, following about half the conversation. He was relieved when one of them got out and the driver drove away.

"I'll just wait for our friend," Sweeny said. He crossed the street and took up a position next to one of the bronze lions. He waved at the policeman, who continued his rounds and quickly disappeared around the far corner.

Because of the cold, the front doors to Fischer's building were closed and Sweeny didn't hear the balky elevator rumble to a halt inside. He didn't hear Alexandra Downing's foot steps on the marble floor until she pushed through the doors and stepped outside.

She climbed down the steps quickly, deep in thought. Sweeny's bald head didn't register on her consciousness until she had reached the bottom step. Their eyes met. The terror of the Excelsior returned to her with electrifying speed.

Recognition bloomed in his eyes. Adrenaline burned inside her. She opened her mouth to scream for help when his muscular arms vised around her. She twisted, but a thick arm tightened around her waist, lifting her off her feet. Another hand clamped over her mouth, muffling her scream.

He was taking her inside to kill her. She resisted wildly. She bit into the flesh of the hand covering her mouth until she tasted blood, but it failed to break his grip. At the doors, she flailed her arms and legs, trying to kick him in his crotch, but he turned to avoid her blows.

"Please take a seat, Mr. Fleming," Fischer ordered. "It will take a little while for my associates to arrive. You might as well make your last moments comfortable."

Fischer's dark eyes followed Jay as he walked slowly toward the desk and sat in a facing chair. The muzzle of the Luger was a third eye, tracking Jay's movements. It gazed at the middle of Fleming's chest after he had seated himself.

The Smith and Wesson under Jay's arm glowed. But there was no way he could relieve the heat. He regretted his decision to leave the Kelvar vest behind. He would never make such a mistake again.

"You're taking a greak risk, Fischer," Jay said.

"Not nearly as great as letting you walk out of here."

Jay's eyes surveyed Fischer, his desk, the distance involved.

"Please don't try anything, Mr. Fleming," Fischer said. "I may be large, but I can pull this trigger before you could get halfway out of your chair. Don't force me to do that, please."

Time dragged slowly by. Fischer's labored, raspy breathing eroded Jay's nerves until he was ready to try anything to escape.

* * *

Alexandra felt the brass door handles pressing into her ribs. The bald man shoved through. The dark corridor inside yawned like the maw of death. His powerful arms could crush her neck like kindling.

Her vision had started to blur from his vise-like grip when she heard the man gasp sharply. Suddenly his grip intensified. Alexandra felt the man's hand pulling back on her neck, while the powerful arm about her waist seemed to be wringing her abdomen into knots. The pain drew galaxies of multicolored pinpoints of light before her eyes. Consciousness slipped gently away like the final moments of ebb tide.

The first step back into consciousness began when the side of her head struck the cold, unyielding granite of the landing. Then she heard a gunshot. Groggily, she struggled to a sitting position. To her left, her assailant cowered behind one of the huge ornamental bronze lions and aimed a powerful handgun at a window across the street. A splotch of blood grew on his back like a spreading disease.

She watched as the bald man raised his gun again and fired once more. The window across the street exploded.

"Die, damn you!" Obsidian cursed quietly as the glass from the bathroom window showered down on him. He had hit the man. That was clear. The woman had been dropped on the steps immediately. From the other side of the men's room, Obsidian heard the excited voices of diners, heard the legs of their chairs scrape against the floor as they rose quickly to their feet. Somewhere amid the noise he heard a glass smash and tinkle. He prayed they would all be attracted by the loud reports of the bald man's pistol.

The woman, who the hell was *she?*

Fischer's head jerked toward the window when the first gunshot cracked loudly down in the street. By the time he returned his gaze to his captive, Jay Fleming had rolled out of his chair and was huddled on his hands and knees at the base of the massive wooden desk.

Jay slipped the .357 magnum from its holster.

"Fleming?"

Jay breathed silently through his mouth. Grunts and groans. A chair squeaking. A heavy metallic thunk against wood. Jay pictured the obese man struggling to his feet. There was no way the banker could accomplish that with a gun in his hand, he hoped. There was only one way to find out.

Fleming launched himself forward, rolled over his right shoulder and sprang to his feet, the muzzle of the Smith and Wesson trained on Fischer's bloated form.

"Don't make a move, Fischer," Jay snarled. "You'd be pretty hard to miss."

Fischer looked once at the Luger on his desk blotter and then again at Jay. With an audible sigh, he collapsed into his chair. Jay stepped quickly to the desk and grabbed the gun. He slipped it into his pocket. "Call your Nazi and tell her to cancel that call."

Fischer looked at him defiantly. Jay leaned across the desk and slapped the banker with his open palm. Fischer's eyes burned for an instant. "Call her," Jay commanded. Fischer looked at him resentfully and complied.

Alexandra's head cleared. She scrambled on her hands and knees to protection behind one of the lions, then climbed behind the base on which it stood. Another shot reverberated among the buildings. She heard excited voices in the street, and then a clatter followed moments later by the sight of a large revolver skidding across the sidewalk and into the gutter where it came to rest.

Timidly, she poked her head around the edge of the stone base and saw the bald man sprawled headlong on the stairs, feet pointing upward. Crimson fled from a hole in his temple.

Someone was pounding on the men's room door.

"Just a moment," Obsidian barked in French and again in German. He quickly unscrewed the long sausage-like noise suppressor from the threaded muzzle of the H & K VP70. Through the jagged hole in the bathroom window, Obsidian watched the bald man topple onto the steps. The woman slowly emerged from behind the lion's base. Men ran up to her, peppering her with questions in a stew of languages. She snatched her attaché case from the sidewalk and ran toward the Pont Adolphe.

The insistent voice sounded outside the men's room door. "Open up!" Obsidian dropped the pistol and silencer into his soft leather briefcase. A man pushed past him and cursed loudly at the mess the bald man's bullet had left in the bathroom.

Obsidian fought through the clot of interrupted diners at the restaurant's entrance just as a Volvo made its way through the crowd. He caught a glimpse of Subasic's furious face. He'd have to deal with him later. He saw the woman vanish around the corner at the Rue Notre Dame. Obsidian turned to the right and walked slowly away as a police car screamed around the corner, going the wrong way on the one-way street.

Chapter Twenty-two

Things were growing clearer now, Jay thought. He sat gazing through the window of the Intercontinental. Beyond the glass, night seeped like ink across the clouds. He was seeing scraps of the true story here and there. But the pieces didn't add up to anything that made sense. He had worried with them for the past two hours. There was something wrong, but he couldn't make it surface. He thought through the afternoon one more time.

Shortly after Sweeny had been shot, Subasic had met Jay in the reception room of Fischer's office. Together they had forced Fischer to make the telephone calls to the Russian and Yugoslavian embassies. At gunpoint, Fischer had informed furious officials that he was reneging on his agreements with them. The banker, then, was theirs, body and soul. His only hope for staying alive was to cooperate. No Tesla papers, no $10 million or assistance in obtaining a new identity. The money, they learned, was a secondary consideration. Fischer was far wealthier than they had originally thought. Assistance in creating a new identity where neither the Soviets nor the Yugoslavians could find him had suddenly become his biggest worry.

Fischer wrote a generous severance check to Mrs. Stahl, whose imperious posture had steadily sagged through the afternoon. By the time they left she was a withered crone.

Subasic accompanied Fischer to his bank to arrange not only

213

for the release of the papers, but to have the banker's assets liquidated in preparation for his flight.

Jay closed his eyes against the approaching night beyond the hotel windows. It *still* didn't make sense. The facts were all there, but something was missing.

He looked at his watch. He had a little over an hour before meeting Alexandra Downing. He turned away from the window and walked into his bedroom. He decided to get dressed and walk down to the bar before Subasic returned. Jay didn't want to argue about disobeying orders to stay in the room.

Subasic had pulled in a favor with the CIA resident at the American embassy in Luxembourg, and had Fischer stashed in a safe house in the countryside. There had been a telephone call from there about half an hour ago. Two CIA men had arrived to relieve Subasic. He was now on his way back to the hotel. Hurriedly, Jay changed into fresh clothes, putting on the brown Kelvar vest.

He peered at himself in the bedroom mirror and ran a comb through his hair. The skin below his eyes had darkened. He looked intently into his own eyes, as if the answer to what was bothering him might be glimpsed there.

He didn't like the way Subasic had left Sweeny's body on the steps. There was such a thing as loyalty, Jay thought. And you always carried out your dead. Subasic had argued that they couldn't afford any complications. And he didn't like the way Subasic had forced the telephone calls on Fischer. It seemed unnecessary now. They had him under guard, would continue to have him under guard until they arranged for his safe disappearance. But Subasic had been insistent, almost as if he sought a brutal conclusion. He explained that the calls would guarantee that Fischer didn't double cross them when he made his arrangements with the bank for the premature release of the Tesla papers. It still nagged at Jay. Subasic seemed anxious to infuriate and embarrass the Yugoslavian and Russian governments. Things just weren't adding up the way Subasic claimed they were.

At the door of the suite, Jay Fleming slipped his hand inside his coat and withdrew the Smith and Wesson. He made sure each cylinder was full.

* * *

The bruise on her abdomen throbbed. It felt like a torn muscle. Alexandra let the hot jets of the shower play on her, wishing they could soothe her tortured nerves.

Again and again she saw the little pinpoints of colored light as she nearly blacked out; saw the determination on his face right before he grabbed her; remembered the red stream of his life as it splashed down the gray granite steps. The blood steamed moistly in the cold air, as if it were releasing spirits.

She shuddered again, then cut off the water. She dried herself quickly and set about making herself presentable.

Alexandra had replaced all her clothes, luggage and cosmetics on a frantic shopping spree that morning before visiting Fischer's office. She looked miserably at the beautiful clothes she had bought. Nothing, nothing at all, would make her feel beautiful after the events of the day, of the past two days. She pressed on dutifully. She had no idea how to gain Jay Fleming's confidence and assistance, but she was prepared to do anything, anything at all.

Chapter Twenty-three

Luxembourg,
December 20

The restaurant and bar of the Intercontinental Hotel were owned and operated separately from the hotel's management, and showed it.

Instead of plastic veneer and fake wood, there were two rooms tastefully decorated in art deco style. The first room served as a bar, the second was for dining. Jay had a hunch that in broad daylight it looked hideous. But in the muted indirect lighting, it all seemed to blend well.

The piano player, a young black man with long jointless fingers, played a Gershwin medley.

Alexandra stood in the doorway scanning the dimly lit tables for nearly a full minute before Jay connected her with the brusque businesslike woman he had bumped into twice before. Gone were the hard lawyer-like clothes. Instead, she wore a knee-length dress made of a gossamer silk-like material which seemed to float around her body like an opaque mist. From the light behind her that outlined the dress and shone through the edges of its fabric, he could tell it was the color of malachite. That was all he could tell. The backlighting blurred the details.

"Alexandra?" he called out. She saw him at once and made her way gracefully among the tables. He was standing by the time she arrived. "I didn't expect you so soon," Jay said as she arrived. And then, "You look stunning. I have to admit I feel underdressed." He took a good look at her now that she was close. She had generous lips and a smile full of bright straight teeth. Her face was tanned as were her legs and arms. She wore no jewelry other than a simple serpentine gold chain about her neck, and no makeup at all as far as he could tell. Her fingernails were unpainted, but shone nevertheless, as if she had buffed them. Her hair fell free of spray. She was singularly free of artifice. Only a woman with her high cheekbones, delicate nose and gently curving jawline could pull it off.

Alexandra smiled warmly as she sat in the chair he held for her. "I've had this old thing forever and I decided I either had to wear it or throw it away."

"Don't," Jay said as he sat down.

"Don't what?" she asked.

"Don't throw it away."

He faced the entrance to the room, and the lights from beyond fell on his face. I wonder, Alexandra thought, if he's aware that my dress is almost the same color as his eyes? No, she decided. Men were unaware of their eyes and how much women liked to look at them.

She reminded herself that she was here for business, not pleasure. And the nature of her business had a sobering effect on her mood. She contemplated asking him if she could sit facing the door.

"What would you like to drink?" Jay asked.

A triple scotch, neat, she thought. "What are you having?" she asked.

"The house red," he replied. "It's a second growth claret. Not bad, really. But if you want wine, we can order a bottle of something better."

"That would be nice," Alex replied. "Do you mind white?"

Jay said that would be fine and asked the waiter for the list. Jay selected a Graves.

It was absurd, she thought, sitting here like a normal person, after what had happened just hours ago. How could she function like this? She felt her mind operating on different levels: Alexandra the frightened woman who only wanted to hide; Alexandra the schemer, trying to enlist this man's assistance; Alexandra the avenger, carrying on a fight that had killed Martin; Alexandra the woman, intrigued more than she liked by this man called Jay Fleming.

She looked at him now, his strong jaw, his steady unwavering gaze, a look that seemed to eschew guile. His hair fell a bit carelessly across his forehead and covered the tops of his ears. She noticed his nose made a faint crooked arc to the left, as if it had once been broken.

A warm feeling swept through her, a comforting feeling. Then abruptly, she caught herself. She was here because of another man, a man hardly cold in his grave. Small faint voices argued within her. One said it was indecent for her to be attracted to another man so soon after Martin's death. Another countered that life must go on. She tried to visualize Martin's face, and couldn't.

Jay was speaking. "I've been here for half an hour or so and I had a good look at the list to pass the time. I know a little about wine and the list is filled with scores of German and Alsatian and Luxembourgoise wines. I haven't tasted most of them." His voice grew embarrassed. "I'll have to admit I picked a safe bottle of French so I wouldn't look like a fool." He smiled.

His voice soothed her jangled nerves. There was something trustworthy about him. She wondered if it was because she *wanted* to trust him, needed to trust *someone*.

"We'll just have to be reckless with the dinner wine then," she smiled. "We'll order something neither of us has heard of and drink the consequences."

The wine arrived, and after the ritual, Jay pronounced it good. Alexandra agreed, and they settled into the biographical bartering of two strangers getting to know each other, trading a bit for a bit, trying to inquire without seeming to inquire, to reveal enough to prevent the other from being cheated without revealing vulnerabilities or fears. The wine massaged and loosened the knots of tension, the strains of the piano washed around them, and the comforting familiar sounds made by other people convivially enjoying an evening drink surrounded them with emotional insulation against the day. It was as if their minds, stretched to the limits of endurance, had called a time out from their deadly game of hide and seek.

Alexandra told him her friends called her Alex, that she had been a reporter, a college professor, now lived on a boat, loved dark semi-sweet chocolate and that she was originally from Ashtabula, Ohio.

Jay told her that his friends called him Jay, that he had been a Navy fighter pilot, was now head of a corporation, lived in a small beach bungalow near Santa Monica, loved sailing, Corn Nuts and was originally from Syracuse.

She did not tell him about Martin or her former husband. He did not tell her about his first wife. They both walked around the question of why each had visited Ernst Fischer.

With all the harmless chips exchanged, they fell silent, sipping wine and noshing on the complimentary paté the waiter had brought. They had run out of safe things to say.

Finally, Jay broke the silence. "You got tired of waiting today. I didn't see you when I left Fischer's office." Had she left of her own will or had the shots frightened her? He watched as her face tightened, her lips pressed thinly against each other.

She fought the panic that welled up inside her, that warned her to flee. Her shaking hand spilled wine. Abruptly she set the glass down on the table and clasped her hands together in her lap.

Jay looked at her with alarm. Her eyes were wide. He wanted to go to her, to comfort her, but sensed she had to work through this herself. He remained seated.

"Is there something wrong?" he asked politely. "Is there anything I can get for you?"

Alexandra felt her face flush as embarrassment replaced fear. She took a deep breath and sighed, looked down at her hands, back at Jay. She sipped from her wineglass.

"There was a man killed on the steps of Fischer's building today," she said flatly, studying his face.

"I know," Jay said noncommittally. She had been carrying a gun in her attaché case. Had she killed Sweeny? Had she carried anything into the lounge large enough to conceal a gun? Small guns could be hidden. The flowing dress? Jay tried to calculate the distance between them.

"You don't seem surprised," Alex said.

If she was there to kill him, it didn't much matter what he said. If she could be trusted, again it didn't matter much. The choice was easy.

"I'm not surprised at all," Jay said flatly. Alexandra tilted her head inquiringly. Her eyes asked "why?"

"People have been trying to kill me for nearly a week now," Jay said.

Alexandra sat up straight. She gaped at him slack-jawed, her eyes bright and even in the dim light.

"You can't be serious!"

"I wish I weren't."

"The man who was killed today," she said. "The one on the steps outside Fischer's office . . ." Her voice broke. She tasted the blood from his hand, felt his sinewy arm lift her from the ground, felt him jerk as the bullet from some unknown assassin found him. She took another sip of her wine.

Jay watched her carefully. She ran her tongue nervously around her mouth, and nibbled for a moment at her lower lip before continuing. "That man on Fischer's steps tried to kill me." And then faintly, like a disbelieving echo, she said again, "He tried to kill me. And last night his friend tried to kill me, only I killed him first."

She was telling the truth. He could see it in her eyes. But how *could* it be? He ransacked his brain searching for some reason, looking for something to say to her. Somehow she was connected with the Tesla papers. Immediately his mind rejected the notion as too fantastic. Then he considered: was there a more likely place to run into someone connected with the Tesla papers than in the offices of the man who was the primary conduit for their transfer? But there was something very wrong here, he thought. There were good guys and bad guys. Subasic and Sweeny and Ante were the good guys. The Russians and Yugoslavians and Fischer were the bad guys. So what was Alexandra? Yugoslavian? Russian? He rejected the notion. If she had been either, Fischer would never have left her cooling her heels. Alexandra Downing was a wild card. A wild card that packed a hefty pistol. In his eyes that made her dangerous.

"You say this man's friend also tried to kill you," Jay began cautiously. He was admitting nothing until he knew better where she stood. "Was he the one whose picture was on the front of all the local newspapers today?"

She nodded wordlessly. Jay bobbed his head slowly as if he understood some connection.

"Why are they trying to kill you?" he asked.

Her mouth opened, and then closed quickly on some half-spoken word. Another decision had been made. "I'd like to ask you why people are trying to kill *you*," she said. "And why you were in Fischer's office. It seems—" She stopped abruptly. "Do you suppose he was waiting for you? To kill you too?"

"Yes and no," Jay began and then changed tacks. "I asked you first, why are they trying to kill you?"

Anger flashed briefly in her eyes before they grew opaque to his gaze. She looked like the sort of woman who could keep a secret, Jay thought. Hers or other people's. There would be no use in trying to pry out information she wanted to withhold. She'd tell him or not tell him in her own time. He had to trade. That was the game. But the ante had risen considerably.

"They're trying to kill me because of something I know," he offered vaguely.

"Who is trying to kill you?"

"I don't know." Jay saw a disbelieving look in her eyes. "Honestly. There were some people from the CIA in Amsterdam. The people in Leiden were also government agents." He described the attacks in Holland, leaving out Subasic. For some reason Subasic had used his men to try and kill Alexandra and he was saying nothing about the Yugoslavian until he knew more.

Alexandra said, "I believe you."

He was astounded. "I hardly believe it myself."

"The same things have been happening to me. Somehow we've been thrown together. Those people who've been trying to kill you . . . it's because of something to do with a scientist named Nikola Tesla. Correct?"

Jay nodded his assent.

"That's why they're trying to kill me too." Jay leaned his elbows on the table, partly to catch every word she said, partly because he needed to lean on something solid and real.

She took a last sip of wine. Jay refilled her glass from the bottle. Her voice was warmer, more expansive. "Several days ago, a friend, a very close friend of mine, said he was going to be killed. He was." She told him everything from the last time she saw Martin until the attack by the bald man on the steps of Fischer's office that afternoon.

Jay felt he had stumbled into a mirror image of his own story. As she spoke, his anger at Subasic grew, and with it his fear. Copeland and Guereri had been killed because they knew of the project. A violation of security, perhaps, but no reason for two covert executions. Unless, he deduced, the project was out of control. He had heard of things like that before, even in his own industry. The rumors concerned projects that somehow took on a life of their own because people or companies had grown obsessed with them.

Suppose the Tesla Project was unsanctioned, that someone had ordered it halted. That would account for Copeland's death. But that also meant that Subasic was working for the same people who had killed Copeland. And now they hunted Alexandra for the same reason.

He would have dwelled on the thought longer, would have tried to figure out what it meant had Bogdan Subasic's silhouette not filled the door to the lounge. For an instant, Jay panicked. Alexandra's narrative had planted fear in his mind. Subasic wasn't who he said he was.

"Excuse me a moment," Jay said suddenly, getting to his feet. "Don't worry," he said, calmer than he felt. He put his hand on her forearm. Her skin beneath his fingers was soft. It felt good.

Subasic recognized Jay's face and strode toward him, his eyes sparkling.

"It's just a business associate I have to see," Jay told Alexandra, then made his way toward Subasic before the agent spotted her.

"What are you doing here?" Subasic demanded. He looked at the back of Alexandra's head. Jay's heart stopped for a moment as a vague look of recognition passed over Subasic's face. Jay took his elbow and led him to the door. Subasic resisted.

"Don't call attention to us in here," Jay snapped authoritatively. "Keep your voice down." Jay steered them into a quiet niche in the lobby.

"What the hell are you doing here?" Subasic snapped. "I left you with strict orders not to leave your room."

Jay interrupted forcefully. "You keep forgetting that I am not in your army. You are not my commanding officer. I wanted to get out of the room, to have a drink. Relax. There's an exceptional piano player in there."

"Who's the girl?"

"Someone I met in the bar," Jay said.

"She might be with them."

"I might be inclined to believe you if you could tell me who 'them' is," Jay retorted. "Besides, I picked her up, not the other way around."

"I don't like it," Subasic said. "Not this close to closing things. Fischer is all set to pick things up at the bank tomorrow afternoon. It cost us a few more bucks, but he arranged it."

"So what do you need me for?" Jay inquired. "You seem to have everything sewed up nicely."

"Wrong," Subasic countered. "Someone has to go with Fischer to the bank to make sure he brings things off as planned. I can't go. If the Russians get a hint that this is a sanctioned operation of the U.S. Government . . ." He shook his head gravely. "That's why I can't be seen with him and neither can any of our intelligence agents here. You've got to go with him. You're a private citizen. The Russians will be plenty mad at you, but it's not an international crisis."

Jay stared at him intently. "Surely the bank will be watched. You'll have to be there to protect me . . . us."

"No one knew where the papers had been placed," Subasic said. "Not even old Mrs. Stahl. Only Fischer. Sure, we'll be keeping an eye on you, but from a distance. If anyone at the bank recognizes us, the stakes go up."

"I'll be ready," Jay said. "Tomorrow morning. Meanwhile, I have to make sure the young woman doesn't lose interest."

"Come on back to the room, Jay." Subasic's eyes pleaded. "You'll be safe there."

"I'm safe here," Jay countered. "Go on up. Don't wait up for me." Jay waited until Subasic headed for the elevators before entering the bar.

When he got back to the table, he found a fresh bottle of wine in the cooling bucket and two fresh glasses filled with an amber wine.

"What's this?" he asked.

"I don't know," she said. "Something from the Loire Valley. I closed my eyes and pointed at the wine list." She paused with a small smile. "Try it," she suggested, "it's really quite nice."

Jay absorbed this latest bit of information about Alexandra. She was an exceptional woman. Capable of recovering quickly, willing to take risks, cool under pressure. His admiration grew. Was she hopelessly attached to the memory of Martin Copeland? He took the glass of wine she had ordered, passed it briefly past his nose and then sniffed it. "Nice," he said. "Good fruit." He sipped, rolled the liquid about his tongue. "I like it," he said. "Well balanced, fruity—"

Alexandra laughed.

"What?"

"You sound like a commercial. Shouldn't you add something like, 'It has a zealous *savoir faire* surpassed only by its . . . its transcendental . . . oh, I don't know, something like that?"

Alexandra watched Jay's face darken.

"I'm sorry," she said quickly. "I really wasn't making fun of you."

"It's all right," Jay said good-naturedly. "I suppose I did sound kind of pompous." He laughed self-deprecatingly. Alexandra laughed along with him. They smiled deeply, genuinely at each other, and then as if on cue, both were aware of the artifice of their situation, both remembered the grave threat.

"Actually," Alexandra said, recovering part of her smile. "I ordered the new bottle because my explanation took most of the first bottle. You've got a longer story and we might as well have something to smooth things along."

Jay nodded somberly. "My whole story," he said, as much to himself as to Alexandra. "I'm not sure you're going to like everything. But here goes." He looked up at the ceiling and took a deep breath. He let it out loudly. His eyes met hers. "The two men who tried to kill you were hired to protect me." She looked like someone had slapped her. Jay put his hand on hers. "Just listen," he implored. "It may begin to make sense. Between the two of us, we might have all of the pieces of the truth to this thing. Now the man I just met . . ."

Chapter Twenty-four

The wine had made him sleepy. They had consumed a third bottle, a fine local red. It went splendidly with their tournedos and mushroom sauce. They finished with a Grand Marnier soufflé and afterward, coffee and cognac.

Jay should have felt good and he did. The dread had lifted for the evening. Perhaps, he thought now, riding alone in the elevator, the information Alexandra had given him together with Doug Denoff's arrival the next day would bring the business to some conclusion.

Jay pictured Alexandra Downing at the door to her room. Her face had lost the angularity that anxiety had chiseled on her features. They had drunk a little more than either of them were accustomed to, but not enough to grow really intoxicated. Just enough to soothe the tension.

He was still smiling when the doors slid open on the eleventh floor. He fumbled in his pocket for the room key. He remembered her eyes when he told her of the excitement he felt flying into combat. No other woman had ever understood. He had also told Alexandra about Helen, about her suicide.

"Thousands of women live with husbands who are fighter pilots," she had told him. "And they don't commit suicide. *You* were not responsible for her death and for you to think you were is just egotism."

Jay had looked at her.

"You didn't kill her. She did. She would have done it if she'd been married to a professional stamp collector."

As he walked to his room, he quietly whispered, "Thank you Alex."

Alexandra turned the deadbolt to the door of her room and attached the chain to the door. She heard Jay's strong, understanding voice as she clicked the brass latches of her attaché case. Inside lay the handgun. She held it. After moving on to the sailboat, Alexandra had purchased a .38 caliber revolver on the advice of a woman friend who had been raped aboard her own boat. Alexandra had read of large boats like hers being hijacked by drug smugglers, who killed owners and crew.

She had gone one step further. She had enrolled in a course, taught by off-duty officers of the San Diego Police Department. But this was a small cannon compared to her revolver. Alexandra tried to get used to the feel. A .44 magnum. She set the "Dirty Harry" gun on the night table and took off her shoes.

She sat at the foot of her bed, fully clothed, staring through the open drapes at the black eye of night. How had she gotten into this mess? Could she have avoided it? She had never been sure what she believed in. Life seemed full of cosmic jokes and fantastic coincidences. Had she been doomed to this nightmare the day Martin Copeland had stopped to gaze at her boat? Why her? And that never would have happened if Martin's wife hadn't left him, and if her husband hadn't died. And those— she shook her head abruptly.

She flicked off the overhead light and climbed between the sheets. They felt soft and cool and welcome. The day had lasted a thousand years, and tomorrow was not so far away. As she slipped gently to sleep, the image of Jay Fleming's face seemed to make it all worthwhile.

Inspector Guy deRoux stepped wearily through the doors of the Excelsior and into the street.

"We are becoming another New York City," he complained to Sergeant Jeantot, who had turned the ignition. DeRoux looked over at the boarded up windows of the Excelsior's restaurant and shook his head sorrowfully.

"This Yugoslavian Dvorak," he said as the car pulled away from the curb. "The poor American soldier, Goldberg. Burned alive. A man named Sweeny, another American, gunned down on the streets of the old quarter. Take me back to headquarters, Sergeant. All the witnesses should be there by now. Our artist will have a very busy night tonight."

As Sergeant Jeantot skillfully maneuvered the Renault back toward the Rue Glesener, deRoux rubbed his eyes wearily. The maid at the Excelsior, the service people at the restaurant, dozens of bystanders on the Rue Beck this afternoon—all had mentioned a woman with extraordinary blue eyes. She seemed American. By midnight, the police artist would have a composite drawing. With better luck, immigration would have a name from passport control.

"What do you make of it all, Inspector?" Jeantot inquired courteously.

DeRoux looked at him for a moment. "Two Americans killed, an American woman seen at the scene of all the murders. Drugs? I don't know." He watched the lights of the oncoming traffic. "And the Yugoslavian. Who knows where he fits in? We may be able to tell better in the morning when Interpol wires us through the information on the dead men . . . if they have any information. The American embassy is using the Americans' passports to try and gather information for us. The Yugoslavians are doing the same, although I'll admit not as cooperatively. Every innkeeper has an alert with the victims' passport numbers. They must have stayed somewhere."

"The demonstrators," Jeantot asked. "Have they been helpful?"

DeRoux sighed heavily and shook his head. "I don't think they know anything. Even the leader. He was used; they were used. They are such naive fools."

They rode in silence for a few minutes.

"Might there be a connection with the body found in the woods south of town?" Jeantot asked.

"Quite frankly I hadn't considered it. So much has happened. So much." He looked down at his hands, which were in his lap. "When we get back to headquarters, Sergeant, contact the appropriate precinct and check on that body in the woods."

Jeantot was pleased. This was developing into a big case, and it could be the one that got him promoted.

The two-way radio called. DeRoux grabbed the microphone. The dispatcher gave him the address where another body had been discovered, a minor employee at the Yugoslavian embassy.

Sergeant Jeantot drove like a man possessed through the thinning night traffic. Three blocks from the scene, they passed a distinguished looking American gentleman strolling sedately along the sidewalk. They took no notice of him.

Obsidian sprawled before the crackling fireplace, sipping cognac. He held the Baccarat crystal up to his eyes and watched the colored flames dance through it.

His escape from the restaurant had been clean. But the experience had exhausted him. A leisurely lunch at a little inn outside the city had given him time to regain his lost perspective. This was a job for the team arriving tomorrow night, not for men such as himself.

From lunch he had gone straight to his quarters. There he'd done nothing since but drink and feed logs to the hearth. This was the time to wait. It had been madness for him even to consider doing the job himself. But madness can be contagious, he thought, as Corundum and Beryl came to mind.

"To tomorrow," he said aloud and raised his snifter in a solitary toast. Then he drained the last of the cognac.

The first thing Jay Fleming noticed as he walked to his room was a rust-colored stain on the carpet. It was the size of a quarter and didn't mean much to him until he had unlocked the door, walked into the room and found more stains in varying sizes all over the carpets, furniture and to a lesser extent, on the walls.

When he recognized the stains as blood, the buzz from the wine vanished. He pulled the .357 magnum from its holster and silently pushed the door shut. No sounds came from the suite. He listened to the swoosh of traffic eleven stories below, the tick of the elevator at the end of the corridor.

Jay looked at the three closed doors leading to the three bedrooms that led off the living room. He crept to the first door, which led to his bedroom. He twisted the knob slowly, then pushed the door open. Nothing moved. No sounds. Swiftly, he sprang into the room. His clothes were spread all over. But there was no blood. Jay quickly checked the bathroom and the closets, even under the bed and behind the drapes, and then returned to the living room.

Both bedrooms were in the same state as his own. Jay inspected the blood on the carpeting in the living room. A straight-backed chair dragged from one of the bedrooms stood at its epicenter. Jay walked over to it. A white splotch on one of the legs caught his eye. On closer inspection, he saw it was a torn shred of adhesive tape. Jay scrutinized the rest of the chair and noticed several thin sticky spots. Someone had been strapped to the chair with tape. Subasic. Someone had overpowered him and tried to beat information out of him. They had also ransacked the bedrooms and then left with the intelligence agent. Was he dead? Alive? Had he told them where Fischer was?

Jay's heart sank. Fischer was due to collect the Tesla papers in less then twenty-four hours. Had the Russians or the Yugoslavians caught up with him too soon? He knelt down and touched a stain. It was still damp.

He locked the door. Then, carefully skirting the straight-backed chair and the grotesque patterns of blood, he sat down on the sofa to think. His first impulse was to flee. It was possible, even probable, that the men would return. But affairs were coming to a head. If Subasic escaped he would expect Jay to be at the hotel where he could be reached.

After what Alexandra had told him about the attempts on her life, Jay had wanted to make sure that Subasic was suitably punished. But not until all was safe with the Tesla papers. He had to save Subasic's life before he could threaten it.

He started to dial Alexandra's room, then hung up. The phone might be bugged. They might be reserving him as a backstop for information in case Subasic held out . . . or died.

He went into his bedroom and straightened up his belongings. He suddenly remembered the diamonds he had bought in Leiden for the bogus policemen. Jay located his running shoes. He inserted his fingers into the toe of one shoe and pulled out a wad of toilet paper crammed deeply inside. The two three-carat diamonds rolled into his palm. Tenderly, he rolled them back up in the paper and crammed them back in the shoe.

He decided to stay in the room overnight. He was tired. It had been a long day. His body still ached from the various batterings it had survived. His head was spinning from too much wine and the adrenaline hangover that always appeared when he was faced with a life-or-death alert. All would add up to disaster if he tried to find another place to stay tonight. Besides that's what they, whoever *they* were, would expect him to do.

He slipped the "Do Not Disturb" sign over the doorknob, then bolted and chained the door. He went into his own bedroom, locked the door and slid the dresser in front of it.

Ten minutes later, with his hand still holding the Smith and Wesson, he slipped under the gentle lapping waves of sleep.

Chapter Twenty-five

Obsidian awoke from a troubled sleep. His mouth and throat were parched. Had a noise awakened him? He lay there for a moment, his tongue stuck to the roof of his mouth. Too much cognac. He heard nothing. It must have been his thirst that had woken him. When he was fully awake, he wearily swung his legs over the side of the bed and waited for a moment before pushing up out of it and shuffling toward the bathroom. He fumbled in the dark, found a glass, fumbled some more, found the faucet. He let it run for a moment to get the tepid warmth out. He jumped at a sudden sound. It was the rush of the water foaming out of the faucet. Edgy old man, he scolded.

The water ran cold. He let the glass fill and raised it to his mouth.

Powerful hands closed around his neck. He clutched at them. The glass shattered in the sink. Obsidian twitched, kicked, twisted. He tried to strike, but his feeble fists fell on hardened muscles. He heard his larnyx cracking. He convulsed, trying to draw air. He was suffocating!

Then everything was bright. Someone had turned on the light. Obsidian beheld Beryl staring down at him.

Chapter Twenty-six

Luxembourg,
December 21

The telephone rang. Jay sprang up, the Smith and Wesson in his hand. Sheets and blanket slid to the floor. His eyes cleared as he sat for a moment. He resisted picking up the receiver. Nobody ever delivered good news at 3:30 in the morning.

The telephone rang once more and Jay reluctantly picked up the receiver and held it to his ear.

"Fleming," he said tersely, his voice sounding ominous in the silent room.

He heard raspy, labored breathing. "This is Subasic. I need to see you."

"Where are you?" Jay asked.

"I can't tell you. The telephone may be monitored. But I'll find you."

"Why don't you come back here?"

"I can't." The earpiece echoed with a wet cough. "There's no time to explain. Take down these directions."

Jay turned on the light and grabbed the cheap ballpoint pen and pad with the Intercontinental's number on it. "Ready," he said.

There was a long hesitation filled with Subasic's labored breathing. "Just off the Avenue Marie Therese, a little west of the Pont Adolphe, a walkway leads down to the valley of the Petrusse River."

"I know the one. With riding and cycling trails?"

"Correct. Walk along the path on the north bank. Don't

cross the river. I'll be concealed. I can watch you if you're followed. I'll contact you."

Jay repeated the instructions.

"Good," Subasic said. "There's not much time. And bring your gun."

Jay swiftly pulled on a pair of Levis, a T-shirt, a long-sleeved cotton shirt and a thin sweater. He buttoned the Kelvar vest over the sweater and covered that with a bulky ski sweater. He adjusted the shoulder holster to fit over the extra clothing, then covered it all with his windbreaker.

Jay tucked Subasic's directions into his pocket, slipped his feet into his running shoes and shoved the dresser away from his bedroom door. He grabbed a handful of extra cartridges for the .357, and headed out the door. Halfway to the elevator, he stopped. If something happened to him, Alexandra would be left alone.

Mindful of Subasic's admonition to hurry, Jay ran back to his room, scribbled a note for Alexandra and slipped it under her door. He felt he was penning his last will and testament.

Inspector deRoux slouched wearily in the chair facing the night manager. He was a reedy nervous man with oily black hair that kept sliding over his forehead. He squinted at the photocopy.

"No. I do not recognize her. Perhaps the day crew?"

"Perhaps," deRoux said wearily. "Keep the photo. Put it up behind the front desk."

"If I may be blunt, Inspector?"

"Certainly," deRoux responded, "nearly everybody is these days, especially with the police. But most aren't nearly as polite about it as you are."

The night manager smiled. "The picture you have shown to me. It is not a terribly professional job. It seems crudely drawn. Perhaps if you had a better likeness?"

DeRoux sighed. "We don't really have a full-time police artist," he explained. "We normally use a professor at the university. Unfortunately, he is somewhere in Switzerland, skiing." The night manager saw envy in the inspector's eyes.

"Some coffee?" the night manager offered. "We always have some going for the night staff."

"Yes," deRoux said, grateful for an excuse to linger. Perhaps, he rationalized, he might catch some sort of clue.

Deep in the back of his mind, though, he knew he was just putting off his return to the dark chill.

He and Jeantot had split up to cover more territory. Police had already visited every hotel, pension, guest house, hostel and other possible place of shelter with the same photocopy of the artist's poor rendering.

DeRoux shook his head sadly. No wonder that people were having trouble identifying anyone from the composite photograph of the woman. The eyewitnesses had trouble deciding what color hair, complexion, clothes she had been wearing. The only thing they all agreed upon was the color of her eyes.

"You should get some sleep, Inspector," the night manager counseled, handing him a steaming cup of coffee. "Milk, sugar?"

DeRoux shook his head and then sipped gingerly at the lip of the cup. He closed his eyes as he swallowed. "Excellent," he said, smiling.

The night manager smiled back gratefully.

Chapter Twenty-seven

Luxembourg,
December 21

The still night air seemed almost solid. Streetlights shone brilliantly and above them the clouds had cleared, leaving a sky lit by the blue pinpoints of stars. There was no moon.

Luxembourg, Jay thought as his footsteps gritted along in the silence, was a heavy sleeper. Nothing seemed to move save for the occasional transport truck growling through the streets. He could hear the faint rattle of railcars in the distance and the plaintive sounds of sirens. There seemed to be an abundance of sirens. Was the violence spreading?

He swung his head alertly from side to side as he made his way by foot from the Intercontinental. Over a little rise he saw the bright lights of the Boulevard Royal. It swept downhill to the Place de Bruxelles where it intersected with the Pont Adolphe and the Avenue Marie Therese. He paused for a moment and looked across the vast sheer-cliffed chasm where the Petrusse flowed.

He crossed the Boulevard Royal, then the Avenue Marie Therese. He found the entrance to the paved footpath easily.

Fleming had been careful to check for tails. He looked about him one last time before plunging into the darkness.

The path switch-backed steeply along the precipitous face of the chasm. Jay's running shoes gripped the ground securely as he made his way down, trying to avoid branches or anything else that might make noise.

Jay was scared. He pulled the .357 magnum from the

holster. Its deadly weight offered scant comfort. Where are you, Subasic? In the darkness the slopes were covered with evergreen shrubs, outcroppings of rocks, remnants of old battlements. He could be anywhere, Jay thought. And so could the people who wanted to kill him.

Rushing sounds floated up from the river and wrapped the night in dark swaddling. The closer he got, the louder the sounds. He wouldn't be able to hear any but the loudest noise. Others would have the same difficulty hearing him. But they were hunting, not trying to hide.

Jay reached the bottom of the serpentine path and stood on the banks of the Petrusse. There was little light here, but he knew from daytime visits that the environs resembled an immaculately tended park set between two sheer stone cliffs. To his left, the battlements of the old city rose above him. Across the river and beyond a flat plain some quarter of a mile wide, a matching wall ascended. A narrow tarmacadam path used in the daytime by strollers, joggers and cyclists reached in both directions. Murderers used the path by night. He heard a thud behind him and simultaneously felt something like stones pepper his right shoe.

He dived off the path into the shelter of a sycamore growing on the bank. Two more metallic thuds reached his ears, slugs smacking into the pavement of the footpath. Someone was using a silencer.

Move, Jay thought, keep moving!

He crouched and ran along the water's edge. After some twenty yards, he cautiously peered out from beside another trunk. Nothing. He made his way back to the path. He couldn't find Subasic skulking along the river.

Jay started off at a quiet jog, the soft soles making muted pats drowned by the rush of the river. Behind him he heard a soft "Phut!" A slug narrowly missed his head. He dropped to his stomach and rolled left into a clump of arbor vitae. A dark shadow moved across lighted shadows in the distance.

Fleming trained the muzzle of the .357 magnum on the shadow, lining up the sights, allowing for his target's motion. He was about to squeeze the trigger when he heard a short surprised cry. A man crumpled to the ground. Jay heard the report of a silenced weapon, then three more muted shots.

"Fleming?" A voice came from the general direction of the nearly silent shots.

"Subasic?" Jay moved quickly, the .357 aimed. There were no guarantees.

Jay heard in the reply the same painful strains of Subasic's phone call. "Up here. There's a set of steps behind you, almost covered with vines."

Jay located the steps. They had been cut into the cliff wall and looked like a natural rock formation. At the top, he found Subasic among a clump of shrubs, propped against a trunk. The air was redolent with the pungent resin of evergreens. Subasic's face was white against the darkness. His head was slumped forward on his chest. For an instant, Jay feared he was dead.

He kneeled beside the agent. "Subasic?" he whispered.

Subasic stirred like a reluctant sleeper. He opened his eyes and sat up straight, though the effort cost him. He tried to smile, but managed only a cordial grimace.

As his eyes adjusted to the darkness, Jay saw cuts, bruises and swellings covering Subasic's face.

"You need a doctor," Jay said. He stood up.

"No!" Subasic grabbed his leg with a grip that began strong but quickly became feeble. "There's no time. There is much I have to tell you."

"Tell me at the hospital." Jay said.

Convulsive wet coughs racked the man. Jay bent over and found his torso sticky with blood.

"All right," Jay said.

Subasic licked his puffy, cracked lips. "In the village of Hamm, past the church on the south side of the road at number thirty-seven is the safe house. You should be there by noon to pick up Fischer. Fischer's friend at the bank has had to rig some time-release device, and you must be at the bank at precisely 3 P.M. or there will be complications."

"Of what sort?"

"That's not important." Subasic took a noisy breath. "The men guarding Fischer have your description, but you will identify yourself as Moonstone."

"Moonstone," Jay repeated. "Who's done this to you? Do you know? Is it the same people who have been after me?"

A crooked smile, full of regret, spread across Subasic's face.

"Lunatics. Corundum, Beryl." His voice began to fade. "Their men. Thought they could divert the papers. Obsidian knew. He tried to stop them, tried to stop us so we couldn't be used by them. He's dead too. They killed him."

"What are you talking about?" Jay asked. "Who are these people?"

"Committee," Subasic said. "Committee of Seven. Must get the Tesla papers to Diamond. No one else but Diamond. He'll know what to do with them."

"Diamond? Beryl?" Jay asked. "They must have names. Who are they? Who is Diamond?" Jay gazed with horror as Subasic's eyes closed. "Bogdan? Tell me! You must tell me!"

"Go away . . . sleep," Subasic mumbled.

Jay grabbed him by the shoulders and shook him gently. It must have jarred Subasic's wounds, for he groaned and opened his eyes quickly and looked around as if he didn't remember where he was. His eyes zeroed in on Jay's face and seemed to stabilize him.

"Obsidian knew Corundum and Beryl were lunatics. Trying to get the papers for their own use. They fooled me. Want to take over the project themselves. About to destroy the important work of the committee, forty years work. Can destroy millions of people. The weather project. Key. Information will be tested at the weather project. And Delta Zeus. Obsidian knew. Tried to kill us to stop Beryl and Corundum. Knew I was too close to Corundum. I wouldn't listen. Obsidian tried to kill you in Holland and after your visit to Emerson's estate."

"Who are these people?"

"Committee of Seven. Shepherd's Club."

They had extended membership to him.

"Beryl is here," Subasic said. "His people grabbed me after I saw you. Good thing you stayed with the girl. Taped my eyes shut. Worked on me. Nazis. I slipped away."

The girl! Alexandra! "Why did your people try to kill Alexandra Downing? Her and Martin Copeland?"

"They knew about the project," Subasic said weakly, his voice slipping again. His eyes vacillated between a sharp, clear gaze and flat unseeing. "Would have exposed the operation. Too much good to be done. Must weed out Beryl and Corundum. Diamond knows. Tell him Obsidian is dead."

Subasic had closed his eyes again. His breath was fast and shallow. He was close to death. "Fire. Mistake. I took care of LeClerc. Silly bastard."

Jay shook him again gently.

"Don't," Subasic complained. "Get to Diamond. He knows what to do. Tell him everything."

"You haven't told me who Diamond is," Jay said. "I can't contact him. Who is he? Who are the members of the Committee of Seven?"

"Obsidian is dead."

"Yes," Jay said patiently. "I know. Please tell me about the others."

"Seven stones, Diamond, Corundum and Beryl were the leaders, and they betrayed him. Jade, Onyx, Topaz, Obsidian, but he's dead now. Just six. Eight original members. Your grandfather was known as Malachite."

"My grandfather? It couldn't be!" Jay exclaimed.

"Liam FitzGerald is Diamond. Get to him. He'll know what to do!"

Liam FitzGerald, the crusty old chairman of Allied Defense Industries, the personification of everything that was wrong with the defense industry. They had locked horns many times.

"Kingsley . . ." Subasic was continuing to rattle off names.

"Graham Kingsley? The presidential adviser?"

"James Rhodes. Wyatt Armstrong. Steven Strand."

"He's part of all this?" Jay hissed.

"Beryl. Strand is Beryl. His ally is Corundum." Subasic's chest was heaving desperately now.

Jay wanted to scream. *Don't die. Don't die now.* Tell me about my grandfather. About Steven Strand. About this Committee of Seven!

"Derek Clifford. Clark Hill. Dead now."

"Hill was Obsidian?"

Subasic's eyes closed.

"What about Corundum?" Jay asked. "Who is he?"

Only faint breaths issued from the intelligence agent's body.

"Who is Corundum?" Jay asked gently but Subasic failed to respond. Jay reached for his wrist and, failing to find a pulse, placed his hand on Subasic's throat. A faint pulse stirred beneath the skin.

Don't leave me like this! Don't leave me with all these questions.

"Jay . . ." the voice was faint as dried weeds rustling in a gentle breeze.

"I'm here," Jay said, leaning close. He took Subasic's battered hand in his own. Everyone dies alone, Jay thought, but another human's touch can't hurt.

"Never forget your grandfather. Don't let people forget my grandfather either."

Jay looked down at the dying man. "Who was your grandfather?"

Subasic struggled to open his eyes, finally succeeded. "Tesla," he exhaled noisily. "Nikola Tesla."

Subasic's hand fell limp in Jay's own.

Chapter Twenty-eight

*Luxembourg,
December 21*

Alexandra's voice was sleepy. "Who is it?"

A shadow passed over the viewing end of the peephole in the door.

"It's me. Jay." If Alexandra had followed his instructions, she would have the .44 magnum leveled at his waist and ready to fire. The slug would easily punch through the door, himself, the walls behind him. It probably wouldn't stop until it exited into the frigid predawn darkness.

Jay heard thumps and scrapes and rattles as Alexandra dismantled the door locks, chains and barricades.

"Come in," she said, swinging the door wide. A wan smile covered her face. Her right arm hung loosely at her side and at the end of it the .44 magnum, pointed at the floor. Alexandra quickly closed the door and relocked it.

The light from the bedside lamp cast warm shadows through the room. A glance of mutual attraction connected their eyes for an instant, but the moment passed.

"The people who tried to kill you are dead," Jay said grimly.

"Did you—?"

"No. Someone else. Sit down and I'll tell you about it."

Alexandra telephoned room service for coffee and crois-sants, and then sat down on the side of the bed on which she had been sleeping. Jay pulled an armchair with casters over to the bed and related the events of the past two hours. Alexandra listened intently, taking notes on the hotel's stationery. She interrupted only to express her concern about Jay's safety.

"They were obviously watching the hotel, hoping that I would lead them to Subasic," Jay said. "But as far as I can tell, only one person followed me to the park."

"Maybe they realize that with Subasic dead you're their only link to the safehouse and Fischer."

Jay nodded thoughtfully. "I considered that. It's the main reason I came straight here rather than going to the room. We ought to get out of here as fast as possible."

"Where can we go?" she asked. He told her about his company's offices and the apartments there.

"It's a risk," Jay said. "They'll surely be watching there. But it's a question of the least of all the evils. Besides, reinforcements should be arriving about now."

Alexandra looked at him quizzically.

"The head of security at my company is flying out today. His plane should have arrived about fifteen minutes ago. I imagine he'll be at the building before we are. He's the best there is. He'll have brought people with him. Once we get there, we're safe."

Alexandra nodded absently. "I think we—"

There was a polite knock at the door. Jay checked the peephole. Satisfied, he nodded for Alexandra to open it. She took the tray from the bellman, while Jay stood guard just behind the door, gun drawn.

They set the light breakfast on a table in the corner of the room. "You were about to make a suggestion when the food came," Jay said.

"Forgot it, I guess," she said with a shrug, then smiled disarmingly. Jay returned it.

A trio of Citröens pulled to a halt at the curb in front of ECM headquarters. Darkness was yielding grudgingly to dawn, but only enough to wash out the clarity of the evening's stars.

The engines had barely died when two men sprang from each car. A pair ran noiselessly north along the street, another pair south, scanning the alleys, the entrance ways, the arches, doorways and other possible places of concealment. The two men in the middle car calmly watched the ECM building and its neighbors.

A short cry followed by the muffled rustling of a street scuffle reached their ears.

"Come on!" Doug Denoff said as he broke into a run toward the sounds of the scuffle. The other man followed. Denoff was a fair-skinned man with sandy hair and an easy handsome smile on a face that exuded confidence and trust.

Denoff's long, lean legs carried him to the deep shadow at the mouth of an alley across from the ECM building. When he arrived, he found his two men kneeling before a prostrate man dressed in casual clothing.

"He was carrying this, Colonel." Denoff's man handed him a Colt Python .44 magnum with a massive cylindrical silencer the size of a soup can. Denoff took it and examined it under the light of a pen-sized flashlight.

"No serial number." Denoff flicked off the light and handed the revolver to the other man. "Somebody's secret service. Probably ours," he mumbled. He turned toward the street. "Bring him along and maybe we can find out where he got his toy."

"Right, Colonel," responded one of the men. Denoff had retired from the Special Forces years ago, but everyone still called him "Colonel." He didn't mind. He had earned the rank.

The other pair had turned up nothing and were waiting by the building entrance when Denoff and the others arrived with their prisoner.

As he followed his men down the stairs to the basement of ECM, Inc., where the security section was located, Denoff softly whistled the opening movement to Bach's third *Brandenburg Concerto*.

The elevator ascended languorously. The hotel had started to awaken. Guests with early travel connections stirred in the dark morning.

Jay and Alexandra looked about, their hands near their weapons, Jay's in his holster, Alexandra's in a large bag over her left shoulder.

It had taken only minutes to gather their clothes and throw them into suitcases. Jay had approached his room with his earlier caution and still found no one there. He quickly went through Subasic's effects, looking for names or other information that might prove to be helpful. But the intelligence agent had been a professional until the very end. There was nothing in his effects to indicate that he was anything more than an American tourist.

The elevator murmured to a halt at their floor and opened lazily. They stepped in and punched the button for the lobby.

The desk clerk looked at them oddly when they stopped to pay their bills while the hotel had the Volvo brought around. Jay put the desk clerk's curious behavior down to the earliness of the hour, his own strained nerves and the fact that the night shifts at even the best hotels tend to attract odd people.

"One moment, please, m'sieur." The desk clerk had returned. "We are having a momentary problem with our computer. It will take a moment to pull all the billing information for you both from our files." He smiled apologetically and shrugged in resignation.

The desk clerk's manner struck Jay as amiss, but he paid no attention when the man went into a small alcove and made a telephone call in a muffled voice.

Jay looked at his watch.

"Everybody blames it on computers," he said goodnaturedly. "But computers only do things that human beings tell them to. Behind every glitch is a human being."

Alexandra gave him a strained smile. The desk clerk had unnerved her. He had glanced at something behind the counter and then at her, several times, as if comparing her to a picture. She felt he had recognized her.

A uniformed bellman gave the Volvo's keys to Jay. "It's just outside the front door, sir," the man said in English. Jay tipped him and returned his attention to the desk clerk. It seemed to be taking an inordinate amount of time to prepare their bill.

In the distance, a siren sounded faintly. Jay no longer heard the clerk's voice. "What gives?"

He strode angrily to the door leading to a rear area. He failed to see the clerk. He lifted the hinged portion of the counter and stepped behind it. "I don't believe this," Jay said loudly as he walked out of the alcove. Then he froze. In front of him, taped to the back of the counter, was a poor drawing of Alexandra's face. He went quickly to it and ripped the page off the counter.

"What's the matter?" Alexandra said, her face wide with alarm.

Jay stared at the picture a second longer. A wanted notice was printed in German, French and English below the drawing. He thrust the paper at her and hurried out from behind the counter. He heard more than one siren now and they were growing louder.

"Come on!" He grabbed all their luggage and ran for the Volvo.

The man behind the wheel coaxed the delivery van through the winding lanes of the old city, a task made difficult by the unusually heavy load.

The man heard sirens. He was concerned. He had a criminal record, and although his errand didn't seem illegal, he knew it must be. Otherwise why would they have paid him so much. The sirens passed, headed for other parts of the city.

Relieved, the driver turned first one corner and then another, stopping every couple of streets to check the map and make sure he was not lost. He located the correct street and slowly searched in the dim light of early morning. He found the right numbers, attached to a solid old gray-stone with three Citröens parked in front.

As instructed, he pulled to a halt directly in front of the building and carried out a large tray filled with day-old pastries and rolls.

The engine in the van was still running when the man walked across the street with his tray of bread and disappeared into the entrance hall of an apartment building. Inside, he quickly set the tray aside and ran down the steps to the basement.

A whisper reached out of the dark. The man stopped and smiled.

"Did you bring the other half?" the man asked the darkness, for he could not see the person who had spoken to him.

"Yes," the voice said. "I have brought you your payment."

The man eagerly stepped forth. A well-honed razor slit him open from his testicles to his heart. He died with the dawn stillborn in his eyes.

Chapter Twenty-nine

Luxembourg,
December 21

Jay saw the flashing police lights in his rearview mirror as he drove into the morning traffic.

"The manager's just run out," Alexandra said. She was kneeling on the front seat facing backward. "He's pointing at us. Both of the police cars have pulled out behind us."

"Hold on," Jay said grimly as he pressed the accelerator to the floor. They had only two places to go: the ECM offices or the safe house. Jay didn't want to lead the police to the safe house, and he hoped against hope that Denoff would have a good idea how to shake the police, at least until after the Tesla papers were recovered.

Morning traffic was still light, and the police were gaining. There was no way to outrun them, not on the wide straight main roads. Without slowing down, Jay wrenched the wheel to the right; the Volvo careened off the Boulevard Konrad Adenauer and into the nearly empty parking lot of the European Investment Bank.

"They're still coming," Alexandra said.

Jay followed the signs to the Nieder Grunewald, a heavily forested park across the Alzette River gorge, on the opposite side of the old city from where Subasic's body probably still lay. The road narrowed as they approached the Rue des Trois Glands.

The Volvo's superior road handling began to tell on the

difficult roads. Soon, the police were out of sight, even on the relatively short straightaways.

The Volvo hurtled downhill toward the railroad arches that ran parallel to the river. As soon as they entered the tunnel-like passage, Jay stood on the brakes. The street ended just ahead of them at the Rue Vauban. The Volvo's rear wheels screamed. Jay felt the rear end of the car sliding. He eased up on the brakes to gain traction, but the hemisphere of light at the other end of the tunnel was growing large faster, as were the cars crossing at the Rue Vauban.

Alternately locking and unlocking the brakes, Jay brought the Volvo to a sideways sliding stop at the bottom of the hill. In the distance, police sirens wailed. The hazardous drive had bought them only a few seconds so far.

Ignoring the stoplight and an angry clash of horns, Jay pulled into northbound traffic, crossed the Rue du Pont, took a left and guided the Volvo up a cobbled street that seemed glued to the face of the cliff.

The nearest police car shot out of the tunnel like a projectile and barreled into the rear of a long stake-bed truck loaded with potatoes. The impact sheared off the rear gate of the truck and unleashed a wave of potatoes that swept down the street like a lumpy brown surf.

"Oh, my God!" Alexandra exclaimed. The second police car skidded into the sea of brown. The car spun once and came to rest against its companion. Alexandra began to laugh.

"Are you cracking up?" Jay asked seriously.

"I know I shouldn't be laughing, but—" She broke up again. She tried to explain what had happened.

A faint smile smoothed some of the tension from Jay's face. He halted the Volvo at a stop sign at the Boulevard Jean Uleveling.

"Roll down your window," he said. "Hear that?" More sirens. "Where are they coming from?"

Alexandra tilted her head and then shook it. "I can't tell."

"No matter," Jay said as he accelerated and turned right, bringing them to the Cote d'Eich. He turned left. The ECM offices were just seconds away.

* * *

"Dumb bastard!" Denoff cursed as he glared at the man they had picked up in the alley. "We'll get the information if we have to kill you!"

The man had resisted telling them anything. He was bleeding from cuts on his face.

"I don't *want* to get nasty with you," Denoff said genuinely. "But I will if you don't cooperate."

Denoff walked over to the narrow half window that looked out of the basement and across the sidewalk. He whistled the flute part of a Purcell concerto as he looked outside, hoping another tactic would come to him before he had to start destroying the man's mind. This was the part he hated most.

"How long's that bread truck been out there?" he barked harshly.

Denoff's men looked at each other. One of them rushed to the window to look. The prisoner smiled.

"Hurry!" Denoff ordered. "Upstairs." And without waiting he mounted the steps three by three.

The squad car picked up the Volvo a block before the turn for Jay's office.

Jay stole a glance at Alexandra sitting stolidly watching the walls of the narrow street rush by like the sides of a tunnel past a train window. His admiration grew. She had *laughed!* He wanted to stay alive so he could find out more about this woman.

The Volvo's steering pulsated beneath his grip, sure-footed even on cobblestones and medieval paving blocks. Accelerate, brake, avoid that delivery truck, accelerate, brake. The police had not gained on them, but were only seconds behind and enjoyed the advantage of two-way radio. At every corner, Jay expected to see another squad car cutting off their advance.

A delivery van pulled out of an alley. Alexandra's shoulder slammed into the door as Jay swerved. The car lurched as its left wheels jumped the curb. Their seat belts kept them mostly in place. Jay maneuvered all four wheels back onto the street, and barreled on down the road.

Jay took the final corner like a base runner sliding home. A van was parked in front of his building. The unmistakable figure of Doug Denoff stood in the street, waving wildly. Men were running in and out of adjacent buildings. Residents across the way watched curiously.

The Volvo roared down the street, followed seconds later by screaming sirens. The squad car took the corner too quickly and crashed into a long line of parked cars. The two officers were unhurt and exited quickly, sidearms drawn.

"Get out of here!" Doug Denoff was yelling. "Go! Hurry!"

Jay skidded to a halt and started to get out when Denoff rushed to the door and slammed it shut before Jay could get out. "Get the hell out of here!"

"But—"

"Don't ask questions. Your life is in danger. Get out of here!"

Jay floored the accelerator.

"Who was that?" Alexandra asked.

"Doug Denoff," he replied.

"Oh."

"Where are the cops?" he asked.

"In front of the bread truck."

Denoff turned his attention to the delivery van. It had been parked on the street far too long.

"The door's locked, Colonel," a beefy red-haired man reported to Denoff.

"You know what this looks like, don't you?" Denoff said anxiously.

"Yes, sir," the man said. "A Lebanese special. I saw a dozen of 'em when I served there."

"Can you see inside?"

"Negative. Windows are taped over with newspapers."

"Has to be a timed device," Denoff said. "Or else they would have triggered it when Fleming was here. The offices must be the target rather than people."

Denoff swiped at his chin. "The ECM offices are empty except for the security staff. Tell them to lock up and come down and help us. Then call the local cops." He looked over at the two officers milling around in a daze. "No, call the Army, although I don't know what good they can be. And then get the bullhorns. We've got to get people out of the neighborhood. If that damn bread truck is full of explosives, it'll level the whole block."

The beefy man ran for the building entrance. He never made it.

Jay had reached the next corner and was trying to figure out where they could go when the rosy hues of early morning turned to a hideous orange that lighted the sky like the interior of a bonfire. A split second later the shockwave hit them, lifted the Volvo up on its nose and tossed it through the plate glass of a small butcher shop.

The last thing Alexandra thought about before she lost consciousness was a picture of a hotel in Beirut that terrorists had blasted to pieces with a bomb planted in a van parked outside of it.

Chapter Thirty

Hamm, Luxembourg,
December 21

"How's your head?" Jay asked solicitously. Alexandra stared up at him from the sofa where she had lain since their arrival at the safe house in the tiny village of Hamm just outside Luxembourg city.

"The aspirin helps."

"I believe they've got something stronger if you want it."

"I want a clear head this afternoon."

He bent over and tenderly examined the swelling on the side of her head. The skin had not been broken, but had turned a deep plum color.

"Have it your way." He smiled and kissed her cheek.

"That was nice," she said, taking his hand. "Let's have another. Purely medicinal, you know."

She looked now at the way his eyes glinted in the sunlight that spilled into the little cottage's living room. She would never forget the emotion that had played through those eyes after the explosion. There was concern, for her and for the people injured in the blast. There had been sorrow after he had returned from the scene. Nothing in the immediate vicinity of the truck had survived. There had been anger and a determination to set things right.

Alexandra watched his back as Jay conferred with Fischer and the two agents guarding him. Something was troubling him, but he couldn't yet put his finger on it.

Alexandra pushed herself into a sitting position. She closed her eyes against the pain. She stood up and made her way toward the bathroom.

She glanced through the drapes that covered the front windows. An empty space stood in front where Jay had parked the car he had stolen to get them out of the city. One of the agents must have helped him dispose of it; no, both agents, she remembered now. Jay refused to leave her. The two agents had been forced to leave him in charge of her and Fischer.

The morning newspapers were scattered on the bathroom floor and made crinkling noises when she walked over them. She looked down at a crude semblance of her face, the same one Jay had taken from behind the desk at the hotel.

They were blaming her for the murder of the man at the Excelsior who had tried to kill her and for Sweeny, who had attacked her outside Fischer's office. Fischer had disappeared and they were blaming her for his possible kidnapping. Jay and the two agents had agreed that someone had been feeding information to the police. The papers had published details the police could not otherwise know.

Jay blamed it on Steven Strand, but she wondered how much of that was fact and how much stemmed from Jay's resentment. Whoever was to blame, they were even suggesting that she had something to do with the death of Lee Goldberg.

"Comrade Belenko, consider yourself under arrest. The charge is treason."

Pasha Belenko turned slowly from his desk to face the man who had burst suddenly and unannounced into his office, General Uri Davidovich, Belenko's superior. Davidovich's arrival wasn't entirely a surprise. Pasha had his own system of informants. Davidovich had, however, arrived sooner than expected.

"Good afternoon, Comrade Davidovich," Belenko said courteously.

"There is no need for you to pack, Belenko," said Davidovich. "We have transport waiting at the airport. Your belongings will be packed for you and forwarded." Davidovich froze when he noticed the battered Nagant 7.62mm revolver in Belenko's hand.

"Please close the door and have a seat, General," Belenko

said, training the pistol on the general's belly. "This will only take a moment."

Davidovich looked tentatively at Belenko, and at the sanctuary beyond the open door.

"Don't try it," Belenko said evenly. "I'd have three slugs in you before you reached the door. You ought to know that. You reviewed my pistol qualification scores." He smiled.

Davidovich pushed the door closed and moved to the straight-backed chair across from Belenko's desk.

"No, this one," Belenko said, indicating with the muzzle of the revolver another chair beside the desk. Reluctantly, Davidovich complied.

The general's huge body overwhelmed the narrow seat. Davidovich wore the dress uniform of the KGB, complete with medals and service ribbons. He was well over six-four, weighing nearly two hundred and seventy pounds. He had a ruddy complexion and heavy gray eyebrows that matched his hair, still thick at age fifty-five. Black eyes burned furiously in his square face.

"Where did you get that relic?" Davidovich referred to the Nagant.

"It was my grandfather's," Belenko said. "I have kept it as a memento." It had first been used by the Tsarist armies.

"A rather dangerous memento."

"I have cared for it well. My grandfather killed White Russians with this gun. My father used it to kill Nazis in World War II. I have used it to execute traitors."

"And you intend to kill a Communist with it, is that the special meaning it has for you now?"

Belenko looked at him through pale watery eyes that seemed diluted by misfortune. "Yes," he began. "I am going to kill a good Communist and a loyal Russian. But first, let me tell you that I am aware of what you have come to tell me, General. By not reporting my contact with the American, I have jeopardized—"

"Ruined."

"I have completely ruined a special and highly secret diplomatic mission which would have helped our relations with Yugoslavia. I have destroyed the fragile trust that, after long struggle, we managed to develop with the Yugoslavians. In a generation they will never come this close to trusting us. Is that what you had come to tell me? And for that I must suffer, and my family? My children?"

"No, Pasha," Davidovich began soothingly. "You have made a mistake. A big mistake, yes. But the arrest is only a formality, to satisfy the higher-ups who are crying for blood. Haven't I been your friend for these many years? Haven't I always supported you? After the furor dies down, the charges will be quietly dropped and you will be reassigned. Your wife, your family will not suffer."

It all sounded so good, so comforting, Belenko thought. But he had told comforting lies before. A man whose life is threatened will say anything to save it. No, Davidovich had nothing of the sort planned for him. It would be a gulag . . . if he was lucky and not sentenced to a firing squad. And his daughter . . . that was what hurt most. She would be ostracized. No more special schools.

"Tell me, General," Pasha continued, disregarding Davidovich's appeal. "What was so important about those papers?"

"Let me answer that with another question," Davidovich said, grateful for the conversation. The longer they talked, the longer he stayed alive and the more likely Belenko was to make a mistake. "What would be the advantage of our disabling every computer in the West?"

Belenko looked at Davidovich as if the man had posed a riddle. He decided to play the game. "Everything in the West depends on computers: the banks, the telephone system, all their weapons systems. They'd be helpless. They've counted on the use of high-technology computers to make up for their lack of numbers against us. Without computers, they would be at our mercy."

"Correct." Davidovich smiled for an instant, then his face twisted into an ugly mask of rage and frustration. "And those papers would have given us that capability. The weapon that could be built from those papers . . . the weapon that could be perfected from the discoveries in those papers . . . would have allowed us to overload and destroy every circuit in every silicon chip in the West. We could have plunged the West back into a pre-electrical age if you had not . . . had not—" The general's face twisted and twitched, swollen with apoplectic rage. Arteries bulged on his neck like thick fluid ropes.

"Calm down, General, before you have a stroke," Belenko said, using the pistol for emphasis.

"Calm down?" Davidovich said in a voice climbing toward hysteria. "You have stolen our greatest chance to crush the West and you ask me to calm down?"

"Yes," Belenko said flatly. His sources had already told him what Davidovich had just confirmed. Belenko had already suffered from the rage of his own hand, had already stared blearily through his sleepless nights, had already lived through a hundred possible lifetimes in a hundred different ways.

"You should remain calm at times like this, General," Belenko said, his voice soft with a dreamy quality that made the general fear genuinely for his life. It was the dreaminess of a man capable of anything. "The training manual tells us to remain calm, to retain our facility for thought and logic, that the battle is not lost until the final second has passed."

Belenko raised the revolver and closed his left eye in order to sight down the barrel.

Davidovich trembled as he watched Belenko line up the revolver's sights. A small corner of the general's mind registered the wet warmth that spread from his groin and pooled in the seat of his pants.

Then Pasha Belenko plunged the barrel of the revolver in his own mouth and pulled the trigger.

Chapter Thirty-one

Luxembourg,
December 21

The ride in from Hamm had been uneventful. They had arrived in a midnight-blue stretch Mercedes limo the CIA had hired from God knew where. The driver managed to find a spot in front of the bank. Two police cars passed, but neither challenged the expensive limo or the occupants who sat unseen behind the tinted glass. Fischer and one agent sat in front. Jay and Alexandra sat next to each other, facing the second agent, who occupied the jump seat. No one spoke. Everyone looked frequently at his watch.

Fischer had shed his sullen demeanor and had begun to enjoy being center stage, joking with the two guards. He still refused to speak to Jay unless absolutely necessary. He would never forget his humiliation at Fleming's hands. Otherwise, the banker seemed to be looking forward to his new life. He had chosen Costa Rica as his destination. The two men from the CIA assured him it was a fine place for anonymity.

"About time." Jay's voice broke the uneasy silence. All glanced automatically at their watches. Fischer nodded. The agent on the jump seat nodded. The chauffeur jumped out and opened the doors for Fischer and Fleming.

The sun beat down warmly. Jay took off his overcoat and handed it to the agent. Jay scanned the street, looking, he hoped, like a man enjoying an unusually warm winter day.

"Come on, come on," Fischer said curtly, "we haven't got

all day. Someone may recognize us." He started up the steps. Jay hurried after him.

Fischer pushed through the heavy glass door and stepped into a dark foyer with a single desk where a uniformed guard sat. Like many private banks in Europe, this one required an appointment. The guard recognized Fischer immediately.

"Good afternoon, Herr Fischer," he said in faultless German. "Herr Neudorf is expecting you." He pressed a button under the desk and the inner door buzzed open. Fischer pushed confidently through. Jay followed him closely. Behind them, the door clicked securely shut.

Neudorf greeted Fischer effusively, one thief to another. Neudorf glanced at Jay, but when Fischer failed to make any introductions, paid him no attention.

Jay stood in one corner of the lavishly furnished office and watched the transactions. At 3 P.M. one of Neudorf's assistants summoned him to the door. There was some malfunction with the timer device on the vault door leading to the bank's trust section. Would he please come and take a look?

Moments later, Neudorf returned with a brown expandable file tied with cord. He proffered the file to Fischer, but Jay stepped up quickly and took the bundle from him instead.

"Sorry, gentlemen," Jay said. "But this belongs to me." Fischer and Neudorf both glared at him, but neither made a move to recover the file. Jay took the bundle to a table in the corner of the office and untied the cord. He carefully removed the contents while Neudorf and Fischer concluded their business. Fischer paid Neudorf his bribe, then took possession of the results of the hurried liquidation of all his assets. The bank had even purchased Fischer's office building and home.

Jay quickly shuffled through the documents he had received from Neudorf. He expected photocopies, but the file contained the originals, most too faded for reproduction. It was possible, Jay knew, that the Yugoslavs had taken care to have special photographic duplicates made. Even so, he knew there would be unreadable areas.

Jay closed out the avaricious dealings between the two bankers as he examined the writings of a remarkable man. Tesla's mind had a grasp of many different disciplines, although most of his fame came from his electrical research. It was said he could actually visualize machines and circuits and inventions working before his very eyes, that he spent hours sketching and describing what had materialized full blown in his brain.

As Jay examined the papers, it grew increasingly clear to him why so many people had been killed to get them. The weapon Tesla described in his drawings and narratives was disarmingly simple, eminently workable. It was frightening. The possessor of the knowledge contained in the documents could irrevocably alter the balance of power in the world. And while it was not the doomsday weapon so many scientists were searching for, its power, in conjunction with a military force shielded against its effects, would be irresistible. And now he had to decide what to do with it.

Neudorf's office was hot and oppressive. He felt the air sitting palpably on his shoulders, moving sluggishly into his lungs. His first inclination was to destroy the documents. But his respect for learning rebelled. He wondered how long it would take before he reached a decision.

The responsibility empowered him, yet bound him as well. The discovery could make him rich. ECM, Inc. had the resources to develop the weapon. But what use did he have for more money? He already had more than he could spend.

He thought about building the weapon and giving it to the United States. But he wondered if cool minds could prevail. The temptation to use the weapon might be impossible to resist.

Subasic's warnings came to him. And what of the massive project described in the documents Martin Copeland had sent to Lee Goldberg? It was plain that someone—the Committee of Seven? Liam FitzGerald? The Shepherd's Club?—had already built most of the weapon, had even tested it in limited ways. The New York Blackout, communications disruptions, the blackouts in Hawaii, power outages, computer failures . . . the list was endless. Was it possible that all were caused not by natural acts or equipment failures, but by the testing of an electromagnetic pulse weapon?

Jay's reverie was interrupted by Fischer's rude hand on his shoulder.

"If you're quite ready," he said. "We can leave now."

Jay hurriedly assembled the documents and replaced them in the file.

Fischer walked somberly out of the bank, holding the calfskin briefcase that now contained his entire financial portfolio, his life. Fischer walked as if the weight of his future was pressing down on him. There was no way he could know that the shabby brown file Jay Fleming carried was far more valuable than a hundred of his own briefcases.

When the outer doors closed behind them, Jay felt as if he had just stepped from a prison. The sunlight lifted his spirits. Perhaps he would find a way to handle the responsibility the papers had placed on his shoulders.

Fischer hurried across the street. Jay followed closely. The driver opened the door for them both.

"Run, Jay!" Alexandra screamed before a hand muffled her voice.

"Inside," the driver said. Jay felt the muzzle of a gun jammed into his ribs. Suddenly, Fleming heard the *sput!* of a silenced weapon, and a short cry of pain from Fischer. The fat man crumpled.

"In, asshole!" the driver shouted as he shoved a knee into Jay's kidney and battered him into the rear of the limo and slammed the door. Jay's face scarcely hit the floor when the limo rocketed away from the curb.

Jay pushed up quickly and earned a blow on the back of the head.

"Slowly, Mr. Fleming," a familiar voice said. "Or we may have to hurt you or the girl."

Slowly, as directed, Jay pushed up and found himself staring into the barrel of a large caliber handgun. That fact didn't hit him as hard as the recognition of the man holding the gun. It was Steven Strand.

Chapter Thirty-two

Luxembourg,
December 31

The Mercedes made its way gracefully into the snarled traffic of the old town. Jay's head spun unsteadily from the blow Strand had dealt him with the gun barrel; it took all his concentration to struggle to his hands and knees. He felt cool hands on his head and shoulders. Alexandra.

"We always seem to cross paths," Strand said evenly. "Please don't try anything rash," he warned. "If you do, Ms. Downing will get hurt. And I'm afraid you'll have to watch. Sit up on the seat with the rest of us."

The agent still sat on the jump seat, holding an automatic pistol. Strand sat by the door with Alexandra next to him.

Jay wobbled on his arms, then collapsed. Alexandra gave a cry.

"Hold it!" Strand ordered her back in her seat. "Let Mr. Fleming help himself. I've listened to his sanctimonious statements about how the arms industry is a bloated monster incapable of standing on its own feet. About its inefficient bureaucracies propped up by government subsidies. 'Welfare for the rich,' I believe he calls it. Isn't that right, Fleming?" He looked down at Jay's inert form. When Jay failed to respond, Strand poked at his head with the sharp toe of a hand-tailored Italian loafer.

"Don't!" Alexandra protested. She knelt beside Jay. She bent low and examined the cut on his head.

When he was sure Alexandra's head and hair obscured

Strand's view of his face, Jay winked at her. She was startled, but managed—she hoped—to hide her surprise.

"You may have injured him seriously," she said when she straightened up and reclaimed her seat.

They sat silently for several minutes as the limo pushed through the traffic.

"I'm going to be leaving you soon," Strand said to Jay's sprawled form. "I am sorry I hit you so hard. I wanted to tell you to your face what a help you've been. In fact, we couldn't have done it without you." He turned his glance to Alexandra. "And to you, dear."

"You will be delivered to the police station in a few minutes," Strand continued. "Fischer's murder will be added to your rap sheet. There are six bodies in Amsterdam, all former CIA operatives. Four have Fleming's fingerprints on some piece of their property. The Dutch police have already been alerted to the locations of the bodies. I imagine they will be calling the police in Luxembourg pretty quickly. Bogdan Subasic reported things fully to my ally on the committee.

"Add up all these various murders, kidnapping, larceny and other charges and I imagine that the two of you will be put away for life." Strand smiled triumphantly. "You can be thankful there is no death penalty in Europe.

"Most importantly," he continued, "the deaths all point to you as renegade thieves who soured the transaction between the Russians and Yugoslavians. The finger points *away* from the United States government or the committee.

"We can't afford to upset international relations. The entire affair will be blamed on a berserk private citizen and his—what shall we call you? His mistress?—who wanted the papers in order to make a profit."

"You can't expect to get away with it," Alexandra said, her voice filled with uncertainty. "We'll testify in court. We'll tell them the true story, we'll tell them about you."

"You just do that, and watch them laugh. Do you honestly think they would believe either of you? You're connected to nearly a dozen murders. You kidnapped poor Mr. Fischer—Frau Stahl will testify to that—and took millions from him. Of course the police will find his briefcase in the car when they catch you. There's more, but I hardly need to go into it. Do you expect them to believe some lunatic story about scientific papers and the Committee of Seven and a secret weapon that wipes out computer chips and electrical circuits?"

He paused for a moment. "Yes, perhaps I'd prefer to see you do that. They *would* think you were insane." He looked down at Jay. "I wouldn't mind the world remembering him as someone who had lost his marbles. He's caused me a great deal of trouble and exasperation. Nearly ruined my own reputation. He's been a thorn in the side of the rest of us in the military industry."

Freed of the thrombosis in the old city, the limo picked up speed.

"You seem to have planned things very well," Alexandra said. "Do you like playing God?"

Strand smiled at her as though she were a naive child.

"Sometimes. Anyone would, but few get the opportunity. To spare lives"—he looked down at Jay—"or to end them if necessary. He was out of his league." Strand's voice carried the notes of remembrance of things not entirely pleasant. "He should never have tangled with me."

"It must take a lot of thought and planning to be God," said Alexandra.

"Primarily good information and the ability to think swiftly and creatively. You maneuvered yourself into all this. I'm just taking advantage of your presence. You lend such éclat to the whole affair."

"But you set up Jay and this Subasic from the beginning?"

Strand nodded. "They are finally playing out the roles I had written for them months ago. The destiny I created for them. Of course there was the matter of the interference of that fool, Hill."

"The one called Obsidian?"

"Very good," Strand said with cynical enthusiasm. "You have a marvelous memory for a woman." The agent sitting on the jump seat chuckled.

"But even Obsidian played a supporting role in the end. I just had to intercept him and write his lines for him."

Alexandra opened her mouth, then shut it quickly, not trusting her own tongue. There had to be a way out of this, but it wasn't going to help things for her to lose her temper. She tried to think of something appropriate to say, but all that entered her head were verbal broadsides. She was not going to give him the satisfaction of seeing her upset.

The limo stopped in a small wooded area.

"I'm sorry to have to leave you, but the next act must begin," Strand said as a uniformed chauffeur opened his door. Through the opened door, Alexandra caught sight of a burnished silver Rolls Royce, its rear door open to welcome the godplayer. Strand handed the brown expandable file to the chauffeur.

"I want no slip ups," Strand said first to the agent in the jump seat and then to the driver. First inform the police, then let them out in the Place de la Gare. It'll make it easier for them to arrest them. The stations are already intensely watched, but it won't hurt to give the police a little extra notice. Dump him on a bench if you must."

Without another word, Strand turned on his heel and disappeared inside the waiting Rolls.

The limo quickly carried Jay and Alexandra down the Avenue John F. Kennedy and sped past the buildings of the European Economic Community.

Time was slipping away quickly. They would arrive at the train station in minutes. The agent in the rear had the muzzle of his gun trained downward on Jay's inert body. He obviously didn't consider Alexandra a threat. Women weren't credible threats to men like him.

Alexandra looked at the agent and then at Jay. "I want to make sure he's still breathing."

"Sure, go ahead," the agent said.

She knelt on the floor of the limo and bent over Jay's body. Electricity seemed to run over the surface of her skin as she summoned her resolve. Now! Her body failed to obey. The gun was pointed down, she knew that. It would do neither of them any good for her to get killed immediately.

Slowly, she pushed away from Jay, this time close to the agent. Close enough so that he had to deflect the gun's barrel to let her up. Intelligence, Strand said, and the ability to think swiftly and creatively. There was no better time than now, she thought.

Alexandra launched herself at the agent, her left shoulder slamming into his gun hand, sending the muzzle upward. In the confined space, the report of the pistol sounded like the rending of the heavens. The slug embedded harmlessly in the ceiling of the limo.

He was a strong man, and he began to shove her away. Before he had a chance to shed her, Alexandra plunged her fist into his groin, once, twice, again, finding the soft semi-firmness of his testicles. The agent screamed, firing two shots wildly.

Jay catapulted up from his prone position and slammed his knee into the side of the agent's face. He felt the bones yield beneath his kneecap. Alexandra grabbed the pistol from the agent's limp hand and trained it on the driver, who suddenly stood on the brakes, slamming her and Jay back. The limo skidded amid the protest of horns.

The limo recovered its equilibrium and surged forward, throwing Jay and Alexandra in a heap on the floor. Then suddenly there was the *basso continuo* of a truck's air horn and the crack of impact as a transport sideswiped the limo, sending it in drunken pirouettes across the roadway.

A wail like a siren reached Jays's ears and then abruptly ceased as the limo came to a grinding halt. It took Jay a moment before he realized the cry of terror came from the driver. Jay struggled to his feet.

"Don't move, don't move!" the driver shrieked, his words engraved in hysteria. The limo teetered and rocked as Jay slowly sat up. The reason for the driver's fright quickly became apparent.

The impact with the truck had sent the limo spinning toward the railings of the Pont Grande Duchesse Charlottee which spanned the hundred-and-seventy-foot-deep gorge over the Alzette River. The limo hung diagonally on the metal-and-stone bridge railing, its front end mostly over the edge. The weight of the engine was dragging it steadily closer to a final plunge.

"Just hang on a moment," Jay said to calm the driver. "We'll move toward the side and balance things out a little better." Slowly he and Alexandra moved to the door. He carefully opened the door. The car seemed to stabilize momentarily.

"Come on," Jay urged the driver. "Climb over the seat. The closer you get to this side, the steadier things will get." The man's face looked like a cadaver's, drained of blood and waiting for the embalming fluid. He seemed frozen to his seat. The limo lurched suddenly.

"Come on now," Jay commanded. "Otherwise we're getting out, and that'll send it over."

Galvanized into action, the agent scrambled eagerly over the seat.

The door was open, and through it, Jay saw people running toward the limo.

"We'll have to jump together," Jay said, "Otherwise the limo might go over too fast. Ready? He looked around. The agent's head seemed to be searching for something. "Something wrong?" Jay asked.

"The briefcase. Fischer's briefcase," the agent said. "It's worth tens of millions."

"Forget it," Jay said. "Pick it up at the bottom."

The agent looked dubiously at Jay and then at the briefcase which lay on the floor in the front seat. He started toward it. The limo groaned like a wounded elephant and pitched violently. Jay shoved Alexandra out the open door and lunged after her. In a roar of metal against metal, the limo slid clumsily off the edge of the bridge. Three seconds later, the sounds of a horrendous smashing of metal reached their ears.

Refusing all offers of assistance, Jay and Alexandra ran from the bridge, the sounds of the agent's scream echoing in their ears.

Chapter Thirty-three

Los Angeles,
January 1

Thank God for KLM, Jay thought as the 747 banked gracefully and then leveled off for its final approach into Los Angeles International Airport. Jay checked his watch. They would be touching down almost within a minute of the scheduled time. He stretched his legs and pushed back against his chair, calling stiff muscles to life. Alexandra stirred next to him, her head pressed sleepily against his shoulder. His eyes were soft and reflective.

The past two weeks had been hard on her. But she had adapted. She turned her anger at being falsely accused into a storm of energy that sustained them when their spirits had begun to flag.

Following the accident on the bridge, they had hurried back into the old town and flagged a taxi to Len Hartkemeier's office. He had been expecting them.

"Word carries fast in Luxembourg," he told them, hustling them out of his office and into his Citröen. After recovering their luggage from the safe house in Hamm, Hartkemeier drove them to a small house he kept as a retreat in the Belgian countryside just across the border from Luxembourg.

Money can buy just about anything, even between Christmas and New Year's Day, as long as you know where to look for it. Hartkemeier did. While Jay and Alexandra hid in the tiny cottage and fed the fireplace hourly, Hartkemeier arranged a visit from a discreet makeup artist from the Antwerp underworld who professionally cut Jay and Alexandra's hair in totally new styles. He turned them both into blondes, right down to their eyebrows and pubic hair. "You can never be too sure," he cautioned. "Some *flic* might decide to strip you and then where would you be?"

Hartkemeier then purchased new identities for both of them, including genuine Swedish passports representing them as a married couple, Lars and Inga Andersen.

"They were expensive," Hartkemeier explained. "New ones always are. Forged or stolen ones can get you killed. Only genuine ones are safe." He wouldn't tell how he had managed to arrange for genuine Swedish passports. Trade secrets, he joked. "If I told you, you wouldn't need me the next time you get into trouble."

The police moved quickly to freeze Jay's corporate and personal bank accounts, but Hartkemeier readily loaned the substantial amounts needed for the passports and the new identities from his own pocket. He refused to take the diamonds Jay offered in exchange.

"You will need them more than I. I trust you. Pay me back when you get out of this."

The landing gear thudded into position. The 747 decelerated and nosed downward. Alexandra stirred.

"We're here?" she said groggily.

"We've been *here* all the time," Jay replied playfully.

"You know what I mean," Alexandra said as she sat up in her seat and looked at him. Her face bore the sleep-creases of his corduroy coat. She brushed a strand of blond hair away from her eyes. "We're finally in LA?"

"Finally in LA." Alexandra gazed out the window as the tiny geometric patterns outlined by the rust of sodium vapor street lights, became houses and businesses and streets lined with palm trees. They passed low over the brightly lit oval of Hollywood Park and caught a brief glimpse of the horses rounding the first turn. Then the 747 plunged on downward, over the stretch of hotels on the Sepulveda Boulevard.

It eased onto the runway, decelerating with the reverse thrust of its four powerful engines.

Alexandra took Jay's hand in both of hers and squeezed hard. Her hands were damp.

"I guess it begins again," she said, peering into his face.

"Yeah."

"It was nice these last fifteen hours," she said, her eyes unfocused.

Jay agreed. "I wish we could just circle up here forever, just you and me."

Alexandra smiled warmly at him. Her lips brushed warmly against his.

"You don't mean that," she said seriously. "People who spend their lives in safe, boring holding patterns are just circling around waiting to die anyway. Life is for living, not for hoarding. We're all going to die sooner or later."

"I'd rather it be later than sooner." He kissed her again. This time their lips lingered and drew a curtain around them that excluded the rest of the world. It was a feeling that had grown quickly during their anxious sojourn in Hartkemeier's Belgian cottage.

They had begun the stay as allies of convenience, two people thrown together who could survive better together than separately, each bringing assets into the alliance. They had approached each other tentatively, wary of exposing weaknesses to the other. But as they passed the long hours in the cottage, talking, planning, trying to invent a scenario for the future, it became apparent that they were not two people thrown together by chance. They were together because of who they were. Had they been two other people, they would not have lived long enough to meet, would never have placed themselves in the situations that had forced them together. The barriers dissolved and they were propelled across vast emotional continents in the past week, sharing an intimacy created by the realization that the next hour, the next fifteen minutes, could be their last ones.

And somewhere in that week and a half of soul searching, a new love found a patch of warmth and light, cleared amid the emotional ruins of the past, and grew. It was a new beginning for both of them, made more precious by the prospect of death.

The tromping of feet echoed through the corridor as the 747's passengers eagerly headed to immigration, and from there to customs to retrieve their luggage. Jay and Alexandra flowed along with the stream of passengers from their flight, trying to remain unobtrusive, not knowing what they'd do if they were spotted.

The crowd soon slowed as other flights disgorged their passengers into the central passport control area. Hanging on to each other, Jay and Alexandra maneuvered toward the lanes for people not holding American passports. Inwardly, Jay smiled. It had been his idea to return on this particular night. He had counted on immigration and customs to be jammed to overcapacity, especially at Los Angeles International Airport— probably the least efficient airport in the world.

Now, as he scanned the crowd through the clear lenses of his horn-rimmed glasses, he saw no one but harried immigration officials, and beyond them, hassled and anxious passengers scurrying to retrieve their luggage. A security agent trying to spot them on this night would have better luck identifying a particular bee swarming from a disturbed hive.

The going was slow, though customs inspectors were rushing people through as quickly as possible. They made a minimum of searches, casting cursory glances at people and their proffered declarations. It took nearly an hour and a half, but Jay and Alexandra found themselves standing on the curb searching for a taxi by 9 P.M.

A long but orderly line waited for those cabs that managed to squeeze through the glacial ice floes of traffic.

To pass the time, Jay left Alexandra in the line and jogged into the terminal to buy the Sunday *New York Times*.

News about Alexandra and himself had faded from the front page, but reporters, like policemen, hadn't forgotten them, merely put them on backburners as more recent disasters competed for attention.

There was a story in the obituary section about Obsidian's funeral. The *Times* called him a "principal architect of post-detente diplomacy" and "a pioneer in developing an American defense strategy that extended beyond mutual deterrence doctrines."

A butcher shop owner who died in Luxembourg as the result of injuries sustained in the December 21 explosion in the old quarter brought the toll to one hundred and twenty three.

Companion stories from Holland and from Interpol head-quarters in Paris reported no further progress in locating Jay Fleming and Alexandra Downing. Jay wished he could believe what he read.

They had managed to read most of the *Times*, including the magazine, book review and the rest of the obituaries by the time a taxi was available. The driver delivered them to a gaudy, tastelessly decorated but astonishingly expensive hotel in Century City just before midnight. They checked into a room, waited for an hour and then sneaked back down to the lobby and took another cab to Anaheim, where they checked into the Disneyland Hotel overlooking the Magic Kingdom. They registered as Mr. and Mrs. Lars Andersen of Stockholm, and then fell into a deep sleep, arms wrapped around each other.

The stars shone like reflections in a cut crystal bowl. It was one of those evenings, washed by the winter rains, when the Southern California sky ran to infinity.

Steven Strand paused at the balustrade overlooking the Pacific Ocean and gazed across at the feline softness of Catalina Island, hunched under the full moon. From his home perched on top of the bluffs of the Palos Verdes Peninsula, Strand's panorama encompassed the shoreline from Malibu to Laguna Beach. He was the largest landholder on this wealthy chunk of real estate. His grounds, including the riding trails and stables, encompassed more than fifty acres. The roof of his red-tiled Spanish mission home covered more than an acre on its own.

From more than four hundred feet below came the boom of surf crashing against the base of the cliffs. The waves reminded Strand of his enemies. He was the land, they were the waves. Perhaps in a million years, they might tire him. But one by one they hurled themselves at him, dying to displace a grain of sand. He thought of Jay Fleming. Not even a grain of sand.

Strand picked out the lights of Avalon at the east end of the island, and then the cluster of lights at the isthmus farther west. Without benefit of glasses or binoculars, he picked out the warning lights on Ship Rock.

West of the Isthmus, high in the hills above Emerald Bay, a group of bluish lights wavered. The Shepherd's Club encampment. By tomorrow night, most of the members would have arrived—by launch, helicopter or limousine.

The media had a field day with the Shepherd's Club encampment every year. Commentators wrote that it was suspicious that so many powerful men gathered in secrecy so often. Despite club pronouncements that the activities were strictly non-business, media sages bemoaned that such a perfect forum decided to conduct the public's business in private.

A scattering of dusty and scraggly protestors carrying signs decrying everything from nuclear power plants to harvesting of whales always clogged the only road in and out of the encampment each year.

They were all correct: the media, the anti-bomb, anti-reactor, pro-marijuana, feminist, what-have-yous. The Shepherd's Club was every bit as dangerous as they said and then some. It *was* a marvelous way to conduct the public's business without the meddling and interference of the public or the media or protestors or any of those other ignorant people who somehow felt that wisdom and judgment can be found in a majority vote.

Strand shook his head sadly. How had they let it happen? How had they let the country slip into rule by public opinion poll? He let his eyes focus beyond Catalina, beyond the space in which he stood and the time in which he breathed. There had been leaders. There had been great leaders, even into the first couple of decades of this century. But somewhere the great leveler of populism eroded leadership, obscured wisdom, shackled the hands that knew how to conduct the public's business. That would change soon. That would change very soon.

He turned away from the midnight vista and walked down two flights of stairs that led to a glass-enclosed room overlooking the ocean. He passed the casual patio furniture, walked to the rear of the room and inserted a key into a heavy oak door.

It swung ponderously open. Strand locked it behind him and descended the cast-iron spiral stairs that led into the bowels of the cliffs. He felt the temperature drop. At the small room at the bottom of the stairs, the temperature stayed a constant sixty-two degrees all year round.

He flicked on the light, illuminating a circular room some thirty feet in diameter and twenty-five feet high. Stone walls vaulted to a point in the ceiling. A round table with one chair before it occupied the center of the room. The walls of the room were covered with iron racks on which rested thousands of bottles of wine. It looked like the interior of some subterranean beehive with bottles resting in the comb instead of honey. A ladder with wheels at the bottom rested on a metal rail which ran completely around the room.

Reverently, Strand walked to a small chest next to the table and pulled from it a starched linen tablecloth. Like a priest before mass, he covered the table with the white cloth and reached back into the chest and withdrew a single wineglass and a sterling silver corkscrew which he placed on the table in front of the single chair.

Like a man in a trance, Strand swept his gaze along row after row of bottles. He knew them by heart as other men knew old friends. He passed over the section in the racks painted olive-green. Those were the wines he served to his dinner guests. They were world-class wines the likes of which even connoisseurs rarely tasted more than once in a lifetime. But they weren't his prizes.

Good wines, in Strand's estimation, was not meant to be drunk as the background to a lot of idle chatter or as the canvas to some business deal. The very best wines, he believed, were meant to be drunk alone, in absolute silence. He even showered before he came to drink. It removed the last traces of cologne or other aromatic contaminants.

After nearly a quarter hour of what some hidden observer might have likened to meditation, Strand stirred. He moved the ladder halfway around the room and stopped it next to a section painted a deep claret-red. He climbed the ladder and near the top dusted off a label. A smile crossed his face. His memory hadn't failed him. He located the precise bottle he desired on the first try.

Lovingly, he brought the bottle to the table and placed it in the center, gazing at it for a long moment. A 1929 Chateau Leoville-Poyferre. He felt his mouth fill with anticipation.

As carefully as an acolyte, he trimmed the foil from the top of the bottle and screwed in the corkscrew. The cork deftly slipped from the neck with a wet pop. Immediately his nose caught the scent of the cabernet grapes. He glanced briefly at the cork, and poured an ounce of wine in his glass.

His eyes fixed on the fine garnet color, his nose on the positively sweet-ripe bouquet. The rich taste and lovely finish lingered in his throat like the memory of first love. For a fleeting instant, he pitied those less fortunate than himself. For an instant. No more.

Chapter Thirty-four

Daryl Barnes couldn't understand the information he was getting. It seemed to make no sense at all. He turned on the printer for a readout. The daisy wheel whirred into position, and began to clack, turning the green letters on the computer screen into black-and-white copy.

Barnes leaned back in the wobbly dinette chair with its rusty chrome tubular legs and brightly colored plastic upholstery. Stuffing was leaking from a gash in the backrest of the chair. The gash had been there when Barnes bought the chair, its three companions and the plastic-topped dinette table that matched them all. He cared little for the furnishings, but they provided a place for him to position his computer equipment with a little space left over to place the cardboard boxes of carry-out food from Humongeous Burger which he ate every night except for Fridays when he brought home the all-white-meat special from Charlie's Lickin' Chicken.

Rummaging in the grease-darkened box, Barnes retrieved a handful of cold french fries and gnawed on them absently. Twenty-four years of fast foods and doing nothing more strenuous than carrying a new disk drive down the steps to his apartment had hung 175 pounds on his five foot-six inch frame.

He was what his friends called a "hacker." He had built the computer system before him from components purchased at various surplus sales, flea markets and Radio Shack stores.

Rensselaer Polytechnic Institute had given Barnes a degree,

but just barely. He had spent his four years there ignoring his classes as much as possible while he and his friends built new computers, designed software and tinkered with bytes and RAMs and ROMs. There had been a girl in that group he had dated twice but they stopped seeing each other when she complained that he didn't bathe often enough. It was just as well. The dates drained off money better spent on equipment.

Thanks to his penetration of the data banks of the Lawrence Livermore Nuclear Weapons Lab, he had been offered a lucrative position with the Defense Department designing security codes for their computers. That had turned into an even more lucrative position with the General Accounting Office, the investigating agency which gathered information for members of Congress. He had no longer lacked money for computer equipment.

He looked proudly at the hard disk drive that sat beside the table. It had come from an old IBM 360/60 system that had been sold for scrap following a minor electrical fire. The acrylic cover glowed softly green in the darkness of the room.

The glowing phosphor of the screen was the kitchen's only illumination and the letters danced off the thick lenses of his glasses, which kept slipping down his nose. He had tacked heavy black felt over all the windows to cut down glare.

The printer zipped out one last line, then dutifully plunked to a halt, ready for the next command. Barnes turned on the small gooseneck lamp over the printer with its 25-watt bulb. He tore off the perforated paper and spread it on top of the Charlie's Lickin' Chicken boxes that crowded one end of the table. A grease spot from a french fry formed on the middle of the statistics page. Barnes wiped his fingers on his blue-and-brown Banlon shirt.

The information was puzzling. Although prohibited from surreptitious entry into other data banks on the GAO computers, Barnes regularly used his own computer system—which he considered superior to the GAO's anyway—to browse around in the computer storage facilities of oil companies, defense contractors, banks, chemical companies and others. When he found something interesting, he usually managed to confirm it through legitimate sources. It had made him a star at the agency.

The paper before him was the result of a summary program

he frequently used to analyze data from several corporations. He found that eleven defense contractors involved in the Navy's ELF program had been using funds to buy equipment for radio broadcast stations in more than a score of countries, many of them Third World enemies of the United States.

Barnes had been working on the ELF program, also known as Project Sanguine, for more than a month now. The Navy was trying to develop a system to use Extra Low Frequency (ELF) radio waves to communicate with submerged nuclear ballistic missile submarines. Barnes shoved his glasses back on his nose and continued to study the data.

The problem with communicating with submerged submarines is the inability of radio waves to penetrate seawater. In order to pick up communications, submarines must ascend near the surface, trailing behind a long wire. They then become vulnerable to enemy spy planes which can better locate and track them, thus eliminating one strategic advantage of submarines—their invisibility.

ELF radio waves, on the other hand, will pass through sea water, but only if they are broadcast from a proper antenna. In the case of Project ELF or Sanguine, the Navy selected a particular geological formation found in the upper peninsula of Michigan and in Canada. The rock formation formed a perfect antenna which could broadcast the ELF radio waves all over the world's oceans.

The earth, Barnes had found out in the course of his research, was a spinning conductor of electricity. But its rock formations had confounded scientists trying to harness its electrical properties for their own use. Even that weird old inventor Nikola Tesla had experimented with the long-range transmission of electrical energy through the earth. Despite his relatively unsophisticated equipment, he had succeeded to an extent that was only being approached half a century later. In the case of Project Sanguine, however, the particular geological formation involved communicated directly with the oceans in such a way that a minimum of energy was lost.

In pursuit of their project, the Navy was digging thousands of miles of trenches, crisscrossing Michigan's upper peninsula. The idea was to bury cables that would broadcast radio waves. Scientists had expressed concern about possible health hazards from high intensity doses of ELF radio waves. Citizens, too, were unhappy about the Navy's plans; so were Congressmen and Senators. That was where the GAO and Barnes got involved.

The program he had written had scanned the equipment purchases, shipments, invoices and requisitions of the companies involved with Project Sanguine and found that they had all been shipping ELF broadcasting equipment all over the world: Angola, Nicaragua, Malaysia, South Africa, Finland, Sri Lanka, the Canary Islands, Brazil, Pakistan, Australia.

There seemed to be no pattern to the distribution. The globe was fairly evenly covered. Barnes examined the printout for another fifteen minutes, then waddled over to the refrigerator and pulled out a can of Coke. He drank thirstily.

Beyond the felt covering Daryl Barnes' kitchen windows stood a man in a three-piece suit, looking up at the numbers on the buildings, comparing them to something scribbled on the back of a business card. He was a tall, lean man in his late twenties with the earnest look you see on thousands of young men who come to the nation's capital to help guide its course.

Daryl was stumped. He didn't like to admit failure, but sometimes it stared you in the face. He grabbed a handful of ketchup- and mustard-stained Humongeous Burger wrappers that nearly hid the black push-button phone and tossed them on the linoleum floor. Picking up the handpiece, he punched a number with a 213 area code.

The GAO had a regional office in Los Angeles, primarily to keep an eye on the massive concentration of defense contractors in Southern California. And like the main office, they employed a number of specialists, including a computer expert like Daryl Barnes.

It was just after 5 A.M. in Los Angeles. Barnes listened to the phone ring, trying to imagine Robert Sansome sitting in front of his computer screen irritatedly turning away to answer the telephone. He did after six rings.

"Hello." Sansome sounded annoyed.

"This is Daryl Barnes in Washington."

"Well, good morning," Sansome said, the irritation turning to pleasure. Sansome swept a pile of Taco Bell wrappers from his plastic-topped kitchen table onto the terra-cotta–tiled floor of his condo in Northridge. He placed the telephone in the newly made space and sat down beside it. "What's up?"

Barnes described his data and his confusion.

"Well, let me go into the spare bedroom and get Arnold ready for you."

Arnold was what Sansome called his Kaypro 10 microcomputer. It annoyed Daryl when people gave names to inanimate objects. But, he supposed, Southern California *was* different.

"Okay, I'm here again," Sansome said, picking up the extension. "Get the old modems hooked up and transmit when you're ready." Barnes heard Sansome's telephone click and snap into the modem.

A knock sounded at Barnes's front door as he inserted his telephone receiver into its modem.

"Just a minute!" he called. Barnes's fingers flew over his keyboard as he instructed his computer to transmit the data concerning the ELF radio equipment to Sansome in Northridge.

The knock came louder and more insistently. Barnes listened to the disk drive whir as it searched for the right information and then began transmitting. Only then did he get up from his chair to answer the door. When he opened it, he found himself looking up at a tall, well-dressed man.

"Mr. Barnes?" he asked, flashing a small wallet containing his FBI identification and badge. Barnes nodded. "Mr. Daryl Barnes?"

"Uh, yes," Barnes said with difficulty over the constriction in his throat. Had they somehow found out about his unauthorized entry into the data banks? The telephone calls to his grandmother charged to Bank of America?

"May I come in?" the agent said politely as he replaced his identification and badge in an inside coat pocket.

"Of—of course," Barnes stammered and stood aside to let the agent in and closed the door behind him. What would they do? He wondered. Would it be like the last time? Would they offer him a better job? Was the FBI going to offer him a job hunting for computer theft? Or did they want to prosecute him? Maybe they just want him to pay back the toll charges to B of A.

Daryl Barnes's mind was racing so wildly he didn't notice the small coil of fine wire the agent had taken from his overcoat pocket. He did look with curiosity as the agent slipped two steel pencils through tiny welded loops at either end of the wire.

As the agent grasped one steel pencil in each hand and stretched the wire to a high pitched twang, a tremor of fear raced down Barnes's spine.

"What can I do for you?" Barnes tried to disguise the tremolo in his voice. "What's that?" he asked, referring to the wire.

"A garrote," the agent said with a smile. Suddenly he moved behind Barnes with the speed and grace of a puma. Barnes felt the wire constrict around his throat. He opened his mouth to scream, but only the faintest of choking sounds reached his ears as the piano wire sliced into the collar of fat surrounding his windpipe.

A tongue covered with the brassy saliva of fear worked feverishly at his lips and at the roof of his mouth as Barnes clutched at the wire and the man's hands. The muscles in the man's forearms felt like an iron railing. A chugging sound filled the room, and Barnes realized after an instant it was the desperate noise made as he tried to breathe through his nose. He had a head cold.

A gray blizzard blew into the room, growing darker and darker. Barnes's arms fell heavily to his sides, felt his knees buckle. Mercifully, he did not feel the piano wire as the agent jerked it taut, slicing cleanly through Barnes's windpipe and severing his spinal cord.

The agent eased Barnes's plump form to the floor and removed the two steel pencils from the loops in the garrote. He placed the pencils carefully back in the leather case which he carried in a pocket inside his coat. He slid the garrote from Barnes's nearly severed head, wiping away with a Kleenex the droplets of warm red blood that clung to it. Satisfied it wouldn't leave a stain on his coat, he returned the wire to his inside pocket. The agent then dropped the Kleenex in the growing puddle of blood by Barnes's body and walked into the kitchen.

He immediately noticed the telephone and modem. He walked over and pulled the receiver out of the modem and hung it up. The computer screen blinked its luminous green eye at the interruption.

"Termination?" the computer screen asked.

The agent smiled as he took a large heavy object from his overcoat pocket. It had a long electrical cord which he plugged into the wall socket. When he sat the heavy object on the top of the disk drive, the computer screen twitched and then filled with a convulsion of letters and characters.

The agent counted off three minutes with his watch, unplugged the powerful bulk magnetic eraser, wrapped the cord around it and stuck it back in his pocket.

As he stepped over the body, the agent looked down. Barnes's eyes were still open. The agent closed the door quietly behind him and stood for a moment watching the threadbare beginnings of a snow shower drifting from the gray clouds. He took a deep breath. It was a good day to be alive, he thought, as he stepped up to the sidewalk and made his way back to his office.

Chapter Thirty-five

The snow on the San Gabriel Mountains was white and fresh and looked like some strange ice cream confection just beyond the balcony. Winter's windy brooms had banished the smutty brown smog. Jay slid open the glass door, stepped out on the balcony and took a deep breath. It was amazing. Even Anaheim looked good today.

Down in the vast asphalt prairie between the hotel and the Magic Kingdom, the cars had started to arrive. He watched a white station wagon with some sort of fake brown wood pull slowly between two parallel white lines. Seconds later, the door flew open and five children and two adults spilled into the morning. Jay heard screams of delight as the children tore off in different directions, then the exasperated voices of mother and father mustering them back into order. The children followed their parents in a straggling line, like a brood of quail.

Jay peeked through the door into the adjoining room. Alexandra lay curled up in the dark, still asleep. He closed the door and turned on the television in his room, the volume barely audible.

Game shows, re-runs of "Gilligan's Island" and a talk show featuring a former anorexic woman touting her book, *The Sexy Oyster Diet*, were all he found. No news. Restlessly he returned to the table where he had been sitting and looked at the sheets of hotel stationery he had taken notes on. He had broken the puzzle into three main parts: the Tesla weapon itself, the Committee of Seven and Steven Strand. The trick was to figure out how they all fit together and how to stop them.

From Martin Copeland's papers, and from the brief glance at the contents of the Tesla papers he had examined in Luxembourg, it was easy to deduce that the weapon was an electromagnetic pulse weapon designed to destroy electrical circuits.

Formerly, electromagnetic pulses powerful enough to generate these effects could be produced only by nuclear weapons, or so common wisdom suggested. But Tesla, writing his theories nearly twenty years before the first successful atomic chain reaction, suggested that a way could be found to unleash the billions of volts in the upper atmosphere in what he described as a death ray, a transcendentally powerful lightning bolt.

The researchers at Colonel Copeland's place of employment, the InterGovernmental Weather Research Center, had determined that the effect was not one of a death ray or a lightning bolt, but an intense pulse of electromagnetic energy even more powerful than those produced by a nuclear blast. Using more of Tesla's writings, the researchers found that certain frequencies of Extra Low Frequency radio waves beamed into the upper atmosphere released the electromagnetic pulses.

Jay leaned back in the chair and plucked a memo out of the pile in which he had placed all of the technical documents relating to the weapons. He smiled as he read what was obviously a scientist's attempt to explain the phenomenon to a layman. The memo was addressed to one General Jerry Patterson.

"The upper atmosphere can be viewed as a giant balloon filled with electricity" [the memo began.] "The electricity is constantly being resupplied by new particles from the sun. The trick is to find a low energy way to poke a pinhole in that balloon so that the electricity can spurt out, directed, of course, at the targets of our selection. To date, ELF radio waves have served very well for this purpose. You are familiar, of course, with the famous New York Blackout of November 1965. This was our first full power test of the ELF triggering system. We were not aiming at New York. We learned that the insertion of ELF waves into one part of the upper atmosphere can result in an unpredictable release of an electromagnetic pulse in some entirely different region.

"Since then, we have applied extensive computer analysis to thousands of tests at lower power, using satellites and balloons from the Weather Service and other civilian and military agencies to measure the effects. There seems to be some kind of harmonic effect at work. The ELF waves are like a stone dropped into a pond. They start the ionosphere vibrating, the waves spread out from the point of contact with the ELF waves, and, depending on other disturbances, may or may not result in an electromagnetic pulse. The pulses seem to happen where the waves in the ionosphere come in contact with some other phenomenon. It's like one of those waves in the pond, generated by a stone, as it slaps up against a piling and splashes it. More work is needed."

The memo was unsigned. But was dated July 2 of the year before.

It was obvious that the scientists had built a weapon which they couldn't aim. But if Jay's memory served him correctly, several pages of equations in the Tesla papers he had examined in Luxembourg dealt with aiming the weapon. If that was correct, the scientists were on the verge of perfecting their EMP weapon, a device that could turn back the clock of civilization eighty years.

That the government might try to develop such a weapon would not be surprising. Even the involvement of the Inter-Governmental Weather Research Center would not have raised Jay's eyebrows. But the fact that it was being coordinated by the Committee of Seven, the steering committee for the Shepherd's Club, was more than strange. It seemed like treason to Jay. That and the fact that they had killed or tried to kill a dozen or so people to keep it secret added up to one of the greak unknowns of the puzzle. Why had the Committee of Seven developed the weapon by itself?

Fleming had no problem understanding how they had kept the project secret even from the vast majority of the people who worked on it. The national defense classification system was so fouled up and segmented, it would provide no trouble to someone of moderate sophistication. But how had they paid for it? The development must have cost billions. You could fool the government with its own classification system, but you couldn't fool your major stockholders. An expenditure that large demanded a profit, or the stockholders demanded new managment.

Jay picked up the ballpoint pen with "Disneyland Hotel" embossed on it and wrote, "What are they going to use the weapon for? Against whom? When?" Those seemed like the most pressing questions. Also the hardest to ascertain.

Finally, there was Strand. A member of the Committee of Seven, the man who had taken the Tesla papers, the man present when Martin Copeland made his fatal revelation to General Patterson, a man who hated Jay Fleming with an abiding passion.

"You're frowning." Jay looked up, startled. Alexandra stood before him, wearing a large baggy sweatshirt—his. She gave a short gentle laugh. "You should see yourself," she said, padding softly over to him in her bare feet. "You look just like a little boy caught with his hands in his mother's purse." She stood behind him and placed her hands on his shoulders, gave them a loving squeeze, and kissed his cheek.

"You're going to kill me before Strand does if you keep sneaking up on me like that," Jay said.

Alexandra pulled the other chair out from the table and sat in it, modestly pulling the hem of the sweatshirt over her thighs. "I've never seen someone get lost so deeply in thought," she said. "I must have been standing there for ten minutes before I said anything to you."

"Why didn't you say 'good morning' or something?"

"Because I was having fun watching you." Never before had she taken pleasure in just looking at a man. There was much to learn about him. The surface was pleasing, but what lay beneath interested her more. The depth was gratifying. Even more significantly, his understanding for her made Alexandra cherish him. When she had told him that first time that she wanted to sleep with him but not yet make love, he had not objected, had seemed almost relieved. They needed, wanted the intimacy of holding each other, comforting each other, awakening in the soft new light of morning to gaze on each other's face peacefully composed, like a promise of the future. But what neither needed was rushed, frantic lovemaking. Both had to exorcise ghosts from the past.

This lack of desperation lent an equilibrium to their relationship that stabilized their turbulent days. It also left them with a promise for the future.

"How long have you been up?" Alexandra asked to break the silence.

"Since a little after seven."

"Made any progress?"

Jay gazed at her thoughtfully. He hadn't really considered that question.

"A little," he responded. "I've managed to bring a little order to things. The organization helps me consider possible answers."

Alexandra nodded. "Why don't you tell me about it over breakfast."

As if on cue, Jay's stomach growled hungrily. They both laughed as Jay got up and walked to the telephone to dial room service. Smiles, laughter, the shared companionship that drew two human beings into that imperfect mortal union—those were the things that really counted in life, Jay thought. Not even bullets could erase those.

Chapter Thirty-six

"Are they still there, Randall?" Daniel G. Fraser, Rear Admiral, U.S. Navy (Retired) called from his teak-paneled study. The study was in the rear of a modest three-bedroom stucco house which sat atop the hills of San Pedro with a panoramic view of Los Angeles and Long Beach harbors. Fraser gazed down and watched a container ship making its way slowly out of Wilmington Channel. His life had always been the sea and would be until the day he died.

An invisible observer looking into Fraser's study at that moment would have seen a man who looked at least twenty years younger than his eighty-five years. His clear piercing blue eyes stared out at the world from a face fissured from experience rather than age. His hooked nose gave him the air of some wise bird of prey. His hair was white and thinning, cut short in the military fashion. Dark age spots were beginning to appear on the backs of his hands.

But despite the age, Fraser was unbowed. He stood erect, his bearing unmistakeably military. An old warhorse, that's how he thought of himself. An old warhorse waiting for the final battle. It would come. It was coming now, he told himself. He could feel it deep inside. A dim frown of regret deepened the wrinkles of his face as he realized that this final battle probably would be fought on land, not on sea.

Behind him, the walls of Fraser's study were covered with photographs of himself with President Roosevelt, President

Truman, and President Eisenhower. In fact there were pictures of Fraser and every President up to and including the bastard who had let his enemies run him out of the Navy. And then there were pictures of Fraser shaking hands with Churchill, DeGaulle, Willy Brandt, just about every leader of every western nation between 1945 and 1980.

And what wall space wasn't devoted to pictures of Fraser and the famous was mostly papered with pictures of Fraser's children: the Nautilus, the world's first nuclear-powered submarine; the Forrestal, the world's first nuclear-powered aircraft carrier; the Long Beach, the first nuclear-powered cruiser. And around them, the succeeding generations of nuclear-powered naval vessels, Trident submarines, Nimitz class carriers. Daniel G. Fraser was the crusty, feisty abrasive father of the nuclear navy.

He had conceived a vast navy able to steam around the world again and again without refueling, submarines that could remain underwater for months at a time. Some thought him crazy, but he circumvented, neutralized or bulldozed them. He made enemies, but he got things done. Every Congress and every President since Kennedy had signed special orders allowing him to remain in uniform long past retirement age. His face was an annual fixture in appropriations hearings, his acerbic condemnation of those who would weaken his—*his, by God!*—nuclear navy echoed from the marbled and paneled committee rooms of Capitol Hill.

And every year, he got what he wanted: more carriers, more submarines, bigger carriers, bigger submarines.

But finally he made one enemy too many. He started to criticize the waste of the nation's defense contractors. As a prominent member of the military industrial complex, he violated the cardinal rule: thou shalt not speak ill of thy brothers.

Fraser lobbied Congress to regulate defense spending, and a whispering campaign against him began. When Fraser released documents proving that defense contractors habitually overcharged the government, sometimes by as much as one hundred percent, a lobbying campaign to get rid of him began in earnest.

Led by members of the Shepherd's Club—which had already dropped him as a member twenty years before—the military industrial complex mounted an elaborate smokescreen to soften his influence, redoubling efforts to boot him out of the Navy and out of their hair. They finally succeeded, and without so much as a thanks, Congress and the President failed to grant him the waiver to remain in the Navy.

The tanker passed the Chevron tank farm, making its way through a flurry of pleasure boats swarming like gnats around the vast tanker.

"Yes, sir," Randall LeBlanc replied to Fraser's question after a long moment. "The one in the tan Ford is still parked by the corner. I don't see the other one. Do you want me to go look?"

"Silly fools," Fraser mumbled as he turned from the window.

"I'm sorry, sir," LeBlanc said, walking into the room. "I didn't hear you. Do you want me to go take a better look?"

"No," Fraser said, looking at the younger man. "That will not be necessary. I imagine they'll take their time explaining their sudden interest."

"Very good, sir." It had taken five years for LeBlanc to stop saluting the Admiral. LeBlanc was fifty-five now, and had served the admiral as an adjutant for twenty years. When Fraser retired, LeBlanc went with him. He was a lean, well-muscled Cajun from the swamps of Louisiana.

One night while the battle of Coral Sea was raging, LeBlanc argued with a man in a sleazy honky-tonk outside Baton Rouge. The other man died three days later. The judge had given LeBlanc a choice of jail or enlisting. He chose the Navy because they had better food.

The Navy agreed with him and he with it. He had obtained a college degree and made his way through officers candidate school by the time JFK blockaded Cuba. He played a small but prominent logistical role in the operation which brought him to Fraser's attention. He had been with the admiral ever since.

LeBlanc served as bodyguard, chauffeur, cook and valet. He had his military pension, of course, but most of his income came from the admiral. Fraser made a great deal of money from speaking engagements.

"Would you like lunch now?" LeBlanc asked.

Fraser shook his head. "In half an hour or so. I still have this"—he swept his hand over a foot-high stack of Congressional Records—"to go over. Though God knows I'll probably lose my appetite reading what those fools in Congress have done now." He sat down at the desk and put on the glasses he used for reading. "You go ahead and eat. Don't let me get in the way of that appetite of yours."

LeBlanc left the room and closed the double doors behind him.

Fraser had just gotten to the speech by the honorable member of the great state of California representing a certain district in San Francisco when the telephone rang.

Jay and Alexandra struggled out of the elevator on the first floor of the Disneyland Hotel and angled through mobs of children, all of whom seemed to have chocolate sticking to their palms. A bronze Rolls Royce limo was parked in front of the lobby and the front desk personnel were buzzing about it. The Disneyland Hotel, fine establishment that it is, caters more to the station wagon–set than to those who ride in chauffeured Rolls Royces.

Jay set down their luggage and, after a struggle, attracted the attention of the cashier.

When the chauffeur of the Rolls rushed up to take their bags, Jay couldn't decide who was more astounded, Alexandra or the cashier. Jay finished paying the bill and joined Alexandra in the back of the car. As the door clicked shut, Jay saw the cashier looking curiously at him as if she wanted to run out for his autograph.

"Where to, sir?" the liveried chauffeur asked after he climbed behind the wheel.

"Beverly Hilton," Jay said, then added, "I trust the telephone works?"

"Of course," the chauffeur said with the slightest of indignant inflections. "You can dial it yourself. It's a cellular system."

"Wonderful." Jay was about to request some privacy when the soundproof glass whispered up. They glided away from the curb.

"Do you mind telling me what all"—Alexandra swept her arm in a broad arc—"all this is about?"

"All this is about the telephone."

"A booth isn't good enough?"

"A booth can be traced. A mobile telephone can't. All they can trace is the base station and the license number of the car. By the time they do that we'll be long gone."

He picked up the receiver. A sharp pang spread through his chest. The sticker on the telephone said it had been installed by Dencom Systems. Doug Denoff had started the company as a way to get out of the dicy world of security. The business had just started to take off. Jay knew his old friend was less than six months away from leaving ECM, Inc. to run the telephone company full-time. That was six months too long, Jay thought as he stabbed at the buttons on the telephone. It rang twice.

"Hello," the voice was gruff and uninviting.

"Admiral Fraser?"

"Speaking. Who the hell is this?"

"Jay Fleming."

"Haven't they killed you yet?"

"Not to my knowledge."

"Good, Goddamned good." The concern was evident despite the gruffness in Fraser's voice. "You realize the bastards are probably listening to us right now, don't you? They've got a couple of boy scouts sitting in their cars outside my house. Started a week or so ago. Probably sitting down in some basement right now smoking pot and trying to trace your call. They all smoke pot these days, even government agents. Makes them more intelligent."

"They can't trace me for a long while, Admiral." Jay explained why.

"Good. Goddamned good!" Fraser said heartily. "Let them run themselves all over hell. I imagine you'd like to get together for a little chat."

Jay said he would.

"Always turn to me when you get stuck, don't you?"

Fraser's jab had a lot of truth to it. Jay had first met the admiral when he was a visiting professor at Cornell. Jay had excelled in the class, and Fraser had taken him on as a protégé. The admiral had convinced Jay to fly for the Navy.

Fraser had kept their friendship a secret once Jay had enlisted, maintaining that Jay would make enough enemies on his own without carrying around an old man's too. Again, Fraser had been right.

And when Jay's parents had been killed, less than a day had

passed before the old man and LeBlanc had shown up at Jay's aircraft carrier. The admiral had billed his visit as a surprise technical evaluation session and spent most of two days prowling around the ship's nuclear power plant, questioning engineers and officers, making notes, dressing down those who were sloppy and handing out, rarely, the highest compliment he could muster: "Shipshape, mister, shipshape." An observer could never have picked up on the love that had flowed between the two men, such as the admiral's discretion. But he had been there when Jay needed him.

"Yes, sir," Jay said. "I suppose you think I call only when I need help."

"Goddamned right!" Fraser said gruffly. "You youngsters just can't fend for yourselves. Now let me think about this one. We've got to do this with those brown-nosing bastards listening."

Jay heard a loud chuckle. He loves this, Fleming thought. He loves rubbing their noses in it.

"Listen, young Fleming," Fraser said. The admiral had known his father and his grandfather and had always called Jay "young Fleming."

"Yes, sir."

"Do you remember the score I gave you on that last exam? Not the final exam, the one before it."

"How could I forget?" Jay smiled. The test had concerned neutron-capture probabilities. Fraser, who graded all the papers himself, had marked one of Jay's answers as an error. After half a day of arguing, including an elaborate display by Jay of equations which covered most of three blackboards, Fraser had conceded the points.

"Damn it, I knew all along that you were right," Fraser had told him then. "But you haven't missed a single question all semester and I thought you were getting a little cocky. I wanted to see just how sure you were of your information."

"Good," Fraser said now. The Rolls Royce gathered speed as it headed up the entry ramp to the freeway. "Just start with that number and let's do a little math."

Jay took the cap off his pen and started to write as the admiral began to describe their meeting place starting with nothing more than an old college test score. By the time the limo reached downtown Los Angeles, they had the directions and the time set.

"You just get there," Fraser said. "You let me take care of the Boy Scouts."

Jay agreed and said goodbye. The last thing he heard from the receiver just before it rested firmly in the cradle was Rear Admiral (U.S.N. Ret.) Daniel G. Fraser barking at the Boy Scouts.

Chapter Thirty-seven

From the passenger seat of the Bell Jet Ranger helicopter, Steven Strand watched the cat's haunches of Catalina Island grow closer. Straight ahead was the semicircular indentation in the shoreline called Shepherd's Cove. Above it, stashed among the arroyos and barrancas of the hillside, were seven clusters of tents painted seven different colors.

Strand squinted behind his sunglasses and made out a perimeter of double chain-link fencing that from this distance was indistinguishable from the thinnest veins in a fresh green leaf.

Inside the fences were four hundred and seventy acres of dry-scrub terrain covered with chaparral, numerous palm trees that had been transplanted from the mainland decades ago when the Hollywood filmmakers needed them as scenery, a small herd of buffalo also imported for Westerns, a few constantly hungry rabbits and an occasional struggling shrub. Also within that perimeter was a gathering of the collective industrial genius of the United States, of the world, Strand told himself. And they were all waiting for him.

The Jet Ranger swept quickly across the channel, passed over the cove and made for the landing pad on top of the hill. To the east, Strand saw a Jeep making a speedy path up the Isthmus to the encampment, spreading dust on the unpaved road. In the warm red light of the sunrise, the cloud of dust looked like fire consuming the land. The helicopter slowed to approach the pad. The Jeep stopped at the gates to the encampment, where it was immediately surrounded by protestors carrying signs.

Strand knew what the scene was like. He had been through it several times. The protestors would be genteel, almost like the loyal opposition. The Shepherd's Club member in the car would be good-natured.

"I already have the stuff you gave me yesterday," the member would say in response to the literature they offered him. "Do you have any new material?" Everyone would laugh; a news camera or two might shoot a few feet of film if it were one of the more prominent members, say the Secretary of State. The protestors would then move aside and let the member pass through a gate opened by the guards. The members of the Shepherd's Cove Action Network would then sit back on their haunches and wait for the next member.

Down below, in the cove, there would be protestors in ramshackle launches and rubber dinghies taking the same actions.

What in hell did they think they could accomplish? Those people had only as much power as people like him saw fit to give them. No less, no more. But let them believe they rule themselves, Strand thought as the pilot brought the helicopter to a gentle landing. They're a lot easier to rule when they think their vote counts.

Strand smiled broadly as he stepped from the helicopter. Their votes would count for a hell of a lot less in the coming months.

Even into his eighties, Daniel Fraser remained physically fit, confounding his enemies and critics, the majority of whom wished he would simply drop dead.

Dressed in a plain gray sweatsuit with the crest of the Naval Academy printed on the left breast of the shirt, Fraser stepped out on his front porch to take off on his morning run.

Fraser glanced at the tan Ford parked at the corner. The two agents in the front seat were looking less than fresh after the sleepless night he figured they had spent making sure he didn't meet with Jay Fleming.

The Admiral stepped off his porch and started his jog toward the car. He heard the engine start as he approached.

"Good morning, boys," Fraser called. Neither of the men's eyes would meet his glance.

The car followed Fraser up the hills, into the countryside that insulated Palos Verdes from the contamination of the rest of the world and then back. As Fraser rounded the corner, the agents in the car saw him stumble, catch his balance and stop. The car stopped. The two men watched as Fraser doubled over in obvious pain. The old man fell to his knees. One of the agents reached for the car radio.

"Let's call an ambulance," he said. His companion placed a restraining hand on the radio.

"Looks like a heart attack. It'll save us a lot of work. Don't call."

The first man hesitated, watching the old man climb to his feet and almost make it to the front steps of his house before collapsing.

"I don't think—"

"Exactly!" the first man's companion said. "Don't think. Don't do anything."

They watched in silence as the door to Fraser's house flew open and the man they knew as Randall LeBlanc lunged out the door and down the steps to the still form of Rear Admiral Daniel G. Fraser. LeBlanc scooped the old man up in his arms and carried him back inside the house, closing the door with his foot.

"Now," the first man's companion said. "Use the radio. Call control and tell them what's happened."

Minutes later, the bright red van of the fire department paramedics screamed up the hill and stopped in Fraser's driveway, the shriek of its siren dying away in the morning like a half-finished eulogy.

The men in the Ford watched the attendants hustle the gurney out of Fraser's house, accompanied by LeBlanc, and into the back of the van, then followed closely as it wailed painfully away into the morning.

Chapter Thirty-eight

A sun which would have been brutal in the summer smiled benevolently on the desert and coaxed people out of their coats and into shirt sleeves. It was the only time of the year that Jay Fleming could tolerate Palm Springs.

He and Alexandra sat in the ice cream parlor just off the main drag, a block away from I. Magnins. Jay searched and found one saving grace to the town: It served as a sort of wax museum for the rich and famous long past their prime. Other than that, Palm Springs was a good place to meet Fraser. During their telephone call the previous day, the admiral had started with Jay's test score, a perfect 100, and through mathematics had described a latitude and longitude corresponding to Palm Springs. A second set of numbers gave him an address. The "31" in the third set of numbers had been pure whimsy.

"I'm going to get fat if Admiral Fraser doesn't show up soon," Alexandra said.

Jay swallowed a mouthful of Rocky Road. "We've only sampled six flavors. We've got twenty-five to go." He plunged his spoon into the dish before him. "Besides, I want to get you fat so I won't have to worry about somebody stealing you away."

She turned to the low-calorie coffee-flavored ice cream in front of her. "What happens if he doesn't show up? What if he can't get away from them? What if they follow him?"

Jay leaned back in his chair. "Without Fraser, what we have to do may be impossible. Right now, we have to stop whatever it is the Shepherd's Club is up to. Fraser knows better than we do who can be trusted and who can't. Without him, we'd walk into a trap, probably sooner rather than later.

"As for what happens if they follow him to us"—Jay scraped the last bite from the bottom of his dish—"let's just not think about it." He shoveled the last bite into his mouth, adding, "Just make sure your pistol is where you can get hold of it in a hurry."

Reflexively, Alexandra's hand closed on her shoulder bag.

"What about FitzGerald?" Alexandra prompted. Jay disliked the man intensely and during their time in Hartkemeier's cottage in Belgium had related some of the many reasons why. Despite that, she had repeatedly urged Jay to make contact, for no other reason than Subasic's dying suggestion.

"Maybe," Jay said sharply. Alexandra was right and he knew it. His anger was directed more at himself for not being able to put away the differences between him and FitzGerald. He knew he would have to eventually. "Maybe not if Fraser offers us all we need. Definitely if something happens to the Admiral."

They sat in silence while Alexandra finished her ice cream. Jay kept glancing anxiously at his wristwatch, the time failing to register on his mind.

Finally, at a quarter after twelve, a red ambulance with the circular seal of the Los Angeles Fire Department pulled slowly to the curb and disgorged a white-uniformed attendant. It took Jay several seconds to recognize Randall LeBlanc.

LeBlanc entered the ice cream parlor, ordered two sugar cones, paid for them and returned to the ambulance. It pulled away from the curb as Jay and Alexandra got up to leave.

They found it parked under a tree half a block down. They climbed in back. As they closed the doors LeBlanc drove away. Sitting in a wheelchair, eagerly consuming a mocha mint cone, was Rear Admiral Daniel Fraser. He jumped out of the chair to greet them.

"As Mark Twain once said, the rumors of my death have been greatly exaggerated," Fraser said gleefully. "Good afternoon, young Fleming. You look like hell! Civilian life and all that, I suppose?"

His face was all scowls and bluster, but Jay could see the joy in the old man's eyes.

"And you, young lady," Fraser directed his attention to Alexandra. "What is a nice woman like you doing hanging around with a reprobate like young Fleming here? Don't you know he's wanted by the police in a dozen countries?" He looked at her for a moment and then continued. "Ah, but you must be the mysterious woman, the accomplice the newspapers talk so much about. There's something tantalizing about murder and foreign countries, especially when there is a beautiful woman involved." He looked at Jay. "Don't you think so, young Fleming?"

Jay smiled broadly and agreed. Alexandra felt her face blush warmly.

"But we didn't come here to talk about that, did we?" Fraser said, assuming his we-all-know-who's-in-command-here voice. He sat back in the wheelchair. Jay and Alexandra sat on a gurney beneath an array of wires, tubes and bottles of various colors and shapes that rattled and swayed as the ambulance made its way through city traffic.

"No, sir," Jay responded. "But I do want you to know that I appreciate your coming out like this. I'd like to make sure that we put you in as little danger as possible."

"Save the speeches for my funeral if you're still around when I kick off. Don't go worrying about me. This is the most fun I've had since those thieving bastards in Washington railroaded me out. It's been boring, goddamned boring, sitting up in that tomb in San Pedro. Oh, it's a nice house and all that, but I'm getting tired of all the horror stories, all of them probably true, well-documented horror stories that people come to me with about the military that I can't do a goddamned thing about except work into a speech to some goddamned Rotary Club. People still call me. Whistle blowers, demoted government investigators, ships captains. Captains of our navy's ships of war, for God's sake! Their own chain of command is corrupt and they come to me."

"Excuse me, sir," said LeBlanc. "Where to?"

Jay gave him the address of a small hotel in Indio.

"Oh, I help now and then. Passing along information to the few people I can trust, calling in the last of my IOUs." Fraser's voice grew bitter. "Like the little charade with the hospital.

People owe me favors. They'll loan me an ambulance. But can they topple corporations?" His eyes grew sad. "I think not. But they do what they can for me. Lately I've stopped asking because the government follows me. They wait for people to come to me and then the agents follow them, too. And those people? They get fired, transferred, demoted, or else they clam up or disappear. I've got a feeling the only reason the government doesn't do away with me is because they need me as an unfriendly Judas Goat."

Fraser's choice of words rattled Jay. Judas Goat. That's how Subasic and Sweeny had referred to him.

"No," Fraser said, "they just want me to die of natural causes. They don't need a martyr. Don't worry about me, young Fleming. This is as much fun as I've had in years, and if something should happen to me, just remember that no show is so good that it can play forever. Just remember that and all the fun this is to me.

"Now," he said rubbing his hands together. "What have you brought for me?"

Jay launched into his familiar narrative. What scared him most was that every time he told it, it sounded saner. And nothing could be more insane.

Chapter Thirty-nine

Most people think of busy dock areas as sleazy, crowded, dirty wharfs teeming with rats and vermin of both the human and animal varieties. Nothing is farther from the truth in the efficient ports of today. Computers, cost accountants, efficiency experts and designers have remade many ports into suburban shopping malls. Long Beach is such a port.

The docks there, rather than being dark and forbidding, are places for families to spend a weekend afternoon, fishing from the jetties or visiting the *Queen Mary* or Howard Hughes's famous *Spruce Goose*.

Jay noticed the *Queen Mary* first as they crested the Queensway Bridge. Its majestic lighting was captivating. Beyond the Queen, to the south, the lights of Seal Beach, Huntington Beach and further south, Newport and Laguna Beach shimmered in the moonless night. Closer were the surreal light towers of the man-made oil-drilling islands that dotted the bay. Straight ahead were the container-shipping terminals bathed in bright pools of light the color of ice. But dominating the entire panorama were the stately lines of the *Queen Mary*.

"It's beautiful," Alexandra said softly. She sat between Jay and Fraser in the rented Chrysler.

"There is nothing," Fraser said in booming words that sounded like they would chisel themselves into granite, "absolutely nothing in the world more beautiful than a ship."

He turned to Alexandra. "You have probably come as close as any human being I have ever seen, but . . . ." He trailed off.

LeBlanc dropped them off at the hotel where Jay and Alexandra collected their luggage and paid the bill. Over LeBlanc's protests, Fraser sent him back to Los Angeles with the ambulance.

The three of them then turned in the Avis car they had rented at the Beverly Hilton, took a cab to the Palm Springs airport and chartered a plane to John Wayne airport in Orange County. There they rented the Chrysler and drove up Pacific Coast Highway to Long Beach. Anyone who had tried to trace them would end up in a loony bin trying to sort out all of the double tracking they had been doing.

"Go straight," Fraser said as they approached the turnoff for the *Queen Mary*. The road banked left along a chain-link fence that looked twenty feet high. Fraser stared intensely at the markings and directions. "Go slow," he ordered. "I've only been here once before. It's coming back to me."

Suddenly, as if he had just remembered an important but almost forgotten task, Fraser twisted in his seat and looked out the rear window. "You're certain we have not been followed?"

"We've been driving around Long Beach for half an hour now. I even drove the wrong way up that one-way street to make sure of things. If we're being followed, it's either from the air or by someone in the trunk."

"Shipshape," Fraser said. "Shipshape work." He returned his attention to the fences and entrances. Jay had slowed to less than twenty miles per hour. A semi screamed past angrily and disappeared through an industrial gate a half mile ahead.

The street gradually narrowed and curved clockwise, ending at a booth in front of a sign that read "Asian Pacific Container Terminal."

Jay slowed in front of the black-and-white-striped gate blocking the road. A hefty woman in an olive-drab security uniform stepped out of the fluorescent lighting of the booth and approached the car.

"I told you I'd remember how to get here," Fraser said.

"May I help you, sir?" asked the guard.

"Modesti," Fraser answered. "Kevin Modesti. Tell him his guests are here."

"If I could have your name, I'll be happy to—"

"Just give him a call, please," Fraser directed.

"Of course," she complied. She returned to the booth and picked up the telephone.

"Mr. Modesti will be in the third building on the right, just this side of that gantry crane." She pointed with a beefy arm that strained at the cloth of her shirt. She then stepped back inside her booth and hit the button that raised the gate. Fraser waved at her as they drove past.

A burly man dressed like a dockworker stepped efficiently from behind a group of ornamental evergreens next to the building's front door. He carried his big body with the grace of a dancer. He motioned for Jay to double park behind a green AMC sedan with government plates. Jay complied and the man stepped back into his invisible post.

"What was that?" Jay asked.

"Security," Fraser said. "You couldn't sneak a gerbil in here without them noticing. And you couldn't sneak anything out unless they had orders to let you." Then, sensing Jay's nervousness, "Don't worry. They don't work for the government. Nobody's going to turn you in."

Jay mumbled his relief as they got out of the car. The green AMC wasn't the only government car in evidence. There was a dark blue Plymouth with the seal of the U.S. Navy on the door and a tan Chrysler that looked suspiciously like an unmarked police car.

"They're all friends," Fraser said, sensing Jay's hesitancy. "All former Navy men who served under me. They all have their loyalties, but above all they are loyal to me. You know about my little group. Well these men form the nucleus. They're on our side. On your side."

Fraser had explained it all to him during the trip from Palm Springs. A small group of men still working in government, aware of some of the activities of the Committee of Seven and the Shepherd's Club. They tried to keep tabs on the organization.

"Let's go," Jay said with more conviction than he felt. "They're holding the party for us."

Kevin Modesti greeted them at the door and ushered them through a crowded warehouse area to a set of double doors at the rear.

Modesti was a slim man of about forty-five with wavy black

hair and sharp intelligent eyes. He blinked frequently, as if he were continually surprised at what the world offered him. Fraser had earlier explained that Modesti had served as the captain of a destroyer in the Pacific fleet, and after taking early retirement, parlayed a minority partnership in a small shipping line in the Asian Pacific Container Terminal.

"I suppose the admiral has already explained to you that I frequently work with the FBI and Navy Intelligence," Modesti said as they made their way among the cardboard canyons of boxes stacked to the ceiling. "I owe the admiral a great deal. Several years ago he asked me if I could set aside a little of my warehouse for the questioning and safekeeping of defectors who jumped ship here in the harbor. They needed a place that was entirely their own, located in the harbor, convenient to foreign shipping.

"We took in quite a lot of the Polish seamen who jumped ship after the military coup there," Modesti continued as he reached the double doors and punched a nine-digit code into a small keyboard. "We continue to process other defectors, primarily from Communist countries, at the rate of a dozen or so a week."

"That many?" Jay asked.

The door clicked open. Modesti held it for them. "We keep things quiet. The Soviets are fanatical about not being embarrassed. Don't embarrass them and they'll let you get away with murder." Modesti smiled.

They stepped past him into an unlighted room. The doors swung heavily shut behind them and thudded locked again.

"Steel," Modesti remarked. "And two inches of armor plate. The walls and the ceiling are the same. The ventilation passes through the most modern filtration system capable of filtering out or neutralizing any poison, nerve or biological agents. Ditto for the water."

Jay's eyes had almost adjusted to the dark when suddenly the room blazed with the white-hot intensity of lights that seemed to come from every surface.

"This is the only entrance in or out," Modesti explained as they squinted against the light. "The lights are to disorient any unauthorized person, and to provide sufficient light for photographs to be taken from every angle. The room is protected against bomb blasts by more than a foot of armor plating. In addition, the entire room is fluoroscoped to make sure nothing is smuggled in."

The intense light faded and was replaced by the gentler illumination of a fluorescent fixture in the ceiling. Jay's face muscles began to relax.

"Good evening, Mr. Modesti." The voice issued from a speaker in the ceiling. "Our examination is complete and the airlock seals are being opened. Mr. Fleming and Ms. Downing are both carrying .45 caliber automatic pistols, 1911 issue. Each has two spare clips of ammunition. You have neglected to wear your sidearm tonight. The pin in the admiral's leg is holding up very well."

"That's enough, Doyle," Modesti said. Turning to the others he said, "He likes to show off. The fluoroscope is so sensitive he could tell you how much change you have in your pockets and other more embarrassing things." The inner doors opened with a hiss.

"The inside of the facility is designed like the production areas of electronics plants," Modesti explained. "We maintain a slightly higher air pressure inside which prevents anything in the outside air from seeping in."

They followed Modesti through the inner doors, and found themselves in what could have passed for a middle-class living room. The door closed with a hiss. Jay turned and saw it was faced with varnished mahogany.

"We try to make things as comfortable as possible," Modesti said. "Obviously, all the security devices are hidden from the occupants, just in case a double agent were able to slip past posing as a defector."

As they walked along the carpeted hallway, Modesti explained that the facility had twelve living suites, each with its own bath, all of which could be secured as tightly as a maximum-security cell. The most sophisticated electronics security and detection systems protected the facility.

"Obviously," Modesti said as they reached a door at the end of the hall, "we can't be hooked up to the police or any other security agency for the simple reason that none of them know about us. This facility appears on no government ledger, or in the master plans of any government agency. It is known only to a handful of people in the FBI and naval intelligence. I built, paid for and financed the maintenance and operation of the facility myself," he said proudly.

His pride, and the similarity to the operating methods of the Committee of Seven rested uneasily in Jay's mind. Modesti threw open the door to a large conference room.

Around the vast table were only three people, all at one end. They stood quickly and looked as if they wanted to salute Fraser.

Modesti made the introductions: Bill Lamb, Naval intelligence, a squat muscular man, about fifty-five years old, almost completely bald, with bright black eyes; George Treadwell, FBI, a dapper dresser in good physical condition; and David Curry, auditor with the General Accounting Office, a soft, slightly pudgy man with thick glasses who could have been anywhere between thirty and fifty.

Fraser took the chair at the head of the table with Modesti and the other three men on his right. Jay and Alexandra took seats to his left. Fraser began with a brief explanation of his relationship with Jay and a summary of events over the past two weeks, as Jay had explained them to Fraser. As always, Jay was amazed at Fraser's perfect recall.

The eyes of the government men around the conference table bore into Jay and Alexandra. Alexandra shivered involuntarily as she tried to avoid looking at their eyes. She recognized their stares: she had seen them on the faces of men who had attacked her in Luxembourg.

It was Jay's turn to take the floor. He produced the documents that Alexandra had taken from Lee Goldberg's hotel room and passed them around with his own notes paperclipped to them. He described what he had seen of the Tesla papers, revealed what Subasic had told him and finally gave the group an assessment of what he felt the Committee of Seven was developing.

Alexandra followed, describing her relationship with Martin Copeland, her trip to Luxembourg, the meeting with Lee Goldberg, his death and finally her meeting up with Jay. All through it, she felt their eyes dissecting her. Most men tried to undress her with their eyes; these men probed her like a laboratory specimen.

She finished and the room fell silent, save for the gentle sigh of the ventilation system. David Curry, the pudgy man with the

General Accounting Office, was the first to speak. "We have been keeping an eye on the InterGovernmental Weather Project for some time," Curry began in a rich baritone. "In fact, we have several of the documents Mr. Fleming has given us this evening. Until now, they were just curious items of unknown significance. But, with the additional information, things are growing clearer." He paused and looked around at each face. "And more ominous.

"It ties in with a recent event that until now seemed just another random act of violence." Curry shifted in his chair. "One of the computer experts with the GAO in Washington, D.C. developed a special program that could scan data banks of large defense contractors and found patterns in their shipments, purchase of supplies, hundreds of other items. Using a sophisticated computer system he built at home, he had access to the most secret files in America's biggest defense contractors. Remember the case several years ago when a college student managed to break into the data banks of the Lawrence Livermore Nuclear Lab?" Heads nodded around the table. It had been a widely publicized case. "Well this is the same lad. It's a good thing he wasn't working for the Russians.

"At any rate," Curry continued, "several days ago, he pulled up some information relating to defense contractors supplying Project Sanguine."

Fraser's jaw muscles tightened, his lips pressing against his teeth. The admiral had long ago denounced Project Sanguine as a massive mistake, a prime example of a defense project that would be obsolete before it was built.

"It seems these defense contractors, including Fleming Industries"—Curry glanced briefly at Jay—"have been sending millions of dollars worth of Extra Low Frequency broadcasting equipment to a large variety of countries around the world. The computer expert showed his information to his superior," Curry continued, his voice growing lower, "and yesterday someone killed him. I'm convinced that somehow the corporations involved learned of his activities and had him silenced. Fortunately for us, the information was transmitted to one of the people in our West Coast office. We have the names of the companies involved and the locations to which the ELF equipment was shipped.

"In light of what Mr. Fleming has just told us, it doesn't

seem out of the question to assume that these ELF equipment shipments will be used to target the electromagnetic pulse weapons. Further, their broad dispersal around the world seems to be an attempt to give their weapon a global range."

"But why?" Jay interrupted. "Why have they built the weapon, what do they intend to do with it? As the members of the Shepherd's Club are, they can't very well wage their own private war."

"Especially when they have been so effective in getting the Government to wage war on their behalf," Fraser said bitterly. "They have the collective political power to compel their surrogates in public office to wage whatever war they want for however long. Witness Vietnam. That was nothing more than a corporate war. It went a long way toward shoring up the flagging corporate profits of hundreds of defense contractors."

"And according to our information," Curry interjected, "those corporations are in an even more untenable position now than they were in 1964. Faced with competition on the international arms market from the Japanese and our Western European allies, and with small, more efficient, entrepreneurial companies—like yours, Mr. Fleming—the big corporations— Allied Defense, Fleming Industries, all the other big defense contractors—are losing big.

"But the political climate has changed since Vietnam," Curry continued, reading from his notes. It was obvious he had reached some conclusion and was slowly working his way toward it. "The government is no longer willing to get involved in a war to bail out the big defense contractors. And increased public opposition to government financial bailouts of aircraft or defense manufacturers is making that a tougher road.

"There is a great deal of frustration in the boardrooms of the nation's largest defense and industrial corporations." Curry's voice grew in intensity, maintaining an irresistible grip on his audience's attention. "They have been frustrated by the increasing manner that government has had to yield to public pressure rather than their own, and they are upset because they are losing the high-tech battle to foreign competition. Japan, as you know, is light years ahead of our large firms in the development of the new fifth generation of computers. The defense industry is increasingly a high-technology industry, and the big, established corporations that have dominated the field since the early part of this century are losing their unchallenged hegemony.

"Before I tell you what I think is happening, I'd like to reveal one more fact that seemed nothing more than a random and baffling piece of information before tonight's revelations." Curry looked around, his gaze asking for permission to continue. He needn't have asked. "Over the past ten years or so, Fleming Industries, Allied Defense and many of the others—all prominently represented in the Shepherd's Club— have been secretly buying and investing in what we could call obsolete technology: non-automated manufacturing plant equipment, machinery to manufacture vacuum tubes, that sort of thing. Fleming Industries"—Curry looked again at Jay— "has gone so far as to invest in new facilities to build vacuum-tube computers. Before the advent of the transistor and later, the silicon chip, a computer that could do the work of the average home computer would occupy a building half the size of a city block.

"Why would Fleming Industries and its other associates in the Shepherd's Club be investing millions in obsolete computers? It would only make sense if there were no longer any silicon chips, or transistors. Low-tech products only make sense in the absence of high-tech products."

Curry looked about the room as the awesome truth began to dawn on those assembled.

"You're suggesting that the Committee of Seven has gathered a monopoly on facilities to manufacture and produce low-tech products because they intend to use the electromagnetic pulse weapon to destroy . . . ." Fraser's voice trailed off.

"Yes," Curry said. "They will destroy what they are unable to compete with. And only they will possess the equipment and resources to help put things back together again. We will be at their mercy. They will have no competition."

"But the outcry will be enormous," Fraser said angrily. "They will be dragged from their boardroom and torn to shreds."

Jay shook his head. "I'm sorry to disagree," Fleming said. "But even if they were not protected by the very fact that the world will need them so badly, I can think of a very easy way for them to accomplish it without anyone knowing they were responsible. Far from being villains, they will be heroes of the highest order." All eyes settled on him, all asking the same question.

"How?" Fraser queried.

"Get me all of the press releases from the InterGovernmental Weather Project for the past couple of years and I'll show you."

Chapter Forty

Jay had been right, and it gave him no satisfaction. A search through the *Los Angeles Times* index for the past two years had turned up several stories about the InterGovernmental Weather Project. Three of the stories had concerned statements by the project's scientists asserting that the seven-year sunspot cycle was getting more and more violent.

High sunspot activity has long been known to disrupt communications as torrents of charged particles in greater numbers than usual slam into the upper atmosphere. For some reason that scientists cannot explain, the number of sunspots goes through a cycle with peaks every seven years.

The most recent article in the *Times* had run on December 30 and quoted a project scientist as saying that, even though they were only six years into the cycle, their instruments had been picking up unusual amounts of charged particles from the sun.

"I don't want to be too negative," the scientist was quoted as saying, "but this next year could see some very significant disruptions in communications. Perhaps even some effects on other sensitive electrical and electronic devices."

They were laying the foundation. Curry's hypothesis had been correct. Unable to compete in a free market, the stumbling industrial corporations of America, led by its mammoth defense contractors, had taken the easy way out: destroying the competition. They had invested too much in the old industrial order to let go without a fight. It mattered not a

310

whit that their survival meant lowering the standard of living for billions of people, turning the world from a path of progress to one of low-tech stagnation.

"What are you thinking?" Alexandra softly broke the silence in their room. Modesti had installed them in a suite in the Long Beach facility. Treadwell and Lamb were in suites on either side. David Curry, the perceptive GAO auditor, was just down the hall. Fraser had taken the rental car and driven home. "I keep telling you, these people don't need a martyr," Fraser had insisted. "I'll be all right, young Fleming. All right."

Alexandra walked over to the chair in which Jay sat, poring over the clippings, and over the reams of information Curry had provided them. The GAO auditor had given his computer expert, Robert Sansome, leave to stay home and use his computer to roam through the data banks of Fleming Industries, Allied Defense and other companies involved in Project Sanguine. In addition, the institutions headed by other members of the Committee of Seven were fair game, to the extent Sansome could break into them.

Like Barnes, Sansome had started his career as a teenage computer whiz who liked the challenge of defeating computer systems. But the penetrations had yielded little more useful information.

"Computers can only do so much," Jay said, looking up at her. "There will never be a substitute for human observation, human thought, for the miraculous way the human mind can leap across vast areas of ignorance and come to marvelous answers, conclusions."

"Profound thoughts," Alexandra said.

Jay pushed his chair away from the table and stood up. He took Alexandra in his arms and held her close to him. He felt her body mold itself to his.

"No substitute for human observation," Alexandra repeated as she looked up at him. "You?"

He nodded. Like a small council of war, Alexandra, Jay, Curry, Treadwell, Modesti and Lamb had spent the afternoon over endless cups of coffee and sandwiches trying to decide what they should do, what they were capable of doing with their information.

"If they have infiltrated the government as thoroughly as we have reason to believe," the FBI agent Treadwell had said, "then there is no way we can involve the Bureau."

"Or the Navy," Lamb echoed.

"Or any one else in the government, at least not in any official capacity," Jay reinforced. "It means that whatever action we take must be entirely outside sanctioned channels, and involve the fewest number of people to avoid the dangers of being discovered. We're fighting an enemy of vast resources and superiority. The best we can do is strike quickly and by surprise."

"Are you suggesting we sabotage the facilities involved with the Tesla pulse weapon?" Lamb inquired.

"As a last resort," Jay answered. "To destroy or sabotage the facilities will only delay things. They can always rebuild. Besides, we don't yet have a clear idea where they all are."

"But it could buy us time," Treadwell said. "Delay the use of the weapon long enough for us to find a more permanent solution. Like eliminating the people behind it all."

"Assassination?" Modesti asked.

Treadwell nodded, then sadly shook his head. "There are too many of them, too well protected. And our number is far too small."

"Not really," Jay said. "The Committee of Seven is the real mover behind this all. And there are only six of them left." Those assembled looked about at each other with embarrassed sideways glances, too ashamed of the idea to look at each other directly.

"But I think that's a last resort also," Jay said. "What we ultimately want is the disbanding of this group. With the leaders gone, there will be a scrambling for power, for position. And while that might help us temporarily, it will not ultimately destroy the organization. We need leadership to convince the others that the organization must not continue.

"In addition to all of which," Jay concluded, "we'd have to get all six remaining members of the Committee of Seven. Any one surviving could keep things moving on schedule. And I doubt we have the resources to kill them all before one or two of them have time to escape and fortify themselves against further attacks."

Heads nodded unanimously around the table.

"What does that leave us?" asked Modesti.

"Exposure," Curry said. "We, that is the GAO, have had some success presenting evidence to the media. We have already prepared an excellent case against the Shepherd's Club and its leaders. We could build on that and release it."

"But could public pressure act to prevent it?" Treadwell said. "And if it could, can it work in time?" He looked around the room.

"There's always the possibility of releasing the information secretly to those who have the most to lose," Modesti suggested. "To the Japanese, whose economy is built so soundly on the computer and electronics industry. The Dutch, the West Germans—all our allies, in fact. They might be capable of acting quickly and forcefully."

"Don't be a fool," Treadwell countered. "About the only time our allies act quickly or decisively is when they respond to pressure from some insane leftist group and kick us the hell out of one of our bases."

"How about our enemies?" Jay asked. "What sort of stake would they have in all this?"

"Well," Lamb said. "Both the Soviet Union and Red China are far less technologically developed than we are. They have less to lose in terms of dependence on high-tech weaponry. On the whole, their strategic positions would be improved by the actions, particularly if they had advanced knowledge.

"And as you know," the naval intelligence officer continued, "the Russians are far ahead of us in producing electronic equipment that is resistant to the electromagnetic pulses from nuclear blasts. If you'll all remember the defection a few years ago of the Russian pilot who flew a copy of the MiG-25 Foxbat to Japan, the press ridiculed the retarded state of Soviet technology because much of the plane's electronic parts were constructed of old-fashioned vacuum tubes. Well, on closer examination, those were new vacuum tubes and, as you recall, vacuum tubes are resistant to electromagnetic pulses whereas transistors and silicon chips are not. The Soviets are equipped to do battle without sophisticated computers and electronics. We are not.

"Given advance knowledge of the use of a Tesla pulse weapon, the Russians might just take the opportunity to roll across Western Europe in the confusion that will exist in the hours just after the pulse is used."

"I have one other possible negative effect of the exposure option," Jay offered. "Although I agree that exposure may be the most powerful threat we have to disband this cartel once and for all, I believe we could do irreparable harm both to the country and to our ability to defend ourselves. There are elements in our society and among the country's lawmakers who would so gravely curtail defense expenditures that we would be left unable to defend ourselves.

"The United States does have enemies," Jay continued. "We have enemies who would destroy us were it not for a strong defense. The exposure of this powerful cartel would be a confirmation of their worst fears, and would probably sway enough public opinion and votes to their pacifist sentiments to effectively gut our national defense and leave us as sitting ducks.

"Additionally," Fleming added, "the people of this country have already had their faith in their government shaken by decades of corruption in government. The exposure of this cabal could be the final stroke that rends the country apart and leaves us ripe for some demagogue, some Yankee Hitler.

"We must be aware, and infinitely careful," Jay warned, "not to kill the country trying to cure this disease."

He stood up. "I agree that all these options we have discussed may have to be used: exposure, sabotage, assassination. But I have one additional ploy I would like to try first. In his dying words, Bogdan Subasic told me that Steven Strand had staged what was effectively a palace coup within the Committee of Seven, and that Liam FitzGerald would be willing, and would know how, to set things right again. I don't really believe it. But FitzGerald is the chairman of this little cartel, and I'd like to threaten him, to make a deal with him. If he takes the lead in disbanding the committee and turning the Tesla pulse weapon over to the Defense Department, we will not present our evidence on their activities to the media or to our allies. If we can do this quietly, we may be able to cure this illness without killing the patient." He looked around him for reaction.

"How do you propose to reach FitzGerald?" Modesti asked.

Jay told him about the Shepherd's Club annual encampment.

With growing horror, Alexandra had listened to the conversation, had disagreed with Jay, had tried to sway him and the other members of the group that one of them, not Jay, should go. She cursed herself for her earlier efforts at convincing Jay that he ought to put aside old enmities and meet with FitzGerald.

But she never thought the meeting would happen like this. The situation had changed, and she found herself using Jay's earlier arguments on why he should not meet with FitzGerald: the unresolved conflicts between them would hamper communication; there was no trust; Jay was a wanted man and FitzGerald could use that against him.

Throughout a long afternoon that had grown interminable, Alexandra found herself on the short end of the debate. Jay and the group had decided he would take one of the launches belonging to Modesti's company and meet with FitzGerald on Catalina Island.

Now as they sat quietly in their quarters, the wine they had drunk at dinner—a fine California Chardonnay from Sattui— buzzing lightly in their heads, she renewed her new line of argument.

"I still want to go with you," she suggested. "I don't want you to leave me."

"I know," Jay responded. "I don't want to leave you either. Not even for a minute."

"Then don't," Alexandra implored. "Take me with you. I don't know what I'd do without you. You've come to mean more to me than I ever thought another person could. I'm strong. I'm in good shape. I'm a good swimmer, a very good sailor." The first hint of tears shone on her eyes. Jay pulled her tightly to him and kissed her.

"I don't know what I'd do without you either," Jay said when the kiss ended. "You've set something loose in me that is very dear and very vulnerable. I've been able to feel things, been able to see things in colors I never knew existed. You've done that for me. I don't know what I'd do if you—"

"I'm not the one that's walking into the beast's cave," Alexandra said sharply. "You're in no danger of losing *me!* Let me go with you, please?"

Jay shook his head. "It could get rough. Physically very, very rough," he warned. "We've gone over it again and again."

"I know. I know!" Alexandra buried her face in his chest. She sobbed convulsively.

Helplessly, Jay held her tenderly against him, ransacking his mind for the right thing to say to her. But there was no right thing to say. He *had* to meet with Liam FitzGerald and he had to do it alone. Tears blinded him and ran down his face and mingled with her hair. Behind her on the bedside table, the red display of the digital clock reminded him that he had a little less than eight hours before he would have to leave her.

Following the afternoon meeting, Jay had sent a telegram to FitzGerald via the executive offices of Allied Defense Industries. "My injuries mostly healed. Apologize for lack of communication of late. Will explain. Must meet soonest. Harbor Reef Restaurant at 8 A.M. Thursday. Subasic."

Treadwell had used his FBI affiliation to check with Interpol to see if any more bodies had turned up in Luxembourg. Some had, mostly victims of the bombing. There had been no mention of Subasic. The Yugoslav had hidden himself well in the brush covering the ledge above the jogging path. His body had not been discovered and probably would not be until the weather warmed up.

Jay was counting heavily on FitzGerald's not knowing of Subasic's death. He hoped that the industrialist, expecting to meet his trusty employee, would take fewer security precautions. His life could depend on that.

Alexandra's sobbing had trailed off to long wet sniffles. She looked up at him, her tear streaked eyes red and forlorn. She saw the dried salty tear tracks on Jay's cheeks and reached tenderly up with one hand and wiped them gently away.

"I love you, Jay Fleming," she murmured.

"I love you too," Jay responded.

She placed a finger over his lips. "Words are for the timid. Show me." She pulled him toward the bed.

Jay let her pull him down on top of her. They kissed wildly and fumbled with each other's clothes like high schoolers in the back of the family car.

Although they had slept together for two weeks, they had

done so chastely, in gowns and pajamas. For the first time he felt the yielding firmness of her warm breasts beneath his hands, heard her soft moans growing louder. Her breasts were fire beneath his hands, spreading like tinder through his body, burning between his thighs. Her searching hands found the fire and fanned the flames.

Dear God, Alexandra thought, this is what making love is supposed to be like. Her skin seemed to glow beneath his touch. She felt him grow hard next to her and with her free hand, fumbled with the zipper of his pants. Never had she wanted anything so much as this. He kissed her, and each spot beneath his lips tingled long after he had touched it. He kissed her again and again, on her lips, her neck, her breasts and as he moved lower, an odd sound reached her ears. It took a long time before she recognized her own cries of pleasure.

They made love desperately, like lovers about to be separated by war. They made love again gently, savoring each other's body. And then they fell asleep, arms entwined, just as they had every night since Belgium. But unlike every night since Belgium, they slept deeply beneath the velvet sleep of lovers who knew that only death could possibly separate them.

"Don't, by God, tell me what I should or should not do!" Liam FitzGerald thundered as he strode angrily back and forth across the wooden planks of the white tent that served as his quarters. Members of the Committee of Seven had the largest tents in the encampment, and as chairman, FitzGerald's was the largest of the large. A wooden platform covered a rectangle thirty feet by forty. A frame of heavy lumber outlined the walls and peaked roof and over that, the securely laced canvas. In the distance came the muffled sounds of an electrical generator which fed the ceiling lights as well as a variety of electrical gadgets. Only the Committee of Seven was supplied with electricity. The other camps made do with gas or, for the newly initiated, kerosene. FitzGerald's footsteps thumped like a faulty bass drum, as the tall angry man strode the length of his quarters, ten steps, turn; ten steps, turn.

Steven Strand sat in a campaign chair next to FitzGerald's desk, his face composed.

"Just because we have the goddamned Tesla papers is no

reason to get careless," FitzGerald said. "There are too many things that could go wrong yet. We have to tread softly. We can't afford to take the risks you suggest."

Strand leaned forward, palms outstretched. How he hated having to deal with this timid fool. "I agree with you, Liam. But you have to agree that Fleming is a threat, a big threat to the project."

"He wouldn't be a threat if you or Subasic had done your jobs right," FitzGerald snapped.

"That may be true," Strand conceded, "but that doesn't change the situation. I'm convinced Fleming is in California. There was no other reason for Admiral Fraser to have slipped away so mysteriously unless it was to meet with his protégé."

"But Southern California's a big place," Strand continued. "That's why we *have* to sweat the answers out of Fraser."

FitzGerald stopped at the entrance to his tent and stared out at the dark night, at the stars and the lights of the Palos Verdes Peninsula barely visible across the channel. He shook his head slowly.

"That old goat is scared," FitzGerald said, turning away from the peace of the night. "Even among members of the Shepherd's Club."

"We can't afford scared goats right now," Strand said drily.

"And *I* say we can't afford a martyr," FitzGerald retorted. "You start fucking with Fraser and you'll have every newspaper and all of the networks on our backs in an instant. And I don't think we need that sort of scrutiny right now."

"I admit it's a risk," Strand said, getting to his feet. "But it's a matter of weighing the risks. Is Fleming a greater risk than whatever scrutiny we *might* get from the media? I submit that Fleming is a greater risk."

Strand and FitzGerald faced each other like two boxers before a bout. Strand's muscularity, his superb physical condition, gave him an aura of power that bolstered his arguments. Others, not realizing it, capitulated before his sheer physical presence. FitzGerald was twenty years older, was nearly as old as Fraser. Maybe Strand was right. Maybe he was feeling a little too much empathy with the old Navy admiral.

"It's possible you could be right," FitzGerald said wearily.

"I just know that we can't have Fraser going to the media and telling them about how we interrogated him."

"Don't worry," Strand said, knowing that he had worn FitzGerald down. "He won't go to the media."

And without waiting for a reply, Strand whirled on his heel and strode from the tent.

Chapter Forty-one

Huge juggernaut swells rolling northward from the Antarctic clashed with winds sent southward by an Arctic high-pressure system. The sailing grounds between the Palos Verdes Peninsula and Santa Catalina Island churned white and foamy as the two great weather systems did battle. Despite the rage of the wind and sea, the sky remained clear, fingernail moon beginning to sink into the horizon.

Across the battlefield, a thirty-five-foot motor launch followed a ragged, battered rhumb line from Long Beach Harbor to the Isthmus at Santa Catalina Island. In calm weather, the twenty-six-mile trip would take less than an hour. On this day, Jay Fleming was determined to make it in less than an hour. He needed the darkness to assure the anonymity of his craft.

Feet spead wide, knees bent, Jay clung to the wheel as the powerful craft growled through the foam at the top of a wave. The twin 454-cubic-inch V-8s roared as the props momentarily lifted out of the water, then quieted as the hull slammed back with a spine-shattering impact. Wrestling at the helm, Jay waited for the wave to break over the bow. Cold water slammed into him, prying at his fingers. He tried to loosen his grasp on the wheel. The frigid water drenched his boots.

It had been like that for half an hour now: up the wave, engine screams, crash over the crest, sea breaks over the bow, fight for control, momentary respite and then the climb back over. Jay refused to return to port or to ease off the throttle.

There was too much at stake to arrive in the daylight. The anchorage he was heading for, known as the Isthmus, would be almost deserted this time of year, and any new boat would immediately be noticed. The darkness provided him with some protection. He also wanted time to reconnoiter the area around the Harbor Reef restaurant. Although he had been there many times during weekend sails, he had to look at it now as a place which could become his grave if he made a mistake.

Jay had been following a compass course since leaving the Asian Pacific Container Terminal half an hour before. Now, as he crested the wave, he steeled himself against the water. He glimpsed the lights at Isthmus Cove before the breaking wave washed his vision away.

Santa Catalina Island—"Catalina" to natives—is nineteen miles long, and, at its widest point, seven miles across. Six and a half miles from the west end of the island are two coves which nearly cut the island in two. The two coves, only half a mile apart, are connected by a broad, low canyon about a quarter of a mile wide.

Isthmus Cove, on the north side of the island, and Catalina Harbor on the south are favorite anchorages for local sailors. The area is not as developed as Avalon on the east end, having only camp-style restrooms and showers, a small restaurant and bar and a general store stocking everything from outboard motor parts to wine. There are no overnight lodgings on shore and only a handful of buildings scattered about the low-lying areas to house the couple of score of inhabitants. It has the rustic atmosphere of an island thousands of miles away from civilization.

Away from the Isthmus, the terrain grows quickly inhospitable with precipitous cliffs and inaccessible canyon mouths falling hundreds of feet into the sea. Other than a Boy Scout camp at Emerald Bay, the only inhabitants of the west end are rattlesnakes, wild pigs, buffalo, a scattering of eagles, an occasional rabbit, and the Shepherd's Club encampment.

The muscles in Jay's shoulders and arms ached from the strain of the pitching trip. Each new wave tried to rip his hands from the wheel and his arms from his body. To distract his mind from the pain, he concentrated on Alexandra's face. He saw the tears again as he said goodbye that morning, he felt her body against his.

For the first time in his life, caution became important. He wanted to return from this trip, wanted to be with her more than he had ever wanted anything in his life. He wondered briefly about Helen. What had brought them together? What had ever made him think they could be happy together? But how could he have known that it *wouldn't* work? He had not known what right felt like until now.

Jay let his mind wander among the relics of the past, steering his attention always away from the pain in his muscles. Soon, the white guano-coated form of Ship Rock loomed out of the darkness and beyond that, the lower discreet form of Bird Rock. The waves gradually diminished as the launch entered the protected waters of Isthmus Cove. The throbbing of the powerful engines diminished and, over them, Jay heard the thundering of surf against the foot of the cliffs that girded the island.

Jay cut the engines to idle and shifted into neutral as he approached a huge white beachball-like mooring buoy about thirty yards from shore. He snared the line with a boat hook on the first pass and made it fast to the bow and stern cleats of the motor launch and then gratefully killed the engines.

The sounds of the sea rushed in to fill the vacuum left by the silent engines. The urge to sleep, to rest, was almost overwhelming, but immediately after making fast to the mooring lines, Jay went below to the cabin and changed into dry clothes. There was no longer any need for the foul weather gear, and he hung them in a wet locker by the companionway to dry.

In a locker in the cockpit, Jay retrieved the Avon raft, inflated it with air from a battery driven compressor, and then threw it into the water. Inserting the oars in the oarlocks, he rowed toward the pier, letting the winds ease him along.

A single member of the Isthmus Cove Harbor Patrol lounged on a tall stool with his feet up on the counter when Jay tied up to the dock. Jay said, "Good morning."

The man returned his greeting along with the information that the coffee shop wouldn't be open until 7:30.

"That's all right," Jay said. "I like to take long walks before breakfast."

The harbor patrol officer told him to have a nice walk, and to be sure to get a landing card when the office opened up.

Jay made his way along the wooden dock and past the landing office to the shore. Dead ahead the unlighted windows of the Harbor Reef restaurant looked like blank eyes. There was a collection of patio tables with umbrellas in a little garden area to the left of the main entrance, and to the right, a screened-in dining area that served as a snack bar. Jay knew the bar was behind the restaurant. The country store rested dimly in the shadows to the right of the restaurant. On the beach between the buildings and the water, a pair of volleyball nets watched over a stone barbecue pit.

The long dark green painted restroom area was to his left, and Jay strolled up the rough path between palms and yucca plants and into the men's room. After relieving himself, Jay paused on the dirt road that ran from Catalina Harbor and looked to the east where sunrise had started to spread above the mainland like a peach-colored border between the black sea and sky. He wanted to share a lot of sunrises with Alexandra.

Beyond the restaurant and general store were the outboard motor repair shop and a scattering of low one-story lumber buildings. A little farther on, up on the hillside, lights blinked behind the windows of a shingled bungalow. The Isthmus was waking up.

Jay circled the restaurant area, finding nothing that surprised him, refreshing his memory from past visits. FitzGerald, he guessed, would probably arrive either by the single dirt road from Shepherd's Cove, or by sea. He wandered down to the beach and took a seat on a low rise that gave him a good view of the restaurant, the dock and the road. He wished FitzGerald would hurry up and he wished he'd never come.

"Give him another dose," Steven Strand ordered. He ran one finely manicured hand through his hair and turned away from Admiral Daniel Fraser's bedside. Fraser lay on the mattress, clothed only in a pair of boxer shorts, his wrists and ankles bound to the bedposts with elastic bandages. In the harsh illumination shed by the 100-watt bulb in the bedside lamp, Fraser's body looked like a grizzled old rooster laid out for dissection. Over the firm muscles kept fit by his regular exercise, his skin hung flaccidly, its elasticity stolen by time. Veins stood out prominently across his biceps and forearms and calves. A black blood pressure cuff compressed his right biceps making the vein bulge at the elbow. Two pieces of adhesive tape crossed over the vein, securing an intravenous needle whose tubing led to a bag of saline hung over the bedpost. A middle-aged man with watery gray eyes sat beside Fraser, holding a syringe which fed into the saline drip. The man had once been a dentist who had specialized in painless surgery. Then three patients died under his anesthesia. After losing his license to practice and spending several months in prison, he found his talents in demand by people who cared little whether or not he had a license. Steven Strand was one of those.

"I must warn you," the man with the watery eyes said tentatively, "we are approaching danger levels."

"He has told me nothing useful," Strand retorted.

"There is an extremely fine line sometimes between eliciting useful information and killing the subject. With him dead, you lose your information forever."

"Let's see if we can walk that line without falling off, shall we?" Strand ordered testily. The man blinked hesitantly at Strand. "Give him more!" Strand demanded. The man with the watery gray eyes nodded rapidly and eased the plunger of the syringe in another fifteen ccs.

"Where is Fleming?" Strand spoke calmly to Fraser's anesthetized mind. "Tell me where he is."

Fraser opened his eyelids and stared sightlessly past Strand. His dry cracked lips twitched.

"Just tell me how to find Fleming and you can sleep," Strand promised.

Fraser's tongue worked at his lips; his eyes closed.

"More," Strand commanded.

The anesthetist complied. Moments later, Fraser's body arched and began to convulse.

"Fleming!" Strand shouted at Fraser. "Where is Jay Fleming?"

Mumbles dripped from Fraser's lips as the convulsions subsided. Strand bent low, trying to catch the almost unintelligible sounds.

From across the room, Randall LeBlanc looked on curiously as a smile grew on Strand's face.

Strand finally stood, nodded at LeBlanc and walked into the

living room and picked up the telephone. As he punched the first digit of the number, Strand heard a crash of furniture from the bedroom. He heard the former dentist start to cry out, then a painful gurgle and finally the muffled cracks of vertebrae separating as LeBlanc broke the man's neck.

Chapter Forty-two

Catalina Island,
January 5

The rising sun was glistening like a carmine oil slick on the unsettled water of Isthmus Cove when a dark forest green Jeep Wagoneer rumbled down the dirt road cut in the cliff high above the water. From his position on the beach, Jay watched it trailing red dust in the sunrise as it descended and then disappeared beyond a grove of eucalyptus trees. He listened as the motor noise diminished and then grew louder again. Moments later, Jay could see the Jeep through the gap between the restaurant and general store as it jounced over the uneven surface and pulled to a halt just behind the restaurant about fifty yards from shore.

A small cloud of dust detached itself from the Jeep and slowly faded to nothing. Through the dust-caked windshield, Jay could make out the dark forms of four people in the vehicle. After a moment, the one sitting next to the driver got out and opened the rear door.

Jay watched as Liam FitzGerald's tall aristocratic form emerged from the rear seat. He paused to exchange a few quiet words with the man who quickly walked around to the front of the restaurant, checked out the still empty snack bar where the cook was readying to open for breakfast, and then, after making a complete circuit of the structure, returned and rendered a report to FitzGerald.

While the security man was making his report, Jay strolled up from the beach and walked up to the counter of the snack bar. He ordered a large cup of coffee and French toast. The young woman at the counter took his money and poured the coffee into a foam cup which Jay took over to a Formica booth in the corner of the long narrow room and sat down to wait for his French toast and Liam FitzGerald.

FitzGerald, as Jay had expected, arrived before the French toast. Preceded again by one of his security agents, FitzGerald entered the room. FitzGerald paused just inside the door and looked around. He then dismissed his bodyguard with a wave of his hand and approached the counter. Dressed in starched khaki's, Topsiders and a broad-striped polo shirt under a poplin blazer, FitzGerald resembled nothing more than the owner of one of the boats moored in the harbor come ashore to eat. Only the knife-sharp crease in the pants gave him away, Jay thought. Small-craft sailors had wrinkles, not creases.

Conflicting emotions swept through Jay in wave after wave as he sipped at his coffee and tried not to stare at FitzGerald. Fleming had always detested the man and what he stood for. He had grown rich by providing inferior weapons to the United States at overinflated prices. He had somehow institutionalized greed of the worst sort.

Yet, Subasic trusted the man, had in his last breaths directed Jay to him. Subasic believed the Committee of Seven had been subverted by Steven Strand, and that FitzGerald—no matter how much Jay hated him—would be a valuable ally. Subasic's earlier miscalculation had cost him his life in Luxembourg. Jay hoped this wouldn't cost him his.

FitzGerald took a container of coffee and walked over to a booth near the door and sat down with his back to Jay. Moment's later, Jay's French toast arrived. He wolfed it down.

When FitzGerald's order of eggs was delivered to him, Jay gulped the last swallow of coffee and stood up. He disposed of his empty plate and took the empty cup back to the counter and stood behind a trio of men who, Jay judged by their conversation, worked at the scuba equipment rental office at the head of the pier. While he waited for the men to order breakfast, Jay glanced nonchalantly through the broad expanses of glass that formed three sides of the snack bar.

The driver of the Jeep lounged on the front fender smoking a cigarette. Jay spotted one of the security agents sitting on a bench near the general store, looking out of place and uncomfortable. The man's head scanned the area around him constantly, like some nervous bird feeding . . . or a falcon looking for prey. It bothered Jay that the third man in the car was nowhere to be seen.

After the woman behind the counter refilled Jay's cup, he took a sip and looked around like a man unsure of his next move, and then walked swiftly to FitzGerald's table and slid in opposite him.

"It's eight o'clock," Jay said, fixing FitzGerald's surprised eyes with his own. "Subasic's not coming."

FitzGerald composed his patrician features instantly and calmly finished chewing. He swallowed, took a sip of coffee, studied Jay's face. Fleming could almost see the man rearranging photos in an album, comparing features, trying to match Jay's with some known image.

"Subasic's dead," Jay said, taking a sip of the coffee. "His body's still in Luxembourg."

"Fleming," FitzGerald said flatly. It wasn't a question.

Jay nodded. "I think we have some business to take care of."

FitzGerald looked at him curiously, making a show of tilting his head, squinting. "I can't say the changes improve your looks," he told Jay. "But I do admit the disguise is effective. I didn't take a second look at you when I came in."

"I know." Jay smiled. A hint of a scowl fleeted across FitzGerald's face.

"You've managed to get yourself into a fair amount of trouble over in Europe."

"No thanks to you and your Committee of Seven, Mr. . . . Diamond."

"You seem to know a great deal, Mr. Fleming. You're a great deal like your grandfather. He too knew more than was good for him."

"I didn't come here to argue with you. I know all about the committee's attempts to get the Tesla papers." Jay paused and sipped his coffee. FitzGerald studied him intensely through hooded eyes. "Subasic was under the misguided perception that you were somehow unaware of what Strand was doing, that somehow you would be willing to correct things, bring Strand into line. But I think you and Strand have been working together all along. I believe that you misled Subasic because you knew he wouldn't do your dirty work for him if he knew the truth."

"I gather that Bogdan told you a great many things before he died." FitzGerald sounded as if Jay had told him something amusing.

"Not as much as he would have liked. Strand's people did a job on him before he managed to escape. He died still believing that the Committee of Seven had a great purpose."

"It *does* have a great purpose. We have as our goal nothing less than the continued security of the western world."

"You have as your goal saving your own clumsy, inefficient, greedy asses," Jay retorted.

FitzGerald smiled patiently. "If you could ever get beyond your juvenile notions of what's right and wrong, you could develop into a leader. You have the intelligence, the energy, the initiative."

"Honesty keeps me from achieving greatness as you define it."

FitzGerald shook his head slowly. "You have some Victorian notions of honesty and propriety. It is not always possible to be totally honest *and* accomplish for the republic what it needs most."

"Does the republic need to be plunged back half a century by your plans to overload electronic circuits with electromagnetic pulses? Is that what the republic needs right now?"

"How did you . . . ?" FitzGerald's face lost its composure. His head jerked to the side for just an instant.

"How did we find out?" Jay asked. "That's not important. What *is* important is that we do know and what we intend to do with the information unless you quietly dismantle your little secret society and return to the government what you've stolen from it."

"You're bluffing," FitzGerald said, his voice wavering with uncertainty. "You can't prove anything."

"Sure we can," Jay returned. "We've got documents outlining what the InterGovernmental Weather Project has been doing. We have names and dates and places concerning the ELF broadcasting devices you and Fleming industries sent all over the world. We have reams of memos, files, invoices— you name it."

"You puny, little, narrow-minded shit!" FitzGerald hissed.

"You do that and you will have destroyed the greatest institution of the twentieth century. You will have destroyed the country! We have worked for forty years to get to this point. Four decades. We have fought relentlessly to make sure that the pacifist elements in government didn't leave the country undefended.

"You would destroy the single most effective force to keep the country militarily strong!" FitzGerald leaned across the table. "For four decades, we have banded together to lobby for what is right, we have exchanged information in such a way as to produce the most effective weapons, we have fought the country's enemies—both from within and without—with an unending vigilance."

"And you've ripped off the military at every turn," Jay countered.

"You simple-minded clod!" FitzGerald snapped. "Do you think we are so inefficient? Do you think that cost overruns are an accident? Don't insult my intelligence by harping about overcharges and such, like those vain mavens of the media do." FitzGerald paused. A tremor ran through his body. With a visible effort, he reined in his fury.

"Do you actually think for a moment that the billions of dollars each year in defense contract cost overruns are an accident?" FitzGerald asked indignantly. "Do you think we'd allow that to happen? Do you think the institution of the cost-plus, single-source negotiated contract was an accident . . . that it just happened because it was a good idea?

"None of the way we do business is an accident," FitzGerald said. "We're not the helpless fiscal giants we make ourselves out to be in Congressional hearings. *We* have institutionalized the cost overruns as a way to finance the research, development and production of the weapons that the Western nations need, but which their politicians are too timid to vote for themselves."

Jay sat up, his anger suddenly chased away by FitzGerald's astonishing revelation.

"In 1947," FitzGerald began, "a distinguished group of men met in secret to discuss an alarming lack of understanding of military matters by the public and their elected officials. It became clear to us that World War II hadn't ended with the signing of treaties, but rather was entering a new, unknown stage. It was apparent to us that the United States and its allies had to maintain a strong military presence in peacetime.

"Your grandfather felt very strongly about this, by the way," FitzGerald said, leaning back against the plastic upholstery of the booth. His eyes searched Jay's face for an instant and then fixed themselves on a spot about two feet above Jay's head, and on an era forty years earlier.

"It was Strand who suggested at that meeting that it would be possible to use the new secrecy laws and a different form of accounting to provide us with the necessary funds to continue to develop and build the weapons needed for the country's defense. At that meeting, Strand also presented us with the remarkable revelation that an obscure scientist named Nikola Tesla had made some vital discoveries that could also advance our cause."

As FitzGerald unspun the snarled strands of events that began at that meeting, Jay sat transfixed, astonished by what he was hearing. In the back of his mind a dim memory began to float to the surface. It was the memory of his father telling a young, curious Jay Fleming about how the young boy's grandfather had been killed in a traffic accident in Virginia on his way back from a mysterious meeting.

"We succeeded in using the Central Intelligence Agency to distribute many of the extra weapons we manufactured," FitzGerald continued as he led Jay through a chronology of the Committee of Seven's history. "In many cases, we have simply stored tanks and aircraft and extra weapons and ammunition in storage depots. The military auditors never count them anyway. They always take our word for it.

"We were ready for Vietnam," FitzGerald said proudly.

"Excuse me, sir." A voice from behind Jay made him spin around. It was the third man.

"Yes?" FitzGerald snapped.

The security guard approached FitzGerald and whispered in his ear. As he did, a broad victorious smile rearranged the deep wrinkles that covered FitzGerald's face.

"Thank you," FitzGerald said and dismissed his employee. "Now," he said, returning his attention to Jay. "Where was I? Oh yes, Vietnam."

Jay noticed a change in FitzGerald's demeanor. He had lost his composure after Jay had revealed their plans to expose the group. Now, following the whispered message, he had regained the composure. What had the man told FitzGerald? What could so suddenly eliminate his fear of exposure?

"As I was saying," FitzGerald continued, "when the government got into that one and needed material immediately we already had much of it in storage."

"And you made a tidy profit selling back to them what they had already paid for through cost overruns," Jay replied.

FitzGerald looked at him, annoyed.

"That's unfair," FitzGerald responded defensively. "We were entering a new era of high-tech weaponry. We needed the additional funds to develop new generations of electronic and computer assisted weapons."

"Which you haven't done very well lately," Jay interjected. "Primarily due to competition from companies like my own."

"You could have been such an asset," FitzGerald said. "We tried . . . how we tried to get you involved. But you and your outmoded sense of ethics . . ." He let his voice dwindle away. Closing his eyes as if reconstructing a distant memory, FitzGerald wiped his face with one manicured hand and then slowly opened his eyes again. "Hindsight should have warned me that you were too much like your father and your grandfather. Your almost successful battle with Strand for the control of Fleming Industries should have told me that.

"We almost lost control of Fleming," FitzGerald said. He shook is head, remembering a close call. "That would have been disastrous."

"We?" Jay said.

FitzGerald studied Jay's face curiously. "Oh surely you didn't think Steven Strand could have done all that by himself, did you?"

The two men regarded each other silently for a long moment.

"You?"

"Not just me," FitzGerald said. "The resources of the Committee of Seven and through it the Shepherd's Club. You don't think we could have allowed such a major defense contractor to fall under the control of someone whose interests were so contrary to our own, do you?"

"No." Jay looked at him vaguely, trying to remember details of the struggle. "I don't suppose you could." Jay felt anger flare briefly through his belly. It was quickly replaced with a feeling of pride. He hadn't been battling just Steven Strand, but the orchestrated efforts of the most powerful cartel in America. The pride faded before the realization that he was now battling that same cartel, trying to force its dissolution. The thought was dismaying. Still, he told himself, he had almost beaten them once and he had not even been aware of their role. Now, he was forewarned . . . and he had allies: Fraser and through him a broad network of assistance. And Alexandra.

"But even with your vaunted power, you've lost the high-tech battle," Jay suggested.

"That's not entirely true," FitzGerald began slowly. "I'll have to admit that we have lost some ground to foreign competition. That is one factor in our decision to proceed with Project Nick. The electromagnetic pulse weapon was more of a curiosity than anything else. Before the advent of the transistor, of course. About that same time—in the early sixties—atmospheric testing of nuclear weapons brought the EMP phenomenon to our attention. But it wasn't until about ten years ago that the omnipresence of the silicon chip began to change military strategic planning.

"Congress was in no mood to appropriate money for a weapon it couldn't understand." FitzGerald rambled easily through his narrative. A faint warning light began to flash in Jay's head. Why was FitzGerald telling him all this so readily?

"So the Committee of Seven instituted Project Nick to develop the Tesla pulse weapon. We intended to present the finished project to the joint chiefs as a way to disable the electronic guidance systems of Russian missiles and bombers before they could be launched against us."

"But somewhere along the line your focus changed," Jay stated. "Why?"

"Partly it was the inability to aim the weapon," FitzGerald said sadly. "As early as 1965 we had the weapon working. But we couldn't aim it."

"With all your scientific genius, you still needed Tesla's mind."

FitzGerald nodded. "He was a remarkable man, but he was a dog in a manger. He wouldn't share any of his secrets with us. He'd have lived a lot longer if he had."

Jay looked questioningly at him. FitzGerald told him.

"That was monstrous!" Jay said. "One of the greatest geniuses of all time, and you killed him to get his papers."

"I admit now that it was hasty," FitzGerald confessed. "But to finish answering your question . . . yes, our focus did change. We were losing our high-tech advantages to foreigners. But along with that came an increasing concern about a situation of our own making—the arms race, nuclear arms in particular.

"War has become too deadly," FitzGerald offered. "The story of history is the story of men's wars. We were—are—concerned that the final chapter of history might be the story of the last war. Aside from that, we all realized that while there was a great deal of profit to be made from conventional wars, a nuclear war would be decidedly unprofitable.

"The use of Project Nick a few months from now will defang nuclear war," he continued, his voice assuming the notes of an orator's final remarks. "All the arming circuits for nuclear weapons, all the guidance systems for their delivery and guidance, all the computers and electronics needed to operate airplanes and ships and submarines will be overloaded, burned up by the electromagnetic pulses we generate. It will be as if a thousand nuclear weapons were detonated in the atmosphere all around the world. But instead of the terrible blasts and radioactivity, only the pulses will be produced. It's ironic that nuclear devices themselves have given us the antidote for global nuclear war. The fact that it will also make the members of the Shepherd's Club competitive . . . no, dominant in world defense is a . . . not unwelcome secondary result.

"And now," FitzGerald said, sliding to the edge of the booth, "it's time for me to be going."

Jay reached over and grabbed FitzGerald's forearm. "Not yet. We still have to talk."

"We have *nothing* more to talk about," FitzGerald said haughtily as he snatched his arm away from Jay's grasp. "You and your munchkins are no threat to me or to the Committee. Do you think I would have told you all I did if you were a danger anymore?"

Jay thought of the impregnable fortress he had left only a couple of hours before. "Sit down, FitzGerald, before you do something you'll regret for a long time." Jay jumped up, but before he could grab FitzGerald, he felt the cold deadly ring of a muzzle pressed into the sensitive skin just below his left ear.

"Be sensible, Fleming," said FitzGerald. "Everything's already in motion. You can't do anything about it." He looked at the Piaget watch on his wrist. "In about half an hour, the Committee of Seven will begin briefing the assembled members of the Shepherd's Club. For decades now, those members have been meeting at these little gatherings to coordinate their activities, and to take the necessary direction from the Committee of Seven that will make our success in the coming months irresistible.

"By tomorrow night," FitzGerald continued expansively, "they will disperse, each to his own company, and set into motion actions that will assure them of the greatest profits and the most enviable competitive position imaginable once Project Nick is accomplished. Do you think we'd just idly use the Tesla Pulse weapon to devastate our competitors without first being poised to take the best advantage of it?" He shook his head. "This is a corporate blitzkrieg, a lightning war that will happen too fast for anyone but our members to respond effectively. Today, tonight, tomorrow. Such a short time for such profound and everlasting results."

"And they're all going to go along with what you tell them?" Jay asked skeptically.

"We have taken care of that," FitzGerald said confidently. "It will be done. Now," FitzGerald said, with a note of finality, "it's time for us to part and go our separate ways." His eyes fixed on something outside. Four uniformed deputies debarked from a black-and-white patrol car.

"They're from the Avalon substation at the other end of the island," FitzGerald said. "I took the liberty of having my men call them. I thought they'd be arresting Subasic." The older man smiled broadly at Jay. "But I don't think they'll be disappointed with you. Especially after they check with Interpol."

The gun at Jay's head said to move toward the approaching deputies, but before he could, a cry sounded. The waitress must have seen the man's gun.

Jay felt the gun muzzle waver at his head, then made a

decision. He dropped to his knees, going for the .45 in his jacket pocket.

The shot boomed like the end of the world. He felt the searing blast, smelled the ghastly stink of his singed hair. Fleming brought the .45 upward and squeezed off two rounds. FitzGerald's bodyguard exhaled loudly as the slugs ripped upward into his solar plexus.

Fleming sprang to his feet, looking for FitzGerald's second security man. He was running toward the snack bar with his gun drawn.

"You're my ticket out of here," Jay said. FitzGerald had seated himself during the scuffle. "Get up and tell these people not to shoot, or you're dead."

FitzGerald gazed blankly up at Jay and made no move to obey. Then Jay noticed the dark splotch in the middle of the navy-blue stripe of FitzGerald's polo shirt just beneath his throat. As Jay stared at him, the white stripe beneath it slowly turned red. The security guard must have hit him with the first shot, Jay thought. FitzGerald smiled victoriously and then closed his eyes.

Then like the sudden opening of a thundercloud, slugs rained through the windows of the bar, filling the air with shattered glass. Jay dropped to a crouch and ran into the kitchen. He prayed there was a back door.

Chapter Forty-three

Long Beach,
January 5

Alexandra sat in the empty dining room. Her untouched plate of scrambled eggs developed a viscous film as they slowly grew cold. Where was he? She sniffed and dabbed at her nose with a paper napkin. This was too much. She was sick of men always leaving her.

"Ms. Downing?"

Alexandra looked up. George Treadwell stood at the door to the dining room.

"I thought you would want to know."

She froze, staring wide-eyed at the FBI agent. "Has something happened to Jay?" she asked in a hoarse voice.

Treadwell shook his head and approached the table. "It's Admiral Fraser. Someone got to him."

"Oh, my God!" Alexandra exclaimed, her right hand covering her mouth.

"He's still alive," Treadwell said. "He's a tough old bird, and they've got him in the intensive care unit at UCLA Medical Center under heavy guard."

"Who?"

"LeBlanc thinks they were Russians," Treadwell said. "He's in the hospital himself. They apparently bagged him with a tranquilizer gun and then started on the Admiral with a strange soup of anesthetics and mind-loosening drugs."

"Dear God!" Alexandra said. "What kind of a world are we

337

living in? We can't escape from our friends or our enemies."
She hid her face in her hands.

"He's going to be all right," Treadwell said. "The doctors
analyzed the mixture of drugs and have been able to neutralize
them fairly well. The types of drugs used backs up LeBlanc's
hunch. They found traces of drugs used only by the KGB."

"Why?" Alexandra pleaded. "He's an old man! He's
retired. Why him?"

"I think you know the answer to that," Treadwell responded. He took a seat at the table. "He might be retired, but
he carries in his head the most confidential secrets of our
strategic submarine nuclear missile forces."

"Did they find out anything useful?"

Treadwell shrugged. "We'll have to wait to see if anything
happens. We'll know better in a little while. They're releasing
LeBlanc this morning and he's going to join us here to make
preparations for moving the admiral here just as soon as he can
be moved. There's a fully equipped clinic here. But until he
gets here, we'll just have to wait."

"Wait, wait wait," Alexandra complained. "All I do is
wait. All we do is wait!" She stood up abruptly. Her chair
crashed over backward. "I'm tired of waiting. I'm not used to
waiting. I'm used to *doing* something."

"That's the reason I came, Ms. Downing," Treadwell said
calmly.

"I'm sorry," she said. "What is it I can do?"

"Sansome's computer search has turned up a series of
strange shipments from Fleming Industries to an offshore
exploration rig owned by Global Energy. The rig is located
south of here, off Huntington Beach. From the other information we've been able to gather about the operation of the Tesla
weapon, I have a hunch that the rig might be involved."

"An oil rig?" Alexandra said. "How?"

"Remember Project Sanguine?" She nodded. "Remember
how they had to bury their broadcast cables in a certain strata
of rock to communicate with the submarines under water?"
She nodded again. "That same type of rock stratum can be
found about twelve thousand feet below the seabed just off the
coast here. I believe they have been using that rig to drill and
plant their antenna cables that will enable the pulse weapon to

overload the circuits of submarines under water just as the weapon will do above the surface."

"What do you want me to do?"

"You're an excellent sailor?" Treadwell asked.

"Yes," she answered. "What would you like me to do?"

"Help us locate that rig and destroy it," Treadwell said flatly. "If we can do that, we at least have the hope of salvaging some of our nuclear deterrent force in case all else fails."

In case all else fails. In case Jay fails. In case Jay dies. She thought of life without Jay. He wasn't dead yet.

"Will you do it?" Treadwell asked. "None of us here are really good small craft sailors. Modesti has big ships and Lamb, well, it's been years since he even set foot—"

"I'll do it."

"Good," Treadwell said simply.

An alarm shrieked.

"What's wrong?"

"I don't know," Treadwell said. He hurried to the door. Alexandra followed.

"This way," the FBI agent said tersely. He made his way toward the front of the facility, unsnapping the hammer strap from his revolver. She felt naked without her .45. Should she follow Treadwell or retrieve the gun? She wavered, then caught up with him.

Treadwell stopped at a heavy, unmarked door with a peephole and a combination keyboard. He punched at the pad and jerked open the door.

The room resembled the control panel of a giant airliner, a television control room. Two men dressed in suits conferred, their hands fluttering across vast panels of switches, indicator lights and other controls. Color monitors covered one entire wall, a glowing mosaic of closed circuit pictures of both the interior and the exterior of the facility. Each was marked with a small plastic sign denoting the area covered. A red light shone beneath a screen that played forth an image of a blank expanse of concrete bounded by a chain-link fence.

"Get us a magnification of that," one of the men said to the other. Quickly the monitor above the red light zoomed in. Fascinated by the technology, Alexandra watched the technicians manipulate the camera, scanning the fence and the surrounding area.

"There!" one of the men cried. "There in the center. Zoom in!" The screen showed a clear closeup of an opening cut in the chain-links of the fence.

"Sector Zeus nine," the man barked into a microphone, "red alert for intruders. All units maximum alert." He hit a green button and the shrieking siren abruptly ceased.

"Check the infrared for evidence of body heat and the motion detectors," one of the two technicians calmly told the other.

"Hello, George," one of the technicians offered, taking note of Treadwell and Alexandra for the first time. "Looks like we've got a little bit of excitement this morning. Looks like one or two men. Nothing to worry about. Security outside will mop things up. But just to make sure, we've sealed the entrance and all ports to the outside. They could fire howitzers at us all day and all that would happen is that the television reception would get a little shaky." He smiled reassuringly, a man who knew his equipment and its capabilities.

There was another siren, another red light under another screen. Then, one after another, the red lights blinked on until the wall of television monitors became a wall of glaring lights.

"Goddamn!" cursed the technician. "I don't see a fucking thing." He covered his ears with a set of bulky headphones. Through the din, Alexandra made out his commands to security forces outside to report their observations. And then the man's face grew ashen.

"No one's answering," he said desperately. "There's no response from any of the units."

"That's impossible!" the other man cried.

"Just give it a try," the first technician yelled angrily, ripping the headphones off his head. While his companion tried without success to raise the security patrols outside, the first man opened the door to what appeared to be a closet and walked in. He reappeared with M-16s and a pile of bulky black vests.

"Here," he said, handing them around. "You may need these." Chivalrously, Treadwell helped Alexandra into the bulky black bulletproof vest.

"Do you know how to use one of these?" Treadwell asked as he handed her the M-16. She shook her head.

"You know how to use any kind of firearm?" She nodded. "Good."

The walls of the facility shook like an animal shedding fleas, throwing them all to the floor.

"Oh, God!" the first technician said. Every video monitor suddenly displayed the same scene: a face leering so close to the camera lens that the facial features were grotesquely distorted. The lips of the face mouthed the words "Goodbye" slowly. Then the screens went blank.

"Someone's jammed the closed circuit system," the first technician said. The other technician opened his mouth, but was silenced as the control panels bleated and blinked.

"It can't be!" the technician shouted over the cacophony. "It would take an army to set off every sensor at once."

"Or someone who knows how the system works," Treadwell yelled in Alexandra's ear. Taking her by the elbow and pointing her to the door, he said, "Let's get out of here."

"Where?" she yelled.

"To a safer place," he said as they left the room carrying their M-16s. Shutting the door to the complex closed off most of the noise. In the rest of complex, only a single siren split the air. Dust swirled in layers, the detritus of the earlier explosion.

"Get to the center of the facility," Treadwell said. He started down the hall at a slow jog. Alexandra followed. Lamb, Curry and Modesti ran toward them, Modesti leading with his mouth moving. No words could be heard over the siren.

The rough cloth of the flak vest rubbed abrasively against Alexandra's neck and cheeks as she ran, and she found herself hoping it wouldn't leave a red mark on her skin. She scolded herself for such trivial thoughts.

The floor heaved under her feet. She was slammed into the wall and then there was carpeting under her face. The explosion racked her entire body. Metal beams groaned as the powerful explosion twisted them out of shape. A hailstorm of plaster and splinters rained down on her. She coughed from the dust. Around her others were coughing, too.

As Alexandra struggled to her feet, she noticed that the siren had changed pitch. Then she realized the siren had been silenced and she was listening to the screams of a human being in mortal pain. Unsteadily, she got to her feet, leaning against the wall for support. White-hot pain blazed in her left knee when she put weight on it, and she cried out involuntarily for just an instant. The pain was bearable, but it had surprised her.

"Are you all right?" Treadwell stumbled toward her through the debris in the hallway. His face was covered with blood. His hair, which had been immaculately combed just moments before, was matted to his forehead by a red paste of blood and dirt.

"I'll survive," Alexandra said. She leaned against the wall to inspect the knee. There was no blood. "I must have twisted it when I fell."

The screams of agony crescendoed.

"Who is that?" she asked him. "We ought to help him."

Treadwell shook his head. "It's Curry. A support beam fell across his hips. Nearly cut him in two. He'll be dead quickly. Someone placed an explosive charge on the other side of the wall. It held, but the armor plating was shattered inside and the pieces cut them to bits. We've got to get out of here before they can set any more charges. Can you move?"

She winced as she tested the knee. "I think so." Biting on her lower lip so tightly it drew blood, she stood.

"Good," Treadwell said, bending over to pick her M-16 out of the trash on the floor. "Wait here for just a moment." With an agility that was surprising for a man covered with blood, he swiftly made his way back to the security control room, emerging less than a minute later with an armload of clips for the M-16s.

"Stuff these in every pocket you've got," Treadwell ordered. "We may need them all." With that, he began picking his way through the rubble. Alexandra gritted her teeth against the intense pain in her knee and followed him.

"Where are we headed?" she asked.

Treadwell was turning to answer her when a blast even more powerful than the first knocked their feet out from under them. As the debris settled once more, Alexandra heard excited voices. She felt a fresh blast of cold outside air, and she smelled fire, the same kind of fire that had consumed Lee Goldberg in Luxembourg. But before the terror could grip her, she felt Treadwell pulling her up, shoving the M-16 in her hands, urging her forward.

Oblivious to pain, she ran from the approaching voices.

* * *

"Okay, asshole, drive the car or die!" said Jay Fleming as he jammed the muzzle of the Colt .45 in the ribs of FitzGerald's driver. With the start of the shooting, the man had gotten in and started up the Jeep. He hadn't expected Jay to come charging out of the restaurant.

"Where?" the man said.

"Away from here," Jay ordered. The sheriff's deputies rounded the corner and loosed a volley of shots. The Jeep rocketed forward, its rear wheels spinning a smokescreen of dust. The driver pressed the accelerator to the floor.

"Toward the encampment," Jay ordered.

"Yes, sir."

Behind them, he saw the deputies racing for their cars. They would be on them in a matter of minutes.

"Don't spare the speed," Jay said. "If they catch us, I'll kill you anyway, so you don't need to be too careful with your driving. Understood?"

The driver nodded.

With one hand, Jay ripped the driver's rearview mirror out of its mounting and then crawled over the back of the seat and into the very back of the Jeep. He opened the back window and tailgate. In the distance, he could see the rooster tail of dust approaching.

"I may jump out," Jay yelled to the driver, "but I'll blow your head off if you turn around. So just keep on driving." The driver nodded nervously.

As the Jeep climbed the precipitous one-lane dirt road cut in the face of the cliff overlooking Isthmus Cove and skidded around a bend that took them momentarily out of sight of the police or any observers near the pier, Jay said a small prayer, tucked the .45 into his jacket pocket and launched himself into the air. If he remembered correctly, this was the bend that overlooked the sheer cliff under which he and friends had done some scuba diving a number of months back. *If* he remembered correctly, Jay would plunge through a kelp bed at the base of the cliff in about three seconds. If.

Jay stabilized himself feet first, got his body as vertical as possible. It wouldn't hurt if he hit the surface vertically. If he panicked, it would be like landing on concrete. If.

Just before his toes plunged through the surface, Jay looked out toward the mainland and, just about where the Asian Pacific Container Terminal should be, he saw an oily black pillar of smoke climbing into the morning sky like a charred finger pointing to heaven. As the surface of the ocean washed past his eyes, he wondered if the smoke was coming from the facility. He hated a world that hinged on "if."

Chapter Forty-four

The constellations rocked gracefully past Jay Fleming's eyes as he lay on the deck looking up at the sky through a small rectangular hatch on the top of the battered landing craft's cabin. Unsettled winds whipped and swirled outside, whistling across the open hatch.

The boat's radio, turned down so low he had to strain to hear it over the louder gusts of wind, reported strong Santa Ana winds building up over the mainland. The unusually dry weather, combined with the hot dry southern gusts, had whipped up disastrous brush fires on the mainland. The rains in Southern California usually start in mid-December. But the odd weather patterns had kept the area almost summery long past then.

A subdivision of expensive homes in some canyon near Malibu had been decimated by one fire, the radio said, and another development near Laguna was being threatened.

The Santa Anas had started to pick up at about 10 P.M., but had still not established their dominance over the prevailing northwest winds. The air chopped and whirled dizzily in every direction as the two winds clashed.

Jay slowly pushed himself up and turned off the commercial radio station. He had heard all the news reports over the sixteen hours he had been cooped up in the old boat. Aside from the brush fires, the radio's main news had been the destruction of the Asian Pacific Container Terminal Docks in Long Beach,

345

still under investigation, and the search on Catalina by local and federal government SWAT teams for a psychotic murderer who killed industrialist Liam FitzGerald on Thursday morning.

They still hadn't used his name. Jay flicked on the switch to the VHF radiotelephone. Either they didn't yet know his identity, or the Committee of Seven was keeping it secret.

By noon the radio was reporting no signs of survivors in the container terminal. Alexandra. He had never known such pain since the death of his parents. The tears came freely for the first time in a decade. He wondered whether it was a blessing or a curse for Alexandra to have unlocked such feelings.

What made it hurt all the more was the report that Daniel Fraser had been attacked in his home by an unknown killer. The admiral was in a coma from which doctors said he would probably never awaken. LeBlanc had also been admitted to the hospital but was expected to be released soon.

He was alone again, cold again inside.

The VHF was silent. He ran the selector through all eighty-eight channels. Other than some conversation on 13 between two freighters somewhere in the channel, the airwaves had quieted. It was a far cry from the first frantic hours after his escape.

The old rustbucket landing craft had been closer to his dive, and Jay knew from experience that the old boat was used infrequently. After breaking into the cabin, the first thing he had done was to turn on the VHF to Channel 16, the emergency channel. The conversation had blazed with traffic. The Harbor Patrol was calling for the Coast Guard, had reported that people had been killed and that the killer was headed to the Shepherd's Club encampment. They had all taken the bait.

Over the next hours, Jay had needed no radio to ascertain what was going on. A Coast Guard patrol boat arrived within an hour, and boats and helicopters from the Los Angeles City and County SWAT teams as well as those from the FBI arrived one after another. Through the dingy portholes, Jay watched them jam the pier and storm off toward waiting vehicles which tore up the single dirt road toward Shepherd's Cove. From the last radio transmissions he had heard, they were combing the west end of the island for him and had taken up positions around the encampment to guard the captains of American industry.

They would be well-guarded, Jay knew, and, despite the flap, would not alter their schedule. To do so would be to admit they could be panicked. These were not men who liked to admit such things, particularly to the media which would be covering the incident for all their ratings were worth.

Jay switched off the VHF and stepped quickly down a set of half-rusted metal stairs into a dank room that smelled of urine, ancient bilge water and gasoline. Navigating by feel, Jay made his way to a ramshackle bench in the engine room. He had explored the area earlier, in the daylight.

His hands groped for half-familiar handholds, his feet searched for the slippery path. He stumbled against something that clattered against the hull and then splashed into the bilge water.

"Shit," he muttered as he felt his left foot slide into murky water. The water squished in his shoe as he finally made his way to the bench. The odor of gasoline grew stronger. He waved his hand about in front of him and finally collided gently with an oblong object that felt like a water balloon hung by a string. The surface was wet with gasoline. Jay probed the exterior of the object and found the source of the leak: a pinhole at the end of a nipple-like protrusion on the bottom of it. He smiled and looked at the glowing face of his watch: seventeen minutes. The others had taken between sixteen and twenty minutes. Consistent enough for his purposes.

Calmly he made his way back to the cabin of the boat. As he gratefully inhaled the fresher air, he thoroughly ransacked the lockers and drawers there.

When he had finished, he had more than two dozen condoms. That would be plenty, he thought as he stuffed them in the frayed pocket of a ragged black plastic slicker hanging next to the helm.

He wrapped the .45 and his shoes in the plastic slicker and tied them in a bundle with a length of frayed rope, and then quietly stepped out on deck. The moon had swelled a bit from the night before but still offered little in the way of illumination.

As Jay slid into the choppy waters of Isthmus Cove, the

sounds of helicopters came to his ears dimly from the direction
of Shepherd's Cove.

"This is blackmail!" complained the florid man with distinguished gray sideburns and black hair. "This is the most
outrageous act I have ever . . . I won't sign it. By God,
You've gone too far this time, Strand! You won't get away with
this!" The man's hands were trembling with rage.

Steven Strand looked calmly at his accuser, the chief
executive officer of a huge conglomerate that owned everything from cupcake bakeries to jet fighter factories.

"Of course you will, Sam," Strand replied. "You will sign
because you know the necessity of making sure that no one can
break ranks. Loyalty must be one hundred per cent. Ninety-
nine percent is a failure."

Sam Gianelli glared silently at Strand.

"Sam," Strand said conciliatingly, "all the paper says is
what we've all known for years. Look." Strand leaned over
and plucked a thick sheaf of papers from his highly polished
campaign desk. He handed the sheaf to Gianelli. "Look
through it." Gianelli held the papers as though they were a nest
of vipers. "Go on. It's my own. I've signed it."

Reluctantly, Gianelli took the papers and looked through
them, his eyes widening with surprise. "You did all this?"
Gianelli said.

"Yes, Sam," Strand said proudly.

Gianelli handed the sheaf of papers back to Strand. "That
puts things in a different light," he admitted. "But I still don't
think we ought to put things like these on paper. If anyone ever
got hold . . ."

"They won't, Sam," Strand promised, "just as long as
every member does his part. You sat through the briefings
tonight. You know how important it is for every member to do
exactly as he's been told."

Gianelli nodded. "But this is a confession," he protested.
"It says that I've been overcharging the government and
diverting the funds into purchases of obsolete steel manufacturing facilities."

"I know what it says, Sam," Strand said firmly. "And you
know what it says. Is there anything in there that isn't true?"

The two men grappled with each other's eyes. Strand pinned

Gianelli in less than a minute. "There is nothing inaccurate," he said.

"But I don't like it put into writing."

"Will you fail to make a handsome profit on your investments once we have disabled the high-tech facilities of the Japanese and German and South Korean steel mills?"

Gianelli shook his head.

"With their advanced mills out of the way, America can't help but dominate the world steel market again, now can we?" Strand persisted.

"Yes, but—"

"No buts," Strand said. "You sat in on the briefings. You know how carefully this entire procedure has been organized. Each piece is vital. And it's vital that no one gets cold feet.

"No doubt there will be some heat from all of this," Strand said, standing up and walking to the tightly zippered entrance to his tent. The fabric walls vibrated and swelled as the wind tore at its surface. "I have had to make sure that when the consumer groups start to whine and stir up the politicians and bureaucrats, and the investigative committees start asking what they think are hard questions, we all hang tough, that no one turns state's evidence."

Strand walked back to his desk, beside which a bewildered Sam Gianelli sat looking up. Strand slapped the papers on his desk with his palm. "These will make sure that we all hang tough. Understand?"

Gianelli nodded.

"Good," Strand said, handing him a pen. "Now sign."

Gianelli complied.

The Santa Anas breathed warmly through the open flaps as Gianelli departed. It seemed to wash away the stink of fear that the man had left behind. Perhaps, Strand thought, they should have recruited the chairman of Gianelli's company instead. Well, he thought, replacing Gianelli's file in its malila folder, it was too late now.

The signed statement, Strand—and he assumed that Gianelli and the rest—knew was only a formality. The Committee of Seven had amassed a remarkably detailed accounting of how, when, why and where each of the Shepherd's Club members had diverted government money. But Strand wanted everyone to acknowledge his personal responsibility.

Strand lifted his voice over the howl of the wind. "Send in Carothers." Moments later, the chairman and chief executive officer of the country's largest telecommunications manufacturer appeared, the next to last person Strand had to deal with that night.

Chapter Forty-five

Isthmus Cove is a protected anchorage, but its east-facing harbor offers little protection from the infrequent Santa Anas that blast warm and hot out of the deserts on the mainland. Most of the smaller craft had weighed anchor and headed for more protection. Only the work boats and other seaworthy craft like the Coast Guard patrol boat remained.

One choppy wave after another slapped into the back of Jay's head as he dog-paddled along the shoreline, trying to keep the black slicker with his gun and shoes from getting submerged completely.

He shivered as his toes scraped against the sand and gravel at the base of the cliffs. To his left, the lights of the pier and its fuel dock lay about a hundred and fifty yards away. A Coast Guard sentry patrolled the pier. Directly ahead, some fifty yards away, was the same vista that had greeted him the night before: the motley collection of buildings, restaurant, outhouses, general store.

Jay balanced motionlessly on his toes, maintaining his balance with one arm as he scanned the shoreline. He looked left and right, letting the more light-sensitive areas of his peripheral vision probe the deeper shadows for signs of a guard. But he saw none. The search and the vigilance was concentrated farther west.

Silently Jay swam on, following the shoreline as it curved slightly west, ending at the small beach twenty-five yards from the volleyball nets. He crawled up on the beach, trying to remain in the scrubby underbrush and grasses that clung to the steep hillside next to it.

Willing his breath to be calm, Jay sat in the brush and with trembling fingers untied the black plastic slicker. His shoes and gun had fared well. He pulled on the shoes, tucked the gun into his waistband, and slipped into the black plastic slicker. Although people moved purposefully along the dock, from there to the latrine area and back, Jay had seen no one near the rear of the general store during half an hour of observation.

Finally, just before his watch read 2 A.M., Jay moved. Running in spurts, he made his way from the brush to a tall palm tree that canted at a very acute angle. From there, he made his way to a pile of lumber and finally to the rear entrance of the general store. The howling wind covered his noise completely. It would also cover any attacker. It whipped at his soaked pants and brought on another attack of shivers despite the relatively mild weather. It couldn't have been less than sixty degrees.

Jay examined the lock on the rear door, and as he expected, it was a single lock in the knob, no deadbolt. The Isthmus was notorious for its lack of crime. Until I arrived this morning, Jay thought.

He grabbed the knob and wiggled it. It was locked. From his side pocket, he pulled the Swiss army knife he always carried when he went to sea, and opened its large blade. An expert could slip these latches in a split second, but he was no expert.

He carved at the doorjamb surrounding the knob until he had exposed the latch. He then slid back the latch. The door opened quietly. Jay swept the shavings into the sand, then stepped inside quickly and shut the door.

Heart pounding, Jay stood by the door to get his bearings. He was in a sort of stock room with boxes and cannisters stacked from floor to ceiling. Would there be a dog inside? Some sort of silent alarm? He thought not. The sort of people who visited the Isthmus were affluent, definitely not burglars. If they were criminals, they were either the white-collar variety, or the shoplifting type.

Jay made his way into the main room of the store, an area which he had shopped in many times. He moved from counter to counter, from display to display to hide him from the view of anyone looking inside through the store's large windows. He had to crawl flat on his belly across the far end of the store where outboard motors were displayed in a large open space.

Jay made his way around the store, taking his booty back to the stock room to examine it more leisurely. In less than half an hour, he had accumulated a backpack filled with cans of sterno, a roll of aluminum foil, nylon twine, matches, a disposable lighter for backup, a plastic funnel, a flashlight and batteries, a roll of black electrician's tape, a half dozen containers of butane for camp stoves, a small hand compass and a topographical map of the island. To them he added the condoms taken from the boat as well as several packets of balloons. Next to the pack sat two gallons of white gasoline fuel for Coleman camp stoves.

Jay crawled behind the checkout counter, and using a screwdriver taken from a sale rack next to the cash register, pried loose a flimsy lock on a cabinet containing binoculars, walkie talkies, watches and other valuable items. He took a pair of binoculars.

Next, Jay foraged in the food section of the store and found six large cans of stewed tomatoes. He took the cans to the employee's bathroom in one corner of the store room and, with the opener on his Swiss army knife, he opened all six cans and dumped the contents in the toilet. After rinsing out the cans, he made several small holes in the base of each one, and crammed them all in the backpack.

The lingering smell of the stewed tomatoes reminded him that he had not eaten all day and probably wouldn't for another full day—if he survived another full day.

Crawling back into the store, Jay raided the cooler of a large lump of cheese, a sack of hard rolls and two large bottles of carbonated water. He set the bread and cheese out on a cardboard box of toilet paper in the back room and opened one of the bottles of water. He took a long draw from the bottle. Then, as he unwrapped the plastic from around the cheese—a huge wedge of Jarlsberg—his mouth watered almost uncontrollably.

He ate quickly, stuck the remainder of the food and water in the bulging backpack and slung it over his shoulders. With a can of the stove fuel in each hand, he ran quickly from one dim shadow to the other as he made a crooked escape from the small settlement at Isthmus Cove.

The road to Catalina Harbor moves through broad flat terrain with only an occasional eucalyptus tree for cover, so Jay decided to head immediately west into the hills. He followed a shallow draw that took him very rapidly upward. Sage and succulents rapidly yielded to cacti and thorns that clawed at his legs and savaged his hands when he used them to climb upward.

The draw flattened out some two hundred and fifty feet above the harbor, and Jay used the respite to pull out the map and get his bearings. He pulled the flashlight out of the pack, inserted the batteries and screwed the light back together. Next he rummaged through the package of balloons and found a red one which he cut with his knife until he had a section that would fit over the lens. He secured the balloon with the electrician's tape, then turned it on. A muted red light that wouldn't ruin his night vision glowed for an instant before he quickly shut it off. There was too much light. Using more of the black electrical tape, Jay covered about two thirds of the lens before he was satisfied that he couldn't be seen.

The red glow softly illuminated the contours of the map. Jay ran his finger west along the northern coast from Isthmus Cove, past Emerald Bay before he found Shepherd's Cove. Pulling out the compass, Jay oriented the map and found that a course roughly north west, about three hundred and thirty degrees, would take him directly to the Shepherd's Club encampment.

From Shepherd's Cove, Jay's eyes wandered south. He needed a base of operations from which to conduct his raids. He found what he was looking for: a steep barranca with what the map showed to be an intermittent stream running down from it. On arid islands like Catalina, the only place likely to sustain small trees and shrubs that offered concealment was in such a gorge. The head of the canyon seemed to be on a bearing of about two hundred and eighty degrees, almost straight west. Jay lashed the cans of gasoline to either side of the pack and pressed on.

The course followed the southern flank of the ridge of hills that runs like a spine down the middle of the island. The moon shone dimly on this side of the hills, and Jay moved in rapid jerky movements from one patch of scrub to another, trying to use the scant vegetation to his advantage. Below him, he saw stunted trees and bushes in the barrancas. He followed them on his map, comparing the veins of vegetation with the twisted lines on the map.

He moved swiftly, covering the first mile in about fifteen minutes, the second in about twenty. His course took him continually upward. He crested the ridge at about 3 A.M. The Santa Anas blasted him in the face while the colder, wetter northwesterly winds hammered at his back. Here on the ridge the two air masses clashed with a continually renewed vigor, sweeping great whirling clouds of dust from the ground and whipping them into the air. The wind cooled the perspiration on his face and coated him with a fine grit. Somewhere in the distance he heard the faint sounds of a helicopter.

Directly below him, across two hundred and fifty yards of barren territory, he could see the first low bushes which he had hoped would clothe the barranca. Further down, the shrubs gave way to what, though stunted by lack of water and twisted by the vicious wind, were, nevertheless, trees.

Slightly to the left, and farther on by a mile or so, was the near perimeter of the encampment: a double enclosure of chain-link fencing lit at each corner, and in between, with klieg lights. The lesser illumination of mercury vapor lights sat atop wooden tripods. Guards moved in the no man's land between the two fences, and on both sides of it. Jay knew that following the shooting of FitzGerald, the guard must have been intensified. Sophisticated listening devices were salted liberally about the grounds. Any detection would be met with instant and irresistible force.

Half running, half sliding down the steep slope, Jay charged over the crest of the hill and hurried down its exposed flank to the protection of the vegetation below him. He had gained about half the distance when he heard the chopping thuds of a helicopter blade slicing behind him.

He was completely exposed, and would be until he covered another one hundred yards. Downhill, he thought, eleven, twelve seconds at most. Just give me a few seconds, God, he thought as he tried to keep his legs under him. The surface underfoot was loose rocks and dirt and sand that gave way with each step. Jay leaped, slid, landed. The protective tangle of brush grew closer as the helicopter grew louder.

He was only a handful of strides from the bush when the helicopter burst over the crest of the ridge, rotors thwacking, searchlights casting a ghastly blue glow over the slope. Jay rolled into the bushes head over heels as the helicopter shot past and then banked.

Had he been seen? Why else would they turn back? The area would be swarming with security men in minutes.

Jay crashed through the low bushes toward the low trees just ahead. The copter had been heading for the encampment. Jay shed the pack and withdrew the .45. If they had seen him, he was dead. But he'd take them with him.

The helicopter droned past to the west of him, and as it did, Jay caught sight of a huge numeral "10" on the side and the caption "Newschopper Ten" just below it. Inside the cabin, camera lights were trained on a well-coiffed man with a bright smile.

Jay's shoulders sagged with relief as his fear turned first to anger and then to thanksgiving. Finally, he began to laugh softly. The chopper had come about so quickly because of flight restrictions over the encampment. No one had seen him at all.

The laughter came in deeper and deeper sobs until Jay realized he was crying. Less than three weeks ago, he had been the owner of a multibillion-dollar corporation, comfortable and secure, if not terribly happy, and now he was a hunted animal on the side of a barren island off the coast of California, the woman he had swiftly grown to love more than life itself now dead, on the other side of twenty-six miles of water.

He lay down on the dusty ground and sobbed convulsively into his hands. "Alexandra," he said as if the sound of her name would summon her, or return him to an earlier hour, when he could have refused to leave her, when they both could have fled to a place where Strand and his people could never find them.

He cried for several minutes. Slowly, like a rising tide, the outside world seeped into his thoughts.

He silently cursed himself. He'd help no one sitting here and crying. He looked around. He was on the side of a steep

avine. Vegetation of all sorts grew up from the floor of the
avine and laced into a canopy against the sky.

Jay dumped the contents of the pack onto the ground. He
paused for a slug of water and another bite of food and set to
work. He had to have all of his tricks ready and going while it
was still dark. Otherwise he'd never get away. By his
reckoning, he had no more than two and a half hours.

Fleming counted the condoms again: two dozen, exactly. He
let his mind wonder briefly about a skipper who would keep a
copious supply aboard a scow like the landing craft. Either a
prodigious lovemaker or a dreamer. Jay tore open the foil
packages and slipped four of them, one after another, over the
end of his flashlight. When he was finished, he pulled the four
thicknesses off, repeating the procedure until he had six sets of
four condoms. He laid them out carefully on the hard earth.
Along the top edge of one of the cans of stove fuel, he tacked
six short pieces of the electrician's tape. Then, he carefully cut
six lengths of twine about a foot long from the ball of nylon
twine and laid them beside the condoms. Next he unscrewed
the cap on both cans of white gasoline stove fuel.

Rummaging among the items he had spilled from his pack,
Jay pulled out the funnel and then picked up one of the condom
sets. Squatting down over his work, he inserted the small end
of the funnel in the innermost condom, and poured about a
quart of stove fuel into it. The soft pliable rubber swelled like a
balloon.

Jay set the gasoline can aside and pulled a strip of tape from
the other can and wrapped it tightly around the neck of his four-
layer condom balloon. Setting aside the funnel, Jay gently set
the gasoline-filled balloon on the ground and tied the neck even
more securely with a length of nylon twine. He then taped over
that to make sure there were no leaks. Not until the right time.
He looked at his watch. 3:15 A.M.

By 3:30, pack re-loaded with his odd cargo, the last of the
cheese and bread consumed, Jay made his way down through
the brush in the barranca toward Shepherd's Cove. He had
about forty-five minutes before the first condom began to leak.
He needed to have them all in place by that time.

The footing was firmer among the shrubs and grasses. Jay
pushed his way confidently downward, knowing the sounds of

his movements were covered by the howling of the winds that clutched and tore at the tops of the meager trees.

The food had revitalized him, the exercise had warmed him and the dry Santa Anas had chased most of the moisture from his clothes. On the whole, he felt as well as a man could expect who was skulking around before dawn on an arid island with a small army hunting him.

After ten minutes, Jay saw the yawning mouth of a corrugated metal culvert. The surface of a dirt road appeared above it. The stream of the barranca was dry now, but without the culvert, the road would wash away during the rainy season.

Jay stopped and listened. The perimeter of the encampment, according to the topographical map, was less than a hundred yards beyond the road. That meant guards and patrols. Danger raised the tiny hairs on the back of his neck and cleared his head.

He listened carefully, but heard nothing. He started to press on when his nose caught the faintest whiff of tobacco smoke. He froze. Turning to face the wind, Jay caught a fleeting glimpse of a bright orange glow that flared and then died. It was up on the road and moving slowly.

Jay tried to merge with the shadows at the bottom of the barranca and watched as two men carrying what looked like M-16s walked past. They moved silently, like ghosts in a dream, the sounds of their footsteps muffled by the wind.

As soon as they had passed out of sight, Jay jogged to the culvert and crawled quickly through it on his hands and knees. A torrent of wind howled.

From the mouth of the culvert, Jay looked out at the double fence of the encampment and the guards. To go farther would be to invite death. But that was fine. He didn't need to go much farther.

Trying to scan the road above him for any sign of patrols, Jay strained his senses and, finding nothing, darted out of the culvert and into the concealment of a scraggly group of shrubs.

Jay swiftly pulled out one of the condoms, one of the empty tomato cans, a can of Sterno and the matches and lighter. With a length of twine, Jay tied the condom balloon to a low branch of a shrub. It hung like some poisonous tropical fruit, about a foot off the ground. Jay checked the surface to make sure there was no gasoline leaking. Then he checked his watch. The first condom in each set was undoubtedly leaking by now.

Speedily, Jay pried off the lid of the Sterno can and placed it in the bottom of the empty tomato can and set them just to one side of the condom.

The wind quickly blew out the matches Jay tried to use. Each one seemed like the firing of a rescue rocket in the night, announcing his position to the world. Jay grabbed the butane lighter, turned its selector to high, and finally managed to light the Sterno in the bottom of the can.

As he had expected, the tomato can shielded the Sterno, which burned steadily at the bottom despite the heavy winds. He covered all but about one third of the mouth of the tomato can with aluminum foil to block the dim purple, blue light from the Sterno's flame. He wasn't worried about the fire going out from lack of oxygen. The small holes he had punched in the bottom of the can would let in enough. Jay placed the can beside the condom balloon and finally pulled out one of the oil filter–shaped cans of camp stove butane and set it below the condom. He stood back several paces and looked at his handiwork. It was nearly invisible to his eye. He reloaded the backpack and retraced his path through the culvert to the other side of the road.

It would get dangerous now. According to his map he had about a mile and a half of mostly open, exposed territory to cross in order to set his devices where they would do the most damage.

At the top, the terrain looked barren and cold beyond the concealment of the barranca. Randomly spaced clumps of sage and yuccas, an odd gully here and there and, about a quarter of a mile away, another brush-filled barranca. Jay looked about him, his eyes transfixed by the encampment. He had once derided those who charged that the club was an evil cartel. He thought it only a group of greedy old men with no other friends. Perhaps a few deals were made among them, but nothing of consequence.

He now had a chance to undo his mistake. He took a deep breath and plunged out of his hiding place, sprinting toward more cover.

The giant hand of the wind tried to push Jay back. He pressed forward against it. Exhilaration coursed through his body, fortified him, almost made him giddy with excitement. Was someone training a night scope on his back at this very minute?

Moments later, the branches of the shabby plants in the approaching barranca reached out to him like welcoming arms. He plunged noisily into their embrace.

Jay sat for a moment, breathing heavily, letting his heart catch up with his swift run. He looked around. Though narrower and shallower, this barranca was a twin of the first. He got to his feet and began another downhill journey toward the road. All the devices needed to be on the same side of the road as the encampment.

Suddenly he froze: things were moving in the darkness. Jay couldn't tell if the movements were only induced by the wind, or caused by animals. The cool shade and the protection offered by the shrubs attracted the island's creatures just as they had him. For the first time, he was aware of the dangers that some of them might present. Rattlesnakes. But it was cool for them. They were sluggish in cooler weather. Still, Jay thought, if he stepped on one . . . He tried to take his mind off the possibility.

More careful now, Jay parted the vegetation, making his way downhill.

He had just caught sight of the road when a cough reached his ears. Jay spotted the silhouette of a man standing on the road. Jay looked at his watch. Time was running out.

Move! Jay urged silently. Go *on!* But the man remained. A stationary sentry. There was no culvert under the road this time. He would have to set the device on this side of the road. Silently, he unshouldered the pack. The branches of trees on both sides of the road overlapped. The fire would spread across the road without too much difficulty. Things could be worse.

Suddenly a clump of bushes next to the road bank rustled. Jay drew out the .45. It would alert the whole island. But if he had to use it . . .

The sentry was looking aimlessly toward the encampment, oblivious to the movement below. Jay dropped to one knee, training the muzzle of the .45 on the bushes. It didn't move like a human being. But it was large. What large animals lived on the island? Buffalo. But this was too small. Rabbits, but they were too small. Suddenly the air was split by a shriek. A black form with curling white teeth charged from the bushes and stopped less than ten feet from Jay.

A boar. A wild boar! Jay's hand shook. He looked at the razor-sharp tusks protruding from either side of the animal's mouth. Jay remembered stories of boar hunters being ripped and disemboweled by these creatures.

The sentry shouted from the road. "Who goes there?" The wind died down, and the metallic sounds of a cartridge being fed into a firing chamber carried through the night.

Jay's hand was steady as he leveled the .45 at the boar, training the muzzle on the big animal's shoulders. It weighed five hundred pounds if it weighed an ounce, and stared malevolently at Jay with yellow eyes that glowed in the dark. The smell of rotted blood and fur matted with offal and excrement reached Jay's nose.

"Come on out and you won't get hurt." The voice from the road was closer now. Moving slowly, trying not to spook the boar into a charge, Jay eased himself into the shadows at the edge of the barranca as the silhouette appeared.

The boar eyed Jay suspiciously, twitching with anticipation and indecision. The boar had smelled man before. Man was dangerous. But it had been days since he had eaten. The dry weather had taken its toll on what the island supported for him to prey on.

The boar strained at some invisible tether, its legs trembling. Jay had no idea whether the .45 could stop the creature before it gored him. And if he survived the boar, what of the sentry?

The boar edged forward.

The voice carried down from the road. "It's a fucking wild pig!" The static of a radio clearing its throat came broken through the night. Jay heard the voice behind him mumble something as the boar moved closer.

Fleming released the safety, and as he felt the sour breath of the boar, began to squeeze the trigger.

Three shots cracked from the roadway. The boar stiffened, turning his grotesque head toward the road.

"Hot damn!" an exuberant voice yelled from the road, followed by the crashing of a man down the incline.

The boar sank to its knees and rolled over. Jay edged farther into the shadows and waited for the second danger.

The sentry reached the boar seconds later. Jay trained the .45

on him as he laid his M-16 on the ground and walked around the boar.

"She-it," the soldier said. "Ain't seen one of you since I was back in the Ozarks." He walked around the dead creature, admiring the results of his marksmanship. Jay followed his every move with the .45, but he couldn't bring himself to pull the trigger. Go away, Jay urged. Just go away.

But the sentry continued to examine the boar he had bagged. Then the radio at his belt brought his attention back to business.

"Unit 33, report."

The soldier plucked the small portable walkie talkie from its belt holster. "Unit 33. All clear. It was a big fucking wild pig. I had to shoot it."

"Maintain your post," the radio's voice ordered. "File a report when your duty is over."

"Roger," the sentry said and replaced the radio in his belt.

The sentry pulled a broad-bladed knife from a scabbard at his right ankle and began to hack at the boar's curled tusks.

But the radio conversation had broken the man's spell, and as he worked, his eyes scanned the area. He saw the pack first. Abruptly, he shoved the knife in its scabbard and picked up his M-16. Warily he looked around him.

Jay felt the man's gaze sweeping over the foliage like the piercing beam of a prison searchlight. He aimed for the man's torso. Still he couldn't bring himself to shoot. This man's only fault was to work for people who wanted Jay dead. He had never done Jay any harm.

The soldier brought the muzzle of the M-16 around as he turned.

They locked eyes.

"Drop the gun," Jay said. "Drop it and you won't get hurt." The man froze. "I won't hurt you," Jay promised. "I'll tie you up. You'll be okay."

"You're the guy who murdered FitzGerald," the sentry said. It wasn't a question. "How am I supposed to trust a murderer? You're probably one of those psychos who'd tie me up and cornhole me and then shoot me in the head."

How could he explain? He had no time. The sentry brought the muzzle of the M-16 around. The first round from the .45 hit him squarely just above his solar plexus, lifted him on his toes, and dropped him in a crumpled pile on top of the boar. The M-16 clattered off into the bushes.

Jay rolled him onto his back. The shot had destroyed his heart. The sentry stared sightlessly up at the constellations. He was no older than nineteen.

"I'm sorry," Jay said to the young man's clear eyes. "I'm truly sorry." He grabbed the radio from the sentry's belt, turned it off and stuffed it in his backpack.

He set the next device as he had set the first, then hurried to the next site.

Chapter Forty-six

Jay suspended the last condom from the branches of a mesquite shrub, set out the last arrangement of Sterno, left the last can of butane and ran as fast as his weary legs would carry him. He climbed a low embankment and sat down to wait. He wanted to close his eyes, to stretch out on the little knoll and rest. But he sat with his back straight, hoping the discipline would help keep him alert and awake.

When the hands of his watch read 4:19, a bright yellow flame spurted out of the first barranca. It flared briefly, like a match struck to illuminate a dark room, then grew, feeding on the tinder and dry brush.

The last balloon burst into flame. Then, almost simultaneously, four more yellow creatures flared to life and began to feed on the land. The flames spread, whipped through the dry brush by the powerful Santa Anas. There were six loud explosions that sounded like grenades. Jay smiled with satisfaction as the butane cans threw flaming debris in every direction, spreading the fire as it did.

He reached into the nearly empty backpack and pulled out the binoculars and the last of his water. He drained the bottle and threw it away. He tore the plastic wrapping off the binoculars and brought them to his eyes. Below in the encampment, men were running wildly—Shepherd's Club members, assistants, security guards.

The sounds of sirens wafted up from the compound. Jay

watched as men, some half-dressed, others not dressed at all, emerged from their tents. Panic ran wild in the lanes among the tents.

Dropping the binoculars, Jay took in the entire scene. The wind was whipping the fires he had set high into the air, sending glowing cinders swirling through the night like swarms of angry fireflies. The first fire had nearly reached the ocean and was burning rapidly to the west in great flowing waves. The other fires had joined in a blazing arc which led to the sea. The encampment was caught between fire and water.

In the direction of Isthmus Cove, Jay heard sirens and horns. Although he couldn't see them, he knew those would be from the Coast Guard cutter preparing to lend assistance in evacuation. The road up from the Isthmus would shortly be crowded with trucks and cars carrying volunteers to fight the fire. If the world was lucky, this was one of those times they would be slow and ineffective.

The sounds of helicopters filled the air as three from television news departments, sent originally to cover the murder and the encampment, swooped and dipped over the tents, ignoring now any restrictions on air space.

The fire had reached the eastern perimeter now, and as Jay watched through the binoculars, he saw security guards fleeing from the advancing flames. A huge gust of wind sent flames leapfrogging over a group of three guards as they ran, engulfing them all. Jay jerked the glasses quickly away from the flaming bodies.

The group of tents nearest the eastern perimeter had caught fire, and Jay watched as the richest and most powerful men in the world streamed down toward the beach like refugees before an advancing army. Stripped of their trappings, their clothes and their pretensions, they were just ordinary human beings.

As he scanned the flaming encampment, he spotted an entourage of four running from a large white tent. Two of them carried rifles, probably M-16s Jay thought, although at this distance he couldn't be sure. He thought one of the unarmed men looked like Steven Strand. Jay squinted to make out the man's face. It was Strand. The man he wanted most was escaping. A large attaché case the size of a small suitcase was handcuffed to Strand's wrist.

Jay watched helplessly as the entourage made its way to the

helicopter pad where a ring of armed guards kept away an angry crowd. The rotors of the helicopter were already spinning.

The entourage forced its way through the crowd with the help of the armed men. Arms plucked at Strand. He struggled with them, yanking the attaché case first from one man and then another. One of his guards started clubbing people with the butt of his rifle.

They hurried toward the helicopter. A guard held the door open. As Strand and the rest of his entourage boarded the craft, the crowd surged forward, faces twisted with fear and rage. Jay looked on, horrified, as the guards ringing the helicopter opened fire.

The helicopter rose rapidly, but not before two men pushed past the guards and grabbed the aircraft's landing skids. It looked like the last helicopter out of the American embassy in Saigon. One of the armed men leaned out of the door and fired a round from his rifle at point-blank range into the heads of the men who clung to the skids. They plummetted out of the field of Jay's binoculars. The helicopter vanished into the darkness, heading toward the Palos Verdes Peninsula.

The fire gained height as the arc closed in on itself and chased the survivors to the beach. People crowded each other into the water, swimming toward the boats and yachts anchored there. Even the protestors were pulling in survivors.

If they only knew, Jay thought. They were saving those who would destroy so much for so many. Suddenly, Jay felt like someone had loaded his shoulders with sacks of sand. He let out a long weary sigh.

Jay reloaded the pack and looked back at the fire. Then he turned and ran for his boat.

Chapter Forty-seven

Huge wind-driven drops rolled off the corrugated roof like a hailstorm of marbles. The rains had finally come, and with a vengeance. Southern California was trying to cleanse itself. A chill blast knifed through one of the few cracks in the planked walls that he had not chinked with old newspapers. Jay shivered for an instant, steeled against the cold, and climbed rapidly out of the sleeping bag and hastened to pull his pants, a shirt and heavy sweater on over the long underwear in which he had fallen asleep.

Only after pulling on a pair of thick wool socks and hiking boots did the chills start to dissolve. He moved over to the Franklin stove and held his hands out next to it as if he were going to stop it from moving. The gray metal surface softly radiated heat. He walked over to a pile of split wood stacked next to the door and selected three medium-sized pieces and brought them back to the stove.

He poked the previous night's coals to life and added the new fuel. Almost instantly, there was a cheery blaze that began to dissolve the chill from the room.

Jay had discovered the one-room shack years ago while backpacking. It was accessible only by foot, and hidden in a tree-shrouded hollow some twelve miles from Sierra Madre. The nearest road, an overgrown forest service fire break, was half a mile away through heavy brush and sheer terrain that intimidated all but climbers who knew how to use their ropes and carabiners on the old pitons which protruded solidly from the rocks.

He came here to think when all of the ivy had been stripped from his life. He had come here when Helen had committed suicide and again when Strand had ousted him from Fleming Industries. And six days ago, after docking his boat at the transient docks in Marina Del Rey, he had the shack foremost in his mind.

The diamonds he had bought in Amsterdam, and which he had carried in his toilet kit, were exchanged at desperation prices, yet had still fetched more than $30,000 cash. Everything else he needed, including the battered four-wheel-drive pickup which was parked at the end of the fire road, had cost less than $5,000.

Opening the front door, Jay stepped quickly through the puddles that clung stubbornly to the weather boards on what served as a porch and grabbed an overflowing bucket from under the drainspout. He took it inside, filled the black metal coffeepot on the top of the Franklin stove, topped up the pitchers he used for washing and for drinking, and then replaced it under the spout to refill.

While the water heated, Jay washed his face and hands, and sat in an aluminum folding lawn chair in front of a small aluminum folding table on which sat a battery-powered television/radio combination the size of a shoe box. The sounds of a television game show filled the room briefly before he switched the selector and tuned it into the all-news radio station.

As he listened to the enumeration of floodings, slides, school closings, murders, traffic accidents, and assorted atrocities, Jay rummaged around in a brown paper grocery sack and pulled out a pumpernickel bagel and a hunk of Monterey Jack cheese. He munched on them while he waited for more news.

There had been more funerals, more memorial services, more bills introduced in legislative bodies providing for stricter punishment for terrorists, arsonists, murderers. But there was nothing new.

The initial reports about the Catalina Island fire had blamed it on what Steven Strand had called "environmental terrorists." Police had arrested every protestor they could find on the island, had raided the offices of Greenpeace, the Sierra Club, anyone else they could think of. Never in all the news reported had Jay Fleming's name been mentioned.

Strand and the surviving members of the Committee Seven had bigger fish to fry than one lonely fugitive. They would use the national outrage over the deaths of twenty-seven prominent industrialists and politicians as an excuse to shut off their most vocal critics.

Jay had not destroyed enough of the Committee of Seven's plans. He hoped he had interrupted them, perhaps delayed their plans for some months. But he didn't know. What he did know as he sat listlessly in the dingy gray shack was that he had brought untold persecution on the heads of innocent people and destroyed thousands of acres on Catalina Island. The invisible mass of the failure was crushing. And the hopelessness, the frustration.

Most painful was the loss of Alexandra. How could someone he had known for such a short time mean so much to him? There must be something he could do. In spite of the incessant rain, Jay daily climbed out of the hollow and took the pickup into Sierra Madre. He did it partly because he wanted to buy a newspaper to supplement the television and radio news, but mostly because the exercise helped tame the snakes that raged in his head, helped ease the torment.

Slowly, an idea had developed. Steven Strand was the key. The Committee of Seven, the entire Shepherd's Club plan, the use of the Tesla pulse weapon, all led back to Strand.

Jay stood up, grabbed a foam plastic cup from the grocery bag and added a teaspoon of instant coffee to it. He walked over to the Franklin stove and filled the cup with hot water from the teapot, then returned to the small table and sat down. Listening to the news with half an ear, he pulled a yellow legal pad toward him and stared at the list written on the first page:

1. Expensive car (Mercedes? Jag?), rented; 2. Explosives (How much will fill up the trunk? Packages filling back seat?); 3. Detonators (get with explosives); 4. Timing device.

The news had been filled with stories of car bombs going off and leveling vast buildings. He had only to remember the one that had killed Doug Denoff in Luxembourg. Somehow it seemed to complete some ghastly cycle that had to be closed before the evil could be contained. The expensive car would get him past the gates of Strand's palatial home in Palos Verdes. He would park it outside Strand's home, and figure out a way to escape. Or if he couldn't escape, he'd take Strand with him.

The conviction that Strand was the key to the entire conundrum had grown stronger each day. Every mechanism, whether it is a mechanical device or a human plan, has a linchpin that holds things together, allows them to work. Without Strand, Jay felt the Committee of Seven would start to bicker among itself, jockeying for power. The vast coordination necessary would be impossible as members of the Shepherd's Club lined up behind one or the other of the factions. Destroying Strand might be all it took to delay the plans indefinitely—time gained to do what? To figure out what to do.

But how to obtain the explosives eluded him. There must be some way of doing it quietly, of stealing them from a construction shack, of buying them from some illicit source. The car and the timing device would be no problem. But the explosives and their detonators were a serious one.

Perhaps he could locate someone who would steal the explosives and detonators and wire it all up. Surely there were criminals who would do that. And Jay had plenty of money.

He sipped at the coffee and stared into space. Like most law-abiding people, Jay had no contacts in the criminal world, and was as likely to run into an undercover policeman as to locate the right criminal. Then the idea struck.

A year or so ago, he and a group of friends had been sitting around Jay's living room reading aloud and chuckling over the classified advertisements in the back of a magazine that catered to mercenaries and other adventurers. Most of the ads were junk, but some advertised "no questions asked" services of almost any type from executive protection to search and destroy missions.

Jay jumped up, slipped on an insulated vest and rain suit. As he headed out the door of the cabin, he wondered what sort of "no questions asked" service he could get for $25,000.

The pickup slipped and slithered down the rutted road. Jay had the transmission in four-wheel drive, but it was all he could do to keep moving fast enough to avoid bogging down, and slow enough to avoid slipping off the path and crashing into one of the huge trees that lined the road like the pillars of a Greek temple.

As he squinted through the smeared windshield, rubbing the condensation off the inside with his sleeve, he made a mental note to buy new windshield wiper blades when he stopped for gas. Anticipation turned his depression into butterflies. Would the drug store in Sierra Madre have a copy of the magazines? Would he be able to find the right person? How did you approach them? The thought that some of the ads might be dummies placed there by law enforcement officers cast a brief shadow across his thoughts.

After driving for about half an hour, Jay spotted the slick shining surface of the paved main road about a quarter of a mile down hill. His grip on the wheel began to relax when suddenly he saw a Jeep Wagon pass slowly by the intersection, back up and turn on to the forest service road—heading straight for him.

Jay's heart stopped for an instant, and then made up for lost time. There was nowhere to go. The road was lined with trees that made for an impenetrable guardrail. There was a turn-around about a half mile up the road behind him. Jay flashed his brights. The Jeep stopped before it had come more than fifty yards. Then it reversed back to the main road to let Jay down.

Jay pulled the Colt .45 from his coat and laid it on the seat beside him. The only person he had ever told about the shack was Fraser. And according to the news reports he was still comatose.

The Jeep was waiting on the shoulder when Jay reached the main road. The driver flashed his high beams and beeped the horn in a friendly way. Jay grabbed the .45 and jogged toward the passenger side of the pickup. The man looked familiar. As he drew near, Jay recognized the face of Randall LeBlanc, Admiral Fraser's trusted right hand.

Fraser must have regained consciousness, Jay thought hopefully, and had sent LeBlanc for him. The strains of dark suspicion in Jay's mind were quickly buried by the thought that Fraser was alive. Suddenly, Jay wasn't completely alone anymore. If anyone could help him figure a way out of the maze he was in, it was Fraser. Jay tucked the .45 back in his vest pocket and leaned over to unlock the door for LeBlanc.

Randall LeBlanc piled into the passenger seat of Jay's pickup truck accompanied by a sheet of wind-crazed rain.

"Jesus!" LeBlanc exclaimed as he pulled the door shut behind him. "I can't believe this fucking weather." He smiled and wiped at his tangled hair with his right hand.

"Good morning," Jay said. The two men looked uncertainly at each other for a moment. Rain scoured the roof of the cab.

LeBlanc broke the silence. "He wants to see you."

"The admiral?"

"How else would I have found you?"

Jay nodded.

"You were the first person he asked for when he came to." LeBlanc said.

"How is he?"

"Weak," LeBlanc responded. "But he's tough. Nobody thought he'd pull out of it."

"Yeah," Jay said, his voice full of respect and concern. "He continually surprises everybody. It's a wonder he remembered this place."

"His mind was clear as could be," LeBlanc said. "His directions were perfect."

"Well, you made it this far," Jay said.

"Glad you came down," LeBlanc said. "I wasn't looking forward to the rest of the trip."

"You ever done any rock climbing?" Jay asked. LeBlanc shook his head. "You'd've killed yourself then."

LeBlanc gave him a hard look that passed so quickly Jay wasn't sure whether he'd imagined it. "So what's the plan?"

They took LeBlanc's Jeep because it was newer and had windshield wipers and a heater that worked. The wipers beat a metronomic cadence that made Jay's eyelids heavy. During the long silences in their desultory attempts at conversation, Jay found himself half dozing, viewing the world through the gauzy vision of half shut eyes. It was going to be all right, he told himself. Between him and the admiral, they'd figure out something.

Chapter Forty-eight

Jay started to get suspicious when LeBlanc took the Torrance exit off the San Diego Freeway. He held his tongue, thinking perhaps that the admiral had been taken to a hospital close to home. The news reports had not specified the hospital he had been taken to. In fact, Jay couldn't remember any mention of who had given the statements of his condition to the media.

When LeBlanc turned up into the Palos Verdes Hills, Jay spoke up. "Where are we going, Randall?" LeBlanc kept his eyes straight ahead and did not reply. Jay persisted. "I asked you where we're going. There's not a hospital up here. The admiral can't be here."

"But he is," LeBlanc replied. "He checked out of the hospital two days ago."

Jay looked at him as if he were a madman. "The news reports . . ."

"There are many ways that many things can be done if one knows the right people and if one has enough money and influence," LeBlanc replied. Jay reached inside his pocket and felt the grip of the .45 solidly in his fist.

"Don't try anything," LeBlanc said, whipping a revolver from between the door and the edge of his seat. He leveled the muzzle at Jay. Jay froze, his hand still gripping the .45.

"Do as he says." Jay whirled around toward the source of a voice behind him. He was soon staring into the muzzle of another revolver. A gaunt man with a scar over his right eyebrow grinned at him. He must have been concealed somewhere in the rear of the Jeep all this time. "Pull out your weapon and hand it to me," the man commanded.

Jay hesitated.

"Don't be a hero, Fleming." LeBlanc's voice was cold. "We can shoot you now."

Reluctantly, Jay pulled the .45 out of his pocket.

"Butt first," the man in the rear ordered. Jay fumbled with the pistol and complied. After tossing the .45 in the back of the Jeep, the man produced a set of handcuffs, crossed Jay's left hand over to the door and cuffed it there. He then retired to a position immediately behind Jay.

"You're a slimy bastard, LeBlanc," Jay spat viciously.

"Compliments won't get you anywhere."

"How long have you been working for Strand," Jay asked. "That's where we're headed now, isn't it? He lives here in Palos Verdes."

"I've worked for Steven Strand for nearly fifteen years now."

"You've been spying on the admiral all this time. He *trusted* you!"

"Spare me the moralizing, would you?" LeBlanc snapped. "For twenty years I've wiped Fraser's nose, listened to his jokes, taken all his shit when no one else would. Haven't you ever wondered why I lasted longer than anyone else?"

"I guess it was naive of me to think it was because you respected him."

LeBlanc's laughter filled the interior of the Jeep. Behind him, Jay could hear the other man snickering. "I did it because Steven Strand *paid* me to do it."

"So you could spy on him."

"So I could help keep the old fart from screwing up Strand's plans."

Fleming was neither angry nor sad nor indignant nor surprised. He was enervated, devoid of feeling, cold. It was all over. He had used up his last chance when he had unlocked the door of his pickup for LeBlanc an hour before. He had always been a fighter, but even a fighter has to recognize when all the options have run out, when there would be no getting up off the canvas.

"What have you done with the admiral?" Jay asked listlessly. He had burned himself out on caring.

"Oh, you two'll meet shortly," LeBlanc said as he turned off the main road and passed through the gate that marked the beginning of Strand's estate. "He's here and in good enough shape to recognize you. Good enough, that is, unless they've fed him some more sodium amatyl."

At the small guardhouse, a uniformed officer with epaulets on his raincoat stepped out in front of them. He glanced into the Jeep, exchanged several sentences with LeBlanc, and then waved them through. Jay saw him pick up a telephone as they passed.

"You and the admiral are two of a kind," LeBlanc said. "You must be the only two people left in the United States who actually do things because you think they'll benefit the country."

Jay remained silent and thought of Martin Copeland. Of Alexandra. Of Modesti and Treadwell and Lamb and all the rest of them. He wanted to tell LeBlanc how wrong he was, but was too tired to argue.

Paralysis crept through Jay's body. By the time they pulled up to the palatial house, Jay found that he didn't care about anything. He just hoped his death would be quick.

LeBlanc and the other man secured handcuffs to Jay's right wrist and clamped it on his left before releasing the first set from the door handle. They were taking him seriously as a threat, but his mind failed to take any encouragement from the thought.

The rain soaked his head and ran down the back of his neck as they led him past the front door and through a small covered walkway to the rear of the house.

Inside, Jay recognized a large pantry and storage area for the kitchen. They marched him through a large modern kitchen well enough equipped to run a small restaurant, and down a hallway to a suite of rooms.

"Clean yourself up," LeBlanc said. "There's soap, a razor, shampoo in the bathroom. Don't get any ideas. The windows all have bars and Guido here will be just outside your door. He's got orders to shoot."

The gaunt man smiled for the first time, revealing a set of crooked yellow teeth. The man's flat icy black eyes stared at him like a predator playing with his catch. And although Guido was tall and thin, Jay had felt the grip of his hands when they had snapped the handcuffs on him. He was strong and he had a gun.

"I understand," Jay replied.

"Good," LeBlanc said with a smile. "The faster you get cleaned up the faster you can reunite with your beloved admiral. We'll all be having lunch at 1:30."

"We?" Jay asked.

"You, me, Strand, the admiral and Maxwell Emerson."

"Emerson?" The name of the European arms merchant was enough to shock even Jay's anesthetized nerves.

LeBlanc turned quickly on his heel and walked down the hallway without saying more.

Trying to make sense of this new turn of events, Jay brushed past Guido and entered the bathroom.

"It's him! It's Jay!" Alexandra whispered excitedly, struggling to retain control over her voice. She started to rise from her crouch.

"Shh," George Treadwell cautioned and placed a hand on her shoulder. "Stay down, you'll give away our position."

She sat back on her heels and watched as Jay, accompanied by two men, passed along the covered walkway and entered the kitchen. Behind her a few yards and hundreds of feet below she heard the fists of the surf battering the shore at the bottom. She could barely hear it over the roar of her own heart.

After a few moments, she began to feel the cool sea breeze again, began to hear the surf clearly. She heard the rain, which had tapered off to a gentle drizzle, tapping against the fabric of her khaki rain suit. She thought of the danger they both were in. But he was in there, alive. He had made her hope when there was no hope left and now . . . she had to be loyal to those hopes.

The waiting had been the hardest part. Since they had escaped from the facility during the attack, she had spent her days trying to control wild mood swings that fluctuated from the deepest of depression to the hottest of anger to an almost uncontrollable impatience that had been leavened only through the patience of George Treadwell.

During the attack at the facility, Treadwell had hurried her into a lower level of the building and finally into the cramped room where the sewer lines exited. There she had found

Modesti and four other men working at a block and tackle to hoist a massive plug of concrete from a tube next to the sewer lines. The tube led down another fifty feet, and then horizontally for nearly a quarter of a mile.

Only Modesti's old-fashioned chivalry saved her life. Once the plug had been hoisted clear, Modesti had urged her into the tube. "Ladies first," he said without being ashamed of his old-fashioned manners. Treadwell went second to accompany her. But even before she had touched bottom, an explosion rocked the room above. There had been a brilliant flash of flame and a concussion that loosened her grip and nearly sent her plunging to the bottom, and then darkness as the huge plug of concrete and other debris covered the entrance. They descended to the bottom of the tube, and then along the gently sloping passage to the end, where they found a small round chamber with one hatch at the top and another to seal off the tunnel. After flooding the chamber and exiting through the top hatch, they found themselves floating in thirty feet of water under the wharf near Pier G.

They had climbed the access ladders fixed to the pilings for the use of motor launches and walked out of the area virtually unnoticed as everyone else crowded the edges of the docks, watching the explosions at the Asian Pacific Container Terminal.

An explosion of improperly stored hazardous materials was blamed for the incident, although local fire and police authorities were baffled at the manner in which FBI and Naval Intelligence officials refused to let them examine the ruins.

Now, as she crouched in the tall weeds and brush that was allowed to run wild at the very edge of the cliff, Alexandra knew that Treadwell's advice and his maddening patience had been right. He had been right about the relatively light perimeter security around Strand's home.

"Americans save all their security for their houses," he said. "Particularly those with a lot of land around their houses. They somehow think that acreage is security. It's a sort of Alamo mentality; fight them off at the doors."

And other than an occasional foot patrol by a uniformed member of a private guard service, there had been nothing to stop them from entering the grounds. They had worked their way to the rear, hoping that the security would be lightest next to the sheer cliffs that led vertically to the ocean. Treadwell, once again, had been right.

Their vantage point gave them a view of the back of the house, and the glass-enclosed walkway that led to Strand's wine cellar. Except for forays to get food, they had been waiting for three days for something to happen, primarily for Jay to show up. They had expected him to enter surreptitiously as they had, not as a prisoner.

"What now?" she asked. "You're the boss."

Furrows of thought plowed verticle wrinkles between the FBI agent's eyebrows. "That's a tough one," he said finally." "I was sort of counting on his help to raid Strand's place. I didn't expect to have to rescue him. We might have to wait until dark so we can get closer to the house."

"But we've already done that," Alexandra protested. "That's why we've been sneaking around at night, drawing this map, isn't it? So we'd have the layout? Think of what could happen to him in the next five or six hours," she said. "We can't afford to wait until it's dark."

"We can't afford not to," Treadwell said harshly. "We'll be no good to him if we're dead."

She looked at him skeptically. "Still . . ."

"Still, we wait," the FBI agent said firmly. "You've trusted me this long. Just a little longer."

Wonderful work in the outdoors. Piss on it, Ralph Knudsen thought to himself as his boots squished across the luxurious sponge of Steven Strand's immaculately kept lawn. The job hadn't been half bad, he thought, until the rain started. After six years on the Long Beach Police Force, Knudsen thought almost anything would be better.

As he walked along the perimeter of the lawn, past flower beds mulched down for the winter and under the overhang of the huge mature palm trees, Knudsen was plagued by the thought that perhaps the police work was better than this. He had almost decided it would be better to be killed by a criminal's gun than to die of boredom in the gilded, rarefied world of the wealthy and powerful.

He stopped, looking out toward the sea. What he really wanted was a cigarette. He cursed under his breath and moved on. The chief of security had complained that they neglected the area to the rear of the house.

"Remember," the chief had said that morning, "we're here to look after every aspect of security, including the physical aspect of the grounds. Keep your eyes open for any sign of earth movement that the rains might have caused, any erosion, particularly along Mr. Strand's driveway, or any hint that tree limbs might endanger human lives."

And look sharp, the chief had stressed. There would be some very important visitors to the estate in the next several days.

Knudsen snorted as he approached the area of weeds and brush that ran wild at the edge of the cliff behind the house. They let it run wild because it was too dangerous to have people working there without a fence of some sort, and Mr. Strand, Mr. Big Fucking Deal Strand didn't want a fence obstructing the view he had paid so much for.

Well, Knudsen thought, if it was too dangerous for gardeners to work there, it was too dangerous for Ralph Knudsen. He'd take a look to see if the cliff was going to slide downhill and then head back.

Chapter Forty-nine

Palos Verdes,
January 12

Guido ushered Jay silently along a hallway covered with thick gray carpeting and lit subtly with small sconces of cut and etched crystal. The clothes that had been left for him fit perfectly: A gray tweed blazer, gray wool slacks, a pink button-down shirt and a rep tie, black Italian loafers, black socks.

There was a very good reason the clothes fit so well. They were his. Strand must have been prepared for this meeting for a long time. It angered Jay to think they had invaded his home, but it shamed him even more to realize how easily he had fallen into Strand's trap. He had been outclassed.

With the deference jailers sometimes show to condemned inmates, Guido opened the door at the end of the hall for Jay. Fleming walked into a large reception room painted a pale olive with darker wainscotting that ran the circumference. A long, polished rosewood table dominated the center of the room, and above it an oak-leaf pattern crystal chandelier. The table was lavished with fresh fruit, crab legs, lobster, shrimp and all manner of cheeses breads and crackers. Silver warming trays contained a smorgasbord of hot casseroles and meats and vegetables.

In one corner, a uniformed bartender stood guard over a small bar. Around the perimeter of the room sat antique tables, chairs and sofas.

There was no one else in the room. Guido abandoned Jay to its furnishings and retreated to a position beside the door through which they had entered. Jay cast covetous glances at the windows that ran along the wall facing Guido, and at the sets of double doors at either end of the room. No doubt well-guarded.

He hesitated for a moment, then made his way past the table of hors d'oeuvres to the bar. He got a glass of club soda with a splash of Wild Turkey Bourbon in it. He noticed the knotted muscles in the bartender's hands and arms and the revolver at his waist. With the bar as a shield, Jay would never make it around in time to take the weapon away from the man. He took the drink back to the table and pretended to study the food. There were no knives on the table, only plastic forks and spoons. There were electric hot plates keeping the warm foods warm, nothing with a flame. They had thought of everything.

There was nothing to use as a weapon, and making a run for things was out of the question. The food was seductive, and Jay had started to reach for a plate when the double doors nearest to the bartender clicked discreetly open.

Jay turned. As the doors opened, he saw first the tall grinning countenance of Randall LeBlanc, then the huddled figure of Admiral Daniel Fraser. Fraser was slouching in a wheelchair pushed by LeBlanc. The old man's body looked like it had been crumpled up and wadded into the chair. His head lolled loosely.

Jay set his glass on the table, sloshing the white tablecloth with the contents and hurried toward Fraser.

"Hold it!" The bartender had his revolver aimed at Jay. LeBlanc smiled arrogantly. "Don't try anything."

"Listen to him," LeBlanc said as he pulled a boxy automatic from a shoulder holster and leveled it at Jay.

"I'm going to talk to him," Jay said with steel behind his words. "Shoot me if you want to." He walked toward Fraser, and as he grew close, tears began to blur his vision. A week ago, this octagenarian had been alert and vigorous and now . . . the slack jaw, moist eyes peering through half-closed lids. On top of the blanket that covered his lap, Fraser's hands fidgeted and jerked convulsively.

With a great effort, Fraser tilted his head to look up at Jay. The admiral's mouth opened, and the jaw worked several times but no sound came out, only a thin dribble of spittle, and then his head fell limp against his chest.

"You've been a great strain on the old man," LeBlanc said. "Why don't you let him rest."

Jay tensed. LeBlanc brought the gun up quickly. "Don't do what you're thinking."

"You're real brave men," Jay said through clenched teeth. "Just look at your power. You've reduced an old man to . . . to . . ." The words clotted in his throat.

Holding the gun in one hand, LeBlanc turned Fraser's wheelchair and pushed it over toward the bar. "There," LeBlanc said like some poor actor playing a nurse, "that'll make us happy now, won't it?" He leaned over the chair and dropping all pretense said, "Won't it, you decrepit old fart? And if you shit in your pants one more time I'm going to beat hell out of you." He smiled obscenely at Jay as he stood by the chair. He seemed to be waiting for something.

An instant later, the double doors at the other end of the room opened. Steven Strand and Max Emerson walked through the doors side by side. Jay watched as an armed attendant reached in to close the door behind them.

"Shouldn't we be hearing hail to the chief or some royal fanfare or another?" Jay asked. Neither man replied.

Emerson's great adipose bulk halted by the table of food. Strand continued until he was an arm's length from Jay, and then held out his hand. Jay looked at him, looked down at the proffered hand, then stepped back a pace.

"Fuck you and the horse you rode in on," Jay said.

Strand's composed face cracked for just an instant. "That's hardly sporting of you," Strand said. "I thought with all your old-fashioned morals and such that you'd shake the hand of the victor."

Jay glared silently at him as he calculated his chances of grabbing Strand and strangling him before his guards could pull him off. Considering Strand's well-publicized physical fitness and the proximity of three armed men, Jay decided he was playing with sucker's odds.

"I was just admiring your handiwork," Jay said. "You do a nice job of beating up old men."

"Unfortunate," Strand said. "Truly unfortunate. But Admiral Fraser had some information we needed badly and was unwilling to tell us. If it makes you feel better, he withstood the effects of the drugs longer than any other man I have heard of.

remarkable mind . . . or rather it was." He looked over to e corner. "I'll have cognac," he ordered and then turned on s heel and joined Emerson at the food.

"We'll be having a rather informal buffet lunch," Strand id as if addressing a lady's garden club. "Won't you join ?" When Jay stood rooted to the spot, Strand added, "You ouldn't want to miss your last meal, now, would you?"

Jay glanced over at Emerson, whose plate seemed to sag nder the weight of a gluttonous pyramid of food. "Never lose our appetite, do you Max?" Jay said.

"You should have joined us when you had the chance," merson said genuinely. "You could have been a valuable part f all this."

"Maxwell's a vital part of the entire operation," Strand said. Vhen he noticed the look on Jay's face, he added, "Of course 's going on as scheduled. Do you think your little foray last reek could have stopped all that? I do have to admit, though, aat you were ingenious, quite creative."

"But we will continue and continue on schedule," Strand aid as he loaded his plate up with crab legs, and walked oward a wingback chair near the bar. "Maxwell here has the vorld's largest inventory of conventional weapons, as well as n enormous supply of military electronics that were con-idered obsolete more than three decades ago. In just about two veeks, he will be the most powerful arms dealer in the world.

"He's a valuable part of our new order," Strand said as he .ccepted his drink from the bartender and settled back in the :hair. "We will return a balance to this country and the world. No more mob rule; no more pretense at egalitarianism. No one vill be able to resist us. But, even more importantly, it will be lecades before scientists, working with crude instruments, :ver discover that we are behind it all. And by then, it will be oo late."

"A new order," Jay said. "I thought you'd be a little more original than that, Strand. I think we heard about that in the last var."

"But we have a far better way of maintaining control now," Strand continued, taking a sip of his drink. "We have a real power that we can exercise directly. Never before has it been possible for so few to exercise so much power without the use of armies, politicians and other untrustworthy intermediaries.

"No," he continued, wiping his mouth with a linen napki "we will not make those mistakes."

"I never would have believed it if I hadn't seen everything, Jay said, "if I had not been a victim and survived as I had.

"That's just the point," Strand said. "That's what will allo us to rule unchallenged. People's minds are too small. Wh seems like the preposterous never gets serious consideratio People didn't believe in the atomic bomb until we dropped it c the Japanese. They didn't believe in space travel, the laser— million other things. People would never believe you even you did manage to get free and spill it all to the media." H looked long and knowingly at Jay. "They wouldn't believe yo because their minds are too small to conceive of it. Only th visionaries—"

"Like you and Emerson?"

Strand smiled indulgently. "Only the visionaries can see a the real possibilities. Napoleon was a visionary, Alexande Caesar and they all had the guts and the talent to build grea empires. Hitler had that vision, but he didn't have the depth c genius and the talent to carry it out. The poor creaky old men i the Politboro also have the vision and lack the talent. Bu we"—he looked at Emerson—"have learned from thei mistakes and will not repeat them. Machiavelli stressed that th securest power is that which is exercised unseen. What bette unseen channel than to bring on terrible solar flare storms ever year or two to make sure that the competition never gets chance to make up for the ground it will lose?"

"You're staking an awful lot on people falling into lin behind you," Jay said.

"See what I mean?" Strand said. "If you had the vision you would see. When the high-tech weapons overload and burn out, the military machines of the world will be forced to turn to us. *We* have the greatest reservoir of the weapons they will need. In some cases, we are the only source. If Western Europe, Japan, the United States wish to have the weapons they need to defend themselves against the Russians and Chinese—who are far less dependent on technology—then they must turn to us. Politicians who don't turn to us will quickly be replaced by frightened constituencies. We will be only too happy to provide those weapons—but political concessions will have to be made."

"Likewise for industry," added Emerson. He had settled his bulk on a small sofa. "Don't forget that while I have been buying obsolete equipment for pennies a pound as scrap and storing it for decades, other members of the Shepherd's Club have been doing the same with low-tech manufacturing equipment, assembly lines, buying up the patents for obsolete processes at ridiculous prices. We will have a stranglehold on both military and industrial sectors. That spells power."

"I knew it must have been something to drag you out of your fortress in Luxembourg," Jay said. "What of your enemies?"

"In a short while, I will have no enemies," Emerson said with satisfaction, then got awkwardly to his feet and waddled back toward the food.

Jay was trying to keep his mind off the battered body of Daniel Fraser when he heard shouts outside the house, distantly at first, then closer. Strand cocked his head. The room was silent for an instant. Fraser gave a groan and jerked convulsively. Jay turned toward him and for an instant saw a glimmer of intelligence in Fraser's eyes, a faint smile on his lips.

The commotion grew louder, from the direction of the hallway behind Guido, and for the first time, Jay heard the agitated voice of a woman. It stirred the dusty dried pot of hope in his heart.

"Go see what it is," Strand ordered. The bartender left his station and took Guido's place by the door. Moments later, Guido reappeared.

"Well?" Strand demanded impatiently. Emerson plunged an entire stuffed artichoke heart into his mouth.

"One of the guards, sir," Guido began, "Knudsen. Discovered two people hiding in the brush near the cliff. A man and a woman. The man fell over the cliff during the struggle. He brought the woman."

Strand frowned for a moment, and then stared across the room meditatively. His face brightened. "Bring her in, Guido. And Knudsen too." As Guido turned, Strand stood. "We have some unexpected entertainment."

Eyes turned expectantly toward the door. Jay felt his legs turn to jelly when Alexandra walked through the door, accompanied by a man in a khaki uniform and a gunbelt held up by a Sam Brown belt. He had a revolver in his hand pointed at the small of her back.

With a great effort, Jay willed his knees to hold him up. It was too much! Too much. He had given her up for dead, and now she was here! Alive, but like him, condemned by Strand. As their eyes met across the room, he tried to sort out the buzzing emotions that swarmed in his head. He smiled. Regardless of what was happening, he was glad to see her.

"Welcome, my dear." Strand walked across the room. "We've been wondering when you would show up."

The bartender walked back to the bar and took up a position beside Fraser's wheelchair.

Strand looked at the nameplate on the uniformed man's breast. "Knudsen. I have to commend you for your excellent work." Looking back at Alexandra, he said, "I assume the man who fell from the cliff was FBI agent George Treadwell. The only other survivor of that unfortunate *accident* in Long Beach?"

"You bastard," Alexandra spat at Strand.

Strand smiled broadly. "You have such good manners. Like your paramour." He looked at Jay.

Jay glared back, then received his second shock as his eyes took in the uniformed guard. Only now did he realize that Knudsen was actually George Treadwell. There was hope.

Guido, LeBlanc and the bartender were armed. Treadwell was armed, and he assumed that Alexandra was also. That left them only slightly outgunned. Emerson was no more a threat than any of the sofas in the room. But that left Strand.

"Officer Knudsen," Strand was saying. "You have performed your duties well. And as a reward, I am going to tell the chief of security to give you a raise retroactive for . . . say, two months."

"Thank you, sir," Treadwell said. "Thank you very, very much."

Strand's smile disappeared when a knock sounded at the double doors nearest to Emerson.

"Who is it?"

"Baxter, sir," came the muffled reply. "I've heard there's been an incident."

Strand looked at Treadwell. "Well, there's your chief now." And to the door, he called, "Come in, Chief."

As the door opened, Treadwell raised the revolver and fired two rounds at it. A scream of pain filled the room and grew louder as the man called Baxter fell forward onto the carpeting, sending the door flying open on its hinges and against the wall.

The room exploded with chaos.

Guido pulled his pistol from a shoulder holster; Jay lunged toward Strand who had started to run toward the open door; the bartender swiftly pulled out his sidearm; Alexandra fumbled with the .45 she had tucked under her foul weather gear; Maxwell Emerson dropped a plate piled high with strawberries and whipped cream and crawled under the table. Only Admiral Fraser failed to move.

The muzzle sight of Alexandra's .45 snagged on the cloth of her pants and then on the edge of the pocket as she tried to drag it out.

In the slow motion terror of nightmares, she watched as both Guido and the bartender trained their weapons on Treadwell. The FBI agent turned from the door and trained his revolver on Guido.

The room was filled with a massive explosion. Just feet away from her, she saw Guido's body stiffen and stagger backward into the wall and slide slowly to the floor. His chin slumped onto chest.

She found Treadwell sitting in a glistening pool of his own blood, feet splayed out like a small child's in a sandbox. His head snapped back as the bartender fired a second shot. A grisly red-and-gray pattern painted the wall and floor behind Treadwell as the bartender's second shot punctured the FBI agent's head.

The bartender looked from Alexandra to Jay and trained the muzzle on her.

"Hold it, Fleming, or I shoot your girl!" the bartender shouted. Jay froze. Strand continued through the door and disappeared. The thumps of hurried footsteps rumbled throughout the house. More of Strand's praetorian guard. They would be there in seconds. And where was Strand? Probably calling the police. The international fugitive had been caught.

"Come on back in, Mr. Fleming," the bartender ordered.

Reluctantly, he walked toward the bartender as directed. The thuds of approaching feet grew louder. Jay approached the bartender and then stopped about fifteen feet away and regarded Fraser's battered face with concern.

"Go on over there with your girl," the bartender commanded as he walked out from behind the bar and stood by Fraser. "We'll just wait for the cavalry to arrive." He smiled.

Jay was about to comply when he witnessed an incredible sight. With a high-pitched scream, Admiral Fraser lunged up from the chair and slammed his shoulder into the bartender's arm, forcing it upright like a Nazi salute. The revolver issued a single round that blasted one of the fobs on the chandelier into a snowfall of glinting shards.

The bartender whirled as Jay lunged toward him. With his left hand the bartender swept Fraser away like an unwanted lap animal. The admiral hit the floor with a smack as the bartender leveled his gun at the charging Jay Fleming. Jay watched the man's unwavering stance and knew there was no way to reach him before he fired.

Alexandra had never let go of the grip of the .45. She tugged desperately on it. Accompanied by the sound of ripping cloth, the .45 suddenly flew free. Using both hands, Alexandra aimed at the bartender's midsection. She fired three times, hitting him twice. He dropped his gun and collapsed on the floor.

Jay looked at her with an unearthly lightness in his chest. She ran to him and they embraced.

"Oh God, oh God," she said over and over. "Are you all right?" She looked up at him. Never had her eyes looked so blue or so bottomless to him.

He nodded. "How about you?"

"All right, I guess."

The shouts of reinforcements interrupted their embrace.

"We've got to get out of here fast," Jay said. He stepped away from Alexandra and knelt beside Fraser. He lifted the old man in his arms and hoisted him over his shoulders in a fireman's carry.

"Get the bartender's gun," Jay said. Alexandra handed it to Jay.

As they reached Baxter's body, the double doors on the other end of the room burst open, accompanied by angry shouts and sporadic gunfire. Jay whirled in time to see Max Emerson rise to a crouch and then collapse on the floor, a gaping red hole in e side of his face. The obese arms merchant had come out of is hiding place during the lull in the shooting and been felled y the new fusillade.

Alexandra returned the guards' fire as she and Jay hurried on rough the door and out of the sights of the approaching guns. Which way? There were enough rooms and hallways to house n army. Jay felt like a rat in a large maze. But wrong moves ere were punishable by death.

"There's a garage in the rear," Alexandra said. "Several ars there. George and I watched them move in and out."

They were soon in the hallway which Jay had been brought rough earlier.

They burst into the cool winter air. A light mist swirled and ainted soggy halos around bright security lights that burned n the house and all around the grounds. A gray blanket of ain-sodden clouds covered the sky and burned slightly righter in the west, a reminder that somewhere above this ness, the sun was shining. The rise and fall of a siren sang a lirge to accompany the percussion of gunshots and shouts.

Behind them, they heard shouts of "This way! They're ere," and then the clatter of feet against the concrete walk.

Jay was breathing heavily now. Fraser was a solidly built old nan.

"Just a little further," Alexandra said. "The garage is just up he way."

They had nearly gained the side entrance to the garage when they heard the roar of an engine. Jay jerked the door open in time to see a Mercedes sedan with Strand behind the wheel backing out of the garage. It was a huge three-car garage. The door to the bay closest to them was open. The Mercedes was halfway through it. Jay raised the revolver he had taken from the bartender and brought it to bear on the car. The first shot tore a gaping hole in the right front tire, the second shattered the windshield beside Strand's head.

Strand jerked his head around. Jay laid the admiral on the concrete floor of the garage and sprinted toward the Mercedes. The car came to a stop. Jay thought Strand was going to get out. Suddenly the Mercedes surged forward. The bumper struck Jay a glancing blow on his thigh. He went down as the Mercedes crashed into the wall at the end of the garage, narrowly missing Alexandra and Fraser. Jay rolled back to his feet as Strand leaped from the passenger side of the car. A dull pain radiated from his thigh.

"In here, you fools," Strand shouted. He dragged a large briefcase from the Mercedes, the same briefcase handcuffed to Strand's wrist as he left the Catalina Island encampment during the fire.

Jay tried to get a shot at Strand, but the older man ducked down between a black limo and an old restored Dusenberg. For a moment, there was silence in the garage. The siren outside had stopped wailing, but from a distance came the more ominous sounds of multiple sirens. The police. He had to get Fraser and Alexandra out of here before the police arrived.

There was a scrambling sound near the far end of the garage. Jay turned. Strand's arm shot upward to hit the electric switch that controlled the door. Jay started for the door when the sound of Alexandra's .45 sounded twice behind him. Strand slipped out the garage door.

Jay quickly returned to Alexandra's side.

"How are you fixed for ammunition?" he asked.

"I have two more clips in my raincoat pocket."

"Good," Jay said. "Take this." He handed her the revolver. "And give me yours."

Alexandra handed over the two extra clips with it. Jay pulled out the partially spent clip and loaded a new one.

"All right," he told her. "When I say so, start firing at the walls on either side of the door."

She nodded. Jay swiftly made his way to the open garage door behind the wrecked Mercedes. Crouching beside the door, he took a deep breath, and shouted, "Now!"

When Alexandra commenced firing, Jay shot out of the open door and around the corner. Six men were squatting on their haunches, one looking straight at Jay. The other five had riveted their attention on the doorway where Alexandra was shooting.

The man facing Jay raised a .30-caliber magazine-fed submachine gun. Jay fired. The slug smashed into the man's torso, straightened him up and then dropped him on the concrete. The other men started to turn. Jay emptied the clip. None of them had a chance. Jay's stomach quaked. The police sirens were growing louder. He had no idea how many other guards Strand had. He had to get Alexandra and Fraser to safety, but there was Strand. And there was still the Tesla pulse weapon that had to be stopped.

Picking up the submachine gun, Jay raced past the bodies of the men he had just killed and into the garage.

He gave the .45 and the final full clip back to Alexandra. Fraser was sitting up now. His abject helplessness had obviously been a ploy.

"The briefcase," Fraser said weakly. "You must get the briefcase."

"No time to talk about things now," Jay said as he leaned over to help Fraser to his feet. "Get in the limo and lock the doors. Strand's a careful man. It's probably armored."

When he installed Alexandra behind the wheel, and had laid Fraser on the back seat, he checked the machine gun and started back to the side door.

"Where are you going?" Alexandra said, concerned.

"After Strand. I won't be long, I hope." He left at a dead run, afraid that if he lingered any longer, he would forget Strand altogether and escape with the woman he loved.

Fools! Idiots! Strand cursed the security guards who worked for him as he ran across the well-tended lawn toward the glassed-in walk that led to his wine cellar and its observation room. If he could reach that, he could barricade himself in until the police arrived.

The attaché case hung heavy in his hand, making his running slow and awkward. But the dossiers inside were all he needed. Project Nick would continue as long as he had the wherewithal to compel the remaining members of the Shepherd's Club to follow through on their assignments. There was enough damning evidence in the affidavits signed by the dead members to compel compliance by frightened executives, men all too eager to avoid scandal or a government inquiry.

Behind him, Strand heard the sounds of running feet, the regular fast breaths of someone approaching. Fleming! How had he escaped from the garage?

Strand continued to run. He skirted the tangle of weeds and brush at the edge.

"Stop, Strand, or I'll shoot," Fleming yelled. Strand continued without hesitation.

Jay leveled the submachine gun and pulled the trigger. Divots of turf danced around Strand's running legs. As the magazine in the gun ran out of ammunition, a slug struck Strand in his right shoulder, bowling him over. Jay had no more ammunition, so he tossed it aside and sprinted toward the fallen man.

Strand rolled into the thick brush, dropping the attaché case. Jay stopped at the case. He briefly considered taking it and leaving Strand to die in the brush. But there was no assurance that Strand was mortally wounded.

Cautiously, Jay followed the trail of bent and broken weeds into a dense thicket. Incredibly, Strand's trail seemed to disappear. The vegetation, along with the feeble winter light, made it difficult to make out anything but the outlines of things. He heard only the surf and police sirens winding up toward Strand's house.

Time was wasting. Every second narrowed the chance for escape. He looked about him frantically. Strand was nowhere in sight.

The pain in Strand's shoulder burned like the fires of hell. As he crouched behind a thick evergreen shrub, he tried to take a deep breath. He felt the wound suck in air as he did. The shot had hit his lung. It was a matter of only a few moments before the lung would collapse, filling with blood. He could not allow Jay Fleming to defeat him.

Breathing through his mouth to remain as silent as possible, Strand watched Jay move aimlessly around the thicket. Finally, he saw Fleming start back toward the manicured lawn.

"Strand?" Jay called and stopped to listen. Nothing. Finally the fear of being arrested by the police, or forced to shoot it out with them, urged him back toward the lawn. He'd take the attaché case. It seemed to be vitally important. Even Fraser thought so. The old admiral must have heard some talk about it during his confinement.

Quickening his pace, Jay stepped past a thick evergreen shrub, and then heard a tiny soft sound, like a body moving swiftly through the air. Something hard and wooden smashed into the side of his head. Jay staggered and raised his right arm.

The hard wooden thing slammed into his forearm and glanced off. Jay tried to turn his head, but the first blow had so upset his sense of balance that the sudden movement sent him to his knees at the axis of a spinning galaxy. He raised his head and found Strand standing above him with a piece of a thick branch.

"Your grandfather and your father couldn't get away from me," Strand said, his voice edged with hysteria. "And neither will you."

My father? My grandfather? Small detached thoughts wandered through Jay's head. They were killed in accidents. Accidents. Jay looked up in time to see Strand bringing the club down on him with two hands. Jay tried to move out of the way. The club crashed down on his left shoulder, paralyzing it for an instant. Then the cold numbness was replaced by daggers of pain.

"It's no use," Strand said.

Was his voice getting weaker? He tried to keep his eyes open for Strand's next blow. My father, my grandfather. A drunk driver. A traffic accident.

Then, like ice water, the realization flooded through him. His grandfather had been killed in a traffic accident, returning from the organizational meeting of the Committee of Seven. It was obvious. They couldn't afford to let him live.

And Jay's father. It was clear now why the drunk driver who had killed both his parents on Christmas Eve had died of a heart attack before being brought to trial. He had been a hired killer. Hired by Strand!

Jay rolled away from Strand's next blow, which thudded impotently into the wet earth. Using a tree for support, Jay pulled himself to his feet. Strand stood unsteadily about ten feet away, swaying slightly like a punch-drunk boxer. A dark stain soaked his coat.

"I know why you killed my grandfather," Jay said. "But why my parents?"

"For the same reason," Strand said, his voice weak now. "He learned about Fleming Industry's involvement with the Committee of Seven. He was going to have me fired. We couldn't have that. Your mother just happened to be with him on the wrong night."

Jay couldn't believe his ears. He walked toward Strand. The older man tried to raise the club to defend himself, but it seemed to have gained weight. It fell from his grip. He backed slowly away from Jay.

"I can make it worth your while," he pleaded. "All this . . . we can have it arranged. You can . . . millions, I can give you millions."

"All I want," Jay said, "is to strangle you with my own hands."

Strand continued to back away as Fleming slowly closed the distance between the two of them.

Then suddenly Strand seemed to sink into the ground amid a thrashing of weeds. He screamed a dying man's scream that grew swiftly faint. Jay walked cautiously over to the edge of the cliff and looked down at the crumpled figure on the rocks below.

Despite being relieved at not having to kill Strand, he felt cheated.

He picked up the briefcase and ran back to the garage. The lights of approaching police cars lit up the night.

"I can get us out through the woods," Alexandra said as Jay opened the door. "The same way George and I got in."

Jay looked at her silently and kissed her. "I love you," he said. "Lead on."

He got Fraser out of the limo's back seat and laid him down on the driveway next to the attaché case. The sounds of the racing motors of the police cars filled the night.

"Give me the .45," he said to Alexandra. She looked on, puzzlement knitting her brows together, as he squatted on his knees behind the Mercedes and fired two rounds. Instants later, gasoline began to pour on the floor of the garage. Jay fired another round at the concrete. The slug plowed across the pavement throwing sparks in every direction in the pool of gasoline, and then the ruptured gasoline tank exploded.

"That ought to keep them busy for a while." Jay returned to Alexandra and handed back the gun. He slung Fraser over his shoulder. Alexandra took the attaché case and they ran for the trees that bordered Strand's estate. As they passed safely into the shelter of the trees, a massive whump came from the garage. They paused and turned. The gas tank of one of the other cars had exploded. Heavy, oily smoke poured into the sky, connected with the garage by greedy tongues of yellow flames that had spread to the main building. Policemen busied themselves with the fire.

After a quiet moment they turned and walked on through the woods. They had a long way to go before they could find safety.

Epilogue

The Caribbean sun glared down from an aquamarine sky. Sweat dripped off Jay Fleming's nose, trickled in rivulets along his spine, seeped into his eyebrows and filled them like an oversated sponge until he had to reach up with a grease-smeared hand and wipe them dry before perspiration dripped into his eyes.

He stood up and stared at the Palmer four-cylinder sailboat auxiliary engine that rested on the low wooden bench. He looked like a frustrated priest before an altar. He wondered if a human sacrifice would free the stubborn bolts that held the engine's cylinder head on. He had in mind sacrificing the sailboat's owner, who had operated the engine without oil until it had frozen up.

Fleming sighed, pulled a stained rag from the rear pocket of his cut-off denim shorts. He looked at the rag carefully, searching for a clean spot. He turned it over several times, folding and unfolding it until he found an area whose stains were lighter than the rest. He wiped his face with the clean spot and then walked over to a bench and sat down next to a fat manila envelope with his greasy fingerprints on it. He tried to ignore the envelope.

A gentle breeze wafted through the open sides of the little tin-roofed workshop he had built four months ago. The four sides of the structure were also covered with tin, and hinged so they would swing upward, taking full advantage of the Caribbean's predictably soothing breezes.

He and Alexandra had happened on Rodney Bay not quite by accident. He had been here several years ago when his aircraft carrier, on a goodwill mission to several small Caribbean nations, anchored just outside of Castries Harbor for a week. He had seized his shore leave to check into a wonderfully simple establishment between Castries and Rodney Bay called East Winds. It had only a dozen small cottages on the beach and it was all he had wanted.

Now, he looked around him and wondered if *this* was all he wanted or if it was time to move on. They had slipped Alexandra's boat quietly from its dock three nights after getting Fraser to the UCLA Medical Center in Westwood. They then took the boat to San Diego to buy a forged set of papers for her boat and to change the numbers on her sails and on the bow. After that, they had headed south, along the western coast of Mexico, avoiding all the places where cruising sailors typically stopped. The search was on for them, but the ocean, as both he and Alexandra knew, was a big place.

They sailed far off shore to avoid tangling with American warships off the coast of Central America, then passed through the Panama Canal.

St. Lucia seemed the ideal place for them to stop. Twenty-four miles south of Martinique, the island is only twenty-seven miles long, fifteen miles wide. The few tourists who stop there are mostly British and German; very few Americans. The government was leaning toward the left, like its neighbor Grenada to the south, and so inquiries coming from the United States government about fugitives were mostly lost or ignored by the island's tiny police agency.

Jay had found work two days after he and Alexandra pulled into Rodney Bay. He was a passable diesel gasoline engine mechanic, and the charter services at Rodney Bay had need of such skills. Marguerite at East Winds remembered him from his earlier stay, and gratefully hired Alexandra to help her keep the establishment's accounts.

The time passed serenely, the most disturbing events being those times when the telephones or electricity suddenly stopped working, sometimes for days at a time, but usually just for a few hours.

Fraser wrote to them frequently. Except for severe head-aches, he had mostly recovered from his mistreatment at Strand's hands. Friends and allies of George Treadwell and David Curry and Kevin Modesti, and dozens of others had stepped forward and taken charge of the attaché case of dossiers Strand had compiled.

Resignations were quietly forced, musical chairs at the top of America's largest corporations quietly shuffled. Uncoopera-tive members of the Shepherd's Club had begun to meet with unfortunate accidents. But, by and large, they were taking things slowly.

The public could never know how close it had come to a coup, how close the foundations of the world's oldest represen-tative democracy had come to crumbling. This ruled out any public disclosure of the plans designed by the Committee of Seven, or any trials of its members.

But continuity of the country's institutions also demanded a gradual changing of the names in leadership positions. It hadn't been easy, was still difficult. The bureaucracies of state and federal agencies, law enforcement departments, regulatory agencies, courts—all were riddled with people who, because of bribery or blackmail, owed their primary allegiance to the cabal of the Shepherd's Club.

Jay looked at the manila envelope on the crude wooden bench beside him. Fraser's San Pedro address was handwritten in the corner. This was one piece of correspondence he wished the U.S. Postal Service had treated with its usual efficiency and mangled, destroyed or lost.

"Bozu."

Jay turned toward the source of the greeting. He saw Alexandra approaching from the gravel parking lot with a covered wicker basket. Parked at the side of the road he saw their beat-up Suzuki Jeep.

"Bozu, yourself." They had both picked up a lot of the native patois in the past four months. St. Lucians all spoke English as an official language, but the natives also spoke a pidgin French. "Bozu" was their version of *"Bonjour."*

"How are you?" she asked.

"Hot and tired." He stood up to greet her.

"You're also very dirty," she said when she drew near. "I brought you some cold fruit juice."

"What brings you out here this early," he asked. She usually arrived with his lunch shortly after noon. "The ice machine at East Winds break down again and Marguerite needs me to fix it?" he asked, taking the basker from Alexandra and setting it on the bench. She took the paper napkin off the top of the basket and spread it on the bench before sitting down.

Jay watched her fondly as she arranged herself. In keeping with the standards of propriety suitable to the island, she wore a light skirt and a modest blouse. Her richly bronzed arms and legs made the white of the skirt and blouse seem to glow in the cool shade of the workshop. Her blue eyes seemed even deeper against the tan of her high cheekbones. She wore her hair pulled back and tied behind her head, and the delicate gauzy pattern of her hairline displayed her face better than the richest frame ever could. He put his hands on her shoulders as he leaned down to kiss her.

"Thank you," she said, "but it won't get you out of repairing the ice machine." She looked up at him and they both laughed. "Now come on," she said, patting the bench beside her. "Sit down and relax for a moment."

Jay slid the manila envelope to the end of the bench and sat. Alexandra's eyes looked at the envelope and then at Jay, her carefree gaze transformed into one of concern. Jay noticed her worry.

"It's just another thick missive from the admiral," Jay said.

"I know, that's what's worrying me," Alexandra said as she reached into the basket and produced two glasses and a quart jar filled with fruit juice and ice cubes that tinkled against the glass. "The letters have been getting thicker and thicker. And every time you get one, you get more dissatisfied with the life we're leading here."

She avoided looking at him as she poured the juice.

"It's mostly good news," Jay said brightly. "All the charges against you have been dropped, the record's being expunged. Everything against me has been dropped except for the incidents in Holland. You know the Dutch. Sticklers for propriety."

"That's wonderful," she said unenthusiastically. She handed him a glass.

"Pineapple and coconut," Jay said heartily after taking a swallow. "My favorite. And the business is doing well. Chris

Carneghie is doing a fine job of managing ECM. Better than I could." Excitedly, Jay set down his glass and grabbed the manila envelope and pulled out a sheaf of papers from it. He riffled through them and finally found the ones he was looking for. A newspaper clipping wafted to the ground. "Here," he said, showing her the papers. "All I have to do is sign these and get them back to Chris, and the courts will release our assets." Jay's stocks and all his bank accounts and real estate had been seized by the government shortly after Strand's death.

"You want to go back," Alexandra said glumly as she sipped at her juice.

Jay slowly replaced the papers in the envelope.

"You know we can't stay here forever," Jay said. "You're wasting your talent."

"Does it really matter whether talent's wasted?" Alexandra said suddenly. "God knows you're wasting yours. But does it really matter? Does it really matter if you squeeze every last fraction of an inch out of your talents? What does that get you? A few fractions of an inch."

She put her glass down and turned toward him. "Doesn't it matter more to be happy? To live our lives together? What can you *do*? You can't change things permanently. Why can't you just *accept* your limitations?"

"I love you so much," Jay responded sadly. "I just wish I could accept things like you can. I know in my mind that you're right. But in my heart"—he raised his hands in a gesture of helplessness—"I just can't *not* try."

Alexandra looked at him and shook her head slowly, her eyes full of love. "You're not an easy person to live with, Jay Fleming." She leaned over and kissed him.

"I know," he said. "I've had to do it all my life." He managed a smile. "I wish I was more like you. Maybe a few years will change me?"

She shook her head. *"Piti has ka-bat gwo bwa,"* she said in patois.

Jay looked at her, confused. "I don't understand."

"Marguerite and I were talking about you," Alexandra smiled. "She said the St. Lucians have a proverb that sums up your philosophy."

"Terrific," Jay said. "Now translate."

"'Little axes cut big trees.'"

"You understand, don't you?"

"You know I do," she said, taking his right hand in both of hers. "And I love you because of the way you are and despite the way you are. Because I suppose that if you somehow didn't feel you had the urge to go out and chop at the dark forests of the world, then you wouldn't be all of the other wonderful things that you are."

He leaned over to kiss her.

The headline on the newspaper clipping that had fluttered to the ground caught her eye. "Oahu Blacked Out When Five Major Transmission Lines Fail." She leaned over to pick up the small clipping. It was from the *Los Angeles Times*, not two weeks old.

"From Times Wire Services," the byline read.

"HONOLULU—Five major electrical transmission lines went out of service in a 'domino effect' Wednesday, knocking out power for most of the afternoon to the 800,000 residents here and to the rest of the island of Oahu, authorities said.

"Hawaiian Electric Co. officials were investigating the possibility that a fire in a sugar cane field ionized the air around one of the transmission lines and shorted out the power system.

"By late afternoon, power was restored to about one-fifth of the island.

"Gov. George Arioshi ordered . . ."

"Jay," she said looking at him, "do you believe the story?"

He shook his head. "We've got most of them," Jay said, "and as far as I can tell, only Strand knew the location of the Tesla papers that were needed to make Project Nick a worldwide phenomenon. But after reading this, I can't help thinking there are some facilities, some people, that we don't know about. Someone's trying to carry on without the last pieces of the puzzle."

"Are you sure only Strand knew the location of the Tesla papers?"

Jay shook his head. "Nor do we have any assurances that the remainder of the group might not make another attempt to obtain copies from the Yugoslavians in some way."

"Little axe chopping at big trees," Alexandra said quietly. "You really do have to go back, don't you?"

Jay nodded.

"We've had a wonderful four months," Alexandra said.

"It's like being stranded on a desert island with exactly the right person."

"Thank you," Jay said. "I feel the same."

"No you don't," Alexandra said. "I've watched you growing antsy."

He placed his forefinger on her lips. "I *have* enjoyed it. Don't spoil the mood. Let me chop at a few more trees and then we'll find another island to get stranded on . . . ah, unfortunate choice of words . . . marooned on."

"Do you promise?" Alexandra asked.

"I promise."